LIGHTHOUSE
ISLAND

LIGHTHOUSE
ISLAND

PAULETTE JILES

wm
WILLIAM MORROW
An Imprint of HarperCollins*Publishers*

LIGHTHOUSE ISLAND. Copyright © 2013 by Paulette Jiles. All rights reserved. Printed in the United States of America. No part of this book may be used or reproduced in any manner whatsoever without written permission except in the case of brief quotations embodied in critical articles and reviews. For information address HarperCollins Publishers, 10 East 53rd Street, New York, NY 10022.

HarperCollins books may be purchased for educational, business, or sales promotional use. For information please write: Special Markets Department, HarperCollins Publishers, 10 East 53rd Street, New York, NY 10022.

FIRST EDITION

Designed by Jamie Lynn Kerner

Library of Congress Cataloging-in-Publication Data has been applied for.

ISBN 978-0-06-223250-2 (hardcover)
ISBN 978-0-06-229359-6 (international edition)

13 14 15 16 17 OV/RRD 10 9 8 7 6 5 4 3 2 1

LIGHTHOUSE
ISLAND

CHAPTER 1

The winds carried dust to every part of the great cities; left it on roofs and windowsills and uneven streets. It scoured glass to an iridescent glaze. The city covered the entire earth, if people think of the earth as "where I live." At night the wind sang through the abandoned upper floors of buildings with a noise like oboes and this erratic music could be heard at street level where people walked in the heat to their work in offices and in the recycling dumps and the cement works, to work on the pumps that kept the water, contaminated with gypsum from Silurian seas, flowing through the pipes. In the interstadial spaces between the borders of gerrymanders, prisoners painfully attended the cactus fields and the soybean fields.

There was not enough pressure to move water any higher than four stories and so upper stories had to be abandoned and demolished and new, dust-leaking roofs built over the remains. Television reports on demolitions were very popular. The city covered mountains; houses were fastened to the steep places and they sprang up in four-story shells along abandoned watercourses and the sinks of vanished springs. The city plated the entire planet if you thought of the planet as "my neigh-borhood," a place where nobody was ever left alone.

On a hot, dry afternoon a four-year-old girl was taken out into a crowded street by her parents and abandoned. It was in the Sissons Bend neighborhood. The girl knew by her parents' manner that some-thing remarkable was about to happen, but she thought as they were walking along that it would have something to do with shoes or maybe a musical toy.

Her parents had given her a coin purse of red leather—in it were five coins—and a note, and another piece of paper on which were drawn the constellations of the Big Dipper, Cassiopeia's Chair, and the North Star. Her mother handed her the paper and said, Look to the North Star and we will always be there. You'll be lonely for a while but things will get better.

Then her parents disappeared in the crowded streets as if they had been teleported somewhere. The girl stood there without knowing what to do. A slow crawling fright rose inside her and it increased with every moment as passersby bumped into her and looked down at her briefly and then hurried on. The girl stared at the crowd as if she had been electrocuted with some kind of cunning electricity that could not be felt unless you moved and so she tried to stand still with the purse and the two papers in her hand but she was knocked down and then scrambled to her feet with gritty hands and stood carefully unmoving again.

The street was choked with people moving to new locations carry-ing children and bags of clothes and solar casserole pots and kerosene cans piled on carts that wove through and around the overloaded buses. The buses ground along in first gear and the little electric Buddy cars were loaded with three and four passengers and their roped suitcases. As far as anyone knew, the world had become nothing but city and the rains had failed for a century. They were on the move because the water faucets had gone dry in one distant part of the city but were rumored to be springing clear and full of pressure out of the standpipes in another. These were ordered migrations and agents in tracksuits paced alongside them. The man of the neighborhood watch saw the girl and frowned. He came toward her.

She was taken to an orphanage where she lived with other abandoned children like herself. She was given porridges and beet tops and a quart of water a day. She sat with the other children in front of a television in a battered wooden chassis. The blue light sucked up her attention like a pulmotor. After a week or so she went blind.

She could not see the eye doctor but he could see her and he lifted her chin and stared into her green-gray blind eyes, her auburn hair sliding in places, and then said, this is going to sting. The day-care attendant said it was for a blood test. The doctor said he was sure it was vitamin A deficiency. Maybe she was especially sensitive to vitamin A deficiency or maybe she had been weaned too early and was raised on bulgur wheat and pastas. Before long, after the paperwork was approved, she would have a prescribed daily dosage of retinyl palmitate. But retinyl palmitate was synthesized from retinol and retinol had to be prepared and transported at very low temperatures in an oxygen-free atmosphere and the industrial unit that made it went through constant breakdowns in refrigeration, the gas-packing apparatus frequently blew its tubes, and delivery by truck was rarely on schedule owing to ruptured tires. In the meantime she must have animal foods. She should be served eggs and cod liver oil and milk. And so he went away.

An attendant patted her shoulder and said it wouldn't be too long before she could watch her favorite programs again and just that brief touch made the girl's heart grow full and she did not feel so desperate. The attendant's name was Shaniya. Shaniya thought of herself as a nurse-practitioner and often gave out medical information that was totally wrong. In this case she held forth on the fact that Raisa's eyes would be weak for the rest of her life. Raisa thought it might be from crying so much so she decided to try to stop crying.

Raisa could hear the television but she could not see it so she sat on the floor and listened intently to the voices because they might say something about what had happened to her mother or her father but in general they were the voices of walking palm trees and animated clocks and cabbages and bright, knowing children.

That's a clock that's talking, one of the girls said. Can't you tell?

She can't see, said another.

Their breath smelled like corn crisps and their fingers felt grimy and when they asked what her name was all she could do was to repeat what she heard her parents say: Raisa. But the way things had changed so quickly she wasn't sure.

She doesn't have any eyes, said a girl beside her.

Yes I do, said Raisa. I have eyes. She put her hands with their pale narrow fingers against her eyeballs and felt them trembling inside the sockets like small infant animals but it was a creepy feeling so she gripped both hands together in a knot and felt tears running in hot streams down her cheeks. They're right in there.

A girl beside her said, They're in there. The girl put her hands against Raisa's eyes. They're inside her head.

See, I told you, said Raisa.

Then why can't she see?

Raisa, why can't you see?

I don't know. Raisa searched for a reason and wiped her face on her skirt hem. Maybe my eyes aren't turned on. My mother is going to come and turn them on.

On the television there were things the others said were magic pencils, a happy spoon named Banji, and a spider, who danced to frenetic music. There were adventures with children who yelled at one another in unresonant voices. They argued about how to do something or which door led to the magic kingdom, or a place where some treasure lay. There it is! shouted an unspecified vegetable. The puppets Pepper Spray and Long Shot exchanged caustic remarks as they rifled a kitchen for cod cakes. Lucy Swiffer and the Space Shuttle Pirates rocketed to other worlds while Raisa came to understand that treasures lay in dark places, behind closed doors, that these doors were reached by perilous journeys through wastelands and clothes closets.

Raisa had thick auburn hair that slipped out of its braids in slick tangles so that her hair was frequently pulled by older children. She could not fend them off. She smelled them in their jammed closeness, their odors of germicidal soap and peanuts. From time to time the television changed to a program about vacations or resorts. She sat suspended in front of the invisible screen where a booming, washing noise sounded.

Whats that? she called. What is that?

The ocean.

What ocean? Where is it? Where?

Somewhere.

Come to Lighthouse Island, said the television.

They were always thirsty and Raisa could hear the building's holding tanks being pumped full and bottles being filled at the tap downstairs, long before the other children. She heard the carts being stacked and put her hand to her mouth. Water time, she said. I can hear them.

I don't hear it, said another girl.

They're coming, said Raisa. I know. And then, just as she had said, the water cart came down the hallway.

Conversations among the attendants left her nervous. She had to puzzle out these words to stay alive. They argued about the food she was to be given and wasn't: the eggs and milk and liver. Adult workers weren't even getting eggs and milk and liver. One attendant said, Why hasn't she been sent to the dryers?

And Shaniya said, Give her a break. She's very functional. The retinyl stuff will be here one of these days. Please.

Raisa liked being alone. She felt her way to a sofa and then crawled into the space behind it. They were being called to come and eat. The children went away. She heard a click and a short, crisp sound, like a quick burning, when the television was turned off. She put her fingertips against each other and fell into stillness. Solitude. In the distance she heard a deep, repeated thunder that rattled the windows in their frames and it seemed to come from a long way away, beyond the street noises. The windows were always open because it was so hot and she felt the puff of air after the explosions.

She hid in silence between the wall and the sofa and listened. The remote sounds of human life were like intricate figures in a textile made up of distant singing and a crowd walking and Buddy car horns and bus motors. She heard televisions from other windows, and pigeons. It was all absorbing and everything mattered in this poised delay where she lived, suspended in hope, which seemed to have located her in spite of everything, hope that her parents would come and for her sight to return.

The attendants were upset when they finally found her. Solitude was the same as hostility. Children were never left alone. Raisa sat and felt about for her plate, her spoon, and tried to eat and drink without spilling but the other children tipped her cup over and laughed and so she flung her grits wildly, hoping to hit them. She was always a mess and she had to be cleaned up. It made the attendants impatient.

Two other girls, June and Nancy, decided to become her protectors and were kind to her. They treated her like a doll. They put the morning and evening water bottles in her hand and said, There now, drink up! They braided her hair and tugged her around the rooms. One time they were given oranges and June and Nancy scrupulously divided an orange among the three of them, an act of generosity that restored Raisa's faith in humanity. They sat her in front of the television and told her what was happening with the sardonic spoons and the hero-children. When the news came on they were all silent and then bored.

For Raisa the stories were all broken and fragmented and incomplete. This kept her anxiously asking, And then what did they do? What are they doing now? They're not talking, what are they doing? So that she was left with nothing but missing links and stories that were mutilated and garbled because she couldn't see expressions or movements or understand what the music meant. She turned her left ear toward the television in hopes of hearing some kind of continuity that the others couldn't and then she turned her right ear toward the screen but nothing helped. It left her with a kind of despair that she could not put into words. She told herself, *It will get better. Life will get better.*

In winter they all left the day-care center and went some other place, some other building. June and Nancy had disappeared. The incessant thundering and street noises grew louder and closer. They were dressed in padded jackets and wrapped in blankets made of an abrasive material. *Step up, Raisa. Here, sit down, Raisa.* As they drove through the streets there was another sound from far below.

What's that? said Raisa.

What's what? She felt Shaniya turning to her.

There's a sound far down, she said. Underneath us. Raisa held on to Shaniya's arm because she was afraid she was being taken to someplace where she would be killed; the thought occurred to her in a kind of evaporating image. The vehicle had stopped to wait for something. Crowd noises outside. It was bitterly cold.

Those are the underground trains, said the attendant. My God, she can hear anything.

Life at the new place started up all over again, just the same. She had to begin again memorizing the number of steps into and out of rooms, into the sleeping area, the eating area, the toilets. She could hear the hissing steam boilers in the basement and the singing of the wind through telephone wires and electrical wires strung from building to building, and the sound of the thick crowds on the sidewalks outside. The television talked about new and deeper wells being drilled, collecting glacier water; it spoke of sex scandals in high places. Crowds applauded, there were dramatic conflicts between men and women in intense close-ups, more Pepper Spray and talking spoons and instructions on the use of solar casseroles.

She became despairing and anxious. They had left her parents behind. She thought of them as still standing at the intersection where they had abandoned her, the last place she had looked at with her terrified and seeing eyes. She thought of them weaving among the displaced crowds, restless and insubstantial. Raisa decided they had gone on, toward the northern stars. They had waited for her but she had not come. How could she? So her mother and father went on through outer space toward the Big Dipper. Her parents would never find her again.

Raisa took hold of Shaniya's hand and said, My mother and dad said if I looked up at the North Star they would be there. Am I not going to be blind someday? Raisa closed her hand around the jingle bell they had tied on her wrist so that everyone knew where she was. She always managed to find silent corners and closets. Happily alone among the mops.

Shaniya said, Well, we're trying to get you some medicine.

Then I could see the North Star. That's where my mother and dad are.

Shaniya said, What mother and dad? You never had a mother and dad.

Raisa said, But I did, I did. She grasped the woman's skirt and jerked at it as if she would rip it. Her fists were bony and white. I did!

Shaniya took hold of her hand and said, Baby, you just listen to all those programs and see. Do any of the children on *Undersea Adventures* have mothers and dads?

No, they did not. So there you go.

CHAPTER 2

Raisa went in a vehicle to a hospital with new papers and a new ID that they told her to hold before herself and hand to whoever asked for them. She had been wearing an eye mask for two weeks. After the retinyl palmitate had arrived, her gray-green eyes were newborn and weak and had to be protected.

Her name was changed to Nadia Stepan for medical care and future maintenance by the Agency for Parentless Dependents. She did not understand this. All hope of her parents ever finding her must now be finally abandoned. They would look for a girl named Raisa. She wasn't Raisa anymore. She was a stunted six-year-old with clothes too big for her and a stiff headscarf and boatlike shoes, a creature that *kindheartedness* and *courage* and *nobility,* concepts that had now become free-floating angelic transparencies, could not locate in this dry and overpopulated world even though they were looking for her, searching everywhere.

Shaniya left her in the care of doctors and nurses and kissed her cheek and went away. The sound of explosions had started up again.

Nadia sat in a room that smelled of antiseptics. Brightness enveloped her but all was silent and so she sat very still.

For a long time she sat, listening to people running up and down the halls, the sound of gurneys on wheels and people crying out, I need some help, here!

When Nadia reached out a hand she touched a water bottle. Down the hall was a television with news: demolitions now occurring without proper forewarning, agency heads responsible arrested. Trials beginning next week. Arraignments. Footage. The Facilitator regrets.

She waited. The water bottle was slippery in her hands. After a while it was clear no one else was there. They had forgotten her. A complete silence except for the announcer's voice on the TV down the hall. Another explosion and rumbling. She sat waiting for somebody to take off her eye mask, for the great revelation, the world of sight.

She called out but there was no answer. She pulled the covering from her eyes herself and tore strands of hair with the adhesive. The light was so dazzling she seemed to be suspended in it. She could hear walls coming down.

She put out both hands and walked into planes of gleaming things. She picked up her feet and put them down very carefully as if she were printing some image on the floor. She came to the room with the television. She sat down in front of it. The picture resolved itself, became intelligible, and she saw a tall, thin tower with a light on top sending out an intense beam and a great sea washing over rocks, curtains of drift.

Lighthouse Island! said the announcer's voice. *Save up your credits and go! See the rain forests!* Trees reared upward into mists and rain, long trunks like the legs of marvelous beings whose bodies were higher yet. *Northern beauty, misted nights!* The revolving light on top of the tower arrowed into the night and the sea.

Nadia thought, *This is the magic planet that Lucy and the Swiffer Boys were looking for in their transformer ship. Searching through a cartoon galaxy. I am supposed to go there.* Ocean spray thundered over the guardian cliffs of the shore. Maybe that was where her parents went. A house of logs with intricately carved eaves and painted decorations and medallions and pointed windows, a fantasy house, resolute and calm with a light shining out of a window, people inside, safe and warm. Kind people.

An ambulance attendant found Nadia in front of the TV, picked her up, and ran with her through descending showers of rubble, into the dry streets.

She said, I am not Nadia. My name is Lucy Swiffer.

They believed her; not for very long, but enough to encourage her in thoughts of deception, altered personalities.

At the beginning of the demolitions of the Three Falls neighborhood many square miles of skyscrapers came down, and people scavenged in the rubble for copper pipes and other fixtures, paneling, scrap lumber, nails and screws and hinges and tile and I-beams and I-tools. Some were legal scrappers but others were freelance and most of those were thieves. In groups of four and five the scrappers wrenched up blocks of rubble and snaked out electrical lines; they came upon dishes and clothes and from time to time the remains of other people.

James Orotov was eighteen years old and had come to love demolition, even the smell of cordite and the dust of test blasts. He was deeply absorbed by the remains of structures where he could see the hidden anatomy of the city exposed like a medical student's cadaver, where he could observe load-bearing beams and ancient water mains and the infill of foundations. He and his brother had the privilege of flying south with the engineers, one of only ten flights that year. In the south one could come across old Saltillo tiles with imprints of the hands that had made them, and paw prints and chicken tracks. James had a collection of these tiles with their fossils of vanished animals and workmen. In a notebook he began to make secret maps; they were tentative and unsure. *Prester John Apartments,* he wrote. *28 degrees 24 minutes North latitude and 97 degrees 45 minutes West longitude.*

He and his brother went out on a balcony of the Prester John Apartments after the crews had taken down the top five stories to see the beams that supported the balconies. His brother dared him to step out on the balcony and so he did. So they both did. They eased through the doorless doorway and onto the balcony and then the balcony gave way. There were no beams. It was only a concrete shelf without supports.

He fell all four stories and landed on top of a pile of mattresses, fans, solar cookers, cacti in planters, wheelie carts for shopping, tools, bedding, and polyester clothes that had been dragged into the street by former inhabitants.

As he dropped through the hot city air a great voice (his own) shouted through his mind like a loud-hailer, *But I never met her!* He fell, windmilling his arms, into the deep canyon of the narrow street, young and strong and in flight for perhaps the last time in his life. Slabs of broken concrete came down with him. He struck the pile of mattresses and clothes and would have survived without serious injury but the remains of the balcony fell on his back and broke his spine. Pieces of concrete hit the street and bounded and shattered into even smaller pieces. His brother hung from the balcony door frame by his fingers and some men ran up the four flights and pulled him in.

The workmen loaded James onto a door and ran down the street with him. They dodged buses and carts. James shouted that he could not feel his legs. His brown hair was glistening with blood. His brother dashed ahead to a telephone exchange booth and called for an ambulance. The operator gave the EMS the corner numbers and James was taken to a hospital and ended up in a wheelchair.

He recalled his descent through the hot afternoon air and his wild thought, *But I never met her!*

Met who?

He studied and attained degrees in both architecture and explosives. He studied cartography on his own. He had brown hair and gray eyes and the cynical and reserved attitude of someone confined to a wheelchair. James often tried to find his way through the antiquated and unstable remains of the Internet, searching for the disappeared. He had once been tall.

James and his brother, Farrell, became closer after the fall. They had lost their father to cancer and so there were only three of them left and one of these in a wheelchair. Farrell was stockier than James and shorter, only now of course James sat in his wheelchair and was shorter than anybody except children and dwarves. Farrell studied meteorology and aviation and became a pilot and a devotee of old weather reports, written in a language so obsolete that few could puzzle it out. Meteorology, an orphan bureaucracy, was always shifted around because the world had fallen into a state of weatherless weather. All was blue seared skies and drought and, in the winter, intense cold because atmospheric water had frozen up in the glacial caps at the poles, plunging the world into a Drought Age. Farrell was given a position in Meteorology and Intrusive Species Identification because he could read the technical jargon or at least was interested in understanding it and could translate the greater part of the reports. He obtained a Ph.D. in aviation and weather, as if it were an award.

Farrell asked agency heads in Wellness and Medical Certification about research into spinal injuries, specifically corticospinal tract regeneration. It was not a high priority and medical research had gone seriously downhill over the last century. Farrell discovered a facility that prepared retinol for stabilization into retinyl palmitate. The plant was laced with great tubes delivering inert gases for gas packing, smoky people in subzero temperatures doing things in white coats, and in the rear a tiny laboratory where corticospinal researchers lived in squalor.

Yes, sir? A woman sat in a busted armchair out in the entryway to the minute laboratory. Her hair was flattened under a dirty white cap, her skin dried into innumerable wrinkles. A cardboard box that said BIOWASTE overflowed onto the floor. He told her why he had come.

She said respectfully, Well, Director Orotov, we may have something. We're trying to find a blocking system for an enzyme called PTEN; it's a cell-proliferation inhibitor. It inhibits a molecular pathway called mTOR, and if we can delete the PTEN, we may get nerve regrowth. Spinal nerves normally don't regenerate but this may do the trick. It has with the pigs.

I see Farrell's dark eyes were fixed on her and very alert. So, this is working on your lab pigs.

Yes, but it may allow for formation of tumors. Other illnesses. I mean, you suppress a cell-growth inhibitor and so you may get all kinds of weird cell growth.

Okay. Farrell nodded. You'll let me know, won't you?

It will be available for severe cases only, at first. An experiment.

And the severe cases are always among people who have connections.

Isn't that the truth?

But you'll let me know? Farrell laid down two Krugerrands. What else do you need?

The woman looked at the gold coins for a long moment. A new centrifuge. The one we have is hand-cranked if you can believe that and the air seal is faulty. The woman put her hand on the coins. This is lunch. For, like five months or so. What do you do, Director Orotov?

I'm in Meteorology.

Farrell and James came from a good family, a privileged family. They had been taught, against all logic, the privilege and responsibility of public service. But the corrosive contempt of the general population for the agencies wore down this concept as if by steel wool.

The brothers often went to the rooftops to talk, to get away from those who might listen in and disapprove and get them arrested. They listened to Big Radio and its cycle of readings: *Here we are at the beginning of autumn when the season turns and the leaves take on color. This is the season for the classic works of Spain and then the unforgettable explorers' tales. Let us begin with* Blood and Sand.

From the streets below came the sounds of the inhabitants of the worldwide city streaming in many directions, thick as boiling grains, dried out and thirsty. Beyond that sound another deep tremolo of trains rumbling underground carrying compressed brewer's yeast, cactus paste in blocks, boxes of soy crumbles, solar panels, pressed recycled cardboard, packets of fish-flavored shreds, rice milk from what used to be St. Louis but was now Gerrymander Seven. The shipments were often stalled for months for lack of paperwork or were sidelined and rifled by professional thieves while neighborhoods quietly starved. Distribution was a chronic problem and a mystery but secret trains full of prisoner-workers bulled their way past the immovable food shippage.

The brothers sat on Farrell's rooftop with a water feature called Eastern Tranquility and listened to this symphonic arrangement of urban sounds and talked. They discussed the human propensity to construct cities and the imperatives of urban growth. James's long unfeeling feet were in house slippers on the wheelchair plates, his hand skipped over his keypad. They talked about heavier-than-air flight, about old movies, about the future of humanity, about forgetting, about the fall of James and the fall of man.

James was one of the top men in his field and he was quietly invited to join the Royal Cartography Society, which was not exactly illegal. After the Urban Wars they had destroyed all the maps, the old place names as well as the year numbers. This left people in a kind of eternal present in no specific place. The maps needed to be recovered, rediscovered, and if they were quiet about it, no problem. Pandrit Yi was an undersupervisor in Urban Drainage and Flow Control in the Eighth Gerrymander who mapped in the wee hours; Albert Burke held some kind of job with Furniture Supply and he actually walked over the rise and fall of the land, house by house, in the far north, Fourth Gerrymander, Neighborhood Fifteen, which was at one time known as Minneapolis, and drew in the topographical lines as things felt and bodily known.

Are we truly born to formulate cities? James had himself driven to the interspaces, traveling by ambulance to the limits of his own part of the city, which was a micronation, or had been, to look out on the slums that lay between while his attendants groused and snorted. To leave the dense city, even to approach the small spaces in between urban concentrations was, to them, like approaching death and starvation. They drove for days, through the confusion of broken freeways, crowded by dense housing.

They drove past hundreds of thousands of workers' barracks crowded and filthy and in other areas dense fields of cactus pads fat with glycerin surrounded by a mineral landscape that long ago had been stripped of soil. They came to a place where winds tore across the interurban deserts and carried with them dust and sand grains and lost kites and clothing from distant rooftop clotheslines and wads of dried grasses as coarse as thatch.

On the edge of the Fourth Gerrymander were one-room shacks spaced precisely three hundred yards apart so that they dotted the landscape in endless squares. James wheeled himself out of the ambulance and down a ramp. He refused to use the electric controls so his arms and shoulders were very strong. He was somewhere in one of the old national entities that had been layered on top of another and older national entity. This had once been Mexico. Then the United States. Then the Western Cessions.

His attendants stood behind him in the unceasing wind among broken walls to look out at the wellheads that drilled for water in a landscape so simple it seemed to have just been made. Dirt. Sand. Rocks. They drilled for the gyppy fossil water of ancient seas that lay in the seeping layers of limestone at fifty-four thousand feet. At this particular place James could see great ships half buried in the sands. A gulf of the sea had drawn off and left them at some ancient port. Their rusted prows rose a hundred feet above gray dunes. The *Shunta Maru,* the *Ramik Fane.*

Maybe we are on Mars, James thought. The wind tore at his short brown hair. That's possible. But then would the Big Dipper look the same? Would Polaris still be in the geographical north? His attendants went back inside the ambulance and played cards and then wrapped themselves in their coats and fell asleep around a catalytic heater. The stars emerged slowly and then James sat alone under a clear black heaven where the constellations took on a fierce intensity, and indeed they were all in their accustomed places with the Dipper on one side of the firmament and the Chair on the other and between the two, Polaris dimly shining.

CHAPTER 3

In the apartment building of the family that had been told to adopt her, there lived an older man named Thin Sam Kenobi who used to sit at the entrance of the apartment building and make disposable jewelry things out of the foil from cigarette packages and soy cheese packages.

Nadia, in the ardor of her orphan heart, decided to love Thin Sam like a father and to think about him and do things for him. She and Thin Sam had made themselves a bench by stacking volumes of scavenged hardback books and putting planks across them. Nadia's hands were short with blunt nails and still brown with last summer's sun. The winter was dry and arctic, so Thin Sam had made a rocket stove for them and they held their hands out to it.

It was only October and bitterly cold but sitting outside was better than inside, the TV on Deafening, all of them drinking up their gin allowance, the air clouded with people's breath and the walls sparkling with frost.

Every apartment was assigned about 20 kWh of electricity per month, which was enough to run the OLED television screen, flexible and thin as paper, and maybe a lightbulb for a few hours in the evenings. Communications and Entertainment made sure every human being in the megacity had access to television. Some people fought for assignments to apartments with a higher allowance, maybe 90 kWh a month, but then you had to pay for it with work hours and the electricity failed a lot. And then there were people who were adept at stealing it, and also tapping into the water pipes. Penalty: the cactus farms.

Throughout the apartment building at least twenty televisions were all broadcasting the same program. Soccer was over (men in shorts struggling in the frozen mud over a ball) and now it was *Early to Rise*, where a group of people in a recycle unit found weird things in rubble and argued with one another and had love affairs, but if Nadia watched the screen for more than five minutes she began to see sparks flashing and weaving through her vision.

So she began to read and memorize whatever came to hand. In abandoned upper stories she found novels, stories in which the characters' actions and thoughts were described and the plot proceeded with a happy continuity. The characters' behaviors were explained and motivations stated so everything fell together. She didn't need to *see* anything. She found herself so grateful for this phenomenon that she fell into novels as if into a well, and into poetry as if it were a river.

We're looking down into a valley, she said to Thin Sam. Under all the buildings there, right? "And travelers now, within that valley, through red-lit windows see vast forms . . ." of whatevers. I love to scare myself. Vast *stinking* forms. Eww. She lifted her dark eyebrows and smiled at him.

Nadia, Nadia, he said. He folded the delicate foil strips in his hard fingers. There used to be a lake down there. Standing water. Dirty but standing. It was called Blue Springs Lake.

Where did it go? She pressed out a foil strip between her cold hands.

We used it up. He took the strip from her hand. For manufacturing. Flushed our waste with it. Then the weather changed. Our ancient imperative for growth. It was supposed to be a good thing. Nobody asked, when does growth stop? And so here we are. This used to be called Kansas City but now it's just city most of the way to Denver and we are called Gerrymander Eight.

And where did the animals all go?

We ate them, he said. And we took up all their space. Except for rats, mice, and the hardier sort of bird.

Nadia handed Thin Sam another foil. She had to press them out smooth and then fold them longways; then he wove them together in diamond patterns. She loved being away from the television and the crowded rooms and passageways. From Thin Sam's cupboard where he lived and drank and had his being, a radio played.

Nadia kept her schoolbooks under the bench and only occasionally flipped through them because they were so boring. She also kept old novels there. Nobody cared if she read. Child welfare didn't care. So few people read that it was of no concern.

Thin Sam Kenobi was loose inside his layers of clothes, several shirts and a tattered sweater and a coat. His knuckles were round as marbles. From below came a deep rumbling. The transport trains. He had taken to instructing her in matters of life, things an orphan girl ought to know.

He said, Always, always hide food. Never, never sign anything.

Why? she said. She rested her pointed chin on one fist and her dark-red hair stuck out in sprays.

Because there are people who would arrest you and take you away. He turned a leaf of foil in his hand. You would be a happy child if only the world would let you be.

This left Nadia confused. Was she supposed to be happy all the time? Would people love her then?

Never mind. So. Thin Sam rooted around in his basket and came up with more foils and handed them to her. And you will see other girls who have parents and good lives, and when you find yourself getting angry, getting envious, say to yourself, Stop, stop. It's a waste of mind. Okay?

Yep, said Nadia. Will do.

From the alcove of the doorway to the Riverdale Apartments they could see down the street where it fell away into the great, broad valley covered in the parquetry of hundreds of thousands of buildings, the city without end. It fell into a haze in the remote distance, a fog caused by the heat inside millions of trashy little apartments. Many blocks were painted with portraits of agency heads several stories high with windows for eyes so it appeared that people lived inside all-seeing brains. Nadia heard the engine of a hang glider carrying a day-flight watchman in thick goggles, spying out trouble, especially young lovers who whispered on rooftops, wanting to be alone.

Sand and dust rose up out of the canyon streets in cold coils. It grew dark and the streets were emptied. Here and there someone walked home late with a pierced tin candle-lantern but most people were inside cooking dinner and watching the advertisements for vacation spots. Not that any of them would ever have enough work credits.

You'll never get there, he said. To Lighthouse Island.

Hey, why not? She shoved her auburn hair back from her face and reached for another foil. Her breath smoked from her nose.

You'll meet some guy. He'll say he loves you and that'll be the end of it.

I'll make you a bet, she said. She was suddenly furious. I'll bet you anything you want to bet.

Nah. If you ever ran away you wouldn't even know where to go. You wouldn't know to go north and find the old Ritz-Carlton building. You're going to take up with the first guy that pays any attention to you. That's because you're an orphan. It's the way of the world with orphans.

Nadia bit her lower lip against the feeling of weeping that crept up her neck and jaw. She was once again dressed in an oversized coat and dress, shoes like wastebaskets, clothing issued for someone her age by mechanical and repeated deliveries every year regardless of her actual size.

Run away? she cried. What do you mean, run away? The way of the world with orphans, oh ha ha.

Just remember what I said. Remember every word.

She crinkled up the foil strips and wiped her nose on her sleeve and felt as if her heart were breaking and from the breakage tears were going to spill out in an extravagant, dehydrating stream because Thin Sam Kenobi sounded like the voice of God. He was wise and old and knew everything. He used tools and made things and he had an actual homemade radio that sometimes worked. It broadcast a voice reading from antique books and poetry and also classical music. There it was now; *So then, they know it and we know it; the time has come for the kingdom of dreams to go on the offensive.*

Listen, he said. It's Sigizmund Krzhizhanovsky. *Memories of the Future.* It's into the Russians now.

I don't understand any of it. She wiped quickly at her gray-green eyes.

It's too old for you.

Where does it come from?

From an old satellite, suspended up there, twenty thousand miles overhead.

Jeez, fascinating. She blinked back tears. Thin Sam Kenobi had made a definitive pronouncement on Nadia's life and against this declaration she had no appeal.

He reached behind the bench into the paper sack of foils and brought out a quart bottle of water. It was partly frozen and wrapped in a woven koozie, strips of bright rags.

Here.

Thank you.

Not a problem. Don't ask where I got it.

Very well.

Very well. He imitated her stiff, choked voice. That's so you can cry. You need more water than you're getting. A young girl shouldn't end up wrinkled like an old woman. You should be able to cry any time you want.

His eyes were Baltic pale and he turned slowly to look at her where she sat wrapped in her layers of knit clothing, a canvas coat and finger-less gloves and her wizened adolescent face.

She said, there's *plenty* of water at Lighthouse Island. I could drown myself in it.

Oh again. Again again. Okay, that's what the TV says. But where is it? He laughed and showed a bridge of ill-fitting steel teeth. It's close to the graveyard, where the daughter of Oceanus watches over the sea. Remember every word.

It's northward, said Nadia. Now, Sam, you show me where the North Star is. Her heart was apparently not broken yet or maybe it had repaired itself in the last few minutes.

You show me first. Go ahead and guess.

There. She pointed to a brilliant light rising over the rim of the valley and all the distant apartments with a pale and somewhat dirty forefinger.

That's an advertisement, he said. And the light expanded, threw out glowing arms that formed into spirals. It's the sky ad for Savory Circles.

Well, then, where is it? She turned up the bottle of water, drank as much as was unfrozen, capped it, put it under the bench.

Hide that better, he said.

She covered it with her book bag.

It's dim, said Sam. He handed her two bracelets and then began to fold other foils into star shapes. It's between two big bright constella-tions. You're so smart, I thought maybe you knew.

Nadia put the foil bracelets into a basket woven from electrical wire that Thin Sam then carried into the streets and sold to women and girls who had neither jewelry nor coins to buy anything but these foil brace-lets and rings that would sparkle for a short while, would lift spirits for a week or so. It was not illegal so far but you never knew. When the people at the top decided, they'd let you know. She clasped her hands under her armpits to warm them. I *am* smart, she said. And you know it and I know it.

All right then, what are these? He laid out the star-shaped foils.

That's the Big Dipper and the Chair and I guess the little one is the North Star.

Good! Okay now, where in the sky is it?

Over Lighthouse Island.

He swept up the foils and crushed them and began folding bracelets again. I told you, he said. You'll never get there.

Oh, how do *you* know! She put both hands in their tatty fingerless gloves over her eyes and fell, finally, into abandoned and hopeless weeping.

I know, he said. He looked down at her. Nadia wiped her eyes and took deep breaths. His thick eyeglasses made his cloudy eyes shift and glint. It's life.

Somebody called, Nadia! Sam! Come inside!

Because the wind is becoming stronger and stronger and supper is ready. Come in. Get away from the street. Hide from the cruising pickup vans. Come in where it was safe from the dark and the things that paced nervously in the dark.

Sam, tell me, she said. If I just *act* happy all the time, will I be okay in life?

You don't know how to be, he said. Orphan child. You don't know who you are. He patted her on the top of her head and it was like being softly beaten with a baseball glove. Just hold out your two hands and pretend there's a light there, and it's all yours forever, and there are these huge stars on your left and your right, whose job is to look out for you.

Nadia thought for a moment. Yes, wait, here, I got it. My mother and dad live on Lighthouse Island. They're waiting for me to get there. She looked up at him with a delight in her own audacity.

He sighed. Okay, he said. Okay, okay.

CHAPTER 4

Nadia slept in a nest of dreams and coverlets. It was deep in the night and deep in a dream of some performance where onstage an entertainer fell into a giant fan and was sliced to pieces. She was supposed to take one of these bloody pieces somewhere so they could put him back together. It was wrapped in a dishcloth. In the middle of all this her curtain was pulled back and a man came into her alcove; it was near Christmastime. He pulled the curtain shut behind him with a metallic sliding sound as the rings ran along the pole and he stepped to her bed.

Hush, he said. Don't say anything. His glasses flashed in front of his eyes. He was dark against the dark and the black wind gnawed at the windows of the long attic. The man in the empty night was a primitive demon come out from under the floorboards.

Nadia sat up as if she had been lifted on wires and her hair crept strangely on her head and she could feel her eyes starting from their sockets. She put out both hands and said, Get out!

She could smell him; it was Thin Sam there in the freezing dark standing over her with his odor of cigarette smoke and oily hair.

Hush, he said. Listen.

One of the other girls across the attic said from behind her curtain, *Nadia?*

She sat unmoving and heard the tinny voice of a radio; not Big Radio but something else. *They are coming to Riverdale Apartments,* the voice said. *Thin Sam, run, hide.*

Loud knocking and shouting and engines in the street below. Doors were smashed open. Men shouting commands.

Thin Sam's voice was a coarse whisper. There's a trapdoor above your bed. Get up, get *up*. Nadia, get out of my way.

She swung her legs out of bed and dragged a coverlet with her. All around the attic other girls woke up and cried out, What? What? Who's there? Tiny lights in pinpoints as girls connected the wires of their battery lamps. Nadia stepped backward in the dark and the curtain tangled around her legs.

Footsteps pounded up the stairs. The door to the attic was kicked open and Thin Sam stood in his broken old shoes on her bed shoving at the trapdoor, smashing at it until the dry plaster sprayed on her bed. In the piecemeal darkness he struck it with his fists while Nadia whispered, What are you *doing*? But then the attic dormitory was full of large agents with flashlights.

Get out of bed! Line up! Who's in there? Get out!

Then Sam stopped with the trapdoor half open. He reached into his pocket and in the broken flashes and noise he took out a small silver thing and handed it to her.

Hang on to it, he said. Don't lose it. It's the sign of St. Jude, patron saint of escapes and evasions.

Nadia shut her hand around it just as the curtain was ripped aside. Thin Sam Kenobi stepped off her bed and held out both hands to his sides. Three men in gray uniforms with clashing belt tools and flashlights laid hands on Thin Sam in her private space, in a crush of loud voices and heavy shoes.

Sam was illuminated by the flashlights like some kind of tramp

celebrity, a joey clown with his two-day beard and glasses and slaty eyes
now filled with artificial light. He threw up a hand to shield his eyes.
An agent struck him behind the head with a heavy flashlight and when
he went down they kicked him and his eyeglasses shot off his head and
his bridge of steel teeth flew out of his mouth in a spray of blood and
saliva. It landed on the linoleum and a girl screamed at it as if it were a
live biting device. They took him away.

Then the agents tore out drawers and turned over mattresses. They
threw boxes upside down and the contents of small treasure hoards
scattered; fortune-telling stones, tarot cards, plastic bracelets and rings.
An old High School Jam eight-ball rolled to the answer, *I've got nerve
and I say no.*

Nadia had to abandon all her possessions on the linoleum, her tin
box of hairpins scattered among perfume sticks, books, and pieces of
fallen plaster. She was shouted at and pushed downstairs in her night-
gown with all the others.

Your name is Nadia Stepan.

Yes, sir.

Parentless dependent child. Adopted by this wacko outfit.

Yes, sir.

A quart a day plus basic shower privileges. Ah, let's see, you're grade
nine, fourteen years old. Hmmmm. PR stream. Ever been interrogated
before? Have you?

No, sir.

Fun, isn't it?

Nadia pulled the coverlet more tightly around her neck and said, I
don't know.

The apartment building's kitchen smelled of kerosene and rose-
mary and was oppressed by the usual low seven-foot ceiling. A windup
wall clock hammered out the minutes. A scorpion eased down between
the ceiling and the wall and inquired around itself to see if the coast

were clear. Nadia held the silver thing in her hand as she had once gripped her jingle bell.

Why was this Sam person hiding in your little place, there?

I don't know. He just came in. I just woke up and he was coming in.

Yes, well, he had a resistance problem. Okay now, so Mrs. Bergolts gave you a lot of extra shower privileges and way over your regular water ration and like that. All you girls.

She did?

Yes. We already know this. So just tell me about this.

What am I supposed to tell you?

Quit crying. Listen here. You knew all about the tap line. The one down in the cooler well.

I did? What's a tap line? I don't know what a tap line is.

Sure you do. Who else was running lines off it?

Off what?

Shut up crying. I hate that. They tapped into an industrial water line and everybody here was living very well. It was Mrs. Bergolts and this Sam person and the Thrane couple and your friend Josie selling it by hundreds of gallons. You all had all the water you wanted while people like me got to get along on a quart a day. Little kids croaking in orphanages, everybody dying of thirst, and a great big girl like you swilling water and playing in a wading pool. Bawling isn't going to get you out of this.

I didn't know they did that. I never heard anything about a wading pool. What's a wading pool?

Rubber thingie with ducks on it. About six inches deep.

You fill it with water? And people stick their feet in it?

Listen, if you weren't in the PR stream you'd be in summer camp right now, did you know that?

No, sir.

Nadia could hear Thin Sam's radio: *Today the sun rose clear and continued so until twelve o'clock when the captain got an observation. This was very well for Cape Horn but the clear weather did not last very long.* It was November and the radio time of sea tales.

The interrogator turned to the door and shouted, Somebody go and shut that goddamn radio off. He returned to Nadia. That radio should be illegal. But nobody cares except weird people like Mr. Kenobi. Tell me about the wading pools.

The agent sounded tired as if even he didn't believe in the wading pools and the rubber ducks. Nadia stared at him with her mouth slightly open, breathing out clouds, wadded in the quilt.

You think it's smart? You see these felons on *Sector Secrets* and you think stealing water is smart?

No, sir, I don't. I don't even watch television.

You what?

I don't watch television. I don't know what they do on *Sector Secrets*.

You don't watch television?

No, sir. I can't. I have eye problems.

Eye problems? Are you legally blind?

No, sir.

Well, let's see. For instance could you see the Thrane couple down in the cooler well running a hose up to the kitchen? Eh?

I never saw them stealing water. I just had my regular ration, that's all.

All right, all right. He cast about for something else. He turned up his wrist so he could see his watch. Now, you have to turn in your papers. Parentless Dependents have to submit all letters and diaries in the event of any arrests in the foster home. Go get them.

I don't have any. You can look.

Well, hell. All right. Here. Sign this.

What is it?

Just sign it.

I don't know what it is.

Nadia remembered Thin Sam's dictum and clove to it like sacred scripture of some sort because orphans do not often get good advice and when they do they grasp it and never let go.

You don't need to know. It's required that you sign it.

But I can't read it. Nadia stared blankly at the form in front of her.

You said you weren't legally blind.

No, sir, I'm not, but I have eye problems. You have to get somebody to read it out loud to me and then I can sign it and they have to sign it too. Nadia was surprised at herself, at her convincing voice.

I can check your medical, you know.

Yes, sir, it says right there on my medical.

Listen, Miss Stepan, if you weren't in a PR stream you'd be in summer camp right now on a pint a day.

Yes, sir, but you have to get somebody to read it out to me. I have the order from my counselor.

Another bald-faced lie.

Ah, you're a pain in the ass. Don't sign it, then. Get out. Tell the next girl to come in here. Get out.

Everybody in the entire building called Riverdale Apartments had to stand outside in the frozen nighttime streets while the arrested ones were loaded onto a truck. Nadia and Widdy and Josie stood holding on to one another, their breath smoking in the cold air. They heaved Thin Sam onto the truck. The body was wrapped in gray and tattered canvas but Nadia could see Thin Sam's shoes on feet that wobbled back and forth loose as rubber and she wept as if she would never stop. He had been courageous. Kindhearted. Maybe noble.

Adults were shoved into the back of a big truck with handcuffs in front of them reflecting and winking in the flashlight beams while the urban windstorm tore at all the girls' nightclothes and fluted and sang around the corners, through the empty upper stories of millions of apartment buildings across the endless spaces of cityscape where the informer who turned in Thin Sam peered through curtains and counted his silver coins.

All up and down the street, blinds and curtains were drawn briefly back, letting out thin spears of lantern light, and then dropped again. It was dangerous to know. There were a few dark silhouettes on rooftops where people had run up through the empty upper stories to the roof to see if they would be next. The ambient light of the urban sky glowed behind them, and below the streets unseen trains rumbled. A bus with peeling advertisements for the Home Heating Department's new Fiberglas Lamp Wicks pulled up in a cloud of exhaust vapor and three people got out but when they saw what was going on they got back in. The bus slammed its door and pulled away. Then a sudden loud roar of airplane engines and the crack of lightning and shouting men. The noise burst from every window. *Still Alive* had just come on.

Nadia cried for days and could not eat. She had been brash and daring with her cranky dark auburn hair sprayed out like wiring and her head full of startling ideas discovered in the stained books others had discarded or abandoned, which others had left behind. Now it seemed all her interior water would leak away and she would mummify herself with sobbing. She knew the possessions of the dead were sold on the street in order to pay the Candyman and the sweets given away but Nadia hid the silver dangle and some tattered foils and wept silently over Thin Sam. After a long time her grieving for him was a kind of melodic, distant echo that seemed very ancient, very far away.

And beyond the trauma a strange feeling of triumph. She had lied to the interrogator and got away with it. And so she became an adult, with an adult's complex attitude of both hatred and fear of the authorities. *And who,* said Riddley Walker, *is the Loakel Tharty round here?*

CHAPTER 5

Abitterly cold February. Another new place, an unknown neighborhood in the overcrowded world of trashy, stacked flats, windy streets, and tired people. Her counselor told the new family that Nadia had been shifted to another foster home because of an unfortunate incident in the last place and that she could not watch television because of her eyes and they felt sorry for her and offered to fill her in on the latest corruption trial, and tell her what had happened to Louvat on *Early to Rise* when he had been buried under a collapsing wall as he was trying to retrieve a cache of I-glasses and I-pods from an old exchange office but she said, That's all right, I never kept up anyway. Nadia bent her head down and sat on her cot and listened. Far away in some other apartment a radio played. She would listen to Big Radio whenever she could because it was a link to Thin Sam and links were hard to come by in this world.

Female Voice One said, in delicate tones, *And now it is time, in the beginning months of the New Year, that we turn to fable, legend, and myth. We step into the land of mystery. We move on to the graceful and moving Nō plays of ancient Japan.*

The night grows late. Eastward the bells of the three pagodas toll. By the moonlight that gleams through the needles of the thick cedar trees I begin to put on my armor.

Nadia could memorize anything and often said long passages aloud to herself because of their beauty, because they were affirmative, because the words lightened her heavy heart. She whispered, *Eastward the bells of the three pagodas toll.*

What do you want to do with your life, Nadia? her counselor had asked. She was a kind person named Caroline with thick and kinking hair.

Well, said Nadia, I want to do a walk across the entire city and then to Lighthouse Island. I could do it for charity. I could raise money for a charity drive. For instance, for the subcommittee on Tourette's syndrome. Promote awareness of Tourette's syndrome. I would do the entire walk on foot. If I had a map. It would be energy-smart and eco-green. She clasped her work-worn hands and smiled brightly at the counselor.

The counselor stared at her. She said, I'm not even going to write that down.

Nadia's new foster family stood in line and did a minimalist bow with their heads when the counselor left, the women in their striped aprons and men in cement-stained clothes from their concrete work. And Nadia watched her go. She thought of the television ad for Lighthouse Island shining from the wooden console with a deep glow as if she could reach into the television screen and take the image in her two hands like a crystal ball and the light of it would flow through her fingers, its magic infuse her, releasing her into her true self, which was a generous and confident girl who lived in a rain forest with a light tower sending out signals across a gleaming ocean.

The counselor clicked away on little heels, down the crowded, noisy street in her gray dress with its soiled white collar, carrying her canvas briefcase full of children's adoption files, reports, assessments, family evaluations, reviews. The files and assessments that direct lives.

She was deeply preoccupied with Nadia Stepan's case. She barely noticed the cold. It seemed persons unknown had attempted to pry into the girl's files. She was a bright, odd girl and the counselor wanted to teach her to exhibit the Five Signs of Superior Intelligence, all the appropriate attitudes to make her way up to an office job, better food, more water and electricity and then onward and upward to private showers and water features, vacation credits to places like Country Gardens or Celebration Cruises. She wanted Nadia to lead a more privileged life in which nothing alarming would ever happen. But this fantasy of walking off across the city could get Nadia certified. It really meant, "I want to escape this life." This turned people into State evaders who lived on the margins like animals, perpetually homeless. Like the savage hippies in the Northwest, who formed cults, fought one another, drowned in their rotting boats, ate raw fish.

But the counselor was afraid she was of no more use to Nadia Stepan than a Continuity Man with his dazzling tarots, fake predictions of love and promotions.

People on the street had all turned and were hurrying, or trotting, toward her and past her. An overloaded bus had come to a halt with the driver standing on the brakes with both feet.

Only the unity of television kept the planetwide megapolis from flying apart into brawls, from bombing each other all over again. The young recyclers who rooted in the rubble on *Early to Rise* were avatars of ancient treasure hunters, of tomb looters from earlier times. The news anchors and panels of experts gave the people the feeling of being informed. Public trials shamed and destroyed those who stole from the agencies. Billions of urban inhabitants watched *Imperial Rebels* as one mind as Captain Kenaty and his men struggled toward some distant abandoned city. They were the heroic soldiers the audience loved to admire. A new flashy quick-bit program called *The Question Freak* showed a crazed Master of Mayhem racing through the sets screaming audacious questions and this satisfied people's need for defiance of authorities. The bearded savages of *Still Alive* instructed them in the depths of human depravity beyond the city where no televisual icons connected all these spilling quinoa grains of persons into something rich and fine.

Men came running down the street with orange demolition signs.

What? she said.

Turn around and get out of here, lady! Run for it!

She turned. The C-4 went off. A shock wave struck her and sent her briefcase flying along with other people and pieces of windowsills and metal shards and rolling plastic wheels from recycle pitches and bits of concrete from telephone poles and whipping electrical wires.

So a great part of Nadia's files flew into oblivion, which probably saved her life.

In the new foster home, in the run-down tenement called Silver Lake Apartments, they gave Nadia a place at the far end of the main hall where there was an overhead storage space. The storage cabinet was so high you needed a stepladder to get into it. There they stored things that had to be kept away from children such as matches and kerosene and boric acid powder. The population density of Silver Lake Apartments was far above the allowable limit but nobody paid any attention to allowable limits anymore. They had become fossil regulations.

Nadia hung a canvas shower curtain with multicolored fish painted on it from the cupboard's edge and behind this she made herself a bed with stacks of books on which she placed planks and a foam mattress. There she hid from the clatter of arguments, yelling children, televisions, crashing dishes. There were regulations about the exact size of the table she was to have, the length and width of her bed and the thickness of her mattress, but nobody paid any attention to those regulations either. She bent eagerly over Wendell Berry's poetry, *Valley of the Dolls, Tobacco Road, Piano for Dummies,* Sylvia Plath, anything she could find. *You do not do, you do not do.*

The sheets they gave her had been freshly washed and so that was good. For warmth in the winter she had her coat and a couple of dun-colored army blankets. The families all drank their own gin and vodka allowances, and then more from the black market, but nobody got violently drunk. From time to time one of the women cooked up crispy fries in hard-to-obtain corn oil and sometimes on Fridays they had orange drink. In abandoned top stories of buildings slated for demolition Nadia found old books in dusty heaps and so life was not so bad.

The books with lurid covers she carried down to start the kitchen fire. They were always the boring ones that left her saying aloud, Come on, come on, I don't believe it. She also had to take the trash and separate it for the recycle bins, light the firebox for the hot showers, and fire up the little coal stove. Mrs. Novgorod was incredibly filthy and always tipping over ashtrays or walking away from sticky crusted dishes. She said, You can do it. You're young and strong. And so Nadia did it but nothing interfered with her obsessive reading.

So she began a Sometime life. Sometimes she managed to see the girls from the last place, who lived in the next apartment block. Sometimes the basic rations were not delivered to the neighborhood for days and they all went hungry or walked for miles, carrying the children, to an emergency supply point. It was said that tons of dried and canned food and shoes and computers were stored underground but the bureaucrats got stalled by paperwork. Sometimes the pipes failed and then water came in tanker trucks; it was beige or yellowish but it was drinkable. Everyone lived with the fear that water would finally and totally run out. The news at six thirty often told them that this might actually happen.

At that point everybody in Silver Lake Apartments freaked out. Then there would be a long confusing interview with the senior counselor for water distribution policy who blamed a lot of multisyllabic factors that did not lower the level of anxiety. So they all lived in a condition of subdued dread and low-tech ignorance as the human world marched steadily forward to the Steady State at the End of the Universe. They did not know where in the endless city they were and no longer cared. The audience was told the city came to an end at the shores of the oceans, where houses like concrete swallow's nests were pegged onto cliffs over a dirty, salty sea. The people who lived there from time to time found themselves sliding into a dishwater surf with all their furniture and babies.

Like the amazing personal technology of Previous Times, all things had within them the digital instructions of their own collapse. The factories that made the devices had gone overseas and died there in televised revolutions. The Urban Wars had destroyed whatever was left on this side of the sea. Nobody knew how to make the devices anymore and worse, nobody knew how to make the machines that made the elements and the components of the devices. And the things that received and relayed the signals of all the personal devices were also missing in action. The petroleum that powered the factories and out of which were made millions of essential plastic things had slowed to a trickle. Thus there was very little plastic for solar panel films, pens and steering wheels, bottles and water pipes and toothbrushes, only some for Buddy car parts and a few computer monitors and keyboards, the police cell phones and of course televisions.

Petroleum became difficult to find and extract because the number of three-cone roller drilling bits with tungsten teeth were becoming scarce. Devices that had kept people together in social networks were gone. So let's sit down and relax from being boiled in the stew of overcrowded streets, sit down with these sportless sports programs and the sitcom characters with their vital miseries, their clean clothes and hygienic studio sets, and with the news and its alarms.

People kept to themselves to avoid the management of public thought and also to blank out local authorities. Neighbors did not react to the sound of smashing glass when a neighborhood watchman drove his club through a kitchen window. He had caught Mrs. Caulder throwing a box of oily rags into the alleyway and she was taken away with a bleeding nose and did not come back for a week. And why not? The woman was deeply stupid and could have set the city on fire. People watched silently and said nothing. Nadia knew to never mention her parents nor should she ever mention that night on the street and the poor shoeless dead. Dear Thin Sam. A traveler now within that valley. She had the silver dangle and often recalled the sound of his voice. She remembered every word and they seemed to be words of power and hope, and therefore rare. Rare as Krugerrands and as valuable.

People disappeared but everybody pretended not to notice and stayed neutral and colorless like fabric lampshades. Mrs. Caulder finally disappeared permanently. She left her teeth behind. Don't Ask Don't Tell was written in their schoolbooks. The only people in the entire city-world who could both ask and tell were the police and the executioners. They were given the gift of openness and weapons.

Nadia plunged into books because there was no danger of fictional characters disappearing, and even better, they were not subject to arrest. They could not reach out of the pages and threaten her or kill her friends and load their bodies on trucks. They were always there: the Highwayman and Anna Karenina and Edwin Drood and Huckleberry Finn and Scarlett O'Hara. She took the books and ran up the stairs to the roof in her stiff clothing and her ill-fitting shoes, her thick auburn hair spinning loose from its braids, lost in the story of Madame Olenska.

The roof, like all roofs, was a place of crisscrossed lines of drying laundry, disintegrating boxes of stored junk, and pigeons tipping on the overhead wires. From there you could see the old Liberty Memorial and in the distance a line of bluffs with unusual apartment buildings where important agency people lived. They were far and sparkling and she had never known anybody who went up there.

Mrs. Bergolts and Mrs. O'Donnell lugged baskets of wet clothes back from the Ocean Breeze Laundromat seven blocks away and struggled up four stories to hang them out and so they were always in a cruel mood when they got there. They called each other names. Irish slut, thieving Russian gypsy. They yelled at Nadia to hurry up with more baskets. You can do it, they yelled. You're young and strong. Dehydration made people irritable.

Nadia put *The Age of Innocence* and *The Master and Margarita* into her already-read stack, in with the science-fiction books. Once she had found a box full of e-books and took one of them apart to see if there were some way it had stored books inside it, but there was nothing inside but things called components. A teacher explained that they didn't work anymore because the books that were supposed to appear on them had to be sent from a cloud that no longer existed. It didn't matter. There were so few clouds anyway in the blazing vacant sky.

Nadia dodged the flapping clothes on the lines and ran back down the empty floors to be on time for breakfast. She understood that Bulgakov had fallen down a virtual cave-shaft and had discovered something that was very old: magic. Toros! Toros! A kind of literary Altamira. Nadia loved how the people changed identities, a man became a cat, the heroine turned into a witch. She fell in love with Bulgakov. She imagined herself the heroine, the target of his wounded desires, and memorized long sections of the dialogue, saying it aloud on the rooftop where she could see other rooftops stretching on and on into infinity.

All the history and technical books had been confiscated a hundred years ago because they were incorrect and had to be modified but they were never reissued because these matters were now presented as tele-visuals so ponderous and jargonistic nobody could remember what was said, or cared, either, and so history was lost; it drew backward like a tide and left nothing but paperback novels gasping on the beach.

The long-forgotten novels taught her about nations and borders and extended families, people who had ancestors and descendants and cell phones, whose cities had named streets, numbers on houses, wide rivers and running streams of water. Every place had a name. They had all the water they wanted. They lived in hamlets amid pastures full of red cattle or they lived in houses and apartments in cities and these living spaces had hot and cold running water and private green yards and fish ponds. Ice seemed to be available at all times and real coffee flowed like wine. Cities had limits beyond which the green countryside spread out and in these discrete cities were restaurants, cafés, and coffeehouses where people met and talked for hours. Nadia had never seen a café or a restaurant.

The characters danced and drank too much at Christmas; they sat in private automobiles and looked at maps and tapped at the keyboards of personal computers and tiny handheld devices that gave you weather reports. They had some kind of tiny eyeglasses called contact lenses. They sailed around the world alone and a crazed dwarf named Quilp drank boiling tea out of a pot. They decided themselves what job they would take and there was some system where you could punch in numbers on a telephone and order a pizza delivered to your house, a kind of meat and cheese pie. They had high-phosphate dish detergent that made surfaces cracking clean. They did not chip pieces of bar soap into the laundry machines. They said anything that came into their heads.

There seemed to be no regulations on anything: the watts of lightbulbs, shoe sizes, per-person living space, possession of window boxes, size of water bottles, and placing of television screens. They had no ration allowances. They owned cats and dogs without the permission of the Department of Livestock and Companion Animals. There were times and places where there were no people: at midnight, among mountains. It was a world of swimming pools and cybertheft and malls, lakes and pets and horses and cows, cowboys, free-running bison, marshes, rain, fog, pear trees, snow, sailing ships, and men in tights. They were spendthrift and wasteful and neurotic. They had devoured the world and left nothing but a dry husk for Nadia Stepan.

CHAPTER 6

One moment Nadia was a common average adolescent inhabitant of the megacity and the next she was running for her life. At eleven in the morning she and several other girls were paralyzed with lunatic laughter on the girls' side of the auditorium, which caused the proctor to stalk toward them with his cane raised, and at twelve noon she was bolting through the streets carrying her life in her hands.

At the noontime bell she left the lecture hall and its fifteen hundred pupils and hurried out to the dressmaker at the Technicolor Cow to try on her graduation dress that a defrocked Lutheran minister had made from pale orange reconstituted polyester. It was small, like herself, an undernourished fabric but bright and gaudy. The thin woman knew all the students, and their waist sizes and their hem lengths, and when she pulled it over Nadia's head to check the fit she whispered,

Nadia, Nadia, fly away home.

What? Why?

The dressmaker pulled the dress off and wrapped it in foolscap and pressed it into her hands. Listen, listen, Child Welfare is demanding all letters and diaries from graduating Parentless Dependents. They are coming this afternoon. Right now. Have to be handed in at graduation, for job assignment.

She had forgotten. It was a new directive. When the people at the top decided, what could you do? She asked, How do you know?

The defrocked Lutheran minister gestured to a strange device under the counter and said, Local radio. Pirate. Go, go now.

Nadia ran out with the package tight in her hands. She bolted past the broken ceramic particolored cow at the entrance and down the narrow streets dodging people and vehicles and street repairmen pouring tar like black hot gluten, slapping her flat oversized Mary Jane–type shoes on the pavement. She shot past a gypsy stall where candies were set out in various glass jars and a sign with a tarot deck that read:

HOBART LASALLE, THE CONTINUITY MAN! FORTUNES TOLD, CONNECTIONS DISCOVERED!

BACK IN 5 MINS.

They would go through her diary, some hideous unshaven Forensics agent with vodka breath would read how she and Widdy had jammed the street water meter with a comb, how she had called Facilitator Stormond Thrum an imbecile and all the agencies bumbling corrupt liars, how the Council of the Executive was fake, how her nose was too big and nobody would ever marry her, how she loved Martin's slanty stance and his *gorgeous* eyes and how she dreamed he would kiss her, how she was possessed by feelings she could never, ever, tell *anybody,* how the news reports were all bogus and so otherwise why did they never report on the superrich people with water gardens and refrigerators who lived in Alpine meadows or that astronauts had been *abandoned* on Mercury and were still alive there sunning themselves beside seas of liquid cinnabar, how she loved Widdy, her best friend, and (later) how she *hated* Widdy and wished Widdy would go fart peas at the moon, how she had taken her pillow in her arms and pretended it was *Martin.*

Her diary would get her arrested and sent to the punishment unit of some juvenile detention facility, which they called summer camp as if everybody sang songs and danced around campfires.

A tall man sat partially hidden by the fish shower curtain flipping through her diary. Nadia saw him down the long hall. She glided noiselessly to one side of the doorway. She heard Female Voice One on the radio say, *Spring opens up with the promise of Easter and the lively humor of* Alice in Wonderland, *excerpts from the gripping fantasy of* Lord of the Rings . . .

The Forensics agent snarled and reached up and ripped out the wires. His lips moved as he read: *Facilitator an imbecile.* Nadia gasped for air and her cheeks were incandescent. *News reports fake.* He nodded and licked his thumb and turned a page. He was dressed in the Forensics uniform of track pants and balloon runners and a watch cap. If only she had not written all that crap, if only.

A stack of diaries and letters spilled out on the floor. He had taken them from other PDs all over the neighborhood. Greasy filthy boor, animal, moron. She was gasping with rage.

Then there was a man's voice bellowing, What are you doing? What are you doing?

Mr. Caulder stormed past Nadia into the hall, drunk at twelve noon and fed up with neighborhood watchmen and informers and petty housing rules and the lectures from sportscasters and a broken kerosene cooker; his wife sent away who knew where leaving him only her teeth, so here he was in the brain-dead world alone, drunk, half dressed and caged like a zoo animal inside his own frustrated rage.

What are you doing, you asshole! Get out of this apartment building! Mr. Caulder's mouth was wide open, shouting; she could see his discolored tongue and his brown, crooked teeth.

The Forensics man looked up. Shut up, he said.

Mr. Caulder tore the fish shower curtain out of its nails and flung it across the hall.

Get out! It was worth it all, just to scream in some smirking official's face, it was worth it. Mr. Caulder grabbed Nadia's diary and threw it and then kicked the whole pile of diaries and letters into the air. Haul your ass out of here, you jackwit, you prick, you goddamned moron, reading girls' letters, picking on women, that's who you go after! Try *me,* try *me*!

Mr. Caulder was incoherent with happy rage. The Forensics agent reached around to the back of his belt but when he stood up Mr. Caulder raised his fist and struck the agent square on the nose and knocked him out.

Come and get me! Mr. Caulder shouted out the dusty window. Come on!

Nadia had no doubt they would come and get him, but now she saw her chance and bolted down the hall, past the bellowing Mr. Caulder, grabbed her diary, and ran out of the Silver Lake Apartments, down the stairs. She made it to the littered street and as she ran she realized a thick journal was going to be very hard to get rid of. But there—she flung the whole thing into the hot tar where they were resurfacing and yelled Oops!

She would never write anything again.

Nadia slunk down in her seat and tried to concentrate on the tedious lesson on standard water allocations. She chanted along with everyone else: *Oversupervisor five quarts a day, assistant director* . . . They had finished the lecture on the Internet, that technological slum that spread pornography and lies and allowed feral gangs to gather and loot and so the agencies had to shut it down. They had heard this every year of their supposedly exclusive education. Widdy and Josie had begun to laugh again, loudly. The proctor stormed past the overcrowded seats toward them with his cane.

Watch this, said Nadia.

Oh, shut up, Josie whispered. Look, he's coming. Nadia, you are always trouble. They'll ship us off on the dead trains. Josie's moon face was sweaty and yellow.

Nadia stood up. Despite her tiny protein-deprived size she took on an air of authority. She became frosty and restrained.

Thank you but I have this in hand, she said.

The proctor stopped. In hand, he said. Oh, really.

The packed benches of girls kept their eyes on the distant screen. The loudspeakers were now bellowing the lesson on the Urban Wars, how the chaos was finally ended by the agencies. The heat was searing.

Yes, these girls are under tutelage supervision, Nadia said. I am with the Personal Student Observation and Auxiliary Advisement Panel. We accompany problem students and direct those with insufficient behavioral adjustment. I think we are quite laughed out now. She looked down at the girls with a cold and stern expression. Are we done with the hysterics?

Yes, ma'am. They nodded and turned back to the screen.

The gray-haired proctor in his gray uniform snorted and tossed his head.

Then where's your ID? he said.

I am not required to show my ID to an education assistant, said Nadia. Go get your supervisor and I will show my ID to your supervisor.

Nadia sat down and primly tugged at the hem of her skirt. He then told her if that was her job then please keep the students from laughing out loud during lessons. He went away and whacked somebody else with his cane. A discordant shriek of pain three rows down.

How do you do that? Widdy asked.

I don't know, said Nadia. Just natural-born genius.

The lesson on televisual values closed with the poetry quote:
The mysterious North, perfumed like a flower,
Silent like death, dark like a grave.
Written by Facilitator Brian Wei

No, it wasn't, said Nadia. It was Joseph Conrad. And it was the mysterious East, not the North. Liars, liars.

And so with school finished she would have to take the first job they offered, any assignment, especially since Mr. Caulder had hit a

Forensics guy and her entire apartment block could be cut off, no food, no water, no hope of ever reaching Lighthouse Island.

Dust accumulated in the innards of the mimeograph machine, on the windowpanes and sills, in the breathless spaces of the office corridors. People at their desks fanned themselves with pieces of cardboard, recycling thoughts in both words and images. How not to be cynical, how to avoid the disparaging tone, how to be sincere and inspiring, how to steal from the office; toilet paper, bug spray, extension cords. If she stole a lightbulb then she had to go stand in line at a recycle place to buy a dead one and sneak it back in to replace the live one. Life was one deception after another. Of not asking why her roommate Annalee Villanueva had not come back from her ID card renewal interview, for instance.

And here it was Pentecost and so Big Radio would soon be into the French, starting with *Les Misérables* and going on to Dumas *fils* and Villon for whom Nadia had actually puzzled out the French, *Dessus rivière ou sus estan, qui beaulté ot trop plus qu'humaine, mais où sont les neiges d'antan?*, but Pentecost and then Midsummer Eve would go on without her, unheard. Nadia the Radioless.

She acquired a suit of office clothing from a *ropa usada* store and washed it and took it in until she looked presentable. Little heels with rosettes and a straw hat with a bow. Her one extravagance was a pair of garnet earrings that she hoped would impart dark and passionate secrets about the world to her unconscious as she walked about the pre-formed concrete building with its slotted windows, beyond which the yellow air was thick with dust and flying trash.

Nadia had started out well in Public Relations but over a period of three and a half years—about one thousand and three hundred working days—she was repeatedly demoted because she could not come to grips with Mandated Error and had also fallen into an injudicious office relationship. She had tried to get access to her records to see what the bureaucracy was saying about her, and since she was over twenty-one, in fact she was now twenty-two, she was allowed to go to the district information-storage offices a mile away, a long hot mile of walking and fighting the crowds. At one point she had a view down the street to the dry riverbed of the Missouri River, now covered with junk housing and above this a line of bluffs. The Bluffs, luxury apartments, staring down at the urban hive and its insect-people. Higher-up agency people.

She found her way to a damp underground facility where jaded clerks sat in front of long rows of computer monitors and entered data incorrectly, mistakenly erased files, and spilled sticky lemon drink on their keyboards. When they were truly bored they invented computer viruses that produced raging fevers within the hard drives.

Nadia realized that in this overpopulated world there had to be a hundred thousand other Nadia Stepans, that she must have some iden- tifying code after her name. She succeeded only in seeing one blurry page on a monitor that had a handwritten note: *Nadia Stepan145900SB. Somebody has improperly opened this file in an unauthorized search; time period minus seventeen years.*

That's it! cried the creepy geek. He was threadbare and rank, and his hair was cut into ladders. You had thirty seconds! That's it, baby!

Nadia was reduced to trudging around the hot hallways delivering office supplies for the Veterinary Recycling Task Force PR Group. The hall paint was a lime green and the whole interior structure was shaky like her evaporating youthful years. She understood that her life was to be plotless, that nothing should ever happen. *To hell with you,* she thought, but she did not know who "you" might be. Some demons of fashion, the devils of chic, the people at the top who decided, a bodiless cabal.

The Question Freak appeared once in a while on television in a neon-blue coat and orange-and-green-striped tie with round glasses, bolting through the TV studios screaming, *Why do we have to suck up to supervisors? Where is here? When are the agencies going to die and leave us alone?* This was supposed to be an escape valve for a negative world, but it just made Nadia feel worse, leaden and dismal.

The sky over the city rooftops was a burnt blue month after month and year after year but Nadia had never known anything else. Her office was only five blocks from the Mermaid Arms Youth Housing units so she never went anywhere. The office drones wrote down ideas for the General Nutrition PR spots about the delicious paste made from pulped cactus, scribbling on their preformed concrete desks. It was not advisable to say "pulped cactus"; the word was "nopal." The spots had to include the trigger words like "smart" and "green" and "healthy" and "safe" and "alternative." Not only were animal products or the animals themselves never mentioned but the *fact* that they were never mentioned should not be mentioned. They had all been eaten long ago so there was no use in the public longing for, say, a dog.

The year cycled around like a big Laundromat washer. The agencies had never abandoned Christmas and Easter and Passover and Pentecost and All Hallows Eve because they evoked strong visual images and these cheerful holidays made up for getting rid of the year numbers and maps and place names. It kept people oriented toward the perpetual present. Years were recycled instead of used up and thrown away.

Nadia stood by her cart with dry lips, thin and small, under her straw hat her dark-red hair gleaming in knotty braids like cranberries, as they selected people for the new seminars from which people never returned. She was single and not essential but somehow they had not yet called her ID number. She had never committed a felony. Having an affair with her oversupervisor's husband was a criminal offense of some kind but not a felony. They had taken her ID for recalibration, they said.

At lunchtime a group of the young men sat in front of the office television to watch soccer; Nadia came to the door to see the advertisement for Lighthouse Island. A clean sea booming against rocks, drifting rain, the Slavic fantasy house with its steep roof, the lighthouse sending out beams of light into the fog, into the unpeopled waste of ocean. Tourists were shown gazing out of the lighthouse tower windows and feeding seagulls. There was a spinning sail of wind art on top of a very tall tree trunk. No televisions, no crowds, no trash. Cool air, rain. Save up your credits and go! Close to the graveyard, where the daughter of Oceanus watches over the bottomless sea.

Nadia sat at the preformed concrete table with the note. It was written on the back of a tin can label that depicted an oyster in a sailor hat. The note said, *pls send felt liners sox p'nut butter mittens pensil paper pls help send to Annalee Villanueva Girls Contemporary Dance Camp Dorm 600 Tundra Blues Ger. 22 by D. Vail he will come 2 U pls. help pls Annalee.*

Nadia raised her head to see her roommate Josie standing in the doorway to their Youth Housing apartment with that tossy-hair gesture and her nose elevated as if she were deeply offended, Josie's only line of defense.

You went and ratted on her, didn't you? Nadia stood up in her striped blanket bathrobe and bare feet like an outraged indigenous person. You thought up something.

Oh, you're always so *dramatic,* said Josie. Why do you always have to go overboard?

But you did! She's in detention. You wanted more room. Josie, you're a criminal. Nadia clutched the table edge. They were all sort of socially bigger than she was, not having lost their parents until they were preteens on that awful night at Riverdale Apartments and therefore had better food as children but Nadia was an orphan born and raised. So they seemed more important than herself but she was at present furious. You're a *rodent,* said Nadia.

Josie kept on with the hair tossing and took up a box of matches. I don't want to be friends with you anymore, she said in a punishing voice. She lifted her cool moon face with the tiny compressed features right in the middle and lit a cigarette rolled in dark brown paper. She pounced to the window where the dust from a building site drifted in. Josie said, She shouldn't have been dating that pirate radio guy. They would have come and got all of us. She thought she was going to be some kind of underground *celebrity,* and we would have embarrassed her in front of all her new friends, her daring new friends.

Nadia started to say *I would like to set you on fire,* but then she might be next on Josie's list. All the years Nadia had known her, Josie had made herself at least briefly important by being offended by nearly anything and extracting apologies from people, but they had all grown wise to the apology scam and now Josie had found a new way to be important. And Nadia had to live with her. There was no place else to go in all the endless city but the housing you were assigned, unless it were alleyways or abandoned skyscrapers slated for demolition. She sat down again and put her head in her hands.

Widdy dashed in from the bathroom down the hall with a saucepan and put it on the stove, in the midst of making some kind of cosmetic. Nadia looked up and then held out the greasy label.

We've got to help her, she said. Widdy, do you hear me?

Widdy slowly turned her face to Nadia while she dropped in red food coloring one drop after another like a slow bleed.

Leave it alone, Nadia, Widdy said. They'll be monitoring this apartment, okay? It probably wasn't Josie. Hey? No, it wasn't Josie's fault, come on, come on.

Widdy wiped a fingertip over her arm and saw it was a nice blush effect. Nadia knew it was for tonight when some guys from the office were coming over; it was Old Movie Night and the television would treat the populace to the story of the beginning of the Urban Wars, *Dr. Strangelove,* and it would be nice to have a social life, wouldn't it? After their childhood of fright and terror and midnight arrests, just to have a damned social life? Widdy said, Leave it alone, Nadia, please?

Nadia said, Were there other messages from Anna?

Widdy set the saucepan on the table. One. We tore it up. Widdy's face became stiff with guilt.

Well, rot in hell! said Nadia. She slammed her hand on the table.

And there was another about old man Kenobi. Widdy washed her hands at the sink. Nadia stared at her. Yes, where he was or was buried. Leave it alone, Nadia. I tore it up.

Josie smirked. She took the label from Nadia and struck a match and set it on fire.

Nadia took hold of the cart handles and started her rounds: the pens, paper, joke books, copies of the *Capricorn Rhyming Dictionary,* and mail packets from the courier. She carried a deep, fatalistic knowledge that she would continue on this downward slide until she hit bottom. An eventless place without joy. The cactus farms.

Nadia hid food and never signed anything. She had an escape kit prepared in case Josie ratted on her or the oversupervisor decided to drop her, Nadia, down the memory hole. She kept a copy of the *Girl Scout Handbook,* 1957 edition, in her large tote purse along with copies of her favorite poems. She had a Day-Glo pink feather duster and a heavy piece of tapestry-like material. Also a little sewing kit in a metal cough-drop box that held needles, thread, and the silver St. Jude dangle. She collected old dimes and quarters because she would have to pay for things on the street. She went without things like new shoes but she carried the tote bag with her every day to the office and wore her garnet earrings. She had thrown away her youth in a brainless affair. Thin Sam Kenobi had been right.

Tucked in her tote was the last note that the Class Two adjective adviser to the assistant secretary for *Cactea Opuntia* Processing's PR group, Earl Jay Warren, had written her.

We can't go on like this, the note said. He was apparently unaware that this had been said before. *My wife knows.* Ditto. *She will destroy you. I have to try to repair what is left of my marriage but I will never forget you and your bubbly personality and your little cart. Likewise our romantic rooftop meetings. Be who you are and the city will love you as I always will from an official distance. In the meantime you had best apply for relocation or she will send you to the dryers. Love is a many splendid thing and fades like the waning moon. May fortune guide you.*

Nadia wadded the note. No point in keeping it, a reminder of grimy tar on a rooftop and a wilted secret flower on her desk like a snigger. He said he and his wife were separated but they were not. Why was the world so full of liars? Why did she always believe them?

Nadia passed by Oversupervisor Blanche Warren's office. The woman looked up with grief and pain in her face and tears in her eyes. A personal fan ripped at the papers on her desk in a way that made it seem that nothing ever written on any sheet of paper mattered anymore, nothing mattered when married love was destroyed, torn to pieces. And here was the guilty Jezebel, the vandal, passing by her door pushing a cart and looking completely normal. The city dying of thirst. What do a lot of stupid papers mean? What do these black marks mean? The criminal must die.

You Jezebel, said Oversupervisor Blanche Warren. You vile dirty bitch.

Nadia hurried on down the hall.

CHAPTER 7

One day in September when García Lorca and Blasco Ibáñez and other Spaniards would have been on Big Radio, Nadia saw the water in her water jug shivering in rings. This only happened when more than five people were running down or up the stairs, which they did at lunch. Ten thirty in the morning meant an arrest crew. Nadia calmly took up her tote bag from the lower shelf of the cart and put on her hat and walked over to a bulletin board and ripped off a notice about the tissue engineering and permissible rage program for young men. A crowd of people thundered like confused beasts into the far end of the hall, carrying balloons and grinning in all directions.

Who put this up? she said to them. Do you know who put this up? This is outrageous.

What?

The man in front stopped in confusion; behind him a woman in a white tunic carried a boxy portfolio that said *Pedicures* in bright pink with cartoons of smiling toes.

Hey! We're here to deliver a birthday party for the oversupervisor! Come on! Only some special people are invited! Are you Nadia Stepan?

Office workers with alarmed faces peered out of doors.

There's a drawing for a pedicure! said the woman. She was trying so hard to smile happily that her lips shook.

Just a minute, damn it, I am going to find out who dared put this up, said Nadia. Somebody's going to pay for this, and I mean *pay*. In a state of near-paralyzed dread Nadia managed to sound convincing.

They stared at her in a perplexed silence.

She picked up her tote bag and stormed off with the bulletin in her other hand, down the stairs, out the front door, and onto the street.

It was not good to move too fast. She wadded up the bulletin and threw it away and sauntered through the crowds, across the street to a notions stand. There was a young girl on the other side of the plank counter. Her green-and-yellow flag hung limp in the heat. The girl shook a fly-brush of newspaper strips over crumbling pies made of rye flour and tapioca and over the green Quench candies, her tin can for contributions to bribe money. A long brown bus was parked in front of the entrance to Nadia's office building and on its side was painted, over windows and all, *Surprise Parties and Special Occasions!* It burned oil like a waste dump and since the windows were closed the temperature inside had to be well over a hundred. People inside it were probably fighting for their lives.

The girl looked at the bus and said, quietly, They dry people out. Then they're like leather.

Nadia watched as more men in blue coveralls got out with balloons. She laid three pennies on the plank. How do you know?

I know, the girl said. They turn people into like thin wood.

Nadia reached for a jar of green candies and shook out three and dropped them from her trembling hand and snatched them up again. They cost either a copper penny each or a hundred Cessions paper dollars. Three pennies on the counter and one in the bribe can.

A sudden noise from up the street sounded like an enormous flock of birds calling. The noise resolved into human voices; voices of alarm, surprise. A dense crowd of people ran toward her down the sidewalks and the middle of the street, slamming into others who had stopped. They were yelling, Premature demolition! Get back!

Women in hats and office dresses turned and ran on their little heels, men in suits and ties, workmen in coarse cotton overalls carrying the orange warning signs, women with their baskets of street food for sale, all running, swarming past the party bus.

A thump sounded, as if the air had been struck with a massive, soft hammer. Bricks and drywall and boards burst up in a grainy giant fountain, far over the rooftops. A mushroom cloud of rolling dust came down the narrow canyon of the street bringing with it bits of cotton from burst mattresses, raining down on the people darting into doorways, alleyways, with their hands over their heads. Buddy cars came to a stop and the drivers got out and ran.

Nadia bolted for a pair of double doors going into a production building. People crowded in after her, coated with a white, fine powder. Nadia's clothes were crumpled, the bow wobbling on her hat but she went on in a calm stride down a long passageway. A woman ran past with her hat askew, asking. Is there another one?

You got me, said Nadia, and kept on walking.

The air in the passageway filled with choking dust but Nadia found a deserted tool room. She went into the room and came upon a glass two-quart bottle of water with the name Joe Fineman written on the koozie. She jammed it in her tote bag.

Now she was a water thief. Now she was in trouble. There would be no explaining this to a magistrate. She had stolen someone's water allowance. Death by *cactea opuntia*.

She casually walked out the back of the building. Dust still hung thick in the air and a siren sounded and she saw a man lying in a heap of clothing and dust along with a purse, a torn package, scattered among fallen brick. She saw a pair of round eyeglasses with tortoiseshell frames and picked them up.

Emergency workers in orange coveralls came running through the dust scrim and shouted at her to go back but she walked on toward them. The telephone poles were down and electrical wires curled in the rubble. Nadia waved her hand and shouted that she was a property accountant for the Interurban Low-Rise Reconstruction Architectural Committee and that she had to make a quick sketch of the remaining foundations. She *had* to. That was her job. Did they want to see her ID? She was bluffing about the ID but she said confidently, Don't try to obstruct me, please.

The ten-story building had collapsed down on its own footprint in a cascade of bricks and flooring. The buildings on either side were also cracked and swaying, and between them a deep hole and someone crying out in long demented moans.

Nadia ran to it. A hole had opened up in the building's foundations. Stuff hung down into it, linoleum and strips of wood and snarled wire. She teetered uneasily on the edge to see that two feet below her, a set of ancient steps marched downward. She sat on the sliding linoleum of the edge and dropped down onto the first step and then the next and the next and disappeared into darkness.

She ran down the stairs past a man lying to one side of the staircase, head-down on a kind of avalanche of broken tiles, bricks, and lathing. She stopped to gasp for breath and swallow. He was lit as if by a spotlight from the sun lancing down the hole. His lips were a bloody, sparkling crimson. A hard hat fallen from his head lay farther down like something from a decapitation.

He said, Are you Medisave?

Yes, she said. How did you get down here?

I was blown down here, he said. He didn't move. He seemed to be able to talk perfectly well. He tried to lift a hand. Get a stretcher.

Is there anybody else farther down? she said. Her voice was not steady and she had to hold tightly to the railing.

I don't think so. Go up and get an ambulance for me.

Okay. She hesitated. You're sure there's nobody else down here?

Not as far as I know. His hand scrabbled in the broken stones and tile, a long slope of wreckage. He said, It went off before they cleared the area.

What is this hole? What was in here?

Old entrance to the trains, he said. Go on. Go up, get an ambulance for me.

I will, she said in a sincere, lying voice, but instead of turning and going back up the shaky staircase she ran on down, into the underground, below the city, descending through archaeological layers one after the other, time reversed, down into the age of the big Urban Wars with its burned soil and brick and occasional unexploded ordnance and then below that the age of cell phones and handheld devices and multiple TV channels and pizza deliveries and then the mysterious caves full of stored food and supplies and finally the squashed layers of LP vinyl recordings and calendars with numbered years. Below that, the train tunnels.

She stood powdered with mortar dust and sticky with cooling sweat on a dimly lit platform. The train tracks were a few feet below her sliding away in dim ribbons. Her heart pounded and she was very thirsty but did not drink from the stolen two-quart bottle. She had no idea when she would get more. A chain of fluorescent tubes lit the tunnel. On the far side of the tracks, in a wall honeycombed with large holes she saw a heap of dirty clothes. She stared for a long time to see if it was a person, or a body, or merely a wad of rags. In her state of cool terror everything seemed removed, or secondhand. Then from a loudspeaker overhead a voice said, Hi!

Nadia didn't move. She didn't turn her head. She said, in return, Hi!

Give me your destination and we'll get started, the voice said.

Nadia said, The old Sissons Bend neighborhood.

A pause.

I'm sorry! That destination is no longer valid. Do you have an alternative?

Nadia thought in a desperate jumble; names, random nouns, anything that could be a destination.

The voice said, If you are unsure of your destination, could you give me an approximate direction? Say yes, no, or I don't know.

North, said Nadia.

Good! That's a start. The next train north is in ten seconds. Step back from the platform, please. Did you know a change in our thinking is coming? Be alert! When you board our special northern service train, you can use the keypad to the left of the . . .

And the rest of the words were drowned out by a deafening roar. A bright headlight shone from far down the tunnel to her right, and then the platform itself was lit up by the intense searchlight on the engine and the noise was terrific. It sighed to a stop and the doors opened. The interior of the car was lit by brilliant fluorescent lights. Bare plastic seats. She hesitated.

Here you are! said the voice. This is the four-twenty north carrying the locomotive post. Here you are. This is the four-twenty north. Watch your step. Watch your step. Here you are!

Nadia stepped in and the doors slammed shut.

There was no one else in the car. It was perfectly empty. She sat down and clung to one of the stanchions. The train bolted forward and increased to what seemed an incredible speed. All the cars ahead of her and behind her were brilliantly lit and empty. She had never ridden in an underground train; she had never known of anybody who had ridden in one; she had never known anyone who had even gone down into the underground system. Everything smelled of diesel smoke and plastic.

She looked for the keypad but there wasn't one.

Wherever it stopped, she would get off, and keep on walking. She would walk north.

Why not just keep on, sidling along like a kind of tidy derelict through the world, unnoticed, unremarkable, unavailable to all the computer records that would contain her entire history, housed underground somewhere? She would be beyond the reach of oversupervisors and arrest teams, beyond the reach of the buses that baked people alive, beyond anybody's reach. To the end of the world. To Lighthouse Island.

After a while she fell asleep and dreamed.

Someone called her by name, an urgent call in a low voice. *Nadia!* She was in youth housing of some sort that was made of glass or crystal, or perhaps it had no walls at all, only a series of steps from one level to another also made of something transparent. It was evening outside and in this landscape leaves lifted and fell slowly in a sea wind, leaves as big as book covers and they were dark green and very glossy.

She didn't belong there but she wanted very much to stay. Then a man came walking down the glass stairs with the most splendid smile. It turned her heart over and she called out to him, *Oh it's you!* He was about to say something important when she woke up, chilled and dusty. She lay slumped over on the plastic-covered seat with her notebook and tote bag fallen to the floor in front of her and her garnet earrings sparkling as if her mind were still on sleep mode and had temporarily lodged itself in the dark gems.

CHAPTER 8

She placed her straw hat with the bow back on her head as pipes and wiring flashed past on either side. She ate one of the Quench candies. She wondered how much time had passed but there was no way to know.

She sat thinking about the incomparable feeling of the dream and stared down the long line of illuminated cars. Her eyes focused. She saw a man sitting in one of the seats perhaps three or four cars down. Just one man. She had not seen him before. She wondered if the train had stopped somewhere when she was asleep.

Nadia watched as he shifted one hand from the stanchion and took hold of it with the other. He was dressed in a sloppy dark shirt and pants. She leaned back, as if to hide. But she couldn't hide.

He turned to look at her and she could see the round white circle of his face and two black dots for eyes. He was staring at her.

Nadia opened her tote and took out her notebook as if she had something important to read. She glanced up. He was now walking forward through the blue-white fluorescent light. His eyes were fixed on her. He turned a handle and passed forward from his car to the next

one and sat down again. He never stopped looking at her. His abnor-
mally large mouth made him look like a lizard. He sidled a knife or an
ice pick out of his clothing.

From under the crushed brim of her hat she watched and the dark
tunnel rocketed past.

She got to her feet. The car lurched; she took firm hold of a stanchion, and the steel was slippery in her hand. The train began to slow
and then it stopped. Three cars in front the empty spaces began to fill
up with a yellow smoke or mist. In the dim light she saw nozzles on
both sides of the tunnel pouring out a fine spray in expanding rooster
tails onto the outside of the train and also into the inside as the doors
opened. The sharp, chemical odor struck her in the face and tears
started from her eyes. She felt an instantaneous urge to throw up.

Then the doors of her car opened and the automated voice de-
clared, *We are cleaning the northbound make sure all personnel are absent
remove all personnel the northbound is now going through the cleaning and
disinfecting process remove . . .*

She leaped for the platform and landed awkwardly, turned her
ankle, and got up and ran limping down the platform. She swallowed
repeatedly. An ochre mist ballooned up and drifted while music from
the loudspeakers blasted out "Not Dead Yet" by a group she hated.

The gelatinous mist lagged behind her like an assailant. She was in
a high-ceilinged tunnel lit by a few electrical bulbs in a long diminishing procession and far down the tunnel were great open spaces carved
in the earth full of pallets of boxes and bags. The famous food storages. She heard footsteps, stopping, starting, running for a few yards.
Stopping. Nadia wept and wiped at her nose and mouth; all her bodily
fluids seemed to be leaking from her eyes and nose. *Don't let me throw
up.* She ran on.

She ran limping but thought of turning around and grappling with
him. Fighting with him. She could throw herself at him, take off one
of her heels, and smash his face. She dropped to a slow jog and turned a
corner and came to a hub where tunnels led off in different directions.

Set in a rough cast-concrete wall was a bank of elevators facing her with scarred metal doors. Lights flashed over the doors: numbers.

She pushed the up and down buttons on every one and then darted down a tunnel. Flattened herself against the damp, rough wall. She took the shoe from her painful right foot.

In the silence the elevator doors wheezed open and then shut again. She waited with her shoe in her hand but when she no longer heard footsteps she knew that he had got on one of the elevators. Nadia put her shoe on again and continued on down the left-hand tunnel, limping and stinking of chemical.

Sometime later she found herself in an enormous cafeteria.

People in coveralls ate from metal dishes and slammed trays down on a long counter that seemed to stretch into infinity. They ate as if it were a job of work, as if they had been assigned this task of shoveling pasty food into their mouths. There were no windows.

The ceiling was low and the cafeteria was lit by hanging lightbulbs as large as balloons. Nadia was still underground and she had no idea how to get out. How to get back to street level. A buzz of conversation hovered over the great open space, the sound of thousands of spoons and forks striking metal plates, the cooks all up and down the line arguing and shouting at one another along with the occasional loud complaints of men and women dressed in various sorts of working clothes.

Overhead, on every wall, hundreds of television monitors were cluttered with images of freight-hauling trains coming in and being unloaded, trains running under the nozzles of spray, numbers in a crawl along the bottom. The cars were all open, nothing more than flatcars with sides one or two feet high, filled with sacks, boxes, bundles.

Nadia strolled up to the hot tables and peered at the dishes that were offered as if she were about to choose one. She glanced at all the people; no one was dressed as she was, in office clothes.

She couldn't just go up to somebody and say, How do I get back up to street level? They would say, Who are you? Where's your ID card? What are you doing here?

Then again, maybe not. She stared at compartments of smoking mashed potatoes. Nobody ever got down here without some kind of special worker permit. It would not occur to anyone that she had jumped down a demolition hole to get here.

A cook came up to the hot tables with a cart of food. He began to ladle some kind of lentil dish into a compartment. He glanced across at her and lifted his nose in the air and took a deep breath.

Woo hoo, you got caught on one of the disinfectant trains, he said.

Yes, said Nadia. Yes, I did. It's actually making me feel kind of sick. She stood unsteadily on her thin ankles and opened her dress-top collar. Then all the monitors went dark. It might mean something was going to happen here and she felt even more desperate about getting out, up to the street. It might have been because they didn't want anybody to see the prisoner trains.

Okay, sweetie, have some lentils.

Other cooks and cooks' helpers pushed past him with carts, up and down the endless line of counters. The overhead bulbs shone in a long planetary array. On a screen up on the wall *Imperial Rebels* was on; the men were arguing about whether to go toward the distant mountains or turn south.

No. I need fresh air. She put one hand on the steel counter and dropped her head. I feel faint. I feel like I'm going to pass out.

Woo hoo, don't do that! Are we short of fresh air down here? Yes, we are; it is a known fact the ventilation is never up to regulations for worker health and safety. He leaned forward and pitched the last of the lentils into the compartment. It sucks.

I need to go the short way to street level, she said. She clutched both hands around the straps of her tote bag, a dried-out and exhausted microwaif.

Woo hoo, is there a short way to street level from here? Yes, there is and is it known that the cooks use it all the time, and do we let a special few use the short way to street level? Yes, we do, give us a kiss or two and I'll get little raggedy-ass Bennie to take you there.

Go to hell, she said. I'd rather faint right here. She gripped the counter edge. Or throw up.

He looked left and right at all the hurrying busboys and the people standing with their trays and metal dishes. He flipped up a section of counter and said, Duck in here.

Hundreds of people in the cafeteria lifted their heads and glanced at the darkened monitors, and then at one another, and then turned back to their food. There was a sudden silence.

Come on, the cook said.

I mean it, said Nadia.

Me too, the cook said. Hey hey, we're harmless. He waved a soupy dipper at her.

Nadia slipped in through the open section of counter and shrank away as the cook took her arm.

Be glad you aren't on one of those trains, he said. Bennie, you little shit, take this citizen to the cold-box elevator.

CHAPTER 9

A nightjar sang out with a throaty, bulbous noise, darting about in the air over the city. Nadia sat in an alleyway and listened to a television. Heavy music with a deep, bumping beat. *Somebody's coming, over the sea . . .* The crowd of people inside the apartment were trying to sing along with it but they only made distressed sounds until they came to one of the exclamations that they remembered and then shouted it out. *Deep black! Deep black sea!* Probably they had already drunk their evening ration of water and eaten their supper and had brought out the vodka. It was time for the story of Adrian's Atoll and all his troubles.

Nadia listened in perfect, ratlike silence. She was relieved to hear the people inside speaking as she spoke, and watching a familiar television program. She had come so far, but it was not over. *Adrian baby, do you love me too?*

Adrian had survived alone on the island for months when three other people washed ashore on a raft made of steel barrels and some kind of floor from an old house. New people; conflict, arguments. They all had to work together to dig for water and build shelters. There was a tiger lurking on the island and Nadia remembered how Josie and Widdy had relished the close-ups of the tiger's beautiful face with the sea lights reflected in his eyes, and behind him the blurry, waving green vegetation and the roaring sound of the dirty, unresting sea. The show confirmed Nadia's view of the world, the ancient view of Earth as a planetary bathtub with a large, careless child splashing around in it.

She did not really understand how she had become friendless and alone on the street yet *again* in this stupid repetitive way when she considered that other people had friends, specifically a haughty wicked bitch like Josie. Finally she decided it was the *reading*. All those novels, all that poetry, the romantic notions and regrettable hopes. Because Nadia was an orphan, shifted from one family to another, she never knew how to behave and so adopted one fervent heroine after another as avatars, and so here she was, a fervent heroine, in flight.

What if I lose myself? she thought. *Totally?* For a second a kind of terminal emptiness opened up at her feet, a cold orbit.

But then the moon came up, a thin curve, its deep blue heart like a darkened spirit held in waiting and it shone down in the narrow space between the buildings. As always the moon had some business of its own, far above the infinite, crowded city, some task to do with the concealment or the enlargement of its soul. Stars trailed after it but they were hard to see. She looked for the Chair and the Dipper to tell her where she was going—north. She was going to Lighthouse Island, with its tall wooden Russian-looking theme-park house, a damp rain forest and long rays of light from a tower, great glassy breakers pouring over rocks. *I have somewhere to get to,* she thought. *Other people don't.* When she got to Lighthouse Island she would become herself.

At first light she drank most of Joe Fineman's water, splashed some on her face and dried off with her handkerchief, ate the last of the Quench candies, and brushed all the weed leaves and dust from her skirt with the Day-Glo pink feather duster. Then she walked out of the alley with a bright, springing step despite her swollen ankle and on down the street as if she were on her way to some employment. She was, actually; and that was to make herself a map. That was her employment. She was self-employed.

She was very thirsty and she had no idea how far she had come on the underground train, but it had seemed to go very fast. She had slept several hours. She had traveled many miles to the north and maybe she had outstripped the arrest crew. Just out of nowhere they wanted to kill you yet kept everything so tidy and quiet. *But I'm perfectly good!* Nadia thought this desperate thought behind her street face. *Why waste my life? I can think and talk and do stuff, I have great teeth, really good peripheral vision.* But millions upon millions had thought similar things and were extinguished anyway. She was still free, still at large, and if she could reach that wilderness place of green and sea she would not waste her own life or anyone else's either. In spite of the hot street and the thick crowds and hunger and thirst the world lay open before her. Her life was in her own hands like an egg and we all have only one each and so we are obligated to save it if we can.

She had to be cautious and appear perfectly at home. A clandestine life, an existence of secrecy and fraud. Hard work ahead. But she could do it. She was young and strong.

She came to a wide street full of people on foot and bicycles and motorbikes and buses and Buddy cars. They were all dressed more or less like herself and she felt a great relief since she had come so far in the underground and who knew how people might dress in this far place, what language they might speak? But here they were, just like her, recipients of the global culture. Like Alice she had fallen down a hole in the earth but unlike Alice she had emerged into a perfectly familiar overcrowded world and it was herself that was strange.

The sidewalk glowed with reflections from broken glass and a sun that hung huge and red over the street-canyons. She and the others hurried on in a crowded, sweaty herd. Overhead a great billboard urged people to save up their credits and apply for a luxurious sea cruise. A flight of sparrows flew like darts past the digital palms and lagoons.

She walked on. In her head the comforting sound of Male Voice One, memorized, internalized, familiar: *Here we are at the beginning of autumn when the season turns and the leaves take on color. This is the season for the classic works of Spain and the unforgettable explorers' tales. Let us begin with* Blood and Sand.

She came to a man squatting beside his motorbike with a screwdriver in one hand performing some kind of furious surgery on the little engine. Vendors with green-and-yellow flags had set up in the abandoned storefronts; a child selling shriveled beets chewed gum in one and in another a woman had fired up her butane cooker and was making fry bread for sale.

Good morning, Nadia said. Excuse me. She smiled and hid her dirty nails by grasping her tote bag.

What? He turned his head up to her and then went back to unscrewing the bolts that held the motor to the frame. He wore a jacket and tie and kept slapping the tie out of his way. What do you want?

What's the name of this street?

He paused in his work. Why don't you know it? He turned to look up at her again.

My agency was moved to around here. They just left us to find our own way to the new offices.

He untied his tie and drew it off and stuffed it in his pocket and then he went back to his work. People hurried past them and bumped into her; excuse me, excuse me.

Oh yeah? What agency is that?

Personnel and Supply for Animal Control. They just put our office equipment in trucks and went off and left us to find our own way.

Animal control. Hmm. He nodded and slapped his hands together to knock off the engine dirt. What animals?

Ah, pigeons, I think.

Why did they move?

The copy-room ceiling fell in. Right on top of the watercooler. Twenty gallons gone to waste! She waved one hand in astonishment.

Well, whatever, he said. They say this is Farragut Street.

Oh, thanks. And so, does it go north? Nadia turned to stare up the street.

North? He sounded incredulous. North?

Just wondering. She never should have said the word "north." Stupid, stupid. She must not be stupid.

I have no idea where north is. The man started the motorbike and kicked up the kickstand and roared off. Nadia walked over to the fry cook and paid two pennies for a cup of hot citrus drink and put a penny in the bribe cup. She sat down on a little stool to drink it, slowly.

The fry cook was queenly in her primitive kitchen, serene, her green-and-yellow flag flying, her permit number painted on the wall and the wonderful smell of crisping fry bread and sugar powder. Her battered wooden TV monitor sat precariously on a shelf, jumping with faded colors. A man that the crawl said was the director of Gerrymander Eleven was complaining about the Young Men's Rioting Association. They were rioting because Captain Kenaty of *Imperial Rebels* had been killed. The director said they might write him back into the script as a concession. The bad color made the director look as if he had red teeth.

Oh, shut up, great director asshole, said the little cook. She took two pennies from an old man for a small cup of tea. To Nadia she said, Get up, let that old man sit down.

Of course! Nadia sprang to her feet and the old man seated himself slowly, all his joints creaking.

What's he on about? the old man asked. When's *Easy Money*?

Soons he shut up, said the woman. Big-talking asshole director.

The fry cooks affected a sort of pidgin English in order to seem foreign and mysterious, as if their fried snacks might be redolent of the spices from some exotic cuisine. They also seemed to say anything they thought without fear of arrest or water cutoff.

Overhead the rickety sound of a hang-glider motor, gnashing along like a sewing machine with a day-flight watchman in it looking down. He might have a list, a flyer with her picture and her name on it.

The man with the motorbike was walking back toward the little cook shop, talking to a watchman who walked alongside him. Nadia froze, but then something fell out of a window overhead and struck the street. It was a can of some kind of porridge slop and the fry cook and several other people screamed up at the window. The porridge fanned out in a sort of mushy star all over the sidewalk. The motorbike man and the watchman stopped, caught up in the argument and the mush. Nadia gave the cup back and hurried on with her hat down over her face, blending into the heavy crowds.

After several blocks the avenue devolved into a slope that allowed her to see a long way. A vista. She gazed out over the massive smoking hive that was the city and all the world, a kind of gray silicate crystallization going on into infinity. It had to be a universe constructed by something other than human beings; people were only minute units in the dry passageways, a hive in the middle of the waterless world.

Nadia could see some kind of center below, a knot of tall buildings. Probably a group of high-up agency office towers because clearly the great buildings had enough water pressure to go all the way to the top floors. The tallest building's outer skin was made of glass, iridescent from long exposure. Much of the glass had been boarded over, with air-conditioning units sticking out.

If she could go up to the roof of that building she could see a very long way. She could plan, think ahead, and even draw a map in her notebook and so she stood primly in the hot sunlight, outwardly calm, with audacious plans developing in her head. She would continue walking north, making a map as she went. She would bequeath that map to generations unborn, who would revere her memory. She would secretly insert herself into the future.

A group of people stared up into the sky and pointed at a jet trail. So Nadia stood with them and said, Oh, wonderful, awesome, and it was indeed an entrancing thing to see the minute silver jet spouting vapor from two engines like a depth charge launched into the latitudes.

One of the men said in an authoritative voice that it was going northwestward and so it was probably the Facilitator going off to smooth things out with the great northwestern gerrymanders and everyone around said, Yes, right. He's gone to see about the big water pipeline from the northwest. Yes, yes.

After a few moments the jet was lost to sight and left behind an expanding cloudy path blown into segments by high-altitude winds. *Northwestward,* thought Nadia. Farragut Street seemed to more or less go in the same direction. Notes for a map.

Two neighborhood watchmen came up and said, What's the problem here?

Everyone said, Nothing, nothing, and hurried on.

CHAPTER 10

The fifty-story building took up most of the block. Nadia turned into the knot of skyscrapers and the wind was torn and intensified by their height. She came to a porte cochere and a five-foot column of squared stone. There would be food and drink inside, buffets, cool air. Nadia was faint, hot, and inelegant. On the column a plaque of worn bronze that said; RITZ-CARLTON. Guards stood at the entrance with blank stares. The Ritz-Carlton. As Thin Sam had said.

She quickly read the notice board as she walked past. It was up on a three-egged display board.

GERIATRIC NUTRITION AND HYDRATION PROJECT,
21ST FLOOR MON TUES WEDS
COMMITTEE ON CLINICAL WORKLOADS, 35TH FLOOR
ALL WEEK
AEROGELS AND LIQUID CRYSTAL DISPLAYS IN
BROADCAST TECHNOLOGY 15TH FLOOR ALL WEEK
DEMOLITION: AFFECTS OF AIR OVERPRESSURE FROM

CLOUD COVER LESS THAN 1,200 FEET IN CONTROLLED
IMPLOSIONS 19TH FLOOR WEDS THURS FRI

If she could reach the top floor and even the roof she could see where she had been and what lay ahead to the north. She decided against the front doors and did not look at the guards but went around the corner into an alley. Somewhere in the back there had to be a way in. She passed the entrance to a kind of courtyard full of garbage containers and bins: the kitchen. In there she saw two guards with a young woman in a maid's uniform held between them. They were pressing her into a long white van. The girl was shouting and calling for her supervisor. Their voices echoed among the recycle bins and air ducts. A guard grabbed the girl by the hair, his big fist tangled in her hairpins and maid's cap. Nadia kept on walking as if she had seen nothing.

She came to a deep bay: a loading dock and a van. The lettering on the side of the van said PROVISIONS AND CATERING, NUTRITION and displayed the Nutrition Department logo, a sheaf of wheat. Her heart was slamming its halves together as if alerting her; *Be afraid*. She ignored it.

She circled around to the back where the rear compartment of the van opened into the loading bay. Guards stood nearby, their heads turned, listening to the noise of the arrest over in the kitchen courtyard. A man lifted steel containers by the handles from the back of the van to a dolly and the containers were spewing straw all over the garage floor, straw to insulate the cold food that Nadia would so much like to sit and devour. *Salmon croquettes, 20 lbs. Carbonation Recharge 20 lb. pressure bottles.*

Here! She stepped forward. You can't do that.

The man dropped the cold food containers and squinted at this frazzled but somewhat cute young woman in a shabby office suit.

I can't do what? He tipped his cap back on his head.

That's twenty pounds in each hand, she said. That's over the limit.

No, ma'am, it is not, said the workman. The limit is twenty each hand for an adult male.

I'm sorry but it's been changed. She pushed her own straw hat to the back of her hair. It's been changed to fifteen for each hand. I can get a copy of the new regulations for you if you want. She lifted her shoulders. I don't make the rules, she said. She glanced at the containers and wondered what salmon croquettes looked like, how they tasted.

Well, damn, he said. It gets crazier every day.

Don't it, said the guard.

A big change in our thinking is coming, said Nadia in a pious voice.

Well, what am I supposed to do? We have three men unloading. Are we supposed to carry one of these cold boxes in both hands? I could lift four of them. Shit.

Wait, she said. Stop. They should have people out here helping you. Let me get somebody.

She walked with quick steps past the guards and found the freight elevator straight ahead. She went into it and then turned and looked out again. How do you work this thing? she said.

A guard came up. His uniform was sweaty and the hem of his pants legs were leaking threads like a fringe. He smiled at her.

All right, all right, he said. What floor?

The Geriatric Nutrition Conference, she said. Twenty-first. We're supposed to oversee the buffets while we're conferencing. Is there a code thingie? She groped in her tote bag and came out with the tortoiseshell glasses and bent over and stared at the keypad. She couldn't see anything but a blur but she understood that the glasses were going to be very useful.

Here, here, I'll do it for you.

He punched in a code and then the button for the twenty-first floor and then threw a lever. As the door closed he lifted his billed cap to her and she smiled, her lovely broad smile that lit up her face, and the door closed and shut him out.

She felt the lift in her feet, soaring as she shot upward, higher than she had ever been in her life. Taken aloft in a dirty box with splintered wooden bumper rails and the blinking lights that numbered floor after floor as if it were some kind of moonshot, outstripping gravity and a life of tedium and/or imprisonment. She sailed into the unseen hot summer sky toward altitude and buffets.

When the elevator stopped on the twenty-first floor the doors opened and she heard a cart rattling down the hallway and somebody yelling Wait! Wait!

Nadia punched the button for the top floor, the fiftieth, and held it in. The doors slammed on the cart person. When it arrived at the top floor she stepped out as if on a stage. At the far end of the hall a great window had been replaced by plywood and in the plywood was an air-conditioning unit spewing out cool air in a steady, damp wind. The carpet was some sort of plush weave in bright blue and dark red. The walls were an unsightly salmon color.

In the ornate hall mirror her hair curled slightly in the chill humidity and she saw that she was a bit shabby, a bit dirty.

She needed water and something to eat, soon. There was the possibility that she could pass out. That would be the end of her because if she were unconscious she could neither lie nor distract nor deceive.

By now her name and photograph would be on the removal list and that list sent all over the offices of the infinite city where dull and witless office slaves spilled citrus-powder drink on their keyboards and accidentally deleted files and made jokes about the faces that came up on the removal list. She herself personally knew office slaves who had seen a face on their fly-specked computer screens and then later came across that very person in a hot supply room and said, witlessly, Don't I know you from somewhere? If this happened to her she had decided to say, Oh, you saw me on *Shoptime,* I got a part as an extra, I was holding up a hat.

Down the hall was a wooden door with POOL AREA stenciled onto it and a keypad with a slot above the door handle. A pool. People swimming in a pool full of water. Maybe a buffet. She must not seem surprised or astounded at anything.

A cat, or something she thought was a cat, came strolling down the corridor. Nadia stopped. She had never seen a cat before except in illustrations. It was an orange-striped cat and held its bushy tail in the air as if it led an invisible parade. Its license tags glittered and jingled. It meowed, an appealing little noise, and Nadia thought perhaps it was saying something but she had no idea what the sound might mean.

A door opened and a woman stepped out.

Come here, she said. Edward, come on. How did you get out? The cat turned to her in a slow, calm way. The woman saw Nadia backed against the wall. She frowned.

Haven't you ever seen a cat before? she said. Who are you? She looked at Nadia closely with narrowed eyes. You stay right there, I am calling security.

Nadia fumbled for the thick eyeglasses in her purse and put them on with laborious gestures.

Oh, it's a *cat*! she said. I am half blind without my glasses. Well. She gazed down at the animal, a live, breathing animal.

The woman picked up Edward. Why are you here? The woman wore dark patterned lounging pajamas and a pair of thong sandals. Her hair waved in the blast of air-conditioning that swept down the technicolor hallway.

Yes, where is the buffet? Nadia wiped the glasses clumsily on her skirt hem to give her something to do with her shaking hands. I'm with the Sylvia Plath Literary Society and I got off on the wrong floor. Our buffet will be nothing but bones and rinds by now.

The woman considered this. Sylvia Plath? I didn't know there was a literary society meeting here this week. The cat hung purring and limp in her arms.

No. We are not very good at advertising ourselves. Nadia folded the glasses carefully. I suppose we should make more of a noise about ourselves. But at any rate.

The woman with the cat in her arms still hesitated. Are you a writer? she said.

Oh no, no. I wish.

There was a short silence. Well, I do like Plath, myself. The one about an icebox. When they had iceboxes.

Yes. "The smile of iceboxes annihilates me. Such blue currents in the veins of my loved one! I hear her great heart purr." Nadia smiled.

The woman smiled and stroked the orange cat.

Yes, that one. She was relieved not to have to be suspicious anymore. She was a person who did not like to be rude or to confront people and especially here where things were secure and comfortable and people could be kind to one another. This minute, drawn, literary person needed kindness. Well, do you have your entry card? There's a buffet down at the pool that's very good.

Yes, yes, I do. Does it work for this floor? Nadia looked from one end of the corridor to the other. What floor is this? She then put her tote bag down on the distasteful carpet with its relentless blue and red and began to unload her purse, a dotty and confused academic. Oh, it's in here somewhere, she said. Just a minute. She took things out as if she were looking for her ID, as if this woman did not have the right to call an agent of Forensics the moment she suspected Nadia had no ID, no place to sleep, and did not belong in the Ritz-Carlton. I changed purses, she said. Just a minute. She had the notebook in one hand and the round tortoiseshell eyeglasses in another. She tried to lay the notebook on one side of the handbag so she did not have to place it on the floor, and then she put on the eyeglasses.

She then took out her little cosmetic case and tried to balance that as well on the tote bag but it fell off. She peered at it through the thick glasses. Oh yes, she said, *there's* my lipstick.

Here, it's all right. Edward, go on in. The woman opened the door and closed it on the orange cat and then pulled a blister card out of her pajamas pocket. This is the fiftieth floor. This is a private floor but it's all right. Nadia followed the woman in her patterned pajamas down the hall. What is the one with the one-eared cat? "It is no night to drown in . . ."

That's the first line of "Lorelei," Nadia said. No, the cat is in "Resolve." "The one-eared cat laps its gray paw . . ." and so on.

The woman laughed. I'm impressed! she said. I'm so glad there's a society just for her!

Yes, Nadia said. Me too.

The woman dropped her card into the slot and the door opened.

Nadia said Thank you so much and stepped through. We also study Farnham, but that's mainly for the men.

CHAPTER 11

She hovered over the platter of what she thought might be tuna salad. There were raw vegetables on ice. She made herself sip slowly, slowly, at a glass of water.

Perhaps you don't care for the yolks? The waiter bobbed around behind the buffet and then slid a spatula under the boiled egg slices. I can give you just the whites.

Oh, it's all right, she said. It's all right I suppose.

Nadia sat with her loaded plate at a poolside table and ate carefully. She was now somebody else and must think of herself as somebody else. She must not wonder if they went to the apartment, if her face were now on a list with an R after it: Ran.

She was anxious for the hunger pains to be gone. In a minute, in a minute. In a minute her hands would stop shaking. She counted to a hundred and then casually strolled back to the buffet table and took more raw vegetables cut into delicate shapes, orange carrots and other things; purple, pale green, bright yellow spirals and orange flowers. Where had they come from?

She couldn't stop looking at the pool and the two children jumping into it. The water was a darkish green color and when the children were in it, she could not see their feet or legs. So this was what water looked like when there was an entire pool filled with it. Like the sea.

Large windows all around the pool room were boarded over and large air-conditioners gusted cold wet air. So many amazing things in a short time, so much danger.

The faintness had gone away and once again she felt like Nadia the Semi-Invincible and so she finished her third cup of coffee and walked back to the dressing rooms.

In the shower room for ladies, there was an attractive girl trying to watch a small screen behind a little rattan desk and fill out some kind of form at the same time. A sign on the wall said there was a dry-cleaning and laundry service. Nadia saw swimming suits for guests in a basket. She took a size small and two towels. There were also steel containers that said *Shampoo, Hair Conditioner,* and *Body Wash.* Was this all free? She reached to take a plastic shower cap and noticed how dirty her nails were.

Oh, look, she said. This is from working in my window boxes.

How nice to have some, though, said the attendant.

Nadia took everything into a glassed-in combination shower stall and dressing room and stripped off her clothes. A sign said, discreetly, that the shower water was nonpotable. The water was hot, the shampoo foamed on her head and ran down her face and all over her body like lava, and she felt she was arising from a half shell. All the street grime and sweat ran down the drain. She felt she must be several pounds lighter. The shower stall filled with luxurious steam and she held her hands to the showerhead and drank from them, which was risky but so was life at this point. It took a while to figure out the hair dryer. She held it to her head as if she were shooting herself with hot air. Her auburn hair flew and was sleek and bright again.

Nadia pulled on the swimsuit and wrapped herself in a towel; she drank down all the water from her stolen water bottle, pulled off the woven koozie, and then refilled it from the sink faucets, also nonpotable. They did not seem to be metered. Then she took her clothes out to the desk and handed them to the girl.

Would you see that these are sent to the cleaners?

Yes, of course. The girl blinked and drew back slightly as she put the clothes in a bag but didn't say anything.

How soon can I get them back?

The girl nodded. We're fast, she said with pride in her voice. About an hour, hour and a half.

Amazing! Medium starch.

Name?

Sylvia Plath. P-L-A-T-H.

Very well, Miss Plath. Who are you with?

The Discovery Group on Nonverbal Rhetoric and Visual Allure, Nadia said. The girl was having trouble spelling and so Nadia took the pen and wrote it out for her.

She waded into the shallow end of the dark pool and attempted a desperate dog paddle that smashed up waterspouts and left her gasping. It was good, very good. Incredible. She got out and wrapped in a towel and then piled her china plate high with white-bread chicken sandwiches and raw vegetables and dried figs. Apparently these people had all they wanted to drink, so she told the waiter she would like a citrus soda and it was brought to her in a glass full of ice. She reached out for it as if it were a miracle in the desert, closing her hand around the beaded cold glass with its harmless volcano of bubbles gliding upward and as the waiter gazed down on her with a concerned expression she said, I should wear my glasses, I guess. He laughed politely.

She was more or less the same in swimsuit and attitude as a table full of women sitting near her. They had their kids with them. They were talking about plans for a new resort of some kind up in the Northwest and the possibility of a vacation there. Get out of the pool, Nelson, get out now. You're all wrinkled.

Nadia smiled at everyone and felt alive again, prepared to keep on lying and conniving for as long as it took.

When it appeared no one was looking she took a plate of boiled eggs and bread and raw vegetables and little sausages and picked up her tote bag in the other hand and splashed with wet footprints into the women's dressing room and found her clothes in a cotton dustcover. The attendant girl was not there. She put on her clean, pressed clothes and took a washcloth and wiped down her tote and everything in it. She packaged the food in the little plastic shower caps. She sat hidden in the shower with all her stolen food, a street princess with ill-gotten goods, and outside the television howled in the dank, enormous pool room with the sounds of a windstorm being reported from somewhere and herself in a life of fraud and flight.

There were peanuts and some kind of crisps at the buffet. Nadia took the entire bowl with her to a lounge chair by the pool where the TV, out of its wooden console, swam with faces.

Then the news came on. It was a scandal trial of two women assistant under-supervisors who the prosecution claimed had been running a drug-and-prostitution ring in the Home Heating Fuels Shipping Department and the studio audience jeered and catcalled, yelled Shame! The two women tried to defend themselves, they were crying, their hair shook, the camera bit into their private spaces like a devouring beast. Nadia stared, silent and frightened, as did the other women. *Somebody wants their jobs,* she thought, and knew it could be any one of them. She opened *The Girl Scout Handbook* and pretended to be deeply interested in it.

Then the Facilitator was being interviewed in an industrial setting for a program called *Watchdog,* a kind of public affairs program hosted by Mark Fontana and Art Preston and sometimes Lucienne LaFontaine-Fromm. It always opened with a dog's head looking out of a circle going Arf! Arf! Nadia tried to appear interested.

He's on *again,* a bony-looking man said. I'm tired of listening to that son of a bitch. The man clutched a drink in one hand.

You're drunk. His wife looked up from her pedicure with an angry expression. Watch what you say.

The man turned to her and his drink slipped from his knobby hand and shattered. A waiter hurried up with a towel and a dustpan while several other men called to him, Watch it, watch it.

I hate that creep. He's not real.

The present Facilitator, who had never revealed his name, was a youngish frail man, very blond, who made hesitant gestures. The interviewer was Art Preston. He was dressed in coveralls and ear protectors but the Facilitator floated through the scene like an elf on the loose. In the background walls collapsed and fountains of dust rose in the air. They strolled along while the Facilitator discussed corruption, and why it was so hard to root it out, the mystery of it.

People know but they know they can't say anything, he said. *How we all wish that our private thoughts and public utterances should be one and the same. We think things but we keep them hidden. But someday, yes, people will say aloud whatever they think, without being shot or arrested, cruel or mistaken as those thoughts may be.*

In your dreams, said one of the men near Nadia. Ha ha, listen to him. Pool water drained from a young girl's hair as she rose gasping from the green water like a seal. *Loved and cared for,* thought Nadia in an instantaneous burst of sheer fury and then told herself *Stop, stop,* and suddenly felt wet and cold as a dishcloth. The text of *The Girl Scout Handbook* was gray, it swam with sparks and Nadia pressed her fingertips against her eyeballs.

They cheat and lie and steal from their agency offices, said the Facilitator as if he had personally seen Nadia copping a three-way plug extension from Supply. *And much, much worse so they end up in scandal trials, which everyone loves, they just love it, we don't understand the minds of the lower-downs, do we? We're taking a risk with televised, public executions. It may change things in ways we don't understand.*

The women had gathered their things and left. They dragged dripping children from the pool. One of the men came and sat beside

Nadia. He had a towel over his shoulders and wore a bathing suit. His thighs were hairy.

You've been sitting here quite a while, said the man.

Nadia sighed and lowered her book. He'll be fine if I leave him alone for a while, she said. Thank you for your concern. She crossed her bony ankles and lifted her book again.

The Facilitator said, *My job is to coordinate between the agency heads, and so public executions, broadcast live, will require a lot of negotiating between C&E and Forensics and Rehabilitative Labor to choose the right persons. This is not something to plunge into without thought. First of all it will kill all interest in our sitcoms. Does anyone realize that? Nothing can compete with something like that. This fact has been known for thousands of years but since people are completely ignorant of all the literature and the thought of the past, it will appear a wonderfully new and brilliant insight.*

Nadia studiously turned another page and said Hmmm! as part of her untidy academic persona and the air conditioners thundered and choked and then went on again.

This guy isn't resonating anymore, said one of the men beside the pool. He's poetic and frail and intellectual but the appeal has worn out.

He's a goddamned egghead. An egghead, said the man beside Nadia.

We need an unclelike masculine person. Live executions are going to require somebody *heavy,* somebody like a kind but firm parent.

Avuncular.

There, yes. Somebody with a double-breasted coat, gray hair, strong, maybe an old war wound.

What war?

Any war.

I got a name.

Yes?

Stanford West.

Good

Onscreen the Facilitator and the interviewer waved occasionally to workmen.

We got disentangled from the numbered years, the accumulation of numerical years, say, maybe, 2130, 2131, 2132, on into infinity. He strode on, slim and agile. *Numbering each year began ten thousand years ago in Sumer and clearly it had to stop. More and more numbers piled up until they begin to have an actual cognitive weight, an oppressive weight. So we are released into an infinitely repeating present marked by the old holidays, and that was supposed to lighten people but you know, you never know, you can't know their minds really. Public executions may create an instability in the masses. Human mudslides.*

And so, said the man beside Nadia. My wife wouldn't come swim. Reading, petting the cat. I was going to get a massage but I thought my gorgeous body might give her ideas.

A masseuse is not allowed to have ideas, said Nadia. They just play with them and break them, perhaps releasing noxious chemicals. Your wife has a cat named Edward?

Yeah, you must be the poetry society lady. The man turned in the plastic chair and regarded her. She said you had thick glasses. But you're reading without any glasses. He stared at her face and then without moving his head stared down at her pressed, starched dress and then her shoes where they stood together, attentive, at the foot of her lounge chair.

The lights had dimmed and the pool water glistened like a lipid; the reflections from the television shone and ran and drowned.

The Facilitator said, *I facilitate between the big agencies and prevent them from forming private armies. Most people forget that. Otherwise the agencies will begin to fight each other and then we're in for more urban wars, and the collapse of the little minor lives we have scraped up out of overpopulation and chronic waterlessness. I am not into attitude enforcement. Acceptable attitude enforcement has to be limited to one agency, one only. Forensics is good at it. Will broadcast, live executions help with the management of public thought?*

The interviewer, Tom Preston, said, *Aside from all that. Let's get beyond all that, sir. Studies show that the executed criminal should be at-*

tractive. Then you have all the billions in the Western Cessions watching as one person. Think of the psychic power this would discharge.

I can read without them if I rest my eyes, avoid emotional scenes, and use eyedrops. Nadia writhed her toes, ate a crisp. *Go away,* she thought. *Go away.*

The men in the pool room were becoming impatient and it was a bad feeling. As long as they were absorbed by the TV Nadia was all right; they wouldn't pay any attention to her, alone with her book. But for some time now they had been drifting away from all the multisyllabic talk.

But would it really be new? The Facilitator was animated now that he was in an argument. *Think about this; from the Paleolithic age every damn thing was always new and it was always historic. Think about it. Pets were new, spoons were new, spears were new, then jewelry was new, plastics, satellites. And so we took a long happy skipping journey out of i-things and toilet paper and wheels, and here we are. Everything was new all the time and it was getting really old.*

Yes, sir; and killing people on live TV will also be a first. And it will never get old.

Won't it?

Nadia wondered where she would go if she had to get out of the pool room.

Maybe some criminals will actually volunteer. The Facilitator looked up into the dusty blue sky, thinking in real time and on live TV. *Sometimes I think we just want to be seen. Sometimes when I know everyone has gone to bed and I am on the air, I feel really lonely.*

Nadia got up in one smooth movement and slipped her feet into the little, worn-out heels. As she did the man laid his hand on her arm and said, Well hang on a minute.

Get your hand off me, she said, and walked away.

CHAPTER 12

She found the stairway to the roof in the middle of the night. She ran up it, her tote in one hand, and when she came to the door at the top she pushed it open without any trouble. She stepped out onto a terrace where the cityscape shone before her in the night.

Streams of bright-lit main avenues shot off to the distant horizon like arrows and in between were millions of points of light from lanterns and single bulbs in rows of windows, the repeating blocks of apartments in a long and barbarous visual rhythm and a smoke haze drifting above it all through which hang gliders blundered. A ceaseless racket of human activity that never stopped. On and on to the end of the world. She held on to the balustrade and the hot night wind pulled at her hat.

Above her the peaked tower and the great clock face shone like a moon. She put her hands on the parapet and leaned back and searched the sky. There were the Dipper and the Chair, reminding her once again of Thin Sam Kenobi's brown hands laying out the foil stars and his patient voice, buried somewhere unknown. Between these great constellations, despite the city lights, she could see the small and timid

North Star, an infant pinpoint circled by its two enormous parent constellations who were so full of brilliant luminaries.

For a moment she was struck by a forlorn feeling, a feeling of abandonment, as if her parents had only now deserted her on the street, this very moment. Immense great windy beings, our parents, the immortal possession or gift or misfortune of every solitary human being on earth, all that were and all that are to come in their billions upon billions.

She walked by potted palms that thrashed in the high night wind and were outlined against the avenue lights far below. She reached out to touch the palms and drew their fringed and sashed fronds through her fingers and was amazed at their complexity and irregularity.

These have to be watered, she said aloud, in a low voice. Probably watered every day. Then she continued to walk around the rooftop garden; *tock tock tock,* her heels sounded on the tile.

Nadia bent over the parapet and searched every dim-lit street and each segment of the horizon. Even if she could have seen her old neighborhood she would not have known it. The apartment she had shared with Josie and Widdy would be far to the south, hundreds of miles away and also the office and Earl Jay Warren and his oversupervisor wife and the young men her own age who spoke in flatlined tones and those who went for the tissue engineering and permissible rage. The unceasing feeling of danger. Of being spied upon. How good to be away from it, if only briefly.

O thank you St. Jude patron semidivinity of escapes and evasions. She bent her head to her hands on the parapet. Sometimes life called for expressions of gratitude sent out into unknown distances.

At one point on the northern horizon she could see a place where there were no lights at all. Just one or two faint orange sparks in a great area of dark. That must be the countryside. The open countryside. Not too far away, within reach.

Her heart leaped with a jet of delight and desire. She was meant to live in a wilderness. She had been born to dwell on an unsettled seacoast or forested hills or dry mountains shouldered by sand dunes or among windy plains and if this included insect life and evil weather that would make her look like crispy fries, there was no help for it. No help at all. The human world was one of metropolii or metropolises and she, on the other hand, was some *Homo ergaster* left behind and in search of the Paleolithic.

Nadia sat on a bench. It could not be helped. It was like being born with auburn hair. There was a certain fold in her brain matter that caused it (or whoever folded the folds). It was not her fault! Why had she not thought of this before?

She put her hands on the crown of her hat and felt the wind rushing through her clothes. It was intoxicating to be up so high and to see the millions of chimneys spilling out vapors into darkness and the crawling single lamps of bicycles and on the great avenues the double cones of bus headlights and among the taller buildings around her the swinging lights of delivery trucks backing up and turning. Spaced throughout the cityscape were turning windmill blades of wind chargers, the flat reflections of solar panels. She felt released.

Nadia listened to the vague distant sounds of a bicycle bell and two men's voices fifty stories below in the street arguing and the sound of pigeons and sparrows talking to one another in their sleep. Here and there giant illuminated billboards rippled slightly in the wind. She sat unobserved and rested. The palms clapped their hands.

Then she heard another sound, a low grinding noise from some-place nearby, here on the roof. She gripped the edge of the bench. A rotational noise, steady and repetitive. It was growling toward her out of the darkness. She listened for a few moments as it grew louder and her heart began to speed up.

The noise was coming straight at her back. She finally stood up and turned, her eyes wide.

A man in a wheelchair was moving toward her. He came steadily on over the tiles and the city lights shone on the spokes of the wheels as they rolled. There was no sound of a motor. His hands rose and fell as he spun the wheelchair rims. His face was outlined against the ambient light and he had a broad nose but other than that she could not see his features.

Well, he said. There's somebody here.

Yes, there is, Nadia said. She shriveled back into Sylvia Plath, poised and neutral.

A flashlight flared in his hand and swept over her from her hat to her shoes.

And so good evening, she said. She wondered if he would go away or not. If he did not she would have to go back downstairs and find some place to sleep like the floor of a shower or some corner of the pool room and take a serious chance of being discovered and questioned. If he did go away, she would sleep up here. She very much wanted to sleep up here and watch the sun come up over the city.

Who are you? The man tipped his head to one side as he spoke and his voice was low and easy. If I may ask, What are you doing up here on the roof?

She said, Just a guest. Seminar guest. I came up for some fresh air.

I see. He regarded her with a wry smile that turned up one side of his mouth. He reached down to the handrims and rolled himself closer. In the dim light she could make out that he had coarse brown hair and a long face, a somewhat broad nose that looked as if it had once been broken and was large at the tip and light eyes that were flat to his face. Limp legs inside thick trousers and neat shoes, a coat wide and ample like a cloak thrown over the back of the wheelchair. His skin was pallid and his hands long and muscular. A bottle of Mamosi glinted in a sort of cup holder on the arm of the wheelchair. He said, So did I.

She lifted her shoulders. She said, The air is swampy down there in the pool room. It's like a marsh. A fen.

Yes, but you don't have to hang around the pool room. Fen or no fen. He was watching her with an interested look.

No, true, true. I came up for the view. She turned briefly toward the parapet and the city lights and turned back again. My room is on the third floor. Not much of a view there, just a wall. Very tedious.

He nodded and was silent for a moment. Then he said, The third floor is all linens and dry cleaning.

Yes, she said. She felt her face getting hot. I meant the thir*teenth* floor. And you are an attendee as well, I guess.

She stepped back because although she was standing he had to remain sitting and it was a way of not forcing him to look up at her.

I am indeed. He turned his head to gaze out over the cityscape. Well, then. Here we have this sector of the city. It goes on forever, doesn't it? Amazing view from up here.

Well, it does seem to go on forever. The question of the third floor sparked and ran between them like a lit fuse. She had made a terrible mistake. Why could she not just shut up and be mysterious? She said, Except there is a dark space over there. I was wondering if that was a recreational, ah, open space or something.

He leaned forward in his wheelchair and rubbed his knees and then leaned back again. You don't know what that is, he said.

No, I don't. What is it?

It's a neighborhood under interdiction. Everything cut off. Water and electricity and so on. TV reception. They are all perishing for want of TV reception.

Oh. She turned to look again at the distant dark space. Well. They can't watch *Barney and Carmen,* then. She felt a sharp, punishing disappointment and knew there might be tears coming to her eyes. It was not the open countryside. No rivers there, no out-of-focus vegetation with tigers, no sea reflections in any tiger's eyes. She bit her lip and looked down at her hands grasping the parapet. What is it called? She said this as if it were a normal thing, to ask for the name of a place instead of a gerrymander and neighborhood number. For some reason she was testing him. She did not know why.

He was silent and in that silence the wind seemed to have increased slightly. He said, It used to be called Soldier Bend. It was a wildlife area on the Missouri River, which at one time made a border there between the old units of Nebraska and Iowa. But of course now it's been swallowed up in apartments and brick factories. They have indulged themselves in strikes and now they're cut off.

Well. Nadia nodded. I guess they will evacuate them.

The man clasped his hands. They are slated for removal. Workers are needed somewhere, so just cart them off. But you must know that. He paused, and then said, In there are some fifteen-story buildings that will have to be demolished. He stared at the dark hole in the city-world. There were not even the dim sparks of kerosene lamps.

Why don't the people just go away? she said. Go away to someplace else?

He turned to her and smiled a wry smile and then said, There isn't anyplace else.

But there has to be.

A person would think so. Depends on what you mean by "else."

I mean, it's the planet Earth, isn't it?

He turned his head up to the thin light of the stars. My dear, we seem to have fallen into a curiously intense conversation here. Within a very short time.

Well. Maybe not a good thing.

Maybe not. The man ran the flashlight beam over the edge of the parapet as if checking it for faults and then clicked it off. You are a curious girl, he said. As in *inquisitive*.

She gripped the edge of her hat against the wind. I suppose I am. And what conference are you with? To prove your point.

He took a deep breath and sighed it out through his nostrils as if he were tired. I am with the demolition people. Cloud cover and air overpressure. I do demolition and cartography. Actually the cartography is a hobby. He grasped the wheel rims and rocked the wheelchair back and forth. His hands were roped with muscle.

What has demolition got to do with cloud cover?

It affects the blast pattern, he said. We don't have much cloud cover in this part of the city but other sections do. Is that comprehensible? The blast goes up, hits cloud cover, and flattens out, and the shock wave goes places it's not supposed to.

She lifted both hands. Got me, she said.

He nodded slowly. Yes. Maybe I have. And so, yourself?

I'm with the poetry people. The Sylvia Plath people.

He tapped his fingers on the wheelchair arm and his expression was not so kindly now and the wind brushed up two spikes of his heavy brown hair.

There isn't any Sylvia Plath group. I must be very direct with you. What's your name?

I know, I know, we don't advertise ourselves. She waved one hand. I suppose we should.

And your name is . . . ?

She hesitated and then said, Nadia.

Nadia what?

Ah, Nadia Stepan.

I see. Mysterious Nadia who walks on the rooftops and wants to know what the dark spaces are. I am James Orotov and I am a solitary and curious man, who blows things up and lives in a wheelchair. Do you know which Nadia Stepan you are?

She said, Fourteen-fifty-nine zero zero SB. So there.

Very good. What's in your handbag?

She bent down and picked up her tote bag. She adjusted her hat. You know what? I think it's my bedtime.

It may be, he said. But I suspect you don't have a bed. You are not here on a Sylvia Plath seminar. Your shoes are very worn. You got them in a *ropa usada* store. Let's go from there.

He did not seem hostile, just deeply interested. Nadia laughed and bent down and brushed imaginary dust from the rosettes. She said, I did not get them from a *ropa usada* store. (But she did.) I am indeed here on a poetry seminar. Anyway, it's late.

And so I suppose you're also acquainted with Ramsey, he said.

Surely you have not shot your wad on one solitary poet. He watched her with his flat blue or gray eyes and a slight smile as if he were some sort of particularly informed social counselor or an interviewer.

No, no, she said. "We knew our way from dawn to dawn, and far beyond, and far beyond."

Ah he said. You do know it. He relaxed in his padded nest. How few people know it.

Poetry soothes the savage breast, she said.

Not always but it's a nice sentiment. It's very hard to find a copy of "Anthem," he said. I, however, have one. Nadia saw that a soft felt fedora was pegged on the back of the wheelchair as if he would, despite his paralyzed legs, appear manly and maybe even debonair.

Good! she said.

Copied it out by hand myself from a borrowed book. "It was the old ones with me riding . . ." Let's see . . . ta dum ta dum . . .

"Out through the fog fall of the dawn, and they would press me to deciding if we were right or we were wrong . . ." And then it goes on for many more stanzas. In Italian sonnets.

You have it memorized. He leaned back against the backrest. How good to hear it.

And how good to meet somebody who appreciates Ramsey.

There's an affinity, I suppose. James ran his fingers over the hand-rims. Because of Ramsey's life in a wheelchair but I am not yet an alco-holic, although I have considered it but it's too debilitating.

Well, she said. Most people who can read are put off by his sim-plicity.

He's not simple. They have the whole thing on Big Radio.

I know. When does it come on? I forget. With Whitman.

June. Narrative long poems, he said. "Ancient Mariner," et cetera. Where does your group meet? He clasped his hands together and leaned forward. What floor? I would love to hear a discussion of "Anthem."

I'm afraid we're all done, she said. Everyone's gone.

There is no group, he said. None.

Why not? She opened her hands. Why shouldn't there be a poetry group?

Because it's not listed. He leaned his head on one hand, the elbow on the armrest. And you slipped up saying the third floor. You're here for the food and drink, I'm afraid.

She sat very still for a moment and then lifted one hand in a throwaway gesture. There you go, she said.

You made it up.

She laughed. Right you are. It's just me. A single, solitary attendee of a poetry seminar of my own invention.

He sat and said nothing for a few moments. He reached into the breast pocket of his jacket and took out a blister card of mints and broke one out of its pocket of foil and put the mint in his mouth. It was the last one. He said, Excuse me, and tipped up the bottle of Mamosi and drank. Then he shut his hand around the empty card. How did you get into this building?

Discovered and unmasked, here at the very start of her journey to Lighthouse Island. She should have hidden the moment she heard the sound of his wheelchair wheels. She should have gone back to her assumed name, lifted it like a domino carnival mask between her two hands and secreted herself behind a potted palm.

On the strength of my charming personality. By the freight elevator.

That's very dangerous, he said.

She turned up one foot and regarded the decorative rosette on the toe of her shoe. Nevertheless.

Are you trying to get into the interdicted area? You have a boyfriend there or something?

No.

Then what? He did a drumroll on the arm of his wheelchair. I have no intention of reporting you.

For what? she said. I came up for air. For the view.

And then what?

She reached up and held her hat against the increasing breeze that smelled of the tar of rooftops and industrial smoke and concrete, hot with man-made energies and sinkholes of dense air. There was a long silence. The man in the wheelchair with his stiff brown hair did not interrupt this silence.

Finally she said, Where does the city end?

Ah. He turned his head to look out over the panorama of lights and the dark area and in the distance the fierce glow of some distant place that was more well lit, a brighter existence there, richer people, riskier lives. The breeze was changing into a hard wind, and it made his brown hair stand up like the crest of an exotic bird or a helmet. Is this just curiosity?

No, she said. No. I am going to walk to the end of it.

The end of the city?

Yes.

James Orotov leaned his head on his hand and laughed. He held the empty blister card in his hand. I am speechless. How odd. He raised his head and regarded her. What the hell will you do when you get to the end?

I don't know, she said. Maybe there will be water there. She noticed he was waiting for her to say something more. Or a kind of desert? Maybe mountains? I would love to see mountains with no buildings on them. No people. The mountains going on without us. There is a poem that says something like that.

The garden, he said.

Yes, the garden going on without us.

And that's it?

Yes, she said.

That's all?

Yes. That's all. She lifted her shoulders in a kind of overdone comic shrug.

Well, strike me dead. He regarded her with a still and expressionless face. Didn't you get any credits for vacation time where you worked?

I did. I did, but then I lost them all on demerits. She clutched her tote in both arms against her chest as if defending herself against marauding demerits. It was just me. I kept getting demoted. I started out well and then just went through life getting repeatedly fired. That's what comes of reading.

I see. And you didn't sign up for any particular vacation? There are ways around that you know, of course you know, you subvert and corrupt the poor fellow making out the precedence list. You choose a plan and lay siege.

Oh yes, certainly, they did have all the plans. There was Country Gardens and Celebrity Splendor cruises and Skateboard Championships and Village Stroll. Where you shop at ethnic food stalls. Let's see . . . Northwest Challenge where you go with Captain Kenaty's men and stay out all night. Locker Room Tour for the guys, and Undersea Adventures, that's an aquarium somewhere, and Lighthouse Island. She ticked them off on her fingers. And I couldn't bring myself to lay siege to anybody and they are all virtual anyway.

He nodded. They are. Well, no. Lighthouse Island isn't. Skateboard and Lighthouse Island are the two that aren't virtual.

Really? Is there really a Lighthouse Island?

He hesitated and turned the flashlight over in his hands. Yes, he said. Yes, there is. In a way.

And that big wooden house?

Yes.

I *knew* it. Nadia clapped her hands together. I knew it.

And you are going to go there and light up the tower.

Is it out?

For now, yes.

Where is it?

You wouldn't know if I told you. He tapped his fingers the way people with operable legs jiggle their feet. North, he said. It's north. So why did you lose all your credits to demerits? Did you strangle your supervisor or what?

I don't work well with others, she said. I look for individual solutions to collective problems. Could I get there if I walked?

Walked. My God. His smile brought out the creases around his mouth like brackets and enlightened his plain, long face. To Lighthouse Island. It would take you two or three years or so, given luck and given help.

You lie, she said.

I don't.

So if I walked north for two or three years I would come to Lighthouse Island. I'm just trying to get this straight.

Ah, probably. It would be in the Northwest.

Oh, said Nadia. I see. Up there among the savage hippies.

That's what television tells us. We are all such innocents, aren't we? He looked at her carefully. For all I know you really did strangle your supervisor, "Anthem" or not. Do you have a leave permit?

Her doubts all came back like rats. It was possible he would turn her in. Report her. Then she would never see a free river or bare mountains. She would never get beyond the dense city blocks and the demolitions and the trucks carrying evacuees somewhere to die. The television going on without us. We are but turnips in the clinches of the agencies, the human spirit as a useful if nonnutritious paste.

So. No leave permit.

She lifted one hand to her garnet earring and then finally she said, No.

Where is your ID?

They took it away.

You can't walk to the end of the city without an ID and in those clothes.

I have to, she said. These are the only clothes I have. I need to look normal.

That's true, that's true. He pressed his lips together, thinking. Go directly northwest, he said. The end of the city is a very long way.

More than four hundred miles. Then there is a sort of interurban area before the next city begins. Massive scrap yards. Then mountains, with mining barracks. He bit his lower lip and then said, You'll end up jailed or killed.

But it ends somewhere, she said. The urban areas end somewhere.

It ends for individuals, he said. When they die.

CHAPTER 13

The wind increased to a ghoulish howling. James shut his eyes against it and said, Come with me. He grasped the right-side handrim and turned the wheelchair on one wheel, spinning, and started away down the tiles, one shoulder to the parapet. She stood watching him; she saw there was a keypad on the wheelchair armrest, and beneath the seat, a motor, but he was not using it. Come with me, he said. There's a place where the wall is higher.

He wheeled down the tiles and around a corner where there was a parapet higher than their heads. It was easier to talk in the wind-shadow. He wheeled himself beside one of the potted palms; its long, barbarous sharp-leaved fronds moved only slightly.

Sit beside me, he said. He placed his hand on the pottery container. Here, wait. He leaned forward and shifted the big ample coat from behind himself and laid it on the edge for her. She sat down gingerly and was again briefly amazed at the liveness of the palm fronds and the way they lashed around and were not torn off the trunk.

So you are going to go marching on.

Nadia said, I have decided that it is compulsive. A brain affliction involving some inherited defect, a fold in the cerebrum, and so it's not really a *fault,* you see; it's a faulty neuron involvement. She paused.

I'm listening.

Well, then, I used to dream of washing up on Adrian's Island, or being Captain Kenaty's secret guide, or being hired to clean the light-house windows. Very adolescent but leading on to flight. She laughed, and as he stopped smiling and regarded her with a more serious expression the laugh trailed away. To live outside the city. I am looking around for a way to say this.

Keep looking.

I just always dreamed of living anywhere there is some kind of natural landscape since I was very small. I was meant to live in the wilderness. I don't tell people this.

He nodded. Well, it argues a certain amount of philosophical stamina. He looked down at his useless knees for a long moment and then carefully placed each hand on a kneecap as if to hold the kneecaps in place. I work with enormous machines, he said. And high explosives. Hydraulic shears, hoe rams. And here I sit. He lifted his head and said, All so strange. Very well, the first interurban area to the northwest is four hundred miles away. Do you know how many blocks to a mile?

No, she said.

About eight, he said. Count them. And so if there are eight blocks to a mile, how many blocks before you get to the thinning-out area?

Let's see. She bowed her head so she could think.

Try three thousand, two hundred.

Oh my God.

And during your long nights sleeping in doorways you might brush up on basic math.

I will. She nodded. His coat smelled of his own lax body and some kind of good soap. She wanted to reach out and take his hand but she was still carefully neutral, pleasant and unruffled. A thinning-out area?

Scrap. Huge scrap piles where they sort and recycle. Not so carefully policed. If you make it to the e-waste scrap piles you might find a way to stow away on some kind of transportation, going on northwest. His hands remained on his kneecaps and he caught his upper lip in his teeth as if it helped him think. Three thousand two hundred blocks. That's if the blocks are regular. I expect you to be dead or ill or arrested within a week. How interesting to meet you. He cocked his head to one side. What do you do in life?

She tapped her fingertips together. I bring in the supplies for a personnel office, personnel for a public information group. I distribute pencils and pens to whoever wants them. Hand them *The Capricorn Rhyming Dictionary*. Refill the paper dispenser. I mean I did.

Which PI group?

Recycling veterinarian supplies. I used to write copy for a *cactea opuntia* processing public relations group, a sub-sub-subgroup of Nutrition and Cleansing. About nopal recipes and so on. I did some TV ads and wrote a couple of jingles, chant things. Then there was some trouble.

Nadia gestured uneasily. So, demotion! Like a regular thing. Down to vet supplies PR, then down to the PR group for *recycling* trash from vet supplies. Can you imagine the state of mind it needs to write ads for recycling used veterinarian supplies?

No, he said. I don't want to try.

Then I was demoted again.

Veterinarian supplies. He cocked his head. An appendix bureau. No use for it anymore but there it still is. Since there are no animals anymore Or almost none.

Nadia hesitated. Does veterinarian mean animals?

Yes. Medical care for animals.

I thought so. Nadia looked off into the distant city and said, There is a woman in this hotel with a cat.

Yes. Takes a lot of paperwork and sensitivity training classes and then you wait for years. He crossed his arms in front of himself and she could tell he was chilled but decided not to try to get him to take back his coat for fear of seeming too solicitous. He said, So you have decided to live under the radar.

Yes, said Nadia. Under the radar tree.

There's more here, he said. You have told me of a pull but there is always a push. That is, some sort of impetus flinging you out of what might have been a more or less normal dull life.

Not really. Don't other people get flung?

Yes, but you don't want to meet them.

No, maybe not. So, okay. I never told anybody I just wanted to walk out of the city.

That was bright of you, he said.

Okay, well, then there was this birthday party bus that came to work and I knew it was a removal bus and so I . . . it's a long story. Nadia clasped and unclasped her hands in a small nervous fit. So.

Something else was going on.

She looked down and banged her toes together. The rosettes on the toes of her shoes wobbled. I had an affair with a married guy in the office. His wife was on the removal advisory committee. In fact she was the head of it.

Foolish girl, foolish girl.

I know it.

And she put your name at the top of the list.

Looks like it. She stretched out her legs and clasped both hands. I won't go into my hellhole life with an informer in my Youth Housing unit. So it was run or off to the cactus farms for me.

Some people survive. What's her name?

Who?

The wife of the married guy you had an affair with.

Ah . . . Oversupervisor Blanche Warren.

He laughed and briefly put one hand to his forehead. An oversupervisor. Damn.

Why am I talking to you?

People talk to me because I'm a cripple.

Well, she said, and could not think of anything else to say.

He said, It makes me seem harmless.

But you're not.

Not entirely.

The wind poured like a waterfall over the tall parapet behind their heads. From a distance the sound of a siren, a subaudial deep thumping bass. He turned to her and bent forward and reached out with one pale hand and tucked a loose strand of hair behind her ear.

He said, What is a person going to eat on Lighthouse Island?

Fish? Nada mentally began to go through *The Girl Scout Handbook*. Go fishing in the sea?

Despite the tall parapet the wind thrashed the fronds of the potted palms. She watched them, so flexible and resilient. Now she had to raise her voice to speak to him over the noise of the fronds and the wind.

You know nothing about the sea, he said. Or wresting provisions from nature.

No, no. Right you are.

Or about basic mechanics of, say, wind turbines or setting gill nets.

No, but that's the least important thing right now. I mean, I'll figure that out later. I do have *The Girl Scout Handbook*, 1957 edition.

Ah, *The Girl Scout Handbook*, he said. Amazing. Bad weather, he said. What will you do when it's bad weather? That is, on your journey to the end of the city?

Get under bridges? Like in *Condemned*.

God save us, you're off walking to the end of the world on the strength of information you get from television programs.

Well, I just saw it once. I don't watch television.

You don't watch television?

No.

Ever?

No, it bothers me. It affects my eyes.

James put a curled forefinger against his mouth and stared out at the city. Go on, Nadia. There's more.

Nadia said, Okay, here you go, so I was blind until I was six so I never watched it when I was young. I can remember *hearing* it. Nadia pointed to her ear with a forefinger. I remember the other kids would stop playing with me or talking to me when it came on like I was a toy they weren't interested in anymore. And I could never understand the stories, about, like, Pepper Spray and Long John, because I couldn't see. The television characters would all go Oh! but I couldn't see what was happening. So I got to where I just didn't sit and watch. But it seems to make people mad. It makes them mad that I don't watch it. I just try to get away alone and read.

Poetry.

Yes. I memorized a lot.

He thought for a moment. You said, when you couldn't see. What happened?

They found something to cure it. Vitamin A. I guess it's a rare substance. And my vision goes bad if I look at the screen anyway.

Probably better. Now that they are considering gunning people down live on camera. I suppose the infidelities of Barney and Carmen were becoming stale.

Nadia turned her head to the city's far-flung lights and so he saw her profile fretted by the light flutter of loose strands of her hair. Will they really?

All too likely. He took the empty blister card and began to split off the back. He said, You might make it to Lighthouse Island. Maybe not. The real problem is what you are going to do when you get there.

What is on the way?

Let's see. On the way. Well, directly north are some abandoned apartment towers. You need to get to the top and see your way ahead.

Yes, said Nadia. Her voice was anxious. See my way ahead, I'll do that. She watched his face. She had a feeling of suspended delight, an uncertain hope. They were actually plotting together.

Make a map as you go.

I already am.

You are? Marvelous. Very good, very good, I am amazed at you. He paused. Just to the north beyond this building is an agency sector. Fairly important agency offices and homes our parasitic privileged moiety, of which I am so far one, so there will be a lot of Forensics guards and you must get past it as soon as possible. Get on the street past the Dollar General and stay on it, that's north. Then there are the abandoned housing towers. They are called Dogtown Towers, I don't know why. Beyond that and near them are chemical factories, pharmaceuticals. It will smell heavy, or I should say rather bready. Don't stay in the towers for very long. They are slated for demolition. Past the chemical factories is an industrial area. Actually, northwest. Past that are the scrap heaps, including the e-waste, and then the big field systems. If you can do twenty miles a day you can get to the interurban area in something like, well, say a month. Now say that back to me.

To the north, a section for higher-ups, agency head offices. Get past that area ASAP. Beyond that the old housing towers, abandoned. Dogtown Towers.

Yes, said James. If you speak with people use local names as much as possible. As if you were from there.

Yes, I will. Then on, drug factories that smell like bread. Then industry then the scrap heaps and e-waste. Then field systems.

That was very good, he said.

And so what are they like? The big field systems.

Mainly just agriculture. Dusty fields going on for miles. Convict labor. Then after a stretch of agriculture, there is more city, another gerrymander. After that some formidable mountains, mining at high altitudes. Then on the other side, more city. And so on. Then you will come to the coast. Then you will cross water. Beyond that is a rocky island in the sea. This is like a video game or a tarot reading James leaned his head on one fist and pressed down his tie. Perhaps they are the same thing. Both based on the ancient quest theme with which I am sure you are familiar, charted out in those tattered little plot books they hand around to apprentice scriptwriters. On the way you must fall in love and be assaulted by doubts and felons. He regarded her and smiled.

But this is not imaginary.

No. It's not. There are very few maps. And there are good reasons for that. Indisputable reasons. Neither you nor I made the city. I don't know how we became so primitive. My brother is head of Meteorology and people in the other agencies think it means meteors.

Does he go up in weather balloons? The hot-air kind. Like Maturin and Diana Villiers.

Ah, his terrible dream, said James. Diana dying with that enormous gem in her hands.

I was reading it in the kitchen, said Nadia. I couldn't stop. I was crying. The semolina burned. I only found five of the books.

James looked into her eyes; he was searching for something. The wild nighttime city shone in his pupils and it seemed to her as she watched him from the shadow of her hat brim that he was knowing and wise and would not betray her. He was a wounded person, stopped and waiting with the enormous gem of human wonder in his hands shining like the blue peter.

He sat back in his wheelchair and said, No, not a weather balloon. He's a pilot. Slowly he stripped out the little foil flaps from the empty blister card and put them in his pocket. I don't know why I'm doing this, he said.

Nerves, she said. I terrify you. I am the Rooftop Strangler.

On the contrary. He separated the two layers of the blister card and handed her the back portion. That will get you out of this building and into almost any building and most vending machines.

She took it and stared down at it in her hand. What? You're kidding.

No, I'm not. And if you're caught with it, it will be serious trouble.

I'm a techie. We do stuff like that out of frustration. When we're bored. Those were not mints. They are a medication that I'm taking. Experimental. Possibly very dangerous but it may allow me to walk again after a fashion or perhaps not after any fashion, but actually walk. And thus my plot thickens.

Walk again?

I took a bad fall when I was eighteen. Maybe someday I will be able to tell you about it. He rubbed his hands together briskly to warm them. You are in serious trouble already.

And you?

Also. Agency politics. My arrest looms in the future but is as yet undeclared. He crossed his arms over his chest against the increasing chill of the night. I am a cripple and a demolitions expert and I have fallen in love only once before in my life. With a nurse. She drank a great deal. She had a beautiful voice.

She sang?

Yes. Very old sentimental songs. "Danny Boy." She could make it sound like "Queen of the Night."

Ah. Nadia lifted her eyebrows. Nothing else sounds like "Queen of the Night.' She reached out and touched his arm and then settled her hand back into her lap and finally tucked both hands into her sleeves. But she was your queen of the night.

James smiled, a slight, glad smile. Very good. He galloped his fingers on the wheelchair arm. I have instantly fallen in love with you. I think I will marry you. I wish I could ravish you and carry you off but being a cripple this limits my options.

Nadia paused, suspended, and finally said, You probably need a drink.

That could be. And visual images do not quench your longing to be out of the city? Long pans over the plains of Central Asia? Captain Kenaty marching steadfastly through cannibal-infested wastes?

Please.

And you are determined.

I said so.

Nadia held the card and couldn't think of anything more to say. If the card worked it was an immeasurable gift and if it did not it was a cruel thing to do to someone. She turned it over in her hand.

Don't mess with it, he said. His tie was flapping in his face. Go around the corner and there is a kind of shed for the gardener.

You mean I could sleep there?

With prudence. Become ratlike. And tell me your name again.

Nadia Stepan. She got up and handed him back his wide-skirted coat or cloak.

That is your real name.

I think so.

Why only think so?

I was in an orphanage. They change your name a lot.

He pressed his lips together and nodded slowly. Yes, they do. Odd, isn't it?

It is odd. There must be a reason.

Yes. Very well. I will see to it we meet again. There will be sound tracks with stringed instruments, intimate close-ups. His plain face and thick brown hair shone with ambient light. Now he was not smiling.

Nadia said, Okay.

He bent his head down to look at one hand. In it he held the flashlight. He handed it to her.

Perhaps at some time this will be a light in a dark place. Good night.

CHAPTER 14

Nadia made herself comfortable in the small potting shed. It had been built to look like some sort of ethnic-looking adobe structure with a fake tile roof. A plaster armadillo lurked near the easily opened door. There was a cot and a sink, stacked clay pots and shelves of tools, a television.

No fear of theft or maybe a gardener was careless. The television was on mute; some panel of experts argued with one another. She threw a piece of sacking over it and then turned to the faucet and sink. It was an unregistered faucet. A sign: POTABLE. She dumped the recycled water she had got in the hotel and refilled it. There were no clicks.

She hoped to sleep but she had James Orotov to think about. An hours-long conversation to go over phrase by phrase in her head as if it were an assigned task. To think about his competent hands and his wide smile and his thoughts and why he was in a wheelchair and what was the medication he was taking and if the card would really work and how she was to make her way thousands of miles to the northwest, to some unknown coast beyond this world in which she was supposed to be fixed for the rest of her life but she would not give in, she would not.

He read books, he knew "Anthem" and "Queen of the Night" and had taken her arm, a warm gesture in a cold and hazardous world, and he seemed to have said he would help her. *I'm an orphan,* she thought. *I'll take up with the first person that comes along.*

The next morning the windstorm seemed to waft her out of the great glass doors of the old Ritz-Carlton, past the alarmed looks of the guards. She held her hat and pressed forward into the crowds and a micronation of four-story buildings, all of them fairly new and exactly alike. It was the higher-up sector James had told her about. The streets were pleasantly uncrowded. Large glass windows looked out at Nadia stalking forward with her skirt flattened on her thighs and her big tote bag nearly torn from her grasp. She held her hat under her arm. There was no way to keep it on her head. A car big enough for four people glided past on thin tires, its brasswork gleaming, and the people inside stared out at her as they rolled down the street through the hard wind that blew dust from under their tires and on ahead of them. The man driving wore a uniform. Agency higher-ups.

Each building was a dark sand color with a small entranceway and upper stories projecting out a few feet into the street, brass nameplates. Doormen or guards shrank back into the entranceways and stared at her as she walked past but they did not want to stand out in the terrible wind with its ammunition of sand grains and try to hold her ID in one hand and shout over the noise of the windstorm. The large windows were tightly shut, which meant there was air-conditioning inside.

She felt innocuous in her office dress and her small heels. Her feet burned on the narrow sidewalks that were now like rivers of hot running dust. Once in a while she saw someone look out a window and then turn away as if revolving in a bell jar. A man in a suit and tie, two women drinking something from shining tumblers.

The windows were gleaming clean, which meant they were allowed enough water to wash them. They would have moved up far enough to have flowerbeds in boxes (succulents only). A water feature in the hall; two gallons recirculating, battery operated. Eastern Tranquility with two three-and-a-quarter-inch chimes. Desert Spring with redstone basin and washable freestanding leatherette lizard, Woodland Pool with plastic water lilies.

The thought of water features made her swallow and at last she knew she had to step into one of the set-back entranceways for a moment and get her breath. Her thoughts were on James and his sharp, inquisitive face and his hand on her arm. She wanted to think about him. She wondered why he had fallen, from what, why. She wished she had kissed him. At present he seemed unreal. Their entire rambling conversation in the dark seemed unreal. But he had said there was a genuine, physical Lighthouse Island, that she could get there, that he would see her again but on the other hand she had an orphan's heart and was so often and so willingly deceived.

She bent her head and groped into a foyer.

The doorman stared down at her and touched his hat while the deafening windstorm shot errant papers down the street and made high-pitched noises at the window frames.

ID? he said in a loud voice.

I don't want this address, said Nadia. I am just getting out of the wind.

Yeah, it's bad. He glanced at her clothes and shoes and her tote bag. Where are you going?

Office of Deregulation and Reassignment, she said. Actually, just the PR department. It's just ahead.

Why are you walking?

Well, she said. The brass plate said that the building contained several councils on assessment of subsurface Kelvin waves; other councils on assessment of the results of neighborhood disbursement of weed control chemicals. Everybody in there assessing away all day long like a lot of maniacs. She looked up at the man and said, I'm not important enough to send a car for.

No pull, eh?

None. Aren't there some empty old apartment towers on ahead, here?

The guard gave her a suspicious look. He put his hands to his face and wiped grit from his eyes. He had a tattoo on his forearm that showed beneath the white shirt cuff. Spider legs, apparently.

I don't know, he said.

All right, well, back into the wind.

Just a minute. What do you do for Deregulation?

Nadia paused. Well, actually I do dressmaking and alterations and Mrs. Flent wanted me to come to her office.

Alterations for who? The guard stared at her. It was because she asked about the empty towers. She should have kept her mouth shut.

Uniform supply, she said. She reached out and touched the man's lapel. His uniform was dark blue with sky-blue piping and on one lapel the piping was loose. You see there, you're coming undone.

His face hardened and he struck down her wrist. Get your hands off me, the guard said. Who do you think you are?

Nadia turned and plunged into the torrent of wind.

She passed five intersections and just beyond the fifth one she saw a very broad entranceway with a brass plate that said: DEMOLITION AND CARTOGRAPHY NO ADMITTANCE. A wheelchair ramp led from the street alongside the steps.

She stopped. Was this James's office? Was that possible? On both sides of the entranceway were long windows, black as petroleum. Nadia stepped inside the little foyer and beat dust and sand from her hat and her face. There was no guard.

She wanted to see James in the daylight, to find out if he would pretend not to know her or would touch her arm and quote some line of poetry or hand her a map of the heavens, an astroscape that everybody could see over their heads every night of the world and in which an infinite geography offered itself to those who lived inside tiny apartment rooms and were trapped inside the canyons of streets. Here, he would say. He would hand her an open book. These are the stories of the stars. Heroes, heroines, enormous wild animals, pursuits, recognitions, courage and nobility and incomprehensible plots.

The door opened.

Get out of here, a man said. He wore a heavy wool suit with thick, brass-rimmed goggles hanging down around his neck. Get out of this foyer.

She ducked out and back into the windstorm and walked on.

The demolitions had all begun at the same time all over the continental city when it was clear there was no longer enough water pressure to pump water up twenty, forty, fifty stories. There had still been some open countryside a hundred and fifty years ago, when the city could build vertically, but now the upper stories were far too high, and water could neither be pumped up nor carried all that way by hand. And at the same time the rains disappeared and the lakes and reservoirs were emptied. Rivers became dry highways. The pumps choked and struggled and failed. All over the universal city people in high places opened their faucets to a weak dripping. So the skyscrapers had to go, in spectacular implosions, dust clouds, massive collapses of the architecture of previous centuries, which was not all that interesting anyway.

The giant forwarding pumps were allowed to operate under high pressure only for socially significant units such as conference hotels and vacation events, for instance Cantrell Falls and hotels like the Ritz-Carlton. From time to time some rain fell and fizzed on the hot pavements and rooftops and made amazing evaporation hazes that the crowds of the overcrowded city stared at in wonder.

Big demolition jobs required weeks of paperwork and mass arrests of citizens for water theft to make up the removal crews not to speak of the initial steps of vermin removal and shutting off the electricity, if there was any, and pulling out the water pipes. Computers only complicated things as they were old and given to crashing. The ranks of geeks in the Western Cessions, what was left of the USA, had thinned and dwindled along with the available computers. The factories to make new ones no longer existed. Because of the Urban Wars there were no longer any bridges over the Mississippi and so, given the disappearance of history and maps and old place names, the two halves of the former USA mostly forgot about each other.

The few computers that Electronics Supply managed to assemble were allotted only to Forensics and to some higher-ups like James, which made his work seem important, whether it was or not. The net connections were called backbones and tapping into them took some effort. James often thought of these backbones as somewhat like his own, missing essential ganglia and constantly misfiring.

After a number of decades Demolition developed an impetus and a rationale of its own and went on as if the agency wanted to blow up the infinite city itself. People were evacuated in the millions and sent to live somewhere else like the erstwhile floods of evaporated rivers.

Cartography remained an appendix agency that lived only on paper and in the minds of a few hobbyists like James. They called themselves the Royal Cartography Society and communicated by locomotive post and sometimes, when they could attain an hour or so on a computer, through the old Fido network. They were not resurveying, but dedicated to pulling together old topographical maps.

It was decided among them that the society would leave everything in the Eastern Cessions to someone named Charles Varner. For James it was to be the Missouri River from Portage Des Sioux, where it joined the Mississippi, to its source in Montana. He knew very well that the society made him feel that he was part of a band of brothers doing something slightly illegal, something a bit risky, even though he was confined to a wheelchair.

Lewis Thayer was taking the Colorado River and the four hundred miles of agricultural land between Kansas City and Denver. The two cities had nearly merged but the Department of Hydration and the Department of Nourishment and Cleansing had kept them separate with violence, forced removals, and hundreds of thousands of acres of wheat, soybean, beets, quinoa, and barley, and hundreds of square miles of dense workers' barracks. The Ag Department, by now reduced through purges, imprisonments, and defunding, could only lend trucks. The Colorado had led Thayer to the empty riverbed of the Rio Grande and thence to the shrinking Gulf of Mexico.

James had fallen deep into the privacy of maps. The Royal Society of Cartography and their salvaging of old maps was not important. Nothing would ever come of it. It was only a hobby. But in some far future surviving *Homo sapiens* might need these ancient skills. The mark of civilized persons. James was glad to leave the eastern rivers (the Connecticut, the Hudson) or any of the extremely complicated rivers of the southeast such as the Tennessee or the Yazoo to others. He was happy with the Missouri River because it seemed like a frontiersman of the old stories, clearheaded and resilient, striding through broad plains and all the descending breaks.

James placed a tablet of the PTEN deletion dosage in his mouth and tipped up a bottle of Fremont Glacier Water to wash it down. The bottle was supplied with its own koozie in braided colors. He spun his wheelchair and rocked back and forth a few inches in front of his office windows with the tumbler in his hands. On the other side of the blackened glass a windstorm churned sand and dust through the streets, a young woman struggled head-on into it with a hand on her hat. A guard sheltered in an entryway with his coat collar up, watching.

James wheeled himself back to his desk and laid aside the portfolio of hand-copied maps and took up a large telephone handset, dialed a long series of numbers, and placed the handset facedown on the coupler. His addresses came up, green on the black monitor. He began to look for what information was available on Nadia Stepan. There was not much. She had apparently reached the Ritz-Carlton from two hundred miles to the south, where her office and residence were listed in Neighborhood Seventy in the Eighth Gerrymander. That had been, at one time, Kansas City but was now thousands of square miles of habitations stretching in every direction until it blended with what used to be Omaha and St. Louis.

His radio was on; the sound was low and the tubes glowed. It was late September and so they were into the Spaniards now: *Here we are at the beginning of autumn when the seasons turn and the leaves take on color. This is the season for the classic works of Spain and the unforgettable explorers' tales.*

Male Voice One read from *Blood and Sand.*

For many years past, ever since he had been given "la alternativa" in the Bull-ring of Madrid, he had always lodged at that same hotel in the Calle de Alcalá . . .

How good it was to name the place where you ate and lived and fought with bulls. A city and a street. James listened and pulled out the original blueprints for the assisted living facility, in other words a jail, in the next gerrymander. They always shifted prisoners out of the places where they were arrested. If she were caught she would most likely be imprisoned in the Twelfth. He needed an excuse to go there. Think ahead, way ahead. The blueprints had come by locomotive post; the portfolio had the old Amtrak logo on it. James went over the jail blueprints and found the strategic points for the charges, the load-bearing walls. He had to requisition the steel-cutting torches and hydraulic excavators and when they were all in the bureaucratic pipeline it would be impossible to stop and then he and she would take flight for Lighthouse Island and the infamous Northwest, all cut to stumps and populated by brutes.

He turned up the radio. Imagine small Spanish villages, imagine religious processions, imagine a city with taverns.

The door flew open and his main director of agency planning stalked in.

Ah, James!

You were expecting someone else? James's grip shut on the blueprint.

The director came and stood very close to him, so close James could smell his lavender soap and his lunch breath. An angry flush rose to James's cheekbones. He was forced to look up at the man with a craned neck like a pet of some kind. The man's nameplate said WILLIAM CRUMM, DIRECTOR OF AGENCY PLANNING.

James, we have an emergency, an emergency here. An unplanned emergency.

The director always had a greedy, cannibal look to his face and deep violet rings under his eyes. The director's dreadful smile was one with lips closed together in the middle and open at the corners which gave him a clownish aspect and behind it this lust for leaning over people, pressing on them, talking down into their faces.

James, they are asking the last full measure of devotion from some of our employees. The director's smile did not waver.

Like shooting them?

Oh no, oh no, just exile! Go away into exile in the far Northwest to work in the lumbering and turpentine! Shooting them, sheesh. Shooting them, what a thing to say, you are an asshole, James.

James sat as far back in the wheelchair as he could. He suspected the director of actually shooting people himself. The man was running his eyes up and down James's body and then he tore his gaze away from James's slack and helpless legs and turned to the window.

What do you want? said James.

You've got to help me with Findlay. The director said this in a low voice and bent and laid his large hand on James's upper arm and pressed himself close, which brought his belt buckle to James's eye level. Hey? Hey? They want men from me and I've got to give them somebody, hey? I tried to get Findlay to go to the wine tasting but he smelled a rat. You, you're the man with the plan and you want the Old Book Dump Jail to go, sorry, Assisted Living Facility, and so you've got to get Findlay to sign over his apartment to me, with the refrigerator and everything. Is he going to use it? No no. He's old, he's *old*.

He's not dead yet, said James. Yet.

Ahahaha! Crumm waved that away. Now if I just *took* it there would be questions, undue influence, superiors taking advantage of inferiors and so on. Crum stroked the arm of James's wheelchair. He said, I have to have that apartment. Big plans here, have to entertain. If Findlay is gone then I get his place. Findlay has this biiiiig dining table and a new refrigerator. And then I entertain the guy in Vacation Assignments, charm him, lay siege to him, and get three weeks at this new resort place in the Northwest; it's called the Last Good Place. See, it all falls together there.

Stand the hell back, said James.

The director cried out, Well, excuse *me*! Oh my, I am being offensive to you in some way! Excuse *me*!

The director stepped back one step in an elaborate gesture. His eyes were glittering and they never relaxed that hungry vigilance for a moment and James did not know whether it was sexual or an atavistic cannibalism. He had decided that if they came for him he would use the dart gun. He would force them to shoot him. Being a paraplegic in prison would mean a filthy and prolonged death.

Is this okay? Is this okay? The director waved his hands on both sides of himself. Back here?

Mr. Director, one of these days you and I are going to get into it, James said.

The director ceased smiling and then came forward and ran his fingers through James's hair. And I'll see your teeth on the floor, he said in a low voice. And this hair stuck with blood on a club.

CHAPTER 15

James's aging assistant shot his head around the door. He had pointy ears and spotty skin and a bow tie. He came in and shut the door and then sat down in the heavy armchair. It was ornately carved and snarled with lion's heads and feral-looking roses. The assistant put his head in his hands and sobbed and then got control of himself and drew in a long liquid breath and cleared his throat.

Yesterday they came and said it was a wine tasting. I wouldn't go. I wouldn't get in the van. But I know it is just a matter of time.

I can't help, said James. He was still trying to overcome his ungovernable rage over the director running his fingers through his hair. That is, I am afraid there is nothing I can do. I am very sorry.

Why not?

They're going to get me too. But first I want to blow up a jail. He put a hand to his tie and pulled it loose.

They are coming! With the arrest warrant! In a few hours! The assistant clutched at his long and wrinkled face.

Thomas, run for it, said James.

Where? Where would I run? To some interurban slum? Pay for

life's necessities in semilegal greasy coins? Live in secondhand clothes and floppy sneakers and eat semolina?

Yes, said James. Exactly. He reached up to a shelf over his desk to turn off the radio. Juan Gallardo the matador, a devotee of Our Lady of Macarena, both of them working class. *Es ella quien nos da nuestro pan diario,* said the radio and then he silenced it.

Oh please, said Findlay.

How about the Northwest? On James's plain face was a thoughtful expression. He said, The city drains out there, drains away and there is only a spotty population and acres of slash and clear-cut mountainsides. Huge pulp mills. The legendary savage hippies, the state evaders.

James, sir, stop, please. Take my wife to a place like that? We're elderly! Do they even have running water? Television? Paved streets?

Apparently, no. James wheeled himself back and forth. And so. What will the warrant say?

Water theft of course, of course. Diverting for personal use, like I had a personal swimming pool! And some sexual charge, that will get people to watch. What sex charges could they make up for an old man like me? Findlay clutched his hands together and answered himself, They'll think of something. And they are blaming us for insufficient warning time for demolitions, what else? So then it would be manslaughter. He looked up with wet eyes and finger-marks on his cheeks. But it wasn't us! It was Removal and Public Safety!

They'll get them too. James held out a remote and the door to his office opened. And they'll get me, too.

You? Get you for what?

Same things. And my maps. Cartographical treason would do in a pinch, I suppose. Come with me.

James rolled out the door and into the hall and as he rolled he heard his assistant hurrying to keep up.

James wondered what it would be like to walk alongside somebody again. Striding, pace for pace. To turn to the side to speak to someone instead of craning his head to look up at them. An injured central nervous system produced antibodies that blocked nerve repair, but the immunosuppressant he was taking prevented the antibodies from forming and allowed his CNS to repair itself. It also opened some cellular door to fevers, infections, formation of cancers, especially blood cancers. It was a race between self-repairing spinal nerves and loitering, opportunistic leukemia cells that lived in his body like rats in a multistory building. James rolled into his private exercise room.

He placed the wheelchair alongside a leather-covered bench and grasped the supports and hoisted his hips onto the bench and then reached down and lifted his legs onto it as well, first one and then the other. It placed him so that he had to stare at the television.

We must bring in the Council of the Executive only on rare occasions. A still shot of them came up. Ordinary-looking men in suits and ties. No one had ever seen video of them. The Facilitator and Lucienne LaFontaine-Fromm sat behind the anchor's desk. *I suppose they will have to sign off on the public execution thing,* said La Fontaine-Fromm. *Are they real? I am asking you before the Question Freak does. You wonder.* She laughed.

The Facilitator lifted both hands. *Lucienne, we were born to image hypnosis. A gift, a ball and chain. Let's talk about that.*

James lay down and began to buckle himself in.

Let me help, said the assistant.

Leave me alone, if you would.

He lay flat for a moment and took a deep breath and then pressed buttons on a keypad and the bench began to lever itself upright with loud creaking noises. He was now in a standing position. He reached for the suspended weights and began to lift. He had always tried to keep up his upper-body strength against the possibility of arrest and being thrown in a stinking prison cell.

What would they do? With a felon in a wheelchair? James said. No cactus farm. For me.

A lawyer, said the assistant. He sat down on the bench of a Volta weight machine. His mind circled around his own dilemma. I should get a lawyer now. Why was I assigned to Demolition, why? It was my doom the second I got the assignment sheet. I always wanted to be a nurse. A male nurse. He ran his age-spotted hand across his bald head.

Won't help. That is, legal representation. James took a deep breath. Will not. Another breath. Do you any good.

The weight cables made whining noises as they ran through their sheaves.

James, I have come to you for help and you're no help! The distracted assistant got up and paced the room. They are going to televise the trials! It's going to be like *Sector Secrets*! My wife and grown daughters will see me groveling in the defendant's chair!

Yes. You will be trashed alive on-screen, repeatedly, all day long, by all the commentators, in the parallel universe. Those accused will become anticelebrities. They invented this in the old Soviet Union. James was breathing hard; it cut his sentences short. Clever bastards. Only thing they did well.

Outside, the windstorm tore at the window frames like a burglar.

Where was the old Soviet Union?

Far, said James. Very far. You can't get there from here. They confessed. He paused, sweating, still in his open-collared shirt and loosened tie. But, after all, they were on TV. Maybe it was worth it.

Why did they confess, for God's sake? Findlay walked up and down making small, under-his-breath groaning noises. What was the point?

They said they'd shoot the wife and children if no confession. And then shot them anyway. Ha ha, say the Fates. Hostages. They'll arrest your wife, Findlay, and then you'll confess to anything. And since you'll be terminated the director wants you to sign over your apartment to him. He'll promise all sorts of help but don't do it.

The assistant halted in midstep. Oh, oh, if that's what he wants, he will have it! Tomorrow!

I said don't do it. He's a liar and a serial killer. A bestial man. Don't do it, do you hear me? It will get you nothing.

I hear you, I hear you. The assistant paced around the room again as if in full flight down some narrowing alleyway. There has to be a way out of this. He stopped. Do you not have hostages?

Hostages? Me? All I have is my brother. He takes care of himself.

I don't believe you, the assistant said. You have someone in secret. While I openly and publicly marry and have children. Go to all the trouble of creating and supporting *hostages*.

On-screen the Facilitator said, *We have no real way to change the occupant of the Facilitator's office without violence, which is a serious structural problem in our societal makeup. I suspect my days are numbered, here on-screen. But before they get me, I'll see that they get you.*

Lucienne smiled and gave a little laugh and her eyes darted to one side of the camera.

James clicked off the TV and wiped sweat from his eyes and pressed back the brown and sweated hair from his forehead. In the dim light of the darkening window he smiled at his assistant. Ah, Findlay. The heart goes out on its own road like a tiny wizened traveler.

The door to the exercise room opened and three men in Legal Forensics Department tracksuits walked in. Glacial air surrounded them as if they had just stepped out of a refrigeration unit. James switched to the ten-pound pressure bar for abs.

Thomas Findlay? said one of the officers.

Oh no, said Findlay. Please no.

It's just a small matter, said one. We'd just like to discuss some things with you for half an hour. It's not about you. Really. Half an hour only. Would you mind?

Yes, I mind! said Findlay. The commentators will destroy me! And then I'll be shot by thugs. And my wife too. He pulled back and one of the Forensics men struck him across the mouth. Blood sprang out of his nose. Findlay began to shake all over his body and one of the Forensics men held him up.

James pressed the remote and the exercise bench slowly levered itself back to horizontal and James sat up.

Stop it! said James. How dare you hit that old man? But he was helpless. His face flushed red as two of the Legal Forensics Department officers crushed his assistant between them and hurried him out the door.

The third officer held out a pen and a clipboard to James.

Would you sign here? Just a formality. It states you have witnessed two Forensics Department officials request to speak to Thomas Findlay, yada yada, use of Forensics Department automobile for one day for transportation for person of interest, and so on and so on, per diem, meals, water, et cetera. We have to have it.

No, said James. He managed to slide into his wheelchair. No. I don't think I will.

We have to have it. The officer held out the clipboard and the pen like a statue with a synthetic smile on his face.

And you shall, said James. Just have your immediate supervisor send me the form with his signature authorizing the arrest and the arrest details and I would be happy to sign the witness blank. Send it by registered messenger. Not one of those street girls.

The officer stared at him and his smile shrank away out of his face. He tipped his head to one side and said, Very well.

CHAPTER 16

James's driver pushed him up the ramp and into the limousine and drove him to his apartment. The apartment was only five blocks away. It was one long, broad hall with wheelchair-high shelves all along one side and the lights reflecting in streaks down the rich parquetry floor.

A mahogany dining table with a chair for a guest stood against the wall and on it the maid had left a late meal for him: a wineglass with a paper lid on it, and a covered plate that smoked in lean wandering columns up to the ornate lamp overhead. There were no rugs or carpets for his wheels to catch on. At each end, tall windows with dark glass stared out on a neighborhood of higher-ups. Under one window, slings and grips that allowed him to lift himself onto the bed and lie down, to relax and open his viewer to his maps or to sleep. At the other end, a door to a large bathroom with a shower and gleaming brass faucets and shower spouts and more slings and grips. His personal green glass water tower that measured his daily use took up the light like something from undersea. He had had his collection of Saltillo tiles with their paw prints and chicken tracks and human fingerprints included among the bathroom floor tiles.

All along the walls were his books: very old ones concerning the fall of civilizations such as the Minoan and Assyrian, their inevitable decline into dystopias after beginnings that involved heroism, ideals, and a kind of general liveliness; his edition of *The Urban Wars,* printed on pasty-feeling paper with blurred print, a collector's item. His photographs of Barbara Smith Conrad as Dido, lamenting, and Lane Frost waving good-bye, the scarecrow from *The Wizard of Oz*, Chaplin roller-skating in *Modern Times* and Cooper in *High Noon* and Errol Flynn in tights leaping from the rail of a sailing vessel. All active people with legs.

He had a signal that allowed him to access the executive channel but now he seemed to have lost all taste for old movies with plots and connected events because he had entered that world himself; a plot was streaming out of the future toward him with the force of a tidal rip. Connected events bobbed and turned on its surface. He turned on Big Radio for the nighttime classical music. Boccherini, "The Night Watch."

He would find out where they were taking Findlay; he would have to try to send him food and clothing, if possible. It was possible that they would use the old man as an experiment; first live execution on TV. But then, the panel discussion last night had recommended somebody attractive. That left Findlay out. James closed his eyes for a moment and listened to the music and then spun his chair around.

The long desk had a green-shaded banker's lamp that threw its glow down on the limp pages of his brother Farrell's report. James had not tried to hide the report. Why bother?

Abandon everything. Run for it. If he had his legs again, nothing else would matter. If he could save her alive, saturated with sentimental poetry and ancient plotlines as she was, they could escape to the margins and live among the seal rocks of Lighthouse Island and never worry about arrest again. Evasion seemed the only answer. They would live on mussels and salmonberry tarts in the mist. He would walk, they would undress each other, casting aside their sou'westers and rainproof anoraks. That is, if she was who she appeared to be; that is, if she stayed under the radar. She might become a hostage and not even know it, or on the other hand the world could fall apart and they could escape in the general ruin. James personally favored the second scenario.

Because look at this, he said to himself. He turned Farrell's pages. The report was sticky with bad toner. It spoke of Kelvin waves that crossed the Pacific Ocean just under the surface, a few centimeters high and kilometers in width. Strange things. He came to charts of the upwelling cold currents along the coast of the geophysical unit once known as Chile. He read of Farrell's puzzlement concerning the appearance of continent-sized cloudbanks above the west coast of South America as reported by somebody named Amanda who lived in the extinct nation-state formerly known as Peru and refused to give her last name. Amanda sent in her observations by short-wave and ground lines and often had trouble getting through.

She said great storms were arriving out of the Pacific with the appearance of personages dressed in sheet lightning and rain like heavy metal pounding down out of a fermenting sky.

Now here. A chart of the Walker circulation spiraling into vast storms fed from caverns in the upper atmosphere; the place where rain was generated and reborn, but for some reason during the past two hundred years the rain had died. Who knew why? Sciences of all sorts had undergone regrettable decay under the Facilitators but there was so much else to attend to: unsupportable levels of population, droughts like humankind had never known, cities sprawling over entire continents, demolitions, enforced population shifts, catastrophic loss of reading skills, cities fighting over water sources, the ineradicable fungus of bureaucratic jargon.

So in terms of transparent, invisible caverns of air in the upper atmosphere where rain was generated, why not? It could all suddenly cut loose. The ironclad high-pressure system that had held the continent in its grip might be dissolving. Anything could be true. Unfortunately.

Appended, Farrell wrote, is a very old discussion of the Madden-

Julian Oscillation by which the author of this report remains confused but submits request for another six months of study of aforesaid plus budget for excavation of NOAA archives (see Appendix; shovels, rock drills, axes, nail bars, rations for scrappers).

We revert to mysteries and Kobolds, Farrell wrote. There are great caverns up there where rain is reborn. Consider Sibelius's "Oceanides" and the seven levels of heaven: the troposphere, the planetary boundary layer, the stratosphere, the mesosphere, thermosphere, the exosphere with its magnetic aurora, and outer space. All these levels with their calculable lapse rates at the Karman line, and the transparent grottoes gravid with rain events. They might be there. It could happen.

It was happening. Rain, love, coincidence, cosmic intersections in the anonymous urban hive. Gifts of synchronicity. The whispers of a Continuity Man and his tarots in violent colors.

James wheeled to his computer and pulled out the bulky keyboard and began to rattle at the brass-bound keys. He crept along the spines of the Fido network, into other gerrymanders. How did you find your way through old records without numbered years? Easily; you bundled months into year-shaped units. He skipped backward in time in twelve-month packets. He found her at age five, suddenly appearing in an orphanage, Nadia Stepan Fourteen fifty-nine zero zero SB. He burrowed into their records. The name change was difficult. But people in wheelchairs have a lot of time in twelve-month packets on their hands and are therefore dangerous to public order.

Finally he managed to get into Nutrition's Public Vending Commission Monthly Usage site. He ran down the hits so far. His card had not been used today. It couldn't be helped. She would be safer on the streets than she would be with him.

Then he stepped out on the familiar road through the backbones and lines to the geography of charts and maps and located the one he wanted. Lighthouse Island and the adjacent coast. It was a marine chart. It did not show the interior. It was meant for sailors and ships so it was studded with fathom numbers and indications of old lighthouses long dead. "Nootka Sound," it said. "Saturday Inlet" and "Lighthouse Island."

The storm peppered his great bay windows with sand. He suddenly lifted his head. His right foot was tingling.

Nadia slept after a fashion in the middle of a cactus garden and the intense wind lost some velocity as twilight poured over the elegant and hostile neighborhood. The last evening limousine with its beveled headlamps purred down the street. Judging from the sound it was a gasoline engine. The driver sat in an open front seat wearing goggles against the windblown debris; he stared at her long and hard. The people in the back were reading newspapers by battery lamp; the limo quietly rolled down the street and disappeared. Nadia sat on a bench among succulents and the fish-hook barrel cactus and thornless prickly pear, Echeveria and agaves. They all had labels and were artistically arranged. The streetlights threw odd shadows.

She lifted the back of the blister card to the light and looked at it closely. In the clear places there was an almost invisible thread. She took out her notebook and ripped out two pages, folded them around the card and placed it in a pocket inside her tote and then zipped the bag shut.

She sat on the bench with her clothes rustling in the wind. When would it stop, when would it stop. If she were found lying down and sleeping on the gravel path she would be taken for a dead person or at the least forced into a homeless shelter. There she would be interrogated and fed potato starch and probably stabbed in her bed.

She shut her eyes. In her imagination she walked alongside James's wheelchair, the sparkling spokes, a flag on a long wand. They walked on a great smooth path between the fir trees of Lighthouse Island and there was a fine mist that diffused the sunlight into something damp and welcoming. They spoke to each other of the difficulties of being lovers, with him confined in a wheelchair. Can't we just be friends? she said. Devoted friends, companions of long hours of talk. They would be utterly loyal to each other, sharing a passionate and unlawful curiosity, fellow tramps in the intellectual slums, asking the criminal questions, inciting passions for the land, alone in their own micronation of love and damp.

A guard strode by with what sounded like rusty ankles. He creaked from streetlight to streetlight making his appearance in every pool of illumination like an actor with many repetitive walk-ons. Nadia sat with her aching feet drawn up on the decorative bench. She watched an enormous centipede questing along through the gravel pause and lift a forked tail. Then another one. Her plan of sitting upright and managing a few hours' sleep as if she were a figurine made of papier-mâché in this little cactus park was not a good one with these centipedes.

The centipede slowly wavered to a rock. It seemed to say, *Nadia, Nadia, you will get there.*

Then a tiny grinding sound and small pipe-heads rose up out of the gravel. One almost at her feet, another in the middle of tiny spineless prickly pears. She froze. Security cameras, they were looking at her through little cameras on the ends of the pipe-heads. The deadly small thing rose up several inches as if inquiring of her. She thought of throwing her sleeping material over it or at least the nearest one but then it began to spray a fine mist.

A watering system.

She refused to move but sat with her material over her and watched tiny water beads collect and stream from the edge. It made her both wet and happy. Then it stopped, and the pipe subsided. All the umbrella-rib arms of the cholla gleamed with drops. Water dripped from the brim of her hat, something she had never seen before in her life.

James was probably somewhere comfortable, being lifted into a bed with sheets. Surrounded by devices. Someone brought him dinner on a tray. She herself was sitting motionless on a public bench like something on *pause* longing for dawn or at least early morning and planning out how she should appear at every hour of the day. She must not walk out on these streets too early. What excuse would she have? When was dawn? What time did the agency higher-ups come to work? Say about nine. She was going to have to sit here until nine in the morning and then get up and walk out confidently and neatly, down the street, as if she had someplace to go. Which she did. It just wasn't where people would think. She needed a compass.

The endless night crept on. The centipedes traveled here and there with their million million legs. Invisible clock hands in invisible places edged upon one hour numeral after another.

By midmorning she had walked beyond the elite neighborhood, past one of the exclusive Dollar General stores that were for upper-level people only, and she did not stare at the people walking in there, past the security gate, their limousines idling outside and maids carrying the children, as if she had never seen higher-ups before. She came upon a neighborhood where there were once again crowds and bicycles and broken windows and the odor of fuel pellets and wood chips burning in the little stoves.

She felt safer but desperately hungry as well as thirsty, and hot. The sun was straight above her and her hat made an unsteady saucer of shade at her feet. She had counted another twenty blocks since the morning. She had to walk another one hundred and fifty-six to make twenty-two miles for the day and she knew she would never make it. She took off her hat and quickly combed her hair back and replaced it and went on with a deepening discouragement.

People wove in and out and around one another in a textile, every mind in every skull preoccupied with thirst, how to get water for self and parents and in-laws and children. Would the water actually finally run out altogether? How to dodge the selections, where to go if your building was demolished. Preoccupied with their ration cards and office bosses and finding blood pressure drugs somewhere and the spare change jingling in their pockets and some hopeless love for someone, preoccupied with the laundry, with credits, with the tragic death of Captain Kenaty and his apparent revival.

Down a side street Nadia saw tanker trucks parked to distribute fuel; they had pulled into a demolition site. On their rounded sides was painted **EMERGENCY HEATING RELIEF Fuel Delivery Task Force** even though it was not an emergency, had not been for a century. People lined up around the block. They carried glass wine jugs and metal cans. In the line she passed several people dressed in brightly colored tights and tunics with sparkles. They spoke among themselves and hefted their empty jugs.

Nadia came to some kind of rise of the earth and out on the darkling plain of the cityscape, alone in the sky, were the great abandoned housing towers. Multistory fading heads were painted on the sides, among them the Facilitator from her grade-school years, Brian Wei. Pigeons billowed in and out of the thousands of broken windows. Beyond them, on a rise, a microwave tower on wooden legs published its police purposes against a brass-colored sky.

From somewhere came the sound of Big Radio. Male Voice One said, *Here we are at the beginning of autumn when the seasons turn and the leaves take on color. This is the season for the classic works of Spain and the unforgettable explorers' tales. We have completed our excerpts from* Blood and Sand *and now let us begin our explorers' tales with Sven Hedin's* My Life as an Explorer.

Late September; soon the weather would change, swiftly and drastically, to cold. Who up in the apartment building cared? Some anonymous person in the hive, a person of like mind whom she would never meet. They were all separated from one another, the listeners. Big Radio was not forbidden since it was considered the addiction of lower-down crazies grumbling about spiritual losses in the stench of their airless rooms. It signified the fascination with an avaricious past and a desire for the personal communication and entertainment devices that had turned humanity into consuming somnambulant narcoleptic zombies. So in the hot street Nadia stood in the shadow of a ragged awning and listened and the words lifted her heart.

Soon I was seated at my writing-table, the first sheet of paper, compass, watch, pencils, and field-glass before me, looking out over the magnificent river, which described erratic turns, as it wound through the desert.

A line of children ran screaming past, followed by harassed teachers.

The landscape came gliding toward me, silently and slowly, without my having to take a single step or rein in a horse. New prospects of wooded capes, dark thickets and waving reeds opened at every turn.

Someone carrying long rolls of paper bumped into her, crying, Way! Way!

Islam placed a tray with hot tea and bread on my table. The silence was broken only where the water rippled around a bight or when the dogs stood in the bow, barking at a shepherd who stood outside his tent, petrified, watching our boats go by. I entered into the life of the river.

A distant river, beyond civilization, peopled by earnest and simple villagers, a last good place. Sven had hot tea and bread brought in by a servant. Nadia thought he could probably have ordered a pizza delivered, too, with cheese and tomatoes and ground animal flesh on it. And with all this he entered the life of the river.

CHAPTER 17

In the century and a half of severe drought and wild seasonal swings
between cold and heat, the Mississippi River had dwindled to a little
apologetic stream and was repeatedly imprisoned behind dams all the
way down from wherever it emanated from. The great swamplands of
Louisiana and East Texas turned into dry palmetto scrub and thorn
plains and along its lowered sea levels forests of mangrove sprang up
that were then ruthlessly cut down for mariculture farms and workers'
barracks. As the water level dropped, seamounts and keys rose up out
of the underwater formation known as the Mississippi Fan. Workers
and prisoner-workers slid down the ropes on which kelp grew for algi-
nate and waded in freezing salt water, in the huge grow-out ponds for
shrimp, sloshing through the algae blooms. They manned the pumps
for the water exchange and were driven to exhaustion on paddlewheel
aerators. They lived in tar-paper barracks and ate fish food when they
could steal it and boiled quinoa and corn when they could not. They
dove into the Gulf's sandy waters to repair the sea bass pens until their
breath left them forever.

The Mariculture Division of Nutrition and Cleansing considered them all criminals deserving whatever they got no matter how often the assigned noncriminal workers tried to remind their crew supervisors that they had been convicted of nothing and were not in fact prisoners, really, sir, it was their work assignment but it was like talking to a stroke victim who could not tell one hand from the other. Besides, Mariculture was trying to become independent from Nutrition and set up its own bureaucracy, its own executive ranks so it could then build its own upper-level housing on the rolling saw-grass dunes of Les Isles Dernieres, now a part of the mainland, in attractive Mediterranean-style architecture with inner courtyards, seawater fountains, tiled roofs, twenty-foot ceilings, and immense windows. The supervisors wanted to live under the fans, enjoy the soft ocean breezes, run barefoot with the dogs down the beach alongside the sea, the beautiful sea.

Mariculture had begun to arm its own Strike Force Teams to defend its autonomy when the Red Disease broke out. Workers' arms and legs became bright red, then they succumbed to fevers and disorientation. More than seven thousand people died and many more became unfit for work so Mariculture sent out urgent requests for fresh manpower to Forensics. Forget the ruses and cheap tricks; get them from anywhere. Impress them, seize them, arrest them if you can find an excuse, kidnap them out of Nutrition's yeast factories or the scrap piles. Start the collection during the live executions, when people are distracted.

In the confusion caused by this emerging local war in Gerrymander Ten, between Nutrition and Mariculture, and the useless workers' attendance sheets since so many were dead, some people seized a boat and loaded it with stolen supplies and set out at night toward the south, where they heard lay the Islands of the Blest. There grew bananas and limes and fat rats, all for the taking, and no agencies. As they shoved off on their mad escape attempt they saw on the far southwest horizon strange-looking banks of clouds, gigantic and solid; they were lit with an interior frenzy of lightning. A few friends saw them off, whispering, Luck to you, and watched them sail out into the moon's path on the sea, the beautiful sea.

And so Forensics's top offices, which lay no one knew where, wearily passed on Mariculture's demand for at least ten thousand workers to Gerrymander Eleven Forensics and it was this slow noise of the collection buses rising in the canyon streets that Nadia heard.

She sat at a stall in a little market area trying to buy a bottle of water. The little market area had been set up in the empty spaces of demolished buildings; awnings stretched from apartment windows and children ran down confusing alleyways.

Around Nadia plastic buckets were stacked for sale, and chipped mugs and wooden toothbrushes. Next stall over, in the market regulator's booth, TV voices blasted at high volume.

All bullshit, said the woman behind the counter. Now, two pints is two quarters.

That's outrageous, said Nadia. She handed her the coins anyway and sat to drink down half the bottle of yellowish water. The soles of her feet were afire and there was so far to go.

Hurry, drink, they see.

Okay, okay.

Nadia sipped at the water and closed her eyes for a moment against the heat and the dust. Lucienne LaFontaine-Fromm was at the news desk. *This is breaking,* she said. *We are now broadcasting the live execution of Parsons and Gamez.*

No! The market woman turned, quickly, her spatula in her hand. From the crowded market came more shouts of No! and They can't! And a peculiar crackling sound of laughter and catcalls. A woman's voice shouted that there were kids here, they can't see this!

Nadia turned to the TV screen in the market regulator's booth; the screen was layered with street dust and flies were crawling over it. On-screen, in colors made up of hard, glaring tonalities, two women were being led to a stack of sandbags by guards in uniforms Nadia had never seen before, high collars and belted tunics. The women were in sacklike dresses. They were fainting and stumbling. The lights were very harsh and since the women were not made up for TV their faces looked raw.

How could they? cried Nadia.

Right in front of everybody, said the woman behind the counter. Right in front of everybody.

The two women flung their hands and arms up in front of their faces and then the sound of gunfire, a rapid light popping noise. The women jerked, their heads flew back and the cloth of their dresses seemed to be snatched at by invisible hands. Big dark spots appeared on their faces, they fell down and continued thrashing around. A roar rose up in the market and its little alleyways and courtyards and from the crowded street, a furious shouting. Someone scooped up a pan full of boiled oats and flung it at the market director's TV screen.

A crowd of people stood in front of every TV screen in the market. Something strange and malevolent had been released into this city-world, set free to travel from mind to mind like a roaming and hungry subhuman thug older than humanity. The women were being dragged away by the feet and a long gray slime from the back of one woman's head slithered after her. A woman in a striped apron cried out, Oh my God!, but kept on staring at the screen. And all the familiar and comforting characters of the sitcoms covered in their world of the imagination; Captain Kenaty and his heroic soldiers, *Barney and Carmen* with their endless domestic conflicts, the young recyclers of *Early to Rise* exclaiming over their treasures all faded to insignificance beside this—real death in real time.

Nadia poured down the rest of the bottle of yellowish water and walked away. She needed some kind of mind-wash to get the terrible scene out of her head. She pressed through the crowd and ducked into an open doorway. It was a storage room. She sat on a sack full of something lumpy and rattling and in the distance heard someone singing, or trying to sing. A bar of sunlight fell from overhead and illuminated a sparrow on a high beam with a wisp of sacking thread in its beak. It gazed down at her with a deep interest and as she watched, a falling drift of dust motes caught the hot sunlight and glittered like stars on their way to the floor. She sat with both hands open in her lap, and the sparrow made a chipping sound like a question or a series of questions.

I don't know, she said.

Then she lifted her head; far down the street the roar of many large engines sent echoes ricocheting from wall to wall. Nadia quickly took up her tote bag and went out of the storage room.

Two buses blocked off each end of the side street where the line for kerosene straggled and chatted. The hang gliders and their watchmen had spied out crowds and lines. Nadia saw the two women in spangled skirts make a run for the cab of the kerosene truck, jerk the door open, grab the driver, and fling him onto the ground, where he was instantly grabbed by a Forensics officer. The women darted inside and hid under the dash.

Confusion, yelling, the streets thick with running people. A Forensics cop walked around and asked in a calm voice, Nadia Stepan? Do you know this person? Nadia Stepan? They looked at ID and then jerked people into the buses by the arms, not caring that the people dropped packages and files and mail and food.

Nadia had no idea where to run. The fry cooks had shut off their burners and fled, the market crowd began to disappear into the alleyways.

She saw a sort of plastic box lying on the ground, dropped from the hands of some unfortunate captive, and snatched it up. It was a high-school textbook with visual inserts. She walked quickly toward the Forensics officer with an unperturbed expression.

She said, Nadia Stepan was taken yesterday in Gerry Eight at 12:45. You can strike her from the list. Nadia flipped open the book and tapped a page. A voice said, *Oversupervisors five quarts a day with twenty* . . . Yes, said Nadia. Our info here says her oversupervisor has been given a bonus of five quarts a day for her apprehension. Nadia slapped the book shut. So you can take her off the run list. Nadia stood calmly in all the screaming and shouts and violence.

Okay. The officer had tissue-engineered jaws square as a brick and eyes of two different colors and a scorpion tattoo on his neck. She saw him hesitate and so she turned and walked away down the narrow street and the biscuit-colored buildings of concrete whose dim and broken windows stared at each other across the pavement.

A hand shut on her elbow and shoved her forward. Nadia turned. A stout Forensics officer stared straight ahead and pushed her on. His gray hair shone short and clean under an old-fashioned watch cap with a bill and his body smelled of sweat and hot uniform cotton. She started to say something, to invent an objection and a story but he said, Shut up. He was not much taller than she was and there was something about him of that proctor in high school so long ago but more unwavering and quiet.

He pushed her into the door of a telephone exchange where the operator held her earphones in her hand with a wide fearful stare. It was a ground-floor apartment in a cinder-block building, trunk lines running down into it like anacondas. There were no lights on all the jacks of the panel and the jack lines lay loose as garter snakes with their metal noses. The primitive telephone system had been shut down. A piece of sacking had been thrown over the television. Beneath the sacking a panel of experts was discussing the bullet trajectories fired during the execution. Above them was the sound of running feet. The Forensics man sat Nadia down on a chair and reached for a spare pair of earphones and handed them to her.

Put these on, he said. He watched without expression as she jammed them down on her head. Listen to me Nadia pushed one of them behind her ear. The chaos in the streets outside went on and on with shouting and blasts of air horns, commands. Dust rolled in through the open door and the operator shrank back against her dead exchange panel.

I'm listening, she said. They were both speaking in low voices.

Stay here, sweetheart. The Forensics officer pulled a cell phone from his pocket and his eyes went from Nadia to the other woman while a drop of sweat ran down his graying temple. Stay in here. This is not how it used to be. He punched in a series of numbers and stood with an abstracted air waiting for it to ring. I remember how it used to be. Hello, Fred. I've cleared the telephone exchange. Two essential workers here. Leave them alone. No, I didn't. Of course it's an order. He clapped the cell phone shut and looked down at her. He seemed bitter and sad.

I'm to stay in here, said Nadia.

Yes. You fooled that young officer for about thirty seconds.

Nadia didn't say anything.

Twenty-five years ago it wasn't like this, the officer said. Our job was bad guys. We didn't grab young women off the street to send them to the work farms. Nobody even thought of executing people live on television. He slipped the cell phone back into its holster and stared out at the street. It was something you would never even think of.

Nadia and the telephone operator sat limp and silent with their eyes fixed on him.

Stay in here until it's dark, he said.

Thank you, said Nadia.

Can't fight them. He shifted and his equipment rattled; the Taser, the cell-phone holster. He moved to the door and pulled down the bill of his cap. There's this thing called Big Radio, he said. I listen to it sometimes.

They sat without moving, wearing the headphones like black tiaras. At sundown the telephone operator took her ID out of her purse and whispered, Stay here as long as you want. I won't lock up.

Nadia waited for a long time, forever, for an eternity. Then she slipped out into the dark of the alleyway, dirty and exhausted. She couldn't keep this up forever, or even much longer.

Nadia woke up among a heap of stuffed animals: teddy bears, plush elephants, fuzzy lavender kittens, and a great many woolly dogs whose leatherette tongues spilled out of their mouths. She was catastrophically hungover.

She was wearing all her clothes, which was a source of some comfort. She lay in the back of a trailer with her arms around a pale blue penguin. There was a view out the open back doors to a wispy cooking fire; in the cool of the early morning a frying pan was being shaken and slid about on the fire grill by one of the women in spangled tights.

She lay and stared for long moments, remembering the labor roundup of the day before, and hiding in the telephone exchange. But after that things became very vague. There was a tiny flipper impression on her arm. She found her water bottle and drained it. Then she found her straw hat. The brim was all bent. From a distance came the sound of a factory whistle and the smell of something like collagen being cooked in huge cauldrons, a breacy smell.

Then one of the women called out, Oho! We're awake! We've been talking all night and now we're back to earth!

Nadia said, I never left the planet. She sat up with her hair half fallen and parts of it still in the pins.

I don't care what he said, you aren't working here, the blond woman said. Her ruffled and spangled collar blew around her jaws. Nadia swallowed desperately and tipped up the bottle for the last few drops. Work here?

Now she remembered. In bits and pieces, anyway.

Empty nighttime streets and thin colorful curtains drawn tight, gleams of light from the sides and cracks in doors. She darted out of the telephone exchange into a jumbled neighborhood with short streets that ran headlong into one another in the dark. Sometimes there were anguished cries from a window overhead, *Hush, hush, we'll find where they've taken her,* but then she heard the same voice a block down the street saying *I'll make it up to her* and realized it was *Barney and Carmen.* Everyone had their TV audios as high as possible and were probably whispering behind the noise. From time to time people hurried past her with their heads down.

At last she came out on a wide street that ran between a factory on one side and ruined houses on the other. There were lights among the foundations. People were living in there. She hurried on and tried to get the desperate look off her face and to appear unconcerned.

From the factory she could smell the odor of chemicals and something muzzy and cooked like a petri dish solution. Ahead were the lights, moving around like ghost-dancers in the foundations of the partly demolished buildings. Various sorts of wallpaper still clung to vanished bedrooms and piping stuck out of the walls and there were pale squares where pictures had hung.

In this space the circus people were setting up. One woman was filling the kerosene lamps from her glass jug. Two others were erecting tents made of enormous used vinyl advertising wraps that had been stripped from billboards. A skateboarder's runners and giant skateboard wheels were propped up by poles. In front of this it said *Zoo.* The women were singing, a capella and in three-part harmony:

Going to the chapel and we're . . . gonna get ma-eh-eh-ried . . .

Another giant billboard wrap, used for a second tent displayed three women in a Buddy car holding up bottles of Fremont Glacier Water. Over it a glittering announcement:

CONTINUITY MAN! ZOO! FORTUNES DIVINED!

The Continuity Man stared out from under the blond, colossal heads of the women drinking Fremont Glacier Water and picked his teeth. The lamps shone upward on his face. He said, Here's one they didn't get.

Two neighborhood watchmen strolled down the street. Nadia turned and gazed around herself in a mild and vaguely interested manner. For a moment she wondered if it were another ruse. Then she took a chance and ducked into the Glacier Water tent.

The Continuity Man said, You got away and now you don't know where you're going, do you?

Well, actually, I'm looking for somebody, said Nadia.

This is where he is. The Continuity Man glanced at her and then at the watchmen. You found the place. He was wearing a dusty dark suit and a metallic green waistcoat and a bow tie in lime green with white polka dots. He leaned over and spat the toothpick on the ground.

It occurred to Nadia that these people were travelers; they had official permission to travel. They would have rumor and information and stories of distant places. She needed information as much as she needed shelter and food and rest. She could pretend to be part of the group and evade the neighborhood watch and buy another day of freedom under the hot sun in this baked and flattened world.

Well, good.

Yeah yeah. You just come along here and we'll give the fighting gopher and the Ph.D. pigeons their dinner and then I'll tell you your continuity and all about who you are looking for truly in your tricky little subconscious thingie.

He handed her the feed sack and then dragged out a jug of water that said ANIMAL HYDRATION LICENSE #C9401.

Nadia quickly memorized the license number, for no reason she could think of. In the dim kerosene lamplight inside the vinyl tent the pigeons sported dyed tufts of feathers on their skulls and bright paper collars. Nadia let the grains spill out of her hands and watched with deep interest as the birds thudded and hammered at the feed with their beaks. Above her the vinyl wrap lifted and sighed in the evening wind.

You tell me who you think you're looking for. The Continuity Man turned to the cages with the gophers. A hand-lettered sign said, THE SI-AMESE FIGHTING GOPHERS! Never mind. Why don't I stop asking. Those labor roundups just send people running anywhere.

The Continuity Man reached into the cage and picked up the

gopher and struggled him into a tiny pair of World Wide Wrestling trunks of gold-and-purple satin and then turned to her. And you, you're not in the mainstream, you're out of the common herd, girl. You're at sea on the streets, lost in the alleyways of the agencies. He leaned close to her in his dirty tuxedo. It smelled like sweat and tobacco.

Nadia said, I see you have deep insights into people. She had never seen a gopher. She waggled a finger between the cage wires to attract the gopher but he wasn't having it and instead buried his face in some leafy stuff, a true wild animal humble among the beet tops with tiny hard paws. Somewhere there was a gopher heaven of jumbled rocks and succulent roots but this wasn't it. His satin trunks writhed. Next door Thelma's lower half was splendid in scarlet and yellow. She stood up in all her unkempt fur, her tail emerging from a hole in the trunks, and lifted both minute paws to Nadia.

Nadia, Nadia, be kind to those who are in prison.

CHAPTER 18

Nadia looked down at the cards: the Lovers and the Hanged Man, a generic Facilitator with a sheaf of reports as the Prophet.

Which I have to have your name to tell your continuity, now we escaped the impressment gang.

Frances, she said. Frances Lymond. Wait. How much does this cost?

Not a dime. We get grants.

They sat on either side of a table with a kerosene lamp between them. The vinyl wrap lifted and fell with the hot nocturnal wind and scattered shadows. His hands were calloused and battered, and he had some kind of tattoo on his wrist, a series of bars that said he had come out of some hard-rock life into this one, much easier, requiring only charm, which he did not have.

Now here is the Popess or the Popette who descries your earthly circuit, he said. You at one time met a man who will reenter your life very soon. All is not lost. At one time you were wearing a blue dress. You got to wear the same blue dress in your next scenic appearance. This would be on the stage set of your life when this bozo you met some time before shows up again stage left. I see a continuity stream of eyes, Frances. Watching you like an informer. Streams of eyes, here.

Surely not, she said.

Yeah, yeah. Calm down. They ain't coming back. He grinned at her and outside the women laughed and banged pots and pans on the fire. The Continuity Man dropped another card. So here you have the thousand-yard stare, the hairy eyeball, the evil eye, *mal de ojo,* the demon glare and so on. Dries things out. The Demon Glare desiccates. He pulled at his bow tie. I look these things up in a thesaurus, he said. Lydia found one in a paper bale. It only goes to T. She also found me a book of well-loved clichés. He dropped another card. It displayed an eye staring out of the palm of a hand. Don't ask me, I just take the cards as they fall, hey? It's weird how they kind of make sense after a while.

Nadia looked back at the eye on the tarot card and then she lifted her head and tried to smile.

And you, she said. You all just travel around freely.

Lydia. He rolled and lit a cigarette. She does the talking, gets the travel permits, thinks up stuff. Why? You're kind of strange, girl. Like out of nowhere. He picked up the cards and began to shuffle them. Most people have made it home and they are hiding out. I bet they've got blankets thrown over the TV. Afraid of what they might see next.

Nadia regarded her new hand of cards. The Hermit stood barefoot and cowled in the dark of the night with a five-pointed star gleaming in his lantern and he was thin and starved for life in the third dimension. This snowy and solitary monk would be in her future or he had been in her past. *It's Thin Sam,* she thought or wished. And so what have you seen in your interesting life?

Lighthouse Island, the Continuity Man said. He snorted smoke.

Nadia lifted her head and her mouth was slightly open. She tried not to appear startled and was, briefly, successful. She closed her mouth. No kidding, she said.

He glanced up at her and saw her sudden interest. There you are, he said. Now this is the important part of your continuity, this right here is in your stars. You got to go there and light up the lighthouse light before you get caught and sent to the Upper Tundra Zinc Mining Units.

I do?

Yah.

But you were really *at* Lighthouse Island?

Yep-*per*. He shifted the cards in his hands. There were deep lines in his face from dehydration. He pulled the bow tie loose.

One of the spangled women bent over and came into the vinyl-wrap tent.

Lydia, he said. This is our only customer. Wine for my men!

Lydia ducked back out under the great red fingernails and came back in with fried potatoes wrapped in newspaper and a bottle of vodka and a grim look at the Continuity Man with his loose bow tie and dirty collar and his attempts to be a mysterious wizard of arcane knowledge.

Nadia lifted the cup and poured down the vodka and was instantly drunk. The lines containing the extravagant, garish figures on the cards threatened to double and triple. The Hermit now had two heads and several hands. I, uh. She stifled a hiccup that had lodged somewhere behind her sternum. She said, It's up in the Northwest. The savage hippies of the Northwest.

He nodded and drank and rolled his eyes. That's what that TV program says. A lot of damn cannibals up there with No Farting tattoos and so on. Now, Frances, let me tell you something. The world is hard and crazy and there isn't no sense in nothing, so people look for continuity and hope in the *weirdest* places. You're a PD and desperate for love and kindheartedness and courage and all that. What I see here is your boyfriend has thrown you out and you missed getting picked up by a hair. But a miss is as good as a Mrs., hey?

Is that who is up there? Really? She stared at him with a grim look, determined.

Up there? You mean onshore?

Well, yes.

He shrugged. People with weird names. Chan the Uncanny. There's a Captain Gandy, got an illegal ship called the *Bargage Maru*. I don't think he's been eaten yet. Salvage rats and these dirty kind of villages on the coast.

You're a world traveler, she said. She tried to look admiring.

Yes, he had traveled far distances, and not first class either. The Continuity Man had fallen afoul of a supervisor and had been sent by a judge to work for Primary Resources, worked on a factory fish processing unit that fished along the coast near the real Lighthouse Island. Long pause. He had seen boats bringing food supplies there, and a lighthouse tower without a light. There was also a wind turbine, blades still whizzing around. A power source for something. So there. Is that what you're trying to find out about?

Well, yes, said Nadia. And, ah, your career in, like, fish gutting.

The Continuity Man shuffled the tarot cards and said that the processing barge he had been sent to, they fished for salmon, halibut, cod, anything that could be reduced to small pieces and canned or dried and then abandoned by the ton since distribution was left to the mentally challenged. Tons of canned fish rusting because they can't get their effing paperwork straight. Primary Resources sucks. Another considering silence, a kind of barely revealed hurt came over his lined face. It lasted only a second but it was about a full-grown man reduced to small pieces and then abandoned. It is a big sea up there and a long way away. Years away, and there were three or four other cities or maybe nations between here and there and it had taken him two years to make it back to here and he'd hiked along like a zombie. Living on whatever came to hand, but in the kingdom of the blind the one-eyed man is, you know, shit out of luck.

Nadia said, I see. She took another sip from her refilled cup and choked again. So resourceful!

Lydia is my mermaid, rescued me from a vodka shop.

He flipped out another card. The Burning Tower, a great office tower being demolished in a controlled demolition and there were clerks and oversupervisors in suits and ties and high heels falling; a storm of paper made up of reports, assessments, minutes of meetings, directives, all snowing down on an ashy landscape. He regarded it for long moments.

Nadia asked, How did you get here?

Where?

Here. Where we are. She felt like a spy in a book, *The Maltese Falcon,* perhaps. And herself a beautiful redhead with a heartbreaking story. Nadia was close to being overcome by drink. She ate a slice of fried potato, carefully, with two fingers. How did you get past the savage tribes and so on? Up there? She wiped the hair out of her face and suddenly felt the cold night air creeping under the vinyl wrap with its huge red-lipped happy women drinking Fremont Glacier Water.

There aren't any savage tribes. They like have houses and stuff. His bow tie spilled down his shirt in a shower of lime-green and yellow polka dots. A pigeon sat on his shoulder. I just say savage tribes because that's what they say on the news. I just say what the news commentators say. Easier, go along, get along. We docked once in a while and walked around, and I swear to you, there was some people that you couldn't talk to unless you were holding this fake *egg.* Chan the Uncanny, this weird guy started the egg business. He laughed. Some old bald guy made this book out of *wallpaper.* And there was nothing *in* it. The Continuity Man laughed again and slapped his knee. Another weirdo in a *top hat,* if you can believe it, said there's a religious colony up there somewhere, or scientists or something, experimenting on goats. It's isolation, they go off their heads. And so where do you expect to spend the night, Frances?

Nadia smiled with a slight weaving motion of her head and said, I'll call a messenger girl to take me to my mother's place.

The Continuity Man said, Sure. Okay. Now, Frances (he had been told to say the person's name frequently), every place I came to I made up some story about where I'd been before. Don't you? Yes, you do. He drank. He laid the Fool before her. You think you are the only person on earth slipping through the grid of the bureaucracies and skipping along like the Fool at the edge of arrest. We all do. Forging ID is risky but I do it. They only last for a few days. Ah, your cup is empty! You must pay attention to Continuity. What did you tell the last person you lied to? Will they trace your pretty face on computer? What were you wearing at the time? Check your narrative sentence by sentence. Never lose your shoes.

Outside the three women around the fire were singing "I'll Be with You in Apple Blossom Time." They were astoundingly good but they sang to an empty street.

Where is here? She said it with an inebriated insistence. She opened her gray-green eyes very wide to look at the cards and hoped he would not grab her arm or try to kiss her, she would then struggle, there would be screams for the neighborhood watch and so on. She was drunkenly walking a tightrope.

You are in Omaha, he said. He stared at her over his tin cup. In what used to be the state of Nebraska. Not too far away from here is the old bed of the Missouri River. Of course, what used to be Omaha is now thirty million people not counting the satellite units. They run into the satellite units of Gerry Eight which was Kansas City and everything's up to date there.

Right, right.

Now, here, this is the Prophetess. She'll tell you where all your childhood friends have gone. Consulting with her is like attending a high school reunion. Human beings can't live without correlation and links and parallels and coincidences. He glanced up at her. I make lists of words like that and memorize them. It helps people, I don't know how but it's a hard world, girl, and people are always trying for the power of positive thinking from some old guy named Norman Rockwell Vincent, but they don't know how anymore.

Nadia nodded agreeably.

And now they're killing people live on television. Think people will ever be interested in my damn zoo when that's going on?

Nadia paused. They looked at each other across the tarots with a kind of mutual knowledge of how serious broadcast executions were; the sea change that had just happened, the paradigm shift.

No, she said, in a low voice. Nothing you do or say will ever be as thrilling.

He also spoke in a low voice. I know it I know it. I don't know what to think.

Did you watch? said Nadia.

No. He bent his head down to stare at the cards and Nadia could see a thick scar right across the top of his skull, through his part. He laid out another card. A blindfolded woman in a long gown stood with one hand on a wheel. He said, That's Dame Fortune, but damned if she don't look like somebody blindfolded for execution.

Put it back, said Nadia, put it back in the pack.

Too late, he said. Then he straightened up and tugged at his loose bow tie and became the weird and wonderful Continuity Man again. Now! he said. On your travels, Frances, have you ever met the same person twice?

Nadia thought, with some difficulty. No, I haven't met the same person twice. She leaned back in the wooden chair. That's why we need Continuity! On the table before her were the Prophetess and the Sun and the Moon in triplicate. The fried potatoes had disappeared. So had the spangled women. It seemed to be late at night. She said, I thought Lighthouse Island was a theme park kind of thing.

He stared at her for a long time in a considering way. The pigeon with its bright blue and yellow head pecked fruitlessly at his ear and then flapped down to the table and began hammering at the remains of the greasy newspaper.

What are you doing? he said. Where are you going and why? Here you are dressed like Prissy McGillis the PR Girl with clearly nobody waiting for you to come home or otherwise show up, in a neighborhood you don't know, and asking me about where is here. Get out of here. Shoo. The pigeon ignored him.

Nadia was as persistent as a zebra mussel. She said, Does anybody live on Lighthouse Island?

He placed both forearms on the table and leaned toward her. The pigeon, in fawning imitation, stared at her as well. No. It's privately managed now. Probably by somebody very rich and well connected. The rich are different from you and me. Money talks but it can't buy love. If you were to get there, like on a fishing boat or a raft or something, you'd be arrested for trespass. You'll never see it. No matter how many credits you save up your whole life there, girl.

But there is one! It's *there*.

Not a lie entirely. They used to go to the real one and then there was all kinds of problems with nature and toilets so they made a fake one. I know. I did the continuity for the set. The fake one is in some gerrymander close to here, about a million miles from the ocean. Then I got arrested on fake charges of theft. Sent up to where the real one is. Gutting fish. I was seasick the whole time and filthy and cut to pieces with fins and knives and I was eating fish-head soup while the fillets went somewhere else to people with forks and the guts cooked down to cat food for people who have got cats. Have you ever seen a cat? He pulled at his loose tie. I'd like to know what kind of spoiled pets people got that was eating that shit.

Nadia lied, out of general principles. No, I never have. *For he purrs in thankfulness when God tells him he's a good Cat. For he keeps the Lord's watch in the night against the adversary:* "Jubilate Agno." Kit Smart. She ran one hand over the greasy cards. What's between here and there, starting with here?

He tipped his head to one side and regarded her with eyes of a thin brown color, as if they had another plane of color lying hidden behind them. The city. Next north is those towers, housing towers, totally empty. Then an industrial area. About two weeks' travel west is the big scrapping heaps.

And e-waste? She said this too eagerly.

Yah. So?

Just, I had heard that.

Well, hear more. Then after that a lot of plains dry as bones and beet fields and prisoners' barracks by the thousands, mountains going up to fifteen thousand feet covered with mining barracks, then more city, guards, watchmen, and Forensics agents and railroad dicks and stoolies.

You've met somebody who has promised to take you to Lighthouse Island, right? He said you and him are going to skip around in the rain forest and swim in the Pacific. Salmon fillets for dinner. He flopped back in his chair. You been asking about it all evening. All it took was for the guy to say "Come with me to Lighthouse Island" and you were snookered. And there it is, off-limits. No trespassing. Reserved for the manager. He lied.

How dare you, she said, for lack of anything else to say that made sense. What a terrible thing to say.

He moved his chair around closer to her. Hey? Think about it. He lied. And you believed him. The Continuity Man shifted the tarot cards. And girl, you had better be very careful about the authorities. Once they start executing criminals live on TV, pretty soon they are going to start looking for more, for any reason. Any excuse. We're talking sacrificial maidens, here. Something tells me you qualify.

Nadia could not think what to say. She knew it was time to get out of the tent but she would not get far wobbling down the street. She had to find a place to sleep and thought, *Close to Lydia. That would be safe.*

Here. He flipped out a card from the tarot pack. Here. Have a Devil.

The goat face stared out of a dark background with the yellow pentagram bright and baleful between his horns.

CHAPTER 19

Far down the narrowing perspective of the street, beyond the pharmaceutical factory district, the great abandoned towers lifted their broken windows twenty stories into the air. Nadia walked neatly onward. Lydia had been so happy to get rid of her that the spangled manageress had filled one of her water bottles out of the animal hydration jug and pointed her down the street. Wherever you are going, she said, keep on. He's a terrible flirt but he's all mine.

Nadia looked increasingly shabby and unofficelike. Hungover and wobbly. The world appeared very seamy. Her failures sliding down in an avalanching ruin made it difficult to adopt that cheery walk, a pleasant face. And they had her name, they were indeed looking for her.

In a few months, if she lived, she would be walking with James in a green world. She would believe this despite the Continuity Man, despite the distances in front of her. Privacy and silence. Running water. How odd, the thought of running water. Where would it all come from? Wouldn't it run out after a while? Her mind was filled with an astringent negative charge.

She could not keep walking in the shoes and clothes she wore. Nadia thought of disguising herself as a boy, in sturdy clothing. She would have to cut her bright auburn hair but if it were short and under some kind of cap she would be more anonymous.

A new billboard on top of some building: Carmen in front of a fan, her black hair flying in ropy sheaves.

MY RAINSTORM FAN!
CARMEN IS BLOWN AWAY BY
THE WONDERFUL SMALL APPLIANCES GUYS!
OFFICE OF PERSONAL HYGIENE AND SAFETY
DEPARTMENT OF SMALL APPLIANCES

She came to an open square. Bare and twisted trees in the center; they seemed to be made of pipe and wire. An old movie theater and *ropa usada* shops and broken storefronts. The apartment buildings were ancient, five-story structures, their roofs joyous with flying laundry and over the entrance of a Basic Rations store was the date, *1932.*

Old signs wobbled on their poles with nearly invisible images: a rabbit in a vest holding up vanished sandwiches and nonexistent loaves of bread. Someone in a furry hood lifting ice cream on a stick. Nadia wove through the crowds and sat down on a bench made of planks and concrete blocks to rest. She drank the rest of the water Lydia had given her.

The park was packed with people and awash in dirty paper and discarded baskets. Over one of the streets leading into the square was an enormous red-and-white banner: It's Awareness Awareness Month! Learn to Focus on Your Focus! Apply now for weekend seminars!

She sat there, irresolute, and then took out the *Handbook* and pretended to read. She had to get somewhere and rest for several days in privacy where there was no neighborhood watch or threat of collection buses, away from the feeling of being observed, of not knowing where she was and living like an actress in public spaces in the cameras of strangers' eyes. The demon stare, the *mal de ojo,* the evil eye. It was terrible not to have any continuity except yourself.

The linear shadow of the ironwork tree limbs fell across her hand. She turned another page. *Explorer. To explore new places is one of the greatest adventures in the world,* it said, in the *Handbook*'s childlike tones. It radiated attitudes of happy, youthful wonder.

Her drained brain slid into despair. The world had grown very cynical and old. Everybody was old, even the young. Children were old. Everyone faded like an old ice-cream sign, sitting in front of television screens as if their muscles ached with age. Where is the refreshing rain? Maybe the planet itself was terminally old. We are all like geriatric patients cowering in front of the male nurse who brings us our new teeth.

Then two watchmen came into the square with staring distrustful eyeballs and so she quietly slipped into one of the *ropa usada* warehouses. No ID needed. Payment in coins. In the big cool space, full of voices and pigeons high up on the I-beams, she joined a crowd of women rooting through the clothes and throwing aside what they didn't want until they had all dug a crater in the middle of the hill of torn evening dresses, pajamas, raveling sweaters.

She found a sturdy pair of pants and a faded, limp shirt. She located a used knapsack and a flat cap and then came upon a box full of new red canvas shoes with black polka dots in all different sizes. Dreadful looking, childish, but she had small feet and was hard to fit and here was a pair that fitted perfectly.

She picked up a device with a screen that lit up in a weak gray illumination and a bar pulsed across it from green to red. For a moment it made her slightly ill to look at it.

At the counter the woman told her the device had been found by scrappers, it was legal, legal, a toy, you could play with it.

Then a brisk, loud gray-haired female official of some kind came into the warehouse and stalked through the piles of clothing insisting that women sign up for Awareness Awareness Month seminars. She demanded ID and shoved her clipboard at people; sign, sign. Nadia said, yes, just a minute, let me go get my sister, I need for us to get our names next to each other so we can get into the same seminar, and she walked away saying, We'll both come and watch your godawful boring stupid video presentation, I can't wait, what? What?

Outside she looked up at the sky where fat round cumulus clouds were starting to clot together. The wind had a damp feeling to it. Very strange.

Good trees! A short, fat woman stood beside her. Old Omaha Square! Real trees!

Nadia said, I thought they were some kind of artistic ironwork.

No! No! Real trees! Dead!

The woman had her hair done in cornrows with little bells tied throughout the braids. Her dress of brightly colored rags fluttered. She kicked at the trash.

Oh, said Nadia.

I'm a neighborhood snoop! Who are you? said the woman in her loud voice. Why are you just standing here?

I am looking for a beauty shop, said Nadia.

It's right there, right there! The woman pointed. In the old movie theater. They turned it into a beauty shop. Are you blind? Hey? Are you blind?

It was dim and cool and restful inside the lobby of the old movie theater. There were ten stations and all of them full. Nadia did not think watchmen or arrest crews would come into this female hive. Noise, babble, hair dryers going, little girls tiptoeing in and out with buckets of water, every drop accounted for. The doors to the amphitheater were barred with large timbers, the seats empty and the screen dead forever. Against the wall was a four-foot television and on it she saw James. She stopped dead and stared.

Take a numbered chair. An older woman, smartly dressed, looked up from a desk. She wore raindrop earrings. I *said* take a number!

Sorry, Nadia said. She hurried to the chairs lined up against the wall and kept her head turned to the TV screen. James had uneasy edges and his wheelchair spokes blazed with the studio lights. *I am amazed, I am amazed.* Plath.

Nadia listened to his impatient voice, the same voice she had spent hours talking to two nights before. She sat down on a wooden stool numbered twelve beneath a faded poster advertising *Thin Edge* with Teresa Guardo, a film that had thrilled audiences everywhere a decade before Nadia had been born. Teresa was in a flying tae kwon do stance, grinning with wrath, her ninety pounds dressed in oily rubber, striking down big men with guns.

Twelve!

Nadia jumped up.

Bella! said the woman behind the desk and her raindrop earrings sparkled. She lifted her manicured hand. Bella! Then she returned to her careful tracking of the little girls and the buckets.

A young stylist in the rear swallowed the last of her noodles and jumped to her feet.

Shampoo? said Bella. Manicure? New haircut style like the savage hippies, asymmetrical, want to see pictures?

Cut and shampoo, said Nadia. She sat down and looked into the cracked mirror to see the television and James. She was desperate to hear him.

Just a trim? Now also we have lead-free nail polish and agave-essentials face renewer for sale here. Also showers, reasonable prices per gallon and *really* hot water. Now, let's trim this.

No, cut it very short.

The girl took up a length of Nadia's hair and drew it out. You don't want to cut this, she said. This is truly great hair.

It's too hard to shampoo, she said. Needs too much water. She lay back in the chair and all her musculature uncoiled. The air was soft and steamy. The smell of the harsh green shampoo and propane was actually pleasant.

I hear you, said Bella. Now, I can give it a nice fall. Long on the sides. Kind of a Dutchboy. Girlish but tomboyish.

Good, said Nadia. I'll go for that.

Nadia squinted at the reflected TV screen as she felt the tug of the comb and the shearing grind of the scissors as her beautiful auburn hair fell in great sheaves onto the dirty floor. James's voice came to her and he was speaking not to her or to the interviewer but to an invisible audience.

The woman at the desk got up and came to Bella's station. You're not from this gerrymander, she said. Are you? The nearby women glanced over at Nadia with some interest.

No. No. I just got out of a terrible argument and I just *left*.

There it is, said the woman owner, in sudden understanding. She nodded her elegant head and her raindrop earrings jumped. Is he looking for you?

Yes. Nadia leaned forward to peer at herself in the mirror. She wiped at her eyes to make it look as if she had started to cry. She said, I'm trying to look different. So he won't recognize me. A convincing sob snatched at her throat and she wished everyone would shut up so she could hear James on the TV but here she was, compulsively telling some involved lie.

We'll make it different, said Bella. It's going to be okay.

No, no, no, said the interviewer on television, whose name was Art Preston.

Nadia was then sorry she had made up this stupid story. Now they would remember her forever. The girl who ran away from an abusive boyfriend and cut her hair off short. They would tell this story to everybody they knew. Every night Nadia spent out of her own sector without a permit, without her ID, the more illegal she became. She sat stiffly and determined not to say another word.

CHAPTER 20

The television said, *There are no more domestic animals. People are the domestic animals.*

James leaned back in his wheelchair with his television makeup and his splintery brown hair and his broad nose, his sardonic smile. The same man as on the rooftop. Over the noise of women chattering and gossiping and the little girls running in and out with their buckets Nadia could finally hear the interview.

The interviewer shifted his feet around, perhaps to show off his excellent leather footwear. He said, *Of course C. and E. has been very good to me, if you insist on being personal. Culture and Entertainment has been very good to me.*

James considered him. *I'm not being personal. I am being insistent, possibly rude. I was talking about my wish to change over to Cartography. Get out of Demolition.*

Yes, but just explain why they never warn people on time.

I have no authority with Neighborhood Emergency Information Services. They are secretive. Maybe bribes would help, I don't know.

You know you are now on public record saying something like that.

What, bribes?

Bribery is illegal.

Bite me, Preston.

Wow, said Bella. Who is that guy?

I don't know, said Maryanna.

He's in deep shit.

Maybe he's been smoking some extraskunky pineapple express.

And your brother is in Meteorology. That's what I would call a sinecure. One of those clueless bureaucracies studying meteors, and he has upper-level benefits for what? Sitting around staring through a telescope . . .

Meteorology is weather, said James. *You're an uneducated idiot.*

How many hours a week? How many meteors show up in the sky per month? At nighttime so he and his assistants . . .

It's weather. Weather. Meteorology means weather and it's part of Intrusive Species so . . .

Probably sleep half the night. What do meteors have to do with weather? What weather? We don't have any weather, this is what you call an appendix bureau.

What it has to do with is that low cloud cover distorts blast pattern, the blast pattern, you see. Anything lower than twelve hundred feet.

We don't have cloud cover, what the hell are you talking about? I know perfectly well what meteorology means.

We do today, said Bella. Cloud cover.

It's so weird, said the stylist at the next station. I mean like it gets dark, these clouds clump up and it's dark. You can see the edge of the cloud shadow moving down the street. It's freaking me out.

Preston couldn't get his head out of his ass long enough to look out the window, said Bella.

Meteor-ology. And now we do have cloud cover. The past week or so.

I know that. I said that. I said meteorology. Interrupting is not the same as a civic debate. I said that. What does this have to do . . .

Listen . . .

You listen, Orotov.

Let me finish. My brother says the weather pattern is changing, actually quite drastically, in several parts of the world. This has not been covered on the news of course. No one will listen to him. Another "of course." We may have very sudden weather changes here, very sudden. In case of floods . . .

Floods? Are you saying there are going to be floods?

James placed both hands flat on the table in front of him. *Yes, yes, and various agencies will have to coordinate and we'll need the old topographical maps, floodplain maps, and there will have to be plans for evacuation, emergency supplies.*

Wait, wait, Preston said. *Maps for vanished rivers.* He laughed. *All gone in the Urban Wars. The Global Positioning System that led our enemies to us and actually led armies to one another. It all had to go. We are not tied to maps anymore. They are constricting and rigid and lead to rigid and incurious thinking. Contemporary men and women need to be flexible, mentally lithe, so to speak . . .*

James turned to Preston with a hard expression. *Like watching executions live on TV? What kind of depravity is that? I will just repeat that there is a weather change happening in many parts of the world, in Peru for instance, listen to me here, just a minute . . .*

Peru? Peru? We don't name nations anymore, James. Borders kill. The world is entirely urban, this is a new world, this is something that humanity has never faced before. We live in historic times. There are no national borders. A border is an imaginary line and a kill space.

James gripped the wheelchair arms. Nadia watched him intently, thinking, *Did you lie to me? About Lighthouse Island?*

A kill space. You don't say. I have news for you the weather pattern . . .

The interviewer gestured wildly. *Okay, this is just a low-rent noontime show, maybe an audience of a couple hundred million or so, it's probably watched by people eating their noodles and hairdressers and street people, so go ahead, insult me. But we have to remember the city wars, we have the archived films of Leningrad, Stalingrad, Nanking, the incredible city warfare,*

Los Angeles, Chicago . . . I mean it was a time of horror, just horrors, Orotov, everybody fought to a standstill and so dividing the world into Eastern and Western Cessions, a desperate attempt to save an overpopulated world, who doesn't remember the films of the bombing and invasions here . . .

James leaned back and stared up at the studio ceiling and its ranked lights.

I'll just talk over you. My brother is a pilot, he has equipped a storm observer prop plane, twin-engine, and truly violent weather is coming . . .

Your brother, I can have you removed, I can do an exposé on your private life, you're a sick man, Orotov. I have the reports here, here . . . The interviewer moved papers around on the table. His gestures were frantic, sloppy, uncoordinated. *Get out. Just get this man out. Why are we live? Why does this shit happen to me?*

A little girl spilled a bottle of shampoo and began to cry loudly.

When Nadia looked back at the screen James was gone and the interviewer was talking about something else. He said, *I never allowed my children to watch television. It damages their brains.*

Honey, honey, don't cry, said a hairdresser. We'll mop it up. The little girl was afraid of the woman who ran the place and stared at the hairdresser with wide eyes while also crying. They'll shoot me, the girl said. They'll shoot me. The air was filled with the sweet scent of the spilled shampoo.

It's okay, baby, said Bella.

Do personal lives have significance? They do if it tells us something about character. Character affects personal decisions. James Orotov is under investigation for premature demolitions. More on this growing cult of Orotov defenders. It's a weather cult, from all reports. There's a growing backlash, however . . .

Her visual field was now being circled by that old familiar bright spark but then she heard the three bell tones that meant a public service message was imminent.

At least they didn't drag in the Facilitator, said Bella. She said it in a low voice. Creepy freak.

Shut *up*, Bella.

The ad opened with a shot of glaciers taken from a helicopter that sailed over blue-and-green ice cliffs. The ice cliffs foamed with blowing snow. From high above there were crevasses in lines like broken white candy. Sibelius's "Oceanides" sang through the dim, perfumed spaces. A voice-over intoned, *I know, I know.* More shots of ice cliffs. The voice said, *Sometimes it seems as if the bureaucracies move like glaciers. Frozen up. Rigid.*

Say it ain't so, said Bella.

This again? A woman holding a magazine flipped pages.

The camera floated down the river of ice from high above and then there was the sound of seagulls. *But together you and I can get them moving.* Shots of enormous sections of ice breaking off and collapsing like public housing towers into the sea, some sea somewhere. *Be brave. This is a new kind of courage. Civic courage. File your complaints against bureaucratic incompetence. Forms available everywhere.* Then a shot of a sailboat with its sails taut and full of wind cutting through green seas and seagulls circling and crying.

I must have heard that fifty times. Bella blasted Nadia's head with a large, clumsy metal hair dryer that she had to hold with both hands. Inside it the wires glowed red with electricity and the cord was frayed. There!

Nadia stood up and ran her hands through her new, short hair.

It's as good as I could make it, said Bella. It's springy.

The owner woman wagged her finger at Nadia. You go home and lock your door and don't give in if he comes around. *Don't* give in.

And all around the other hairdressers and the women said, She's right, she's right.

Nadia pulled out a Western Cession dime and handed it to Bella. I'll never speak to him again. I mean it. Now, how much is a ticket to the showers?

LIGHTHOUSE ISLAND / 167

Nadia walked north toward the abandoned towers. She was hungry and she thought about the human necessity to *eat* something every day, every damn day. It was a curse. At least she was clean from the hot-water shower and she had a neat haircut.

She continued on and kept the afternoon sun at her left hand. It was cloudy and the air felt damp. By late afternoon she came to a Buddy car repair shop and recharge station. It took up the whole first floor of a long building. It was very noisy. A thin, coughing guard in a worn brown uniform stood at the entrance. She walked over to him and felt a kind of hungry trembling all through her body and was afraid she might faint.

She said, Are there any vending machines inside?

Yeah. They take ID or coins of money.

Well, can I go and get something from them?

The guard gestured toward the low doorway beyond the gate. Don't go any farther than that main room.

He turned back to a little portable TV where the Sunshine Boys were playing the Neutro-Rockets.

Nadia entered the square, bare room that had another door on the far side, leading back into a work area. There were four vending machines. She put her tote bag and the knapsack on the floor and knelt down to find the blister card. There were bootprints on one side of the sandwich machine as if people had been kicking it.

The machine exhibited a running crawl across the top that said THERE IS NO "AWAY," REUSE RECYCLE RECOVER ***PAN-URBAN RECHARGE AND REPAIR DEPARTMENT ***PRESS PLAY TO SEE VIDEO ON HOW WE DO BATTERY RECYCLING. She inserted the blister card. The crawl changed: UNIDENTIFIED NO ID NECESSARY CHOOSE PRODUCT. She pressed a knuckle against the number for a roast beef sandwich. She didn't want to leave a fingerprint. The machine rumbled as something wrapped in brown paper fell into the tray. It worked, it worked, it worked.

Audio came on: tinkling, sweet harp music, and then a voice said, *Hey! Try this! The National Council on Water Security urges you to join with your neighbors in making your own waste-water purifier!*

She pressed the STOP AUDIO button but it kept on.

Get a group in your office together! It's easy! Fill out an application! Over tea and snacks you can all discuss . . .

She hit the button again but the loud voice kept on, urging her to have tea and snacks and join with others and something about using old bathtubs.

Stop, dammit, she said.

The rear door opened and a man came in. His face was dark with metal dust and he was white around the eyes. Goggles hung around his neck and his dusty green shirt and pants had burn marks.

Here, he said. He stood back and kicked the machine solidly with his workboot heel. The voice slowed and gargled *toooogethuuur yoooo annnd yooooor . . .* and stopped.

Put you around the bend, he said. He stuck his ID in the slot and then shoved coins into another slot and a bottle rattled down. Is the air weird out there?

Weird how? she said.

Wet. It's wet air out there. Clouds.

Yes, she said. It seems wettish.

Well, I never thought I'd see it.

He went back through the door with the bottle and slammed the door shut.

Nadia inserted the blister card again and pressed for another sandwich, and then the almondless Almond Delights. She pressed the numbers for a bottle of Mamosi because it had a screw cap and she could reuse it. She tried for soy cheese product but then it said NOT AVAILABLE.

Very well, very well. Nadia was elated as well as hungry.

If she could find vending machines she could stay alive and fed. There would be no vending machines on Lighthouse Island. It was a wilderness, after all. But they would figure it out. And now James would know she had used the card, he would know where she was.

CHAPTER 21

The abandoned public housing towers became taller and taller by the block. The sidewalk was still thick with sweating, hot people and it seemed even hotter now with the unusual humidity. Some were hurrying from one factory office to another with things to be read or signed, applications for vacation time for husband and wife to be granted at the same time, for increased water rations for a new baby; others had got out of work early and were treading along with string bags of things for supper. Girls raced past delivering messages: *Can u come drink rice wine tonite, watch dynamos, Ken. I saw u w/ Brin-duh want to break up or not, † 2 U. Lecia. Borrow ½ gal kerosene pls? pay u back Thelma.* The message couriers made shrieking noises on their tin whistles. She passed gypsy women on their way to their stalls and a woman sitting on the pavement in front of a pile of used stuff, selling the possessions of some recently dead relative in order to pay the Candyman. Beneath the lines of washing strung across the street from apartment window to apartment window were small puddles of dripping water and therefore happy, grateful sprigs of grass were growing up through the cracking asphalt pavement, destroying it inch by inch.

Nadia sat at a hot-drinks stand solving, moment by moment, the eternal problem of street people, which is how to kill time in public without appearing odd.

It was already dark. She was not afraid of the night streets. Half a century ago during the Square One campaign they had executed anyone arrested for sexual predation and/or drugs and/or common theft and a great many other transgressions, like having fatherless children. The impoverished world could no longer afford bad behavior, nor the feral street gangs. The O'Donnells said there were public trials of the most degenerate people imaginable. It was riveting TV. So those genes were removed from the metropolitan population. This also gave many people a way of getting rid of personal enemies by false denunciations but hey, neither you nor I made the city.

The television at the hot-drinks stand sat behind the stove counter; *Railroad Blues* came on. There was the wise old conductor who could be counted on to straighten everything out in the end, and the flighty girl in the dining car who was always stumbling and spilling pasta onto some important higher-up. Part of the attraction of *Railroad Blues* was watching people devouring green salads, tomatoes and roasts, fresh vegetables and yeast bread. These dishes were all whipped up by the crazy cook who hid his gin bottles in the cold locker with the fish (real whole fresh fish). There was a young baggage handler in love with the flighty girl in the dining car, named Pamela, and all the peculiar people who got on the train at various places. There was never any scenery where they stopped. Just train stations of various kinds, clean and generic, numbered but not named. The characters were not constantly assaulted with televisual admonitions and urgings or live executions. The people on TV never seemed to watch TV.

Nadia paid for her weak cup of tea and got up. The man in the hot-drinks stand had finally become impatient and suspicious so she had to go.

Through open windows the wise old conductor shouted at the

flighty girl in a cracking voice. The previous episode had ended with the passenger train speeding toward a crossing where a concrete-mixer truck had stalled. At the time the conductor was drinking something from his thermos and joking with the baggage handler as they unknowingly sped toward destruction and at the last moment the conductor cried out a desperate warning. Just ahead of her the two neighborhood watchmen leaned in a window and called, Did they hit the truck?

The towers whistled in the evening breeze like great wind instruments. The spaces between them were confused with the sastrugi of broken sidewalks and tossing shadows of weeds. Nadia slipped through a rent in a chain-link fence.

Pigeons spoke to one another inside the stairwells in tones of maidenly alarm as she passed. She came to the nearest tower and took out the flashlight James had given her. She put her fingers over the lens and allowed only the faintest beam of light to lance out. She looked up to see the stars and the sky. The enormous tower with its broken tiers of windows appeared to be sailing like a stained and misdirected cruise ship through the galaxies. She imagined herself as a passenger on it with a ticket or a passport in her hand, voyaging to love in a time of officialdom. The tower would land on a glacier that capped some distant planet; it would be flown by James in his wheelchair with his hands on the starship's controls. She would say, *There's nobody else here, nobody, nobody,* and he would say, *I know. I know. The universe is ours.*

She went on with a batlike confidence in the power of night.

Up the echoing dark stairwell floor by floor. At last Nadia came to the twentieth landing. She stepped into the abandoned hallway with all its grit and dirt and she could see in the dim city illumination that the consoles of fluorescent lights had come loose and were hanging down, trailing wires. The hallway floor was littered with pieces of plasterboard and twigs from pigeons' nests and shattered tubes. She banged against glass windows, frames and all, stacked against one wall. People had stripped out and stacked them to come for them later. Maybe tonight.

The door on her right was open: apartment 2055. The flash of a mirror hanging half off the wall, a torn ottoman, and some broken dishes on the floor as if people had fought with one another or the police before finally being evicted. The bathroom door was open and it was very dark inside because there was no window but from the intermittent flashes when the Cantrell Falls billboard drew back to show the rushing white water she could see that everything had been torn out. Marks on the floor where the toilet had been, and on the wall where a sink had been. The bathtub had been too heavy to move.

The low clouds moved in, the color of peaches. At an empty casement frame she leaned out over the city. She saw the fifty-story Ritz-Carlton far away to the south. That building was behind her. Her journey was ahead.

Lighthouse Island: no buildings, no water rationing, only landforms and random plants, fossils, silence, solitude, mountains on the horizon with all their authority and secrecy, fauna, a lighthouse beam turning on hidden bearings and the booming evening seas washing in, over and over, lit up repeatedly by the singular ray. Danger, magic. And James, a companion of the heart. She leaned on her thin hands and stared out.

Ahead to the northwest, on the very edge of the crenellated horizon, shone the lights of the heavy industry area. As she stared at it an intense detonation flared up and then subsided; blasts of illumination from what she guessed were smelting plants washed the hard walls in seductive and magical light.

Nadia tore the brown paper from her roast beef sandwich. She wasn't sure she liked the taste and the meat inside seemed like it must have come from a tire. She needed a knife and spoon and some kind of bowl. She sat with the Mamosi bottle in her hand, in the dim lights coming through the broken window, and drank it all down. She jiggled her foot. It made a gritty sound on the floor so she stopped. The cool night wind hooted at the windows and all the holes and broken places of the towers. She still had a bottle of water and the empty Mamosi bottle now but no idea where she could get more. It didn't matter. She was recovering her self, which was as famished as the tarots for life and the ruined choirs of sweet silent thought. She was the sole inhabitant of this great tower: the Oversupervisor of Empty, the Queen of Ruin.

She opened her knapsack and at last changed into the secondhand boy's clothes and they were so oversized that she felt quite diminished. Then she folded everything she possessed, including the tote bag, and jammed it into the knapsack.

She had to start on her map. A cartographical adventure. Samuel Hearne in the infinite city, Sven Hedin on his river, or Captain Bligh on the trackless Pacific, guiding with an astrolabe his shallow boat over the ocean that was like an atmosphere, and beneath him great drowned cliffs like towers, from one of which she gazed out over the brown and glowing air of the metropolis.

She blew dust from the table and wiped it with her sleeve and then got out her pencil and sat down on the ottoman, alive with liberation and dreams.

She drew an asterisk at the top of the page for the North Star.

To begin she noted at the bottom of the page the name of her apartment building, the Mermaid Arms Youth Housing units. The place she had shared with Josie and Widdy and Anna Villanueva. *Home,* she wrote. Then the dismal office only five blocks away. Then, above that, the demolition dust cloud, the opening to the underground. Then the train north. A long arrow and a man with a pale, evil lizard face riding the arrow. The dead train, over which she put an X. She didn't know how else to signify it. She scribbled figures. Say, five hours. Train: 40 mph?

She had never traveled on anything faster than a city bus, which, as she had seen standing behind the driver, went no faster than 20 mph or an alarm went off. So 40 mph. 40 x 5 = 200 miles. The underground cafeteria and the cook finished that page.

She turned to a new page and again drew in the asterisk, the North Star at the top of every page.

Northwaite Court where she had more or less managed some sleep in an alley and listened to Adrian's torments. Then the wide street the man with the motorbike had said was Farragut Street, licensed for food shops. Then she drew in a jet airplane indicating the place where she had stopped and looked up to the sky to see the jet trails. Then the fifty-story building with the clock: the Ritz-Carlton. Just under the clock two wheels with a stick figure, sitting. James in his wheelchair.

She drew the agency sector and the cactus garden and the centipede with its stitchery of legs. Then the market and the terrible TV broadcast that she did not even like to name. And then the escape from the impressment gang, the telephone exchange. The Continuity Man and the vinyl-wrap tents; her tarot cards: the Devil, the Hermit, the Burning Tower, Dame Fortune blindfolded as if she were about to be shot. Plush elephants. Above that the movie house-cum-beauty shop, Arbor Square and its bituminous trees, then the hot-drink stand. She sketched in this tower where she now sat, and northwest of that, a very long way, the big scrap heaps and the industrial area, little coils indicating smoke. Finally a large arrow pointing upward and a question mark: Lighthouse Island?

The billboard light illuminated her map and then left it to the dark and then lit it up again.

She tried to recall some old story about two children lost in a great, endless park who left crumbs behind them to mark their way because their parents had abandoned them. They wandered around a Grimm forest on high speed like Toto toys. She tried to remember the details. It seemed to her they ate a house.

At first light Nadia stood at the window to look out over the megapolis and under an armada of spaced clouds the heat-haze intensified the smell of leaded gasoline and other combustible fluids. She heard bus horns and shouts and saw the winking flashes of windshields and the dense, packed crowds in the streets, the tops of people's hats bobbing along in their foreshortened hurry. The parachutes of hang gliders glistened and rippled tautly in the early-morning updrafts and the whine of their motors could be heard above the crowd sounds; the day-flight watchmen sailed along with their goggles and their binoculars, spying out violations.

She kicked off her red polka-dotted canvas shoes and leaned against the wall and read from the *Handbook*. *You will find it a great deal of fun to have a garden,* it said. There were drawings of lettuce and onions and cauliflower. It spoke in cheerful sentences about growing fruit trees and beekeeping and chickens and dairy cattle. Nowhere in the *Handbook* did it tell her what one did with animal waste or where these animals got their water.

Then she heard the chugging motor noise of a hang glider coming closer. She ducked barefoot into the bathroom and pressed her back against the wall.

The hang glider slid past the twentieth story. The watchman was looking into the windows out of his round goggles. The machine tipped from one side to the other on a stiff parachute and fought the confused winds swirling around the towers.

From her dark recess Nadia saw the man though the slit of the partly open door, the tattoos on his arm under his rolled-up flapping shirtsleeve, his desire to catch somebody at something, and his pebbled-leather helmet. Behind him fleets of cumulus clouds skated along with flat bottoms on some invisible surface and the city rooftops glinted.

The machine lifted above the level of the window and then dropped back down again. It hovered and bounced on the updrafts.

Nadia could hear his radio crackling. The watchman listened and then flipped down a monocular eyepiece and turned his head, one eye staring through his thick spyglass. He was looking into the windows, her window. He hung there for a long time staring and quivering and the engine backfiring. He moved a wing vane and turned his machine. At last the motor faded away.

CHAPTER 22

J ames rolled up to the doctor's desk to look at the prosthetics mannequin. It was a repellent thing that came apart in sections according to where the desired amputations would take place and the overhead fluorescents made the plastic body appear necrotic. James regarded it without expression and then rolled back.

So here, you see, as I do this, if we amputate just below the knee, said the surgeon. A transtibial amputation. Ahem, excuse me. He was a tiny, dry man with crinkled skin and an irritating habit of clearing his throat. James watched as the surgeon deftly removed the mannequin's legs at the knees. The mannequin was about a foot and a half high, gender neutral, and naked as a baby rat. It was joined in sections with steel pegs. Its arms could be removed as well; everything came apart but the head, for obvious reasons. Behind the surgeon was a glass-fronted cabinet containing prosthetic arms, legs, hands, and feet, all very abandoned looking. Eff, eff, ahem, excuse me, now give me your attention.

Why do you think I am *not* giving you my attention? James straightened his tie and tipped his head. You're excused.

The surgeon nodded and said, Very well, now, this would be a surgery needing only a couple of hours. Extended flap and bone bridging. And when this is accomplished then we can fit you with prosthetics and with crutches or a walker and you will be able to walk after a fashion, which you can't do now, can you? You can't walk now, can you? He smiled in an artificial way, as if his smile was itself a prosthesis.

Clearly not, said James. What an ignorant question. He leaned to one side and presented the surgeon with a face of stone.

It *is* an ignorant question but we need to reiterate. The surgeon smiled again. Ah, ah, let us establish that you can't take a step the way you are now but you have to get into some new thinking. A new way of thinking. We can fit you with prosthetic legs and off you go. After some time in rehab and therapy courses, and then, well, it's off you go for you. He tapped his pointed fingers together and then picked up one of the mannequin's lower legs.

Stop talking to me as if I were an idiot, said James. He ran his hand through his spiky brown hair. Why would I be able to move my thighs?

No, it's not good to talk to people as if they were idiots. No, no indeed. But you see I'm talking to you as if you were a rational being. Now be brave and realize that a change in your thinking must be forthcoming, Director Orotov. We know that people want to retain useless legs because they're attached to them; that is, they are attached to your body. Ahem, pardon me. You have a sentimental outlook on your legs but they are, you know, totally useless. He took up one of the plastic lower legs and turned it over and looked at the sole of the foot. Paraplegics often attempt to refuse this very sensible operation. But I am very good at it. I've done hundreds, hundreds! When he lifted his head to return his gaze to James there was a kind of wicked delight in his eyes. You move your thighs by swinging your upper body. You'll see. So prepare yourself, here.

I think I'll refuse, said James. He said it evenly, but fear had struck him. He felt he had been dropped from a tall height into the knocking ice of glacial waters.

You think you'll refuse, well. You know, I don't think you really can, James, said the surgeon. This is a surgery order from your superior, William Crumm, Director of Agency Planning. May I call you Jim?

No.

I see. The surgeon sifted through some papers. Well, then, you will have to go to counseling on this matter. He carefully laid the plastic lower leg down on the papers, which were rattling in the breeze from his little fan. He said, The counselors have been through all this many times.

The man was a lower-level surgeon, far down the food chain of the Orthopedic Trauma Task Force and Limbless Reconstruction Council. James had been forced to sit in a cramped waiting room with a loud television blasting in his face along with other patients in their carefully repaired clothes and various forms of limblessness, a sign of his descent from privilege to proletarian misery, of which he should not be contemptuous, except for him the consequences of official poverty would be fatal. He was here on orders from the assistant director of the enormous umbrella organization called the Habitation Bureau, which controlled his own agency. That assistant director was an A43, same as himself, but James supposed he had issued the order because he had somehow come to an agreement with Crumm.

His private physician was no longer available. It didn't matter that James had already had his yearly physical. The order for another examination, to be done by a surgeon this time, had come to his office via courier. James couldn't get anyone to return his phone calls and when he called repeatedly to protest, his calls were redirected from Employee Health to Dietary to Wellness and Medical Certification to Workplace Well-Being and, finally, to Dry Cleaning. They wanted to cut him off at the knees. And after that he would find the prosthetic legs and promised training and therapy were all delayed and delayed and delayed. Maybe he would die under the anesthesia. If they even gave him an anesthetic.

It's *my* life, said James. My legs. He shut his hands firmly on the armrests and fixed his gray eyes on the surgeon.

It *is* your life and of course it *is* your legs, but we have to think about optimizing your vocational abilities. The surgeon, with his cheese-colored skin, stared around his small office. There were crocheted seat covers and a waterfall calendar and a clunky handset phone, which had just lit up with a blinking orange light. The surgeon jammed down on the button as if it were an insect. It stopped blinking. He said, You see these very realistic prostheses, James. He gestured toward the display case. Retraining with these new legs is brief, intense, and very successful. Look at this. I want your full attention, please. *Hmmmmheh!* Pardon.

You're repeating yourself, said James.

Now, now, the thing is, you won't be costing the city all this money as you are at present with this wheelchair. The surgeon presented his delicate hand to the wheelchair. Now you see, James, the truth is that you're going to find it increasingly difficult to get upkeep and repair on your wheelchair. Tires, possibly lithium-ion batteries for the keypad? Whatever. You do very much need a pair of *legs*. Then he paused and stared at James as if just now seeing him.

What? said James. His planed face was expressionless as limestone. He dropped one hand on his water bottle with its woven cover.

The surgeon leaned forward and said in a low voice, I saw you on television. It really is going to start raining, isn't it?

James considered what to say. Finally he said, Eventually.

And flood. We'll all drown if there are heavy rains. Everywhere. Right?

What does this have to do with this examination?

The surgeon said in a low, secretive voice, That experimental ag station, a resort. It's supposed to be someplace up in the Northwest. I just want to know if it is really going to start these, you know, torrential rains, flooding! I'll make an application to go there myself. Like all the rest of my superiors. They say they are selling management rights. I could get a little beach house, a little condo or something, up there in the Northwest, mountains, out of the flooding, eh? And what do you think of these public executions? They're going to want more and more . . . The surgeon paused. So I have you here, *aaaahem*, the horse's mouth, animal metaphor there, just for my personal information.

The rain is a supposition, said James. It's merely a projected event. And yes, the television will want more. And more. That is not a supposition.

The surgeon was silent for a moment. I see, he said, in a low voice, and then in a normal voice, Very well. So. Now here. He lifted a box from a shelf in a delicate gesture. Take this videotape home. It shows the whole operation. You may find the noise of the oscillating saw and the blood spraying around a bit off-putting but better you know than not know. Then, you'll see patients running, jumping, dancing and so on with their new legs. Here, take it. Take it home and watch it. Now, your patient record says you aren't taking any medication at all. Is this true?

Aspirin, said James. Once in a while. This was all covered on my last exam. I think you have the file in front of you.

Why am I getting these hints that you have accessed some sort of experimental drug? It's here, right here. The surgeon lifted a page and adjusted his glasses. It says "private informant relays dubious information from Nutrition's retynil palmitate"—that's a derivative of vitamin A— "labs of unauthorized investigational preparation used on pigs with spinal injuries that has been illegally forwarded to patient Orotov."

What labs? Where? said James. The question Where? nearly always stopped people. Nobody knew where anything was and didn't usually even know where they were, as if the entire world was a sitcom set of generic nowhereness.

I have no idea where! The surgeon glared at James. Now, do you have any feeling in the legs at all? The surgeon shot his wheeled office chair backward and turned to a Formica counter. He picked up a steel pin that looked like a pushpin. He walked over to James.

No, James lied. Same as always. No change, no feeling.

Well, let's do a quick check. He jammed the pin into James's thigh. James did not move or react even though it was extremely painful.

He said, Doctor, there is no need for this. You must take my word for it, he said. But the surgeon was now jamming the pin into James's lower right leg, and it made a sound. Blood appeared as dark spots on James's trouser leg but he neither moved nor cried out by fixing his eyes on the pin and preparing himself.

Stop! James said. Look, dammit, there's blood. This is septic.

Then he shot out his hand and gripped the surgeon's wrist. James's hand was thick with muscle; from his knuckles to his wrist the muscle stood out like ropes. This from twenty years of spinning the wheelchair rims. He crushed his hand around the surgeon's wrist with great force. I'll break your hand, he said. I swear I will. Do you hear me?

Let go. The surgeon dropped the pushpin on the floor. Let go! Ah, ah.

James opened his hand.

The surgeon darted behind his desk, holding his right wrist in the other hand. How dare you! he said. *Ahhemmmmmm!* Now I'll need the consent form in a month. I'm giving you one month. That's enough time. Get back to me within a month. Do you hear me? The surgeon glared at James through his flashing glasses and held his fractured wrist.

A nurse entered the examination room. She had three steel teeth in the front of her mouth and was still swallowing her lunch.

Your time is up, she said to James. You can go.

No, it's not, said James. I have . . .

Get out, said the nurse.

James used his battery-powered motor to roll through the crowd in the Dollar General. The uniformed girl at the entrance swiped his card and the message on the monitor said, *Hi James! Hope you enjoy shopping with us today!* instead of *Hello Director Orotov Welcome to Dollar General.* He was quickly sliding down the greasy chute of social destruction, which inevitably preceded arrest. He passed several people he knew and they turned away and pretended not to see him. He was becoming socially toxic. If he was forced into an operation to cut off his legs he was done for.

James used his motor instead of his hands because it made him less noticeable. He rolled past the home décor department with its rustic fence around the water features, past the foods, down the aisle of re-frigerators and fans and even one air conditioner, while his thigh and lower leg were shot through with pain; past housemaids in slovenly gowns printed with bright flowers pushing carts full of paper towels and dish soap in bottles and cat food and bright toys, all unavailable to the masses. Also available to people with the right ID card were booths that did dry cleaning, shoe repair, barbering, and hair and nail beautification. These people came to meet friends and chat and wander about in the cool air. It was 103°F out on the streets today where Nadia must be trudging on like a desert explorer in search of the Lost City of Rain.

He came to the shoe repair shop and presented a ticket to the girl behind the register. She went to the back and signaled him to come around the counter and into the rear where a man with thick black hair sat over a pair of high-heeled shoes. The man looked at James and said nothing and moved the high heels aside. Then he reached beneath his workbench and pulled out a box containing a pair of stout lace-up shoes, handmade. These were for the day that James would walk the disordered terrain of Lighthouse Island, if indeed he had any feet to put in them. Sorrow flooded him for a moment like a heavy drug. The shoes were so hopeful, the odds were so great. They were made with thick rubber soles from new tires, the seams tight and the leather oiled and the stitching minute. The shoemaker's hair fell in his face as he gazed at James and shook his head.

For you?

James leaned back and closed his eyes and then said, No, they're for a nephew, and handed the man two tickets to the audience section for a live taping of *News Interns*. He's been assigned to limestone mining management for the concrete people. He has to be out with the crews.

You just had to lie, lie, lie all the time.

In the linens section a day-flight watchman came to stand beside him.

Well, it looks like she's in there, he said. Sir.

How do you know? James took down a thick towel and then put it back.

Well, I saw a backpack and some books there. Like you said, *The Girl Scout Handbook*. Up on the twentieth floor. A pair of red canvas walking shoes, women's size. He spoke in a low voice.

James slammed both hands down on the wheelchair arms. What the hell is she doing going barefoot?

Well, sir, said the watchman. How am I supposed to know?

He was a youngish man with white untanned circles around his eyes where he wore his goggles and the tattoo of an abstract eagle on one arm. His khaki shirt smelled of cooled sweat. He said, Probably just resting her feet. That was yesterday. Nobody saw her go out as far as I know but you know the ground guys; they're holed up in some alleyway drinking.

James's heart failed when he thought of her slipping out of the abandoned towers at night, into an unknown world. All right. I'll have your army knife here in a minute. I will meet you up in front. You know the penalties for buying for outsiders here.

I don't want it, sir, said the watchman. That's not what I want.

James's expression became formal and blank. That's what you're going to get, he said. Period.

No, no, I just want you to go talk to your brother for me. Sir. Sir, I'd give anything to learn the big ones. Anything, just to get some instruction on a real prop plane. I'll clean his house, sir. I mean it. I'll wash his windows and mop his floors. Talk to him for me. I don't want the army knife, sir.

Are you serious? Do you know how precious those things are?

Yes. If he would just let me hand tools to the airplane mechanic or something. Anything.

How do you know about my brother?

He's on the alert list at the neighborhood stations. Farrell Orotov, pilot, it says. Just an alert. Not an arrest or anything. Per Director Crumm.

No kidding, said James. And me?

No sir, nothing. Not yet.

All right. I'll remember. Now go on.

James tried to buy the Vercingitorix Army Knife with its ten blades, whistle, flashlight, awl, and scissors, but the clerk ran his ID card through the slider and said, Not authorized.

James did not argue. It was time to stop arguing. It was not an easy thing to abandon everything, all he had ever known, his disappearing social circle, his comfortable apartment, his work, his books, the carefully arranged life that enabled him to function in a wheelchair. To launch himself into an unknown country with nothing but a few survival items and his maps, some experimental medication and a girl he barely knew, but there had been other people at other times who had also hesitated, even in the face of the sure but steady crushing of their lives. They had hesitated and hoped that official protests and moral arguments and legal representation would save them. Those people were all dead.

He was going someplace where social prestige did not matter. His privileges were gone. In the world to come much would depend on physical strength and field expedience, risk taking, weapons, brains. His heart bounded ahead like some beautiful, long-limbed animal gathering itself and flying over a fence in a cascade of shining hide and muscle, a creature beloved of the sun and the open spaces. It landed in a field of grass that seethed like a sea and Nadia walked along beside him and there were others, men of old. That phrase was from some song or poem, what was it? *Men of old* . . . ta dum ta dum . . .

He rolled toward the exit through the cool, swampy air with his shoebox and fresh celery and jicama and wine and a set of batteries. He came to the exit card-check and a small but intense light began to flash.

Sir, sir, your permission chip to enter Dollar General has been canceled, the girl said. I'm sorry but this is your last visit until you update your chip.

CHAPTER 23

Nadia slipped out of Dogtown Towers in the dark and into streets of the neighborhood to the north. A moon came up but it was the rice milk advertising moon with the cow jumping across it and a dish and a spoon running after the cow. *Good as milk!* Then the real moon came up, and it was a crescent diminishing into a sliver and it was faint and undecorative compared to the advertisement moon.

She fell asleep on a roof in her boy's clothes and the red polka-dot canvas shoes, leaning against the parapet, wrapped in everything she had. Drying curtains floated on lines, solar casserole pots were washed and ready for the next day. Nothing in them. She checked.

In the first pale light she woke up and climbed down the fire escape ladder. It was a strange gray morning with drooping clouds and the feel of water in the air.

She was unsure of how to walk or act as a boy. The thing was to bring as little attention to herself as possible, and find some means of transportation, to make it to the e-waste area. James was the man who lived in the rice-milk moon, he was the voice of the dazzling glaciers, the brown-haired man who would rise from his imprisoning wheel-

chair, where he had been confined by enchantment, and take the rudder
of a sailboat over the glassy seas until the lancing beam of Lighthouse
Island swept across their sails.

A bus came slowly around the corner. It bumped over the curb of
the sidewalk. It was painted sky blue with pictures of Savory Circles
on the side but passersby shrank against the walls, women with their
secondhand briefcases and children going to school and men in carefully polished shoes ducked into doorways, fled down alleyways. The
entire crowded street drained away as if somebody had pulled a plug.
They knew all the hiding places and boltholes but Nadia did not. As
she tried to open the front door of an office building, a door that had
been slammed shut in her face, the bus stopped and a Legal Forensics
Department agent got out in his uniform of track pants and jacket and
a watch cap with F on the front.

Nadia pulled out the little device with the bar and ran it over a
nearby wall.

You, he said. He walked over to Nadia.

I'm checking cable, she said. Look, I have a job to do, okay?

The officer took her by the wrist and jerked her toward the bus.
It made her cap fly off. They had seized two others along with Nadia
and were cramming them all into the narrow door. Nadia fell on the
steps and then clawed her way upright by holding on to the belt of a
man in front of her. Somebody behind cried out in a strangled sound
and clutched the back of Nadia's shirt. Nadia tore away and fell into a
seat. It was dark inside. The guards shouted and bright fractions and
splinters of powerful lights fled over their faces.

Wait, said Nadia. Wait, wait, I have a job! I have to report in!

A heavy flashlight struck her across the mouth and she bent over
holding her face. A woman sitting beside Nadia was uncontrollably
weeping. After an hour of traveling, maybe more, somebody in the
back said, This old man's dead.

Shut up, said the guard.

He's had a heart attack.

The guard came back without saying anything and jammed the Taser into the woman's stomach and she shrieked in a high-pitched blast and leaped almost out of her seat.

I said shut up.

Each person in the bus held his or her life closely in two hands as if it were a bird's egg or a hazelnut, as if it were all of creation and indeed it was, so easily broken within an instant. The smell was terrible. Nadia sat staring straight ahead as the flashlight illuminated one face after another, and then hers, a light so powerful that she was blinded.

Where's your ID? said the agent.

I lost it. She decided to remain quiet and to show no signs of panic; the guards were on some kind of sadistic trajectory where they needed to kill. Her lips were dry and her hair had fallen in her face. She felt shrunken inside the boy's shirt. She said in a calm, reasonable voice, Listen, I'm late for work. Look. She held up the device with the gray screen. See?

That's your job?

Checking cable, finding outages, yes.

The agent stood very close, looming over her and said in a low voice, You got three hundred?

I don't have that kind of money. Nadia said. Her voice became unintentionally loud and the agent jammed his flashlight against her shoulder.

Tell everybody, why don't you?

They traveled a long time. They were struck if they tried to talk to one another. From time to time somebody passed out from lack of water and air. The bus lurched along at twenty miles an hour, through noisy, narrow streets and around sharp corners. Sometimes the bus stopped and the guards jumped out and grabbed passersby. There appeared to be no rhyme or reason to the arrests. It was as if they were on a hunting-and-gathering trip.

The guards and the Forensics men scribbled on forms and handed them to those who were conscious.

That's your arrest sheet! they yelled. Hand them in when we arrive! Any goddamned questions?

There were no questions.

CHAPTER 24

Keep to the white line, a policeman said. He herded them along with light taps of his club. Nadia stared straight ahead at the policewoman sitting behind the computer screen. One side of her face felt tight and hot as it bloomed into a great bruise.

I have to get out of here, I have to get out of here, the words set off galloping through her head like a film clip of wild horses. *How do I get out of here? By being nobody.*

But then all her records said she was somebody.

Nadia tried to hear what was being said to the policewoman but hundreds of voices made a wall of noise. Prisoners crept past sweeping and their brooms raised dust clouds. The high ceiling sagged with hanging electrical lines and ripped patches of plaster.

The policewoman behind the computer monitor at the head of Nadia's line lifted a cup of coffee to her lips without taking her eyes off the screen. After speaking with each woman in turn, she indicated with a quick gesture for her to go to another area. Names were being called. *Brown, Margaret! Ortiz, Jane!* A good-looking young woman clutching a string bag of market purchases stood shaking in front of the line. She had fine blond hair under a bright flowered head wrap.

The policewoman squinted at her and then said to a guard, Take this one for a screen test. She's got a good TV face. The policewoman rattled at the keyboard. Try her out for trial and execution.

A guard told the girl, This way. He took her by the arm and led her toward a high, broad doorway where a man in a suit and tie sat behind a desk. Beyond the desk Nadia saw daylight, outside light. The doorway out of this place.

The girl held on to her string bag and cried out that she wanted her arrest on record, weren't they going to identify her? She had her ID, right here, please. The guard shoved her ahead and the women in the line turned and stared at one another.

Nadia was now standing at the front of the line.

Right hand here, the policewoman said. She tapped a pad beside the screen. Hurry up. Are you deaf, goddammit?

Nadia placed her hand on the gray pad and it was slightly warm as if it were made of flesh. The pad turned green at the bottom edge and then the green color rolled up and under her hand and took her fingerprints.

The policewoman had not taken her eyes off the screen. Huh, she said. Then she shrugged and said, Your name is Sandra . . . no, *Sendra* Bentley.

Nadia said, That's correct.

You are employed at the Urban . . . The policewoman paused, and then leaned forward to look at the screen and then began again. The Urban Geospatial Utilization Institute under the Department of Non-utilized Urban Housing.

That's right, said Nadia. Her bruised face was still and she did not miss a beat.

Research.

Yes.

Research, ah, the Anthem Advisory Council.

Nadia's heart thudded one great smacking wallop and then quieted. Yes. The Anthem Advisory Council. She licked her dry lips.

Give me your arrest sheet. Nadia handed over the wadded and sweat-stained paper.

The policewoman tapped at the heavy brass keys. She wore small sparkling stones in her ears. Her gray uniform tunic was too tight and her fingernails were bright red and perfect. The nails made little clattering noises on the keyboard. *Sendra,* Nadia said to herself. *Not Sandra, Sendra, Sendra. Become Sendra. You are Sendra.*

She heard the hissing vacuum noise as the metal detection doors opened and more people were shoved into the great hall along with flying scraps of food wrappings. The echoing babble sounded like an enormous evil bus station. James had tagged her fingerprints, triggered them to switch names and personal histories.

A guard walked through the area behind the desks and slapped the policewoman on the back and it made her cup jump in her hand and drops of coffee sprang up like bingo chips.

Goddamn it, the policewoman said. Quit that. It's sprayed all over. The policeman made kissing noises as he walked on. The policewoman muttered as she disabled the keyboard and wiped it off and then plugged it in again.

Research, I am doing urban geospatial utilization research. I can do that. I can make that kind of stuff up. She made herself memorize the words. Urban. Geospatial. Utilization. Somehow James had reached out to her through the crooked tunnels in what was left of the Internet into Forensics and had deceived the beast.

All right. The policewoman stared at Sendra's sheet. Looks like they've got you down for no permit to leave your sector; no residence registration card; no ID; and unauthorized entry into public buildings scheduled for demolition. You may or may not be charged with all or any of these things.

Nadia nodded. I understand, she said.

No special dietary requirements, medical condition is good, last examination two months ago . . . wait. Your pelvic examination shows some lesions. It's on the x-ray. You may have to have another pelvic examination and a biopsy.

They never told me that, said Nadia. Now that she was hidden behind another name her mind began to emerge from a suspended state of shock. Now that she, Nadia, was once more not Nadia Stepan. She stood on tiptoe, trying to see the x-ray on the screen. That's not right. Her voice was cautiously argumentative. She did not want to have a pelvic examination in a jailhouse.

These are lesions. I don't care if they told you or not. If you feel I am incompetent to read your x-ray you may fill out a form. It is ten pages long and may take up to a month to process. As she said this she groped with her right hand for her package of sunflower seeds.

Nadia stood as high as she could and leaned to one side to look at the screen. Coffee droplets arced across the monitor. The stupid woman was reading them as if they were images on the x-ray. Beneath the dark drops, somebody else's pelvic bones were stark and white in the pale matrix of flesh, somebody else's thigh bones lay helpless on the screen. Somebody named Sendra Bentley.

Oh, wait a minute, that's the damn coffee, the policewoman said in a low tone. She was angry. She glanced up with a haughty stare at the line of women to see if anybody had heard her but the women behind Nadia all looked down or away, sweating, some stained with the blood of others, some with their own. The policewoman wiped the screen with her arm. You are in male attire. Her voice was now sharp and harsh. Do you wish to be sent to the men's barracks?

Nadia said, No.

The woman clicked on a No box. Do you wish to be issued any prescription medication?

No. Another click on another No box.

Proceed to your left and enter the processing center.

CHAPTER 25

Nadia was shoved into a great hall full of women; she was made to strip and change into a gray dress, handed straw slippers. The prisoner woman behind the counter found her knapsack and stuffed Nadia's clothes into it, tagged it, shoved it onto a shelf along with thousands of other bundles.

Then a long confusing march with twenty other recent arrestees through hallways, down stairs, up other stairs, and all the way Nadia counted every step and memorized every turn.

They came to a very large, malodorous room painted a dark gray full of cots, people, and a television screen the size of a Ping-Pong table. Two policewomen sat on chairs outside the door and pressed a button on a small remote as the prisoners were marched through the doorless doorway because there was some kind of photo-cell beam there they had to walk through without triggering an alarm.

This is an assisted living facility! It's a jail, girls, not a prison! You will remain here under quarantine until we are sure you have no communicable diseases! Then at some time you will be informed of your meeting with your counselor! Your counselor will inform you of your charges and then you will be sent to one of the work farms or solitary confinement or you may have a screen test for television appearances depending on how your offense is categorized! This building is a maze and if you decide to try to run you will not, repeat not, find your way out! You have been given your cot number and sufficient clothing and personal items for reasonable comfort! There is a signal that will activate a siren if you step beyond this door! You have been assigned a cot, find it! Obey the rules!

Their faces were plump and smooth from plentiful water rations. They were all overweight.

Nadia could see out a scraped place in the painted-over windows if she stood on a cot. She could get enough to eat if she fought her way into the line. She would be able to sleep if she jammed wads of unraveled blanket threads into her ears.

A five-foot television screen carried their minds away into other and more pleasant places, and on a table in front were stacks of applications. It was a gray ward and a gray life. The only color was on the television where actors and commentators wore richly toned clothes and moved in spacious interiors. The ward was packed with more than a hundred women, shouting and arguing and pleading for silence to hear the dialogue on *One Thin Dime*.

Pipes overhead were rusted at the joints and the walls were greasy at head height where women sat on the cots next to the wall and leaned against it. Drying clothing steamed where it drooped from the windowsills. Before it evaporated from her mind Nadia made a map in her head. She shut her eyes against the noise and voices and arguments and gripped the heavy coarse blanket with a hand to each side of herself. She started with the big entry hall. The number of steps. The turns, the stairs. Then here.

Nadia pulled her legs up on cot number thirty-four and wrapped her arms around her knees and wondered which one of these women knew of an escape route, a way out, a guard who could be bribed. She prayed to some divine force that she was not attractive enough to be sent for a screen test. She pulled the blanket over her head and tried to bring up images of Lighthouse Island, of James.

The third morning an older woman came and sat close to Nadia and talked about her orgasms in a low, urgent voice. Her lips were deeply pleated and they worked as she spoke in muscular spasms. She stared intently at Nadia and spoke of her own orgasms, other people's orgasms, the noise they made in the night.

Get away from me or I will hit you, said Nadia. Get away from me. She wanted to shove the woman off the cot next to her where she sat but somehow she knew the woman would like that. I'll report you, she said. I'll report you for abuse.

The woman laughed and then walked away still laughing.

James knew she was here, James would help her, somehow. She had to keep thinking this because otherwise her soul would shrivel. Nadia liked her soul, she believed in it, as she believed in James and his ability to reach her here in the crowded hell of the lowest ring of the world.

The latrines were in a stinking section of the building, twenty commodes in a line. They squirted 50 percent muriatic acid in the rank toilet bowls and inside the tanks and burned themselves. Their skirts looked like they had welding-spark pinholes. Nadia shuffled from toilet stool to toilet stool in the sloppy jail slippers, head down, trying not to bring attention to herself.

They had to look inside the tanks and behind the commodes and turn off the overhead lights and then unscrew the lightbulbs and check around the fixtures for hidden notes or food: prisoner contraband stashes. The guards yelled if Nadia lost one of her loose straw slippers. They hit her and shoved her to the floor. She got back to her feet in a flash before she could be hit again and counted steps and memorized turns. Like everyone else she had bruises on her arms and legs.

She worked alongside a black-haired girl who said her name was Charity, a thin, mean little survivor. Despite a black eye and probably a broken rib or two she clumped along behind Nadia with her jug. Her hair was a frizz of black spiderwebbish tangles. She had feet like pie plates.

Bitches, fat bitches, she said. They drink gallons every day, taking water away from us ordinary people. She said this in a flatlined voice, without stress or intonation. They want the pretty girls for TV. To shoot them. If I had a gun I'd blast them right in their faces.

Shut up. Nadia stepped back from the volatile fumes. You want to get beat up.

Yeah, yeah, Charity snorted and her black hair shook out over her forehead. I get out, I'll catch one of them in an alley and kick their asses so far up their collarbones they'll have to take off their shirts to shit. Then she said in a oddly pleasant voice, Say, Sendra, would it be okay if I traded cots. I could be next to you and we could look out for each other. There's criminals here all mixed up with people like me who didn't do nothing, really. Charity turned to her. Nothing.

Nadia hesitated. Well, okay.

The bruise on Nadia's cheekbone faded to yellow and her hair turned to dirty red sticks before she found a way to get a comb. One of the women carved them out of wood with a sharpened metal kitchen spoon she kept hidden in her mattress. A comb cost two days' water but Nadia paid it and shrank inside her gray uniform and during those two days suffered through the dizziness of dehydration. But she managed not to fall, not to lose the jail slippers. She knew if she went down they would beat her unconscious. It seemed to be some kind of custom or rule. She watched the guards, when they changed shift, how they shut off the electric eye when they came in for inspections.

Once a week the prisoners were led into the showers, where the spraying heads hit them with lukewarm jets of great force, lasting,

Nadia was warned, exactly three minutes. They handed in their dirty tunics and skirts at the entrance and were handed others going out. They showered in their underwear, scrubbed their underpants and tatty brassieres. The guards made the old woman who talked about orgasms go in last, by herself, and her mouth muscles worked and leaped as if she were speaking to some interior demon.

They cupped their hands and drank the almost undrinkable recycled water. Those who had combs raked tenderly at their wet hair. Nadia held her hands to the water and knew she was inhabited by a constant, subdued rage. It was going to make her sick; it would do something terrible to her. She stood in her soapy underpants and gray brassiere and glanced at Charity through the stinging jets. Charity's tattoos were not only extensive, mainly composed of magical animals such as unicorns and flying kittens, but beneath her shoulder blades she had instructed the tattooist to include the cost:

INK: FORTY DIMES
LABOR: NINETY-TWO DIMES
TOTAL: 132 W.C. DMS

A team of men slogged up a mountain pass and from time to time the straggling line was obscured by blizzards. Feral humans with green gummy-looking teeth charged at them from the forests but the Imperial Rebels soldiered on.

I thought they all got killed, said Nadia. She had learned to speak in the accepted flat voice, bare of interrogatives, emotionless. Watching the television made her feel better but soon her eyes would develop a glittering field of sparks and then pain. She looked down at her hands. The crowded room full of women stared resolutely at the TV, which was what they were supposed to do. It made the guards happy. They yelled at a very young girl for dancing and the old gypsy women playing some kind of game with bits of pilot biscuits.

That was the guys that went AWOL, said Charity. This is Captain Kenaty's unit. They are trying to get to the AWOL guys and get their cell phones. But they don't know the AWOL guys got killed by the savage hippies. They put the captain back in because the young men were rioting over it. Listen, the guard that comes for you is named Terminal Verna. The one that takes you away for death row.

A gypsy woman sitting near them said, Big tall woman. When they send her for you it's all over. They give you your stuff and say, Here's Terminal Verna, come to take you away. She laughed silently with her lips shut. It's blotto for you. But maybe you get to be on TV. You get to be a star for about ten seconds.

Charity rested her chin on her fists. Terminal Verna needs her throat slit, she said. The Facilitator needs his throat slit.

Nadia clapped her hand over Charity's mouth and whispered, You're going to get killed, you're going to end up in the dryers.

Nadia sat on her cot with its unraveling gray blanket and the dirty sheets and tried to help women fill out applications. The guards sat at the wide entrance to the Q ward watching *My News, My Day*. The jail authorities had just thrown any kind of application in a pile on the table: applications for clothing allowances, for Buddy car repairs, for lightbulbs and pet ownership and divorce and vacation time and study programs and small appliances. The women simply wanted to be heard by some official somewhere. They wanted their name in a file so they did not disappear altogether.

Okay, so you have to give your reasons here, Nadia said. The noise of the television and the hundred or so women in the ward was so loud she had to raise her voice. The air stank.

You write it, said a small blond woman. She was crocheting a cat out of blanket threads. You can write it; you know how to say it right. The young woman's voice was light and childlike.

Well, what kind of toaster do you want?

202 / PAULETTE JILES

Oh, one for bread.

All toasters are for bread. You'll have to apply for a yeast bread allowance.

Oh, well, let's do lightbulbs, then.

Nadia turned the application over and crossed out *toaster* and wrote in *lightbulbs* with her pencil stub and said, Why are you in here?

The small blond woman said, I helped my boyfriend with his pirate radio station. They tracked us down somehow. I don't know how they do it. She smoothed out her crocheted cat and regarded it and then began on the tail, looping the blanket threads on a fork tine. And you? What about you, Sendra?

I messed up at my job, said Nadia. I worked at a special memorizing section. She wrote down, "Request for three 25-watt lightbulbs for reasons of deficient eyesight." I didn't recycle my trash. Threw it all out the window. I was drinking wine at the time.

Memorizing?

I had to memorize poetry.

What's going on here, what's going on here? shouted the fat guard that everybody called the Lard Queen. The guard bulled her way into the listening crowd, grabbed the application from Nadia's hand, and tore it up. The Lard Queen had grown bored with her news, her day.

Often Nadia was so thirsty she briefly considered drinking the water in the toilet tanks. Briefly. They were to be sent to a work farm somewhere but here they were already, slaving like Orcs in the Mines of Moriah. Nadia asked Charity, Am I talking in my sleep? I am dreaming so intensely. I dream about this man that I met and I am laughing with him, there's an ocean and then other things.

No, said Charity. If you do I'll whack you on the arm.

What if you're asleep.

I'll wake up.

Listen.

What.

I think that's rain on the windows.

Charity lifted her head. Is it possible?

There had to be a way to get out of here, by lying or adopting some disguise or murdering a guard or hiding in the garbage. And then going on as she had begun, to the north. She bent her head and tried to see it in her mind and not the brilliant and professional images of sitcoms and *Sector Secrets*.

Does the sea remember the walker upon it?

Supper and the water ration arrived in a noisy trundling as the barrels were rolled down the hall to their ward and other wards on the Q ward. The water seemed more vital than food. Everyone grabbed their metal cups and shoved into line and some women staggered; their blood pressure was low from dehydration. Nadia learned that standing up quickly made you faint. She stood up slowly. Charity held out her cup as if it were a chalice, trembling.

One night when the guard at the door had fallen asleep and was lightly snoring the small blond woman whispered, Recite. You said you memorized all these poems.

What

Anything. Anything you memorized.

And out of the unresting crowd of women with their arms or sheets thrown over their faces voices spoke up: Yes, yes, recite, give us a poem.

Nadia rustled around in the files of her memory. It was a moment of strange elation and she realized it was because she and the women in the ward were together for themselves, just this short time. The guards

were not the focus of their attention. She put her hands over her eyes
and whispered,

> *The souls of those I love are on high stars.*
> *How good that there's no-one left to lose*
> *and one can weep. All created in order*
> *to sing songs, this air of Tsarskoye Selo's.*
> *The river bank's silver willow*
> *touches the bright September stream.*
> *Rising from the past, my shadow*
> *is running in silence to meet me.*
> *So many lyres hung on branches here,*
> *but it seems there's room for mine too.*
> *And this shower, sun-drenched, rare,*
> *brings me consolation and good news.*

And all around them women sat up in their beds and listened. The
woman who had strangled her twins and the woman who had made
false invoices, the one who had lost her ID, the girl who spoke on pirate
radio, the gypsy women who were not gypsies, all tortured with one
another's endless proximity but now each one listening for herself alone
to the words, things rising from their pasts like silent running shadows. What was a harp, what was a tree. Consolation. Good news. Then
it began to rain lightly, as if the world had just remembered how. It
tapped at the painted windows as if it wanted in.

CHAPTER 26

The sons of bitches and the bitches got to jam themselves into everything we do. They listen to everything we say.

Charity stopped muttering long enough to eat half of her black bean and corn patty. The kitchen was blasted with the theme music from the new program called *Things You Cannot Say*. The atmosphere was heavy with steam and food odors, as if the air had weight and mass, as if it had color and the color was of some sour, tarnished metal. They were sitting on upturned buckets eating their midday meal, on work assignment in the big kitchens.

Nadia had stolen one kitchen worker's pair of coveralls and she could steal a second pair given the opportunity. She was not going to wait any longer for some kind of message from James. He would not understand how she was slowly going insane here. The heroines of the escape novels she had read were always as beautiful as clothing models in essential occupations, with significant villains after them, the center of high-level conspiracies. She was a nobody and she was determined to remain a nobody. That way she might stay alive.

What happened? Nadia said. Why were you arrested?

A donkey. I had a donkey. Charity ate quickly. They had fifteen minutes. She wiped her tiny mouth and said, He was about two hundred pounds underweight; I was going to fat him up but they got me for animal abuse. I was going to fat him up on cake batter. I knew where to get old expired sacks of cake batter powder. I knew how to forge his license and all the permissions stuff.

A donkey. Nadia laughed, as if she were laughing at a yelling woman on *Things You Cannot Say.* The woman was in a shouting fury at a street vendor. Nadia's tunic collar was sticking to her neck and her feet ached from the straw slippers and she had come to hate the sound of them, *slop, slop, slop,* gray uniform lives and gray slopping noises like walking rinds. The semolina was like gluey sand. I can't believe it. A real donkey.

Yeah, yeah. I got him way up north. I was traveling at night but there was some guys from that venomous natural substances program or natural poisonous pest program or council or task force or some shit like that, out looking for scorpions with blacklight flashlights and they nailed me. Bad paper. They said they had the power of arrest and detainment. Liars. Charity snarled over her black bean patty. Liars, liars.

Are people different out there in the field systems? asked Nadia. I mean, more resourceful, more hopeful and, you know, just different?

Shit, I don't know. Why ask me. They are goddamned prisoners for God's sakes, Sendra.

Around them the kitchen workers slung pots and pans into the thirty-gallon sinks full of soapy water and sliced open packages of semolina and tapioca, bags of sugar, emptied them into bins. At the door a dehydrated old woman held out her cupped hand and asked for half a cup of water. Kitchen Head shouted Get out, Granny. Get your ass out of here.

Nadia clasped her hands together to keep from walking up to Kitchen Head and smacking her. To speak like that to an elderly woman look at her hands, a woman who had worked hard all her life and God knows why she was here. Nadia shut her hand around her fork and opened it again and shut it again and told herself to stop it.

She leaned closer to Charity. Could you go through that again?

Yah. Way north. A million miles north. There's some open places up there. Past the Mon Debris Soybean Farms. There's two-three donkeys up there. They took him away in a yellow bus. She bent her tangled head over her black bean patty.

Took who.

My donkey.

Okay. Are you from the North? I mean, why were you coming south to this area?

I was born up there on the Jolly Green Giant Essential Grains headquarters; my mother was a free worker. She said my dad was a guard. I just go around here and there. One place and another. I can't stand being in one place all the time. I been arrested four times now. I got to find that donkey. His name is Homer.

Did you ever hear of Lighthouse Island?

Shit, yeah, it's on TV.

Well, is there e-waste up there? North of here?

Sure, before the farms. From here north there's a kind of snooty neighborhood then scrap, then the paper mill. I know where north is, you bet your ass. Charity tossed her black hair. I know where south is, too.

Nadia saw Kitchen Head looking over at them and quickly smiled and gestured at the screen where a man on the street was shrieking at a bus conductor. There was no voice, just a sound track: *Bridge Over Troubled Water*. It was a very popular program since it showed ordinary people going into emotional states of rage, caught on camera, and the only other place you could see ordinary people instead of higher-up celebrities was on *Sector Secrets* where they were being arrested or dragged bloodily from bus wrecks. Nadia laughed in a false voice at a tiny enraged woman on the screen. Her Dutchboy haircut fell in hanks around her face; she saw herself in a shining steel pot. She looked like a fiercely intelligent floor mop.

Did you escape, when you were in jail before?

Charity stared hard at Nadia. No. But. She was silent again for a moment. I am ready to this time. The garbage chute, eh.

Exactly. Nadia forked down a crisp edge of black bean patty. We can do it in kitchen worker coveralls. I already have one pair.

If we're caught they'll kill us right there. We won't even get a screen test. Charity laughed.

I don't care, said Nadia. I don't care.

That evening two guards came and took away the little pirate radio blond woman, the one Nadia had helped fill out applications. Her face was vacant and stunned, her blue eyes wide with fear. Good luck, the other women whispered. Good luck.

The next day Charity managed to steal a second pair of kitchen worker's coveralls from a locker and then used them to mop the floor as if they were a wad of mop rags. Afterward Charity took them to the shower with her under her own clothes and washed the filth away.

It grew colder and from time to time they could hear light rain pinging at the painted windows. This would be a good time to try the garbage chute. It would not be festering with flies. Charity said, Wait, wait. I know when a good time is. Trust me.

It was close to All Hallows Eve and soon Male Voice One and Female Voice One would begin to read all the sea stories—Joseph Conrad and Melville and *The Golden Ocean,* which read aloud so well, and *The Voyage of the Liberdade*—and they would play the ballad "the Wreck of the Edmund Fitzgerald," which always made her cry. From time to time in the evening she found herself staring at the gray-painted windows in all the noise and smells while she beat her fists on her thighs in gentle repetitive thuds.

She whispered to Charity, When?

Next week. New guard is coming. Doesn't know her way around.

That night the guards smirked as the *Trials and Tribulations* program came on. There was the little blond woman in the dock, shrinking away from a shouting prosecutor and the camera, fighting for her life.

CHAPTER 27

Big shots having lunch with administration, said the head cook. All the good girls get to take it up and serve it. Hey? Fancy offices. Air-conditioned. Bad girls don't get to go. Hey? She turned to Nadia. And what are you?

I'm a good girl, said Nadia. *And may God forgive me for groveling.* She went back to scraping the oily crust from the inside of a twenty-gallon rice pot. *A good girl, a good girl. Very unattractive. Poor camera quality.*

Nadia and Charity and two others shoved the lunch trolleys on the freight elevator and stood braced while they and the rattling dishes shot upward. They were dressed in new, pressed jail uniforms. They were strictly clean. Nadia counted the floors. Seven. In another day she and Charity would get out via the garbage chute and then, if they were caught appearing among the slop, start accusing whoever was standing around of poor safety practices and demand an investigation and then in the confusion get onto a food delivery truck. If they were caught the essential thing was to create as much confusion as possible.

The guard whispered, *Head guy from the top Demolition offices. Came on an airplane, imagine, an airplane.* She flung open the doors to the administrator's office. When Nadia and the others pushed the trolleys in she saw James.

The two halves of her heart struck together like a bell. Her mouth opened. Then she suffered through a little cough. She flushed red. Her ears were burning. James turned in his wheelchair with an attitude of mild interest and looked into her eyes half of a second. His eyes were a rainy gray. It was the first time she had seen his face in daylight and he gave nothing away. Then he glanced at all the other women prisoners and returned to a diagram.

Kitchen Head stepped forward and laid paper placemats of blue-and-beige stripes in front of James and then the administrator. The administrator regarded the women with a blank antiseptic stare. Kitchen Head ignored the administrator's assistant who clearly expected to be ignored and was regarded as a sort of wastebasket or perhaps a human in-out box. He sat against the wall, a meager sour man in a spindly chair. James took up his fountain pen and began to doodle on the placemat.

I know, he said, but we've already designed the C-4 placements. We have designated five thousand drilled holes and twenty-one miles of detonating cord.

There's nothing wrong with this building, nothing, said the administrator. The assistant said *indeed there is not* with little minimal sentences of body language. A minute head toss.

The women all stood silently behind the lunch trolley with their pressed jail clothes and clean nails while overhead fans beat the office air into waves like heartbeats. Nadia gripped a slotted serving spoon, poised over a mound of tapioca topped with maraschino cherries that looked like toy nipples. James had three thick folders laid out on the table. The jail administrator pushed them around as if they were giant playing cards.

Nadia could not take her eyes from his face for long moments and then remembered and looked down at the slotted server. She saw the silver trembling with little lights.

You're using water like there is no tomorrow, said James. We have authorization from the highest level to consider plans for a more hydro-efficient unit somewhere else. I mean this building is ten stories high, you're using huge amounts of electricity to pump, and it's just one inefficient unit tacked onto another. As far as I can see the original building was a library, a hundred years ago, and now it's surrounded by add-on after add-on serviced by very old leaking water pipes. James tapped his fingers restlessly over files. He took up his pen and doodled a stick figure roller-skating on the placemat.

I saw you on television, said the administrator. You claim your brother, some kind of rain man, a storm expert, is saying these disastrous rains are coming. We've had three little rains and he's talking floods! Should I be thinking about where the high ground is? Eh? Should I go and buy a rubber dinghy? Where's the drainage maps for this area? Shouldn't I be thinking about whether to save myself and my family and just leave all the prisoners to drown in their cells? Now where's your water problem?

It was merely a theory, said James. Meteorology is a notoriously inaccurate science.

Well, here's lunch, said the administrator. His voice was unnatural with rage but he spoke in a false, inviting voice. Look here, brought up from our own kitchens. Very good. These are excellent provisions. This establishment does not need demolition. It does not. Here, have some of this beef stew, genuine cow beef with fresh peas, carrots. From a cow. I have all the figures you want. We're doing our own scrapping to make new pipes, prisoner labor, cheap, cheap.

The room smelled wonderfully of furniture polish and detergent and clean air. Nadia envied the prisoner women approaching the table and watched as James accepted a soup plate of beef stew. Nadia would not be asked to serve until the dessert. Meanwhile she could simply steal glances at him. His muscled but pale hands, the healthy and coarse brown hair and his very ordinary profile. He was real. He sat there in his wheelchair with an alert look on his face as if he were paying attention to the administrator. Taking up space, weighing a certain amount, breathing in and breathing out. He wore a watch on a leather band.

Look at this room! said the administrator. Just redone this month! And this is all going exploding into the air? Oh my God, this is unreal.

No, it will implode, not explode.

According to your brother, who is notoriously inaccurate, I might be paddling downstream!

Nadia glanced quickly from one side to the other. The entire room seemed to be electrified, its photons and electrons and atoms and beige-and-blue-striped curtains in a slubby weave were all charged with desire. With potential and kinetic love. With poetry and antique emotions. With faith, hope, and Charity, who was standing quietly by with a bread knife in her hand thinking of slitting the administrator's throat.

James said, The choice was between taking down the top three stories and taking down the whole thing. His voice was mild and full of authority. He had strong, deep lines around his mouth and between his brows and on his face a flat expression, a hard-set, a ram-you-damn-you look. He said, And in addition to the jail there are problems with the entire water sector. Never mind the rain predictions. This sector, including the paper mill, is over its allocation. Something's got to go. You've got to go.

What about them? Why don't they go? said the administrator. He was a moderate-sized man with very large ears and fine, thin blond hair who knew nothing of love. Of imprisoned girls who were covert royalty. Reduced to slaving in the kitchens of loathsome fortresses. Drugged by magic devices. Prepared to undertake their own rescue given one small hope, one small hope.

Can't, said James. They make paper.

Be damned to you, said the administrator. You're one of the people on the problematic distribution list, aren't you? Those people are usually arrested.

No. Demolition doesn't distribute anything. We don't produce anything. On the contrary.

It doesn't matter, the list is the list.

I see. James's pale eyes were unreadable and flat to the plane of his face, his lids hooded. I want you to call for recyclers to start stripping this building immediately, get out all they can use and then we'll begin assessment of the structure. You will have to distribute your prisoners.

You're in trouble yourself! cried the administrator and his reedy assistant flung himself about in his chair and made hushing gestures. I don't care! I can say what I want! This is my building, my jail! You'll never get set up, never; you'll be arrested before you even get in a scrapping crew!

At a signal Nadia stepped forward with two servings of the glutinous tapioca. Her straw slippers shuffled over the carpet. She put the first one in front of the administrator and then gave one to James. She stood very close to him and sat the dish down on his paper placemat. She could take in his scent, of good soap and clean linen and something that was just himself. He had written *Uphusband not well* on his placemat. *Changed files. I have one week.* Then he kept on scribbling and wrote over the words.

What's that? The administrator said. What are you writing?

Calculating primer cord costs, said James. When will you start moving your prisoners?

Moving? You are living in a dream world. You see how well they serve, said the administrator. They get good training here. Excellent training in the food services, janitorial work. If these buildings were to be demolished they would be parceled out. Probably thrown into the mines! Women! In the mines! Dragging carts of coal!

Women, being shot on television, said James. For invented crimes. Maybe they'd prefer dragging carts of coal. What do you think?

Nadia paused a fraction of a second before touching him. Before saying, Director Orotov, would you care for coffee? But if she opened her mouth it would be the end of her. She stepped back to her place behind the trolley.

And poetry? said James. He laid the pen down and took up the dessert spoon in his fine, long hand.

What? The administrator looked up. Poetry?

Why not? I suppose they could be given some training in arts and culture. He dipped his spoon into the dessert. Shame to waste educated people, intelligent and creative people, in such minimalism. Our fine art is in a perilous state. You should be assessing each prisoner's abilities before reallocating them.

Arts and culture? The administrator stared at James. Educated people? Prisoners? You are living in some kind of a bubble. You need to be removed! You have no business trying to expand your agency by destroying my building! You've gone too far! The administrator's voice cracked at the exclamation points.

Try me, said James. He leaned back and pinned his mild gaze on the administrator. Nadia felt the tension between the two men like some kind of bitter odor in the air. Then to her amazement she saw James lift his right foot and put it forward on the footrest, lifting the toe of his shoe up and down. Then he dropped it down on the footrest again.

The administrator said, Maybe I will.

As they wheeled the carts out Nadia kept saying the puzzle words over to herself. *Uphusband not well. Changed files. One week.*

That evening the head guard, the Lard Queen, got in a shouting match with their night-shift guards over showing the execution of the blond woman. The TV screen shone out in blue tones that flickered and jumped over the faces of all the women in the Q ward. Nadia found herself sitting on cot number thirty-four between Charity and one of the gypsy women. They were gripping one another's sweaty hands without ever realizing they were doing it. The screen was hostile, a man-eating thing, a predator. They watched the little blond woman led into the execution chamber, pressed back against the sandbags in her loose shift. She was pleading in a long, babbling scream. Then the Lard Queen settled the argument by ripping the plug out of the wall.

Thank you, thank you, the women whispered.

CHAPTER 28

Early the next morning the guard yelled out that cot number thirty-four was to come to the door and be escorted to her counseling session.

Nadia stood up. There had been no warning. The guard handed her her knapsack as she came out the door and, from the other women in the reeking and dirty Q ward, little faint good-byes. Too bad, said Head Prisoner. She meant that Nadia had to go and face whatever she had to face with no breakfast, no water.

Because she had been handed her knapsack out of wherever they had stored it Nadia knew that she was going somewhere else after the counseling session. She was leaving the quarantine ward.

Live it up, Sendra, said Charity. Luck to you.

Nadia's escort guard said, I'm going off shift. There'll be another guard take my place. She'll be waiting when you get out of your session.

I see, said Nadia. Her heart seemed to freeze in place for a moment and then went on normally.

So here you are. Now you can tell your side of it, can't you? The guard smiled at her and in a moment of sympathy patted her arm. Tell how you're innocent and everything.

Nadia was so relieved to find herself in a counselor's office instead of some kind of screen-test room that she felt giddy. She took hold of herself and stood calmly on the thin carpeting.

The counselor was a youngish pale woman with blond hair tied up in rough plaits, and no wedding ring. Her computer screen was guarded on either side by pieces of cardboard that said LAUNDRY POWDER INSTITUTIONAL USE ONLY. There was a half-eaten sandwich on the counselor's desk and a handful of candies. Nadia came in and stood. It was very cold and the carpet was dirty and the windows were painted out here as well. A large glass paperweight held the files down against a blowing current of cold air from the ventilation system. Inside the paperweight were a girl and a bird.

Sit down, the counselor said. My name is Jeanne Uphusband.

Nadia sat down. She put her knapsack on the floor. It was the name James had written on his placemat.

You say Yes ma'am! Jeanne Uphusband turned to her, and for a moment wavered.

Yes ma'am, said Nadia.

The counselor was dressed in the same uniform gray color as the prisoners. Except her tunic top was faced with green piping and she wore a white blouse underneath, and an ID badge on a string. Her little felt hat with a veil sat on top of the computer monitor.

You're charged with not having an ID, being out of your sector without permission and no residence permit. You were seen coming out of off-limits abandoned housing and you were dressed as a boy. The counselor paused. Ah, yes, um, residence permit. This is the reality of it. So? A boy? What were you thinking? Good Lord. The counselor's head wobbled slightly.

What's wrong with field research? said Nadia. Ma'am? I hope you don't imagine all research is done on a computer.

We contacted your supervisor by e-mail. He said the same thing. I gave him hell for sending you out on such an idiotic task. Hey, this is a genuine word here. You people in sociological research think you can get away with anything.

You contacted my supervisor?

Yes. Our supervisor Thomas Stearns Eliot.

Right. Nadia nodded, no hesitation. Well, I was just observing the area. Specifically, the abandoned apartment towers. Dogtown Towers.

Let's get to the truth. Your backpack had no ID in it whatever.

Well, then, someone stole it. Nadia crossed her ankles. Having spent the last three weeks in quarantine I have heard a great deal of talk of a black market in phony IDs. I have had an interesting time in quarantine. So where did it go? Nadia had recovered her lost interrogatives; they came back like the pigeons to Dogtown Towers.

The counselor stared back at her. Nadia detected a slight hesitation.

How would I know? said Jeanne Uphusband. You'd have to make that claim on an official form. We have to stay in touch with the actual, here. The counselor's head wavered and she closed her eyes and took deep breaths.

Nadia hesitated and then leaned toward Jeanne Uphusband. Are you all right? You seem faint.

I know. Jeanne Uphusband's manner changed for a moment. I had some altercations with my superior and got cut back to one pint. My overly strong objections to these new screen tests. But never mind that. Never mind. We are all prisoners of thirst. I want you to explain what you were doing in abandoned public buildings with no ID and so on and so on . . . She trailed off and then bent forward and inspected the file that had come up on her monitor. Your record isn't all that good, you know.

Nadia said, My record is perfectly good, ma'am.

The counselor said, With your education you could have worked your way up you know. Earn credits, private apartment, a hundred kilowatt-hours water features. Two-gallon recirculating Bubbling Woodland spring with leatherette fish or whatever. She wiped her face.

Her fingers skipped clumsily over the keyboard and she looked at the monitor and stopped typing. Who is this? Why is this on here? She turned the big wooden monitor chassis with the flapping laundry-box wings so that Nadia could see it.

There was a photograph of a young woman Nadia didn't know, with the name Nadia Stepan at the top, and an ID number. Nadia felt her veins beating in her neck but she said, I don't know. How am I supposed to know who that is?

But Nadia knew it was Sendra Bentley. She gazed coolly at the monitor. Also under the name Nadia Stepan was a notation: *Arrest when found. Theft of gov't property and marital endangerment. Ref: Oversec. Blanche Warren. Keyword: Slut.*

Wait. There's more in that file. The woman bent to her keyboard again and the first key she touched caused the photograph to disappear and then a PDF file came up. Author Sendra Bentley.

Ah yes, said Nadia, and she bent forward and read some of the first page. Yes. Nadia read quickly. It contained phrases such as *the politics of renaming,* and *disappearance of the homeless as an analytic category* and *collective identification of objectives in utilization of marginal urban spaces.*

How did that happen? cried the counselor. Why is that there? I never brought that up!

I have no idea. Nadia read on. I loved writing that paper. Marginal urban spaces are the least known and the least explored. We tend to ignore them; I suppose it's our celebrity culture.

Celebrity culture. The counselor was dubious. Perhaps.

Nadia said, Arbor Square and the abandoned public buildings there are an extremely rich field for spontaneous vernacular management of disregarded areas. It is exciting.

The counselor reached for her metal tumbler and turned it up from habit. There was nothing in it. Write out an explanation. Someone educated like yourself, I don't see why you have to go running around in boy's clothes in abandoned buildings. I forgot about the boy's clothes.

She looked up but her eyes were not focusing well. The judge will hand down your sentence.

I thought you said there would be mediation.

It's just a word. They like it. Doesn't mean a damn thing. Sounds good. You're going to have to spend quite a lot of time in solitary. Down in the refrigeration units. Then corrective labor. Good for you. Builds character. Only your supervisor's intervention here is preventing something worse.

Nadia paused, thinking, *Worse how?*

I know what you're thinking. The counselor braced her hands against the desk and a drop of sweat trickled down from her hairline. I know, I know. The guards are making jokes. Want to be a star? Want to be on TV? God. She wiped away the sweat.

Nadia said, How long in solitary?

Shortest, a year. Longest, five years. Jeanne Uphusband's head was unsteady. She looked up and did not quite focus on Nadia. I'll call the guard. The counselor stood up. The motion of suddenly standing up made her blood pressure drop like a stone. She took one step clear of the desk and fell, making a soft thump on the ragged carpet.

Nadia rose from her chair and stood for a moment, wavering. Paused. Listened. Nobody at the door. Then she bent down and stripped the tunic with the white dickie from Jeanne Uphusband, jerking at the flopping, limp arms. She took the ID badge on its string. Then she ripped off her own jailhouse tunic and wrestled the unconscious woman into it. She was almost panting with nerves and animal fear.

Nnnnngaaaahh, said the counselor. She opened her eyes halfway and her pupils were rolled up in her head.

Nadia grasped the paperweight and struck the woman on top of the head. The bird within it flew through the glycerin and hundreds of bits of bread drifted around the girl's head like snow.

Silence.

Well, there you go, Nadia thought. *I've killed her. I've killed her.*

She put on the counselor's tunic and adjusted the little white dickie. Jeanne Uphusband made a snoring noise and one of her arms twitched.

Nadia had to calm down; she had to appear only a little flustered by the fact that a prisoner had fainted.

She would have to leave the knapsack here on the floor. Nadia pulled the tote bag out of the knapsack, shook the tote open, and stuffed the *Girl Scout Handbook* into it. From beyond the door she heard voices. A loud, harsh laugh. A new guard. She grabbed her dress top and her little heels with the rosettes, her straw hat and the journal. She jammed them into her tote-bag purse and then the horrible red polka-dotted runners. Then she dropped to her knees and grabbed everything she could; the blister card and her money and the feather duster and the tortoiseshell glasses and her combs and the precious flashlight, the crocheted cat, the water bottle and its woven cover. The sewing kit in its little tin had spilled open; leave it, leave the electronic thingie too. She grabbed up the silver St. Jude dangle on its chain.

She took the counselor's hat and the stack of files. She took the counselor's shoes and shoved her own straw jail slippers on the woman's feet. Nadia turned to the chair she had been sitting on and knocked it over to the floor with a loud thump. She opened the door and looked at the guard with an irritated little shake of her head. Please, she said.

Terminal Verna stood up her full six feet. She had teeth like burglar bars. She had a nightstick and handcuffs and deep sunken green eyes. Hands like front-end loaders.

What?

The detainee has fainted. Please remove her and her effects. I believe she goes straight to solitary.

Well, damn. Terminal Verna loomed in the doorway.

How can I interview detainees when they are not being given enough water to think properly? She didn't even make sense.

The big guard walked into the room on her thick shoes and looked down at Sendra Bentley.

Please call medical, Jeanne Uphusband said and hurried off down the hall.

CHAPTER 29

Most escapees spend many hours and days planning an escape from their immediate detention but then have no further plans once they get out. Where to go. How to blend in. They simply parade down the street in a state of delirious joy at being out of confinement and enforced hebetude and back into the skin of their own selves. They laugh, they skip they sing, and their speech is alive with exclamation points and interrogatives. They are quickly spotted and rearrested. Nadia, however, sank deeply into the persona of Jeanne Uphusband as if into the cushions of a luxurious conveyance and planned on driving this conveyance for as long and as far as she could.

Nadia hurried along that latticework of remembered paces and turns, counting her steps, into the great main hall, prisoners lined up in front of the monitors, shouts and commands. She bent down the brim of the little hat and pulled down its veil. She walked through the big doorway to the screen-test room, nodded briefly to the C&E guy at his desk, and headed for the outside door.

When she stepped outside she calmly flipped open a file and even though she only glanced up briefly she could tell that something was different with the world since she had been in jail. It was cloudy and very cold and a bitter thin drizzle was falling that seemed to threaten to actually turn into sleet or cold rain. Everything looked washed. She checked the files, nodded to herself, and strode on in Jeanne Uphusband's shoes. They were too big. She had to curl her toes at every step to keep them on.

She was in a courtyard and the only way out was through the courtroom building.

At the entrance there was a security gate with a metal detector; as she approached it she saw a man go in ahead of her with a metal sippy cup in one hand. The alarm did not go off. It was just for looks. Nadia held up her badge on its string and showed it to the guard and he barely lifted his eyes from a TV screen.

She saw other women counselors dressed like herself look at her curiously and Nadia thought, *Somebody is going to recognize this hat, the picture on the badge is not me, I have to get out of here. Where is an exit?* Nadia heard the women talking about shopping at the New Curiosity Shop and filed it away; local information, specific places.

She kept her head down but watched on all sides for bars of clouded, outdoor light that would tell her there was an exit, an open door into the street and the wide world and freedom. The accused slumped guiltily on benches alongside their lawyers. Their tattered shoes said, *There is no way out.* Messenger girls slunk along respectfully; in this legal atmosphere they had lost all their street brash.

Nadia saw a man with a white cane approaching her through the crowd of people. People bumped into him. She could use this man to get out of here.

She came up to him. She laid a hand on his shoulder, her tote-bag straps on one shoulder and the files in her other hand.

Can I help you?

Yes. Yes. Help me find the men's room.

Nadia patted him on the shoulder. It's all right. I'll find somebody. Just a minute.

She reached out and stopped a lawyer. She hoped it would not prove to be Jeanne Uphusband's boss or boyfriend or brother.

She said, Look here, this man needs to find the men's room. The one near the exit.

Certainly, glad to help. Here, sir, I'll take you.

Nadia followed them at a distance. After a while the lawyer and the blind man turned into a very wide hall and headed toward a large open portal that led to the street. She heard a bleeping sound behind her coming from some hidden loudspeakers. People stopped and looked up, then at one another. Nadia glanced down at the ID badge. The little purple light was blinking. She walked out of the entrance in a slow, self-assured pace mainly because Jeanne Uphusband's shoes wallowed around on her feet.

In the street she bent her head against the bitter wind and the fine drifting mist in the air. It was terribly, startlingly cold. She looked weird without a coat. She had to hold on to her little felt hat with the veil against the wind and after a block she stopped at a street vendor's cart. The street vendor was selling hot drinks at prices now far beyond Nadia's reach. As she bent over to look at the coffee and hot tea containers she deliberately caught her badge string on the push-handles and tore it off.

Whoops! said the vendor.

Oh, it's always catching on things, said Nadia. So irritating. She took it in one hand so as to cover the blinking light and went on. In a crowd of people who had lined up for something she saw a woman with a toddler in one arm. She was peering ahead at the line.

Cute kid! Nadia said and slipped the badge into the toddler's baggy pants.

The woman glared at her. Get one of your own, she said.

Blocks went by. Five, seven, nine. Then ahead of her she noticed a building with a peaked roof and white stone facing. Outside people were sitting and smoking on the steps. It must be noon. They were on their lunch break. Over the double doors: Urban Print Regulatory and Security Directorate.

This was where books were transferred to memory plates to save them for the archives, for some putative future generations who might care to read books. Even though there was no way at present to replay the memory plates. People were sitting around outside taking a break and cigarette smoke drifted around their heads.

Are they hiring? Nadia said. She paused with an ill-fitting shoe on the step. She had to get off the street. She strode on so fast that she was temporarily warm. She had to get rid of her counselor's tunic and get into her old street clothes. She put her hands in the pockets.

Yeah. Just temps. You don't have to have a work assignment card. Alls you need is an ID. A young man threw down his cigarette and stepped on it. The smoke and ashes streamed across the steps in the nipping wind.

Oh good, she said.

He said, Looks like you work for Forensics?

Yeah. A temp. I do temp work for anybody.

She walked into the building. Transferring books to archival memory plates was low-level work, they weren't going to be too choosy but on the other hand she had no ID and she was tortured by thirst and the thought of those hot drinks in the vendor's carts. An entire silver quarter apiece. Never mind. She had to get rid of the gray tunic. She was no longer Jeanne. Jeanne was in a baby's diaper. She slipped into a janitor's closet and changed. The khaki top was wrinkled as wadded paper.

Inside the computer room she spotted an empty chair in front of a monitor, one in a long line of monitors and busily typing people. She edged her way down the line and sat in the empty chair, pulled out the keyboard. She put the veiled hat on top of the computer tower. She bent down and took out her own high heels with the rosettes on the toes and kicked the counselor's shoes far under the desk and out of sight.

A young man with a crafty expression and dark hair falling in his face was poised with arachnid fingers over the brassy keyboard. He hoarded a pile of Quench candies to one side. He turned to her.

Are you a temp for Julie?

Yes. She continued to stare at the blank monitor. Then down at the keyboard.

You go up there and the desk lady gives out the books, said the man. People hammered away at keyboards, and sighed, and pressed their hands against their eyes, blinked, looked away and then back to the open book on the stand and the monitor in front of them.

I still have my book from last week. Nadia reached into her tote and took out *The Girl Scout Handbook*. I took it home with me. I love reading. She opened it at random and read out loud:

A shadowgraph screen may be as simple as an old sheet stretched across the doorway, with newspaper covering the space above and below the screen.

Hmmm. Then she said, Oh, I forgot to show my ID to the desk lady. She slumped in her chair. I'm tired already. It's only just after lunch and I'm tired.

The young man said, Nah, you don't need to. Just slip it in there. He pointed to a slot below the Menu button. He didn't ask why she didn't know that but stared at her curiously.

Oh, right. She sat there and wondered if she could pretend to type. People to either side of her couldn't see her screen.

Then she thought of the blister card. She groped around in her tote bag and found it wrapped in a crumpled page and jammed safely inside the notebook. She slid it into the slot. After a few moments the screen lit up with a dull gray light. Letters swam across it. *Welcome to the Urban Print Regulatory and Security Directorate.* She watched in a kind of tired fascination. It worked. The card worked here as well as in vending machines.

She turned to the young man. He gazed at her with a loose, fascinated smile.

You're cuter than Julie, he said.

Thanks. I guess. She smiled back. Are there vending machines around here? I have one bottle allowance coming to me.

No, sorry, not in this building. He reached down and lifted a two-pint bottle of water and handed it to her. There. You can owe me.

She tipped it up and tried not to appear too thirsty. She felt him studying her in her wrinkled khaki top and the gray prison skirt. Her little hat with the veil poised on top of the monitor.

There's vending machines at the bicycle repair. The water is two silver quarters.

Good Lord! Well, I'll pay you back tomorrow, she said.

That's a deal. Go ahead, it's yours. I got a quart coming tonight.

She finished it and handed him back the glass bottle. She felt water flowing into her veins and arteries and flushing her skin. The relief was unbelievable. She sat stunned for a moment and then said, Thanks. Thank you so much, and as she turned back to her monitor there was a loud explosion.

It was a hard, deafening crack and a flash of intense light through the windows, and then it rumbled on and on. Everyone in the room ducked, and then turned to stare at one another.

What the hell was that? said the young man.

Thunder and lightning, said Nadia. I read about it once.

CHAPTER 30

On her screen a sentence appeared:

Nadia you r safe where you r 4 about 4 hours. J.

She stared at it.

Nadia r u there

The whole enormous room full of typers and enterers buzzed with the shock of the lightning. After the screams they all slowly went back to work. Nadia glanced at the young man to her left and the older woman on her right. Both clattered rapidly at their keyboards on the big brass-bound keys that used so much finger-muscle in pressing down and they were frowning and from time to time glancing uneasily at the windows.

She glanced over at the *Handbook* and then typed:

Yes, I am here. Who r u? Get off my monitor. I'm trying to enter a book here.

Don't be coy. This is James. I have no idea how u got out but you did. Go north, Crow Creek Valley, scrap heaps.

How do I know you r James?

No way I can prove it we just have to go on here.

How could you have known where I wz?

The card.

Of course.

U r safe there 4 a few hours. Then get out out ♋♋ ♍■♋♋□♒
hey r starting a search at the other end of street this program is degrading.

I couldn't believe it was u there. I saw u move yr foot.

Yes. Later. U must get out of the area.

Nadia flipped a page of the handbook as if she were copying it.

Which way is north?

When u go out of the directorate main entrance turn right.

Tired. Jail terrible. Can't get much farther. Minutes away from some disaster.

I admire u, brave girl. Go on. ♌❖♑ *Keep on. You must, you can.*

The black-haired young man sighed and stretched his arms, locked his fingers behind his neck, and turned his torso from side to side.

What are you entering? he said. He smiled at her.

The Girl Scout Handbook. She smiled back. What's yours?

He rubbed his eyes. William Cobbet's *Rural Rides Volume I.* It's so boring. I just enter a page or two of wingdings or a letter, like D for instance. Hit copy over and over. Who's to know? Hey? And so where do you live?

Nadia turned back to her screen. Down the street, she said. Near the New Curiosity Shop. Four of us. Amanda borrowed, ha ha, my water this morning.

A punishable offense.

Am I going to turn in one of my roommates?

Nah, nah.

I better get to work here.

They keep a lot of records here. The young man pulled at his tie and smiled. More than books.

Really?

Yeah. In the basement archives. Four million laws. And all the ordinances and regulations.

Oh. Nadia felt something coming and was a little nervous. Who knew? she said.

He jumped around in his chair and waved one hand in a circle. I mean there are so many laws and regulations everybody breaks them all the time and they don't even know it. You could be breaking a law right now, just sitting there.

Nadia typed busily. No kidding.

Someday a bunch of us are going to go down there and erase them all from the computers. Zap. Phhhhht. Gone. Including the new one allowing public executions. He sat up straight and smiled at her. Hey?

I don't want to know about it, she said. I'm busy. *And afraid.* Nadia turned a page of the *Handbook* and pretended to read. Then she typed:

I can't do anything else. Now heavy charges.

I know. My arrest is coming, problem with surgery, explain later don't ask. I have arranged a ride 4 u in the e-waste so ◆●♍○&□□▱⊡ □◆□♍○

Losing you.

Program degrading.

I don't want u 2 b arrested. U r my hero, my savior. Could not believe u were there. How did u do that?

Always wanted to blow up Old Book Dump Jail there in Cheyenne. Where u r now, Cheyenne Wyoming. Demanded random inspection, including kitchen # 14 just so I could c u.

Good to c u.

Nadia. *Leave* ♋◆○ ♌♌☒ □□◆◆■.

U switched files. S.B for me.

Yes. Memorize this. U r much farther N&W of dog town towers. 320 miles. Scrapping and industrial area ahead about 15 miles, follow H.J. Road and stay nw. Come to old riverbed, stay north. This program has a short kill time. Memorize please.

Done.

Electronic scrap yard. Enter with the card. Find van # GAN22VP1–928-LES. Get on the van. Memorize the #.

Done.

♋◆□■•   ♎●○   □♏♍□♏♋◆   *repeat r u sure?*

Sure.

This is the only time I will be able to give you that number. In a moment I will erase it.

Done.

Big rain coming. Move fast.

OK

Signing out now. I will get u 2 litehouse island. I will take u if I am not arrested 1st.

How?

A flight.

Is this 2 good 2 b true?

Put cursor on this ~~~~~ and bring up map of island. Marine chart but will have to do.

She did so and there it was; strange numbers were on it and peculiar lines. A coast, an island, an asterisk for the tower light and around it the blue paper sea said forty fathoms, sixty fathoms where at some time in the distant past people had been able to measure the depth of the sea.

What was the medication in the card? Why r u taking it? Dangerous?

Yes, dangerous but a chance for nerve regeneration in my legs. More later.

Why me?

Have 2 make choices. Mon choix est fait, tant que je vive. Do u know French?

Some. This, yes. Pour nulle vivant, tant soit and so on. Riche de hault lignaige. Dunnett. Lymond.

Get out of there now.

OK. R u sure u can delete all this.

Deleted. Bye.

Bye.

She turned to the young man. Do these print out?

Yeah. He was disappointed that Nadia was not interested in zap-ping the four million laws. In a resigned voice he said, You need to go up to the desk and get a permission slip.

Ah well

Nadia dug the pencil from her tote bag and made a quick sketch of the map of Lighthouse Island and then deleted the map on-screen. Everyone turned to the window. Another blast of thunder made people cower and rain came down in a pounding intensity, a noisy waterfall at the glass.

Happy Jack Road was a small villagelike quarter within the greater overcrowded megacity, and its street-side buildings were no more than four stories high and did not seem to have ever been decapitated. People stared out of the upper windows into the cold with curtains streaming around both sides of them and called down to people on the street. Nadia knew that this made the area dangerous. They all knew one another.

There were a great many shops with green-and-yellow banners, offers of handmade jewelry and hats and boots. The agencies were more lenient here, obviously. Maybe police surveillance wouldn't be so intense. Everything streamed in the wet. Shopkeepers ran out to grab at their displays and signs and things made with feathers and silver and beads and wide-brimmed hats on display, things she vaguely recognized as "western."

Nadia ran into a fire shop, printing wet footprints and dripping.

Rain! she said.

I got eyes, said the woman behind the counter.

Nadia took out her coin purse and counted her dimes as if she were about to buy something. In actuality she was checking out her possessions and glancing out the dusty window for any sign of Forensics agents. She stood among the shelves of matches, kerosene lamps and glass containers of kerosene, candles, rolls of lamp wick, candlesticks, and pierced tin candle-lanterns. The shop woman sat with her hands inside her sleeves and shivered and stared, fascinated, at the drops rolling down the front window.

They had left her almost everything except the coins. They had stolen all her coins; no, there were five dimes and some pennies and nickels that had fallen to the bottom. Almost everything else was there except the sewing kit, which she had left on the floor of Jeanne Uphusband's office.

You don't have an umbrella or something? said Nadia.

The woman laughed.

Nadia bought two candles for a penny and said, A person can't go anywhere without spending something.

The shop woman said, So?

CHAPTER 31

JUNQUE, the sign said. STUFF. I-GLASSES. The permit number was painted over the door. Nadia ducked in, wet and freezing. She had to get out of the cold and the rain even if only for short while. A bell rang as she stepped in.

A white-haired man sat behind a counter with a tiny screwdriver in his hand, taking apart a bird toy. Maybe it was a stuffed bird. It was yellow and black and feathers were dropping from it.

May I help you?

Yes, said Nadia. She tried to quiet herself and act normal. She took a long breath through her nose. I was wondering if you had a compass somewhere.

A compass.

Yes.

Why? Where are you going?

Nadia tucked her hands in her sleeves. She was shaking very slightly with the cold and with nerves and she could see a lock of hair in front of her eyes trembling. She pushed it back under Jeanne Uphusband's hat and looked around at the displays of old framed pictures, vise grips, boxes of nails and screws, old wood-cased TV monitors, tin cans full of kids' school awards badges, cracked chairs and scrap paper, birdcages, and broken lamps. Hats that she knew must be cowboy hats and old spurs and branding irons, painted dishes. A box full of I-glasses of all sizes and strengths. There was a door in the back.

Nowhere. Nadia peered at the stuffed bird. What's that? She bent over the counter, wet and shivering.

A clock.

A bird clock?

Yes. It tells the time. "I am time, grown old to destroy the world, embarked on a course of world annihilation!" He threw the stuffed bird onto the counter. Why do you want a compass?

I am going down to the creek valley, that's why. To the riverbed.

What for? I have a right to be a busybody. He laughed and performed a little writhe and his white hair tossed like silk.

I was told to go north up the old riverbed. Nadia smiled at him and then looked down at all the heaped cheap jewelry under the glass counter.

Told by whom? By a sadist. It would take you through the scrap yards, an entire universe of junk being recycled by gnomes, by dwarves. Swarming over the heaps like unhygienic humanoids seeking . . . what? Things.

I know.

Why?

I am looking for my father's bones. In the river. And so I need a compass.

Child! he cried. He dropped both wrinkled hands to his sides and stared at her.

Nadia shifted her tote bag. Yes. He was murdered north of here and they never found his body. *I should shut up now, now.*

The man opened a drawer and took out a handful of buttons and let them slide through his fingers, slowly. The buttons clattered. And what is your name?

Sonia Hernandez.

A common name, Hernandez. Why don't you have a coat?

I haven't bought my winter one yet, she said. You're nosy. I just want a compass.

Where was he murdered, O son of Hernan?

Ten years and seven months ago.

Child. He leaned with one elbow on the countertop and stared at her with narrowed eyes. His worn suit coat rode up on his shoulders. You wish to distract me with this story. You have been *sent*. You would have been quite young. How do they know he was murdered?

Nadia said, The man confessed. She smiled, a fatherless but brave girl, a daughter of tragedy. It might take me to the end of the city altogether. She walked down the counter and pulled out a drawer. Buttons, old playing cards, nozzles, and faucet handles.

The end of the city! You must not! It is not allowed. The things! The alien tribes! What will you eat? There is nothing to eat but roots and bark and alien tribal people lurking in rocky declivities and so on! You would be stooping over the miry, unclean riverbed in search of your father's bones. "Full fathom five thy father lies, of his bones are coral made, those are the pearls that were his eyes" and so on. Epic. That would be the land of faerie, beautiful and dangerous where bones are turned into sea limestone. Come. I will see what I have. You are really escaping to the Great Northwest, are you not? Where the ancient hippies live as true believers still, and fishes with gold coins in their mouths leap into maidens' laps.

Do they? She looked up at him.

Who knows. He stalked to the back of the shop and began to root through a canvas sack. I saw a beautiful young woman shot dead on live TV, anything is at present possible. A communal grief inhabits us. And now for myself.

Yourself? I just thought you might have an old compass.

You have told me about yourself. I will tell you about me.

That's okay. I shouldn't have told you all about myself. Nadia turned and surveyed the shop. She was looking at the back door, an escape route. She was still shaking and couldn't seem to stop, even in the comparative warmth of the Curiosity Shop.

He opened up an ancient microwave and looked inside and drew out a box with small devices in it. He said, I am probably the last person alive to have seen *The Barber of Seville* performed. Probably the last. My name is Roman Durban Gallegos.

Happy to meet you.

Nadia heard crowd noises outside, street kids yelling. They always did that when a pair of Forensics agents came along.

The elderly man hitched up his pants and pulled at his tie. He said, It was at the Midnight Cowboy Theater, which had a proscenium, and in the opera season they rolled up the film screen and the Sector Zero Opera Company performed. Yes. They were awful. Awful.

Where was the Midnight Cowboy Theater? Nadia moved to the bureau and yanked open a drawer. At the first noise of the jangling doorbell, at the first sound of an official voice, she would bolt through the back door.

I don't know. It's confusing. I get confused now after the invasion and the bombing, they insist it be called the Urban Wars, so whatever. Perhaps Omaha, could have been Denver. I was evacuated on a night train. It was different then! Now here! There. He handed her a compass. Are you happy now?

Nadia reached for the small round object and held it in her upturned palm. Oh, it's lovely, she said. It shone with brass and delicate lettering; *NSEW,* it stated in bold capitals. It's beautiful. How do you work it?

Work it?

Then the front doorbell jangled as the rickety old door was pushed open and two Forensics officers walked in. Their breath smoked; they were very large and heavy with all their belt equipment.

One of them said, Well, Mr. Gallegos. Do you have that tureen for my wife yet? Hey, how about this rain?

Raindrops stood out on their watch caps and sleeves. They stood with their hands behind their backs, trying to smile and set the small elderly man at ease but one of them was going through tissue engineering and his face was like hard plastic and his eyes glittered with permissible pointless rage.

Bing will have it soon, he said. My ceramics scrapper. Soon! And so, did you come to the neighborhood just to ask about the tureen? Mr. Gallegos appeared elaborately surprised. Just to see me? He smiled and backed away one foot, two feet, slowly.

No, no. Looking for somebody and found her. Hiding a stolen ID in her baby's diaper. She's off to jail and the baby to an orphanage. They both nodded together. The tissue engineering did something to their understanding or maybe their perceptions. They became inarticulate, they repeated themselves. She waited, holding her breath.

Yes, baby to an orphanage. They nodded again and drops flew from their watch caps. Then the near one shot out a hand so fast it seemed a blur as he caught a cuff link that Gallegos had knocked off the counter in his nervous crabwise backing. There was nothing wrong with their reaction times.

I don't care, thought Nadia. *I don't, I don't. It was her or me.* She tried to fade into the background, become neutral, mild and gliding. She put two dimes on the counter and then turned away from them to look at a framed print of a little girl in a birch wood, staring up at a bird and then found something interesting near the door.

Your lives are full of drama, said Mr. Gallegos. Lives of theatrical intensity. He nodded and straightened his tie. I was the last person ever to see a live performance of *La Bohème* at the Midnight Cowboy Theater; it was the Sector Zero Opera Company, that was drama, that was romantic intensity. De Lara sang "O Soave Fanciulla"; it was an assault on the senses.

Nadia smiled and nodded to them all and stepped to the door. The stuffed finch on the counter began to sing. *Five o'clock! Five o'clock!*

Gray clouds pouring out from the northwest and a fine drizzle. A ruinous neighborhood with broken pavements or biscuit-colored dirt, hard as concrete and now steaming with damp. Great wet boulders of granite sat between buildings or in front of them as if they had come as invaders from down below in the Land of Underpinnings where rock lived. Untidy apartments pressed against one another down steep slopes and made narrow canyons. Blackbirds wheeled overhead and sang songs to one another in the cold, nebulous light of early morning and from every window shone the jewels of television screens on which glaciers broke apart into the arctic seas and a voice said *I know, I know.* Bowls of grain porridge and hard biscuits with margarine were eaten on doorsteps and smoke from wood fires bannered up from rooftops. Nadia had spent the night under the piers of an ancient bridge structure that spanned a narrow dry wash, listening to other people who had crowded under it, as they shifted and turned and talked among themselves. They were heaps of heavy clothing, breath clouds, the occasional flash of a match. Nadia held her tote bag close and sat awake long into the dark.

As soon as it was light she pulled the big boy's shirt over her dress and put on the red sneakers. She was still cold, and her shivering was wearing her out, exhausting her. She felt abstract, slow, lethargic.

Where are you off to?

A young woman sitting beside a fire of scrap lumber called to her. A frypan sat over the flames on two bricks and bannock rose and browned inside it as if the girl commanded the ministering spirits of baking powder, the toasted odor and crack of vagrant drops of rain that fell on the pan. She cut a triangle of bannock and wrapped it in brown paper. Two pennies!

No, thank you. The smell made Nadia light-headed. She had so little money left. At a distance she heard a crushing noise as ceramic refuse was ground to powder. The cold clouds poured by heavily in sagging corms.

They had stopped looking for her as far as she knew. For Sendra Bentley with Nadia Stepan's face or maybe by now somebody else's face. Nadia wondered which mattered most, the name on an ID or the face.

Maybe neither. Underhydrated Legal Forensics employees with minimal typing skills hit Ctrl/Enter instead of Shift, plus some other key and everything disappeared. Or they thought it had disappeared; what they had actually done was brought up a blank page. *OMG it's all gone!* Their first objective was to hide this from their section manager by claiming they had received a notice: *Case no longer relevant.* Then delete everything. She was not important enough to pursue but James was. And James could not take to the streets and disappear as she had; he could not run for his life; he could not hide. She stopped and put one hand to her forehead. Let him escape. With or without me. Let him live.

A valley, Nadia said. A good view.

Yes, yes! The young woman turned with her to look out over the valley. We all have good eyes here. From looking a long ways all the time. And there are some live trees! Also special are our boulders. You don't want this? Just two pennies.

No, I'm not hungry.

The young woman wore a worn canvas coat with a flannel lining and a heavy skirt with two pairs of woolen leggings and thick leather shoes. Her hair and eyes were black as carbon. She clasped her knees in the cold dawn. Clouds! she said. Rain! First I ever saw! Where you off to?

Nadia said, I am looking for the Laundromat. Nadia's little hat brim jittered in the wet breeze and far away at the edge of sight, in the great valley, were dully glittering mountains of what must be broken dishes rising up out of earth colors of walnut and umber and smoke drifting from the distant foothills textured with the thousands of living units and along the dry wash a few bare trees that seemed to be living yet from some secret source of water far below the surface.

It's on down there. The girl pointed. That's Crow Creek.

It's a beautiful view, said Nadia.

The young woman pushed the ends of scrap lumber farther into the fire. We had a poet laureate here in our neighborhood that made up a song about us, about the Crow Creek Valley, thirty-two verses, he said it over the pirate radio, but he was arrested.

Angela! An older woman leaned out of a glassless, sashless window up on the third story. What are you going on about?

She might think Nadia was some kind of inspector or spy, looking for signs of a pirate radio station. Nadia called up, Is Pamela still on crutches?

Yeah, for a couple of weeks, said the woman. She was somewhat mollified. They're going to show the wrecked train cars being dragged off. And now, who knows? Killing women live on TV. Maybe real dead bodies, real train wrecks. She pointed a finger at Angela. Look after that fire.

Angela handed Nadia the wedge of bannock.

Bye. Take it anyway. Bye.

It took a few minutes before Nadia was able to understand how the compass worked. She held it as she walked. She expected something to light up, she had hoped for a noise or a voice saying *You are headed north now, you don't have far to go. Turn right, turn left.* But it was silent. There were the letters *NSEW* and numbers on the decorative bevel and a central rosette of beautiful spikes and leaves.

The needle floated free and it was up to her to turn her body so that the needle slid around to the N. And then she was facing north. She stood with it in her hand and by the long shafts of sunlight stabbing through the cloud cover she saw that the sun was settling in the late-afternoon at west-northwest. The four directions were standing at the corners of the sky, the maharajas of the world. She and the inhabitants of this open valley of debris were tramping along some latitude and some longitude that crossed each other like a gunsight, looking for sanity and peace.

She came to a scrap-metal reduction yard with the repeated, fierce light of a reducing furnace and a little building with vending machines. The guard allowed her to go in. The bannock had barely touched her hunger.

Looks like you could use a bath, he said. Hey? Just go and stand out in the rain. He threw back his head and laughed.

She came away with a bottle of water, wasabi peas, and a pita wrap with some unnamed filling and the knowledge that she had sent a message to James as to where she was, if he were not arrested, if he could still access a computer.

She walked on toward the Northwest. Up and down the coast behind Lighthouse Island would be settlements of Primary workers or unofficial villages, savage hippies. A man named the Uncanny with some kind of talking egg and a man with a top hat and a demented bald man with an empty book made of wallpaper, a religious colony that sacrificed goats to the mountain gods. Her kind of universe, her kind of world. She ate as she plodded on, running down like some malfunctioning film clip.

Mountains of clothing and bedding, a cornucopia of discarded textiles. Scrappers packed up clothes and cheap quilts, stained sheets, tablecloths, pants, socks, and underwear in bales and strapped them tightly. Then heaps of broken furniture that people were binding up to sell for kindling. In the topmost twigs of the bare trees black-and-white birds teetered back and forth in the drizzle, occasionally lifting their wings to balance themselves and they called to her, *Nadia, Nadia, stop and rest.*

I can't, she said. There is no rest for the wicked.

CHAPTER 32

Nadia slept curled in the seat of a front-end loader among the mountains of scrap. The machine was abandoned, rusty; waiting for repairs, for a part. The rain had its own voice and spoke all night long in running streams, in a light tapping on the windshield, drips from the rusty arms. The bucket was filling with water like a rough chalice offered up. The next morning Nadia changed into the boy's pants in the biting, damp cold and filled her water bottles out of the bucket. She could not let James see her like this. How to talk her way into a Laundromat?

She asked a man picking through a heap of paper bales where the Laundromat was.

The man straightened up in his wet rags with a stack of cardboard in his hands; thin, addicted, larcenous. He gave Nadia a long considering stare from under a drooping rubberized hat brim. She was soaked through and a thin layer of sleet had rimed her hat brim and her shoulders and she was shaking, her lips blue.

Washateria right up there by the paper mill. They use the last rinse of the pulp. Good water.

She stood in line with about ten other women, shuffling forward over the sticky clay of the wet earth, pushing their baskets ahead of them. Above them on the hillside the great paper mill poured out steam and mechanical noises. Nadia's red shoes made sucking noises in the mud and she was shaking so much she could hardly hold on to her tote bag.

The girl attendants in their candy-striped uniforms kept their eyes on Nadia, the crazed homeless person with no ID who had forgotten her pills. Your pills! Your pills! One of the girls had said in a loud voice. Your medication!

You mean the blue ones? said Nadia, with large empty eyes.

Whatever!

A woman in a bright headscarf who stood behind her in the line said, Oh let her in, let her in. Come on, just do it. Two young women laughed at Nadia and elbowed each other.

The girl paused over her form and everyone in the line sighed and kicked their baskets. They were standing out in the rain and were dripping and cold. The girl said, Yes, but what gerrymander are you from?

Dogtown Towers, said Nadia, and put a knuckle to her mouth. I think. I forget where I am.

That's Gerrymander Eleven, said the woman. Just let her in.

And so they had allowed her in and marked down on the form that she was indigent. Nadia walked into the main room where a TV shouted out an exercise program and several women were doing dance moves, and felt the hot air in her face, and fainted.

It was as if someone had opened a drain inside her and her consciousness all poured away. She never knew where her mind went at that time. Her joints came unstrung and the dirty floor rushed up at her face as if the whole building had tilted.

When she woke up, the woman in the flowered headscarf was sitting beside the old couch where she lay and was holding a pottery cup of something hot and sweet. There was some kind of a big torn quilt thrown over her and she felt dangerously weak. This was frightening because she had to go on, she had to.

Drink it, the woman said. She had Oriental eyes and small hands. Sugar. Good for you.

The air was warm and steamy and the whole building vibrated from the washers and dryers. Rain splattered the windows. Now the big television in its wooden chassis roared with some kids' program. The candy stripers were watching it nervously, afraid that another execution might be announced in front of the children. But it presented a jolly world of flat colors; animated spoons did headstands, a wastebasket danced some kind of cha-cha, a tiny pink Buddy car did wheelies and a group of children watched it all, still as death.

Thank you, she said. Nadia lifted her hand but it fell back of its own accord. In a minute, she said.

My name is Bing, the woman said. What's yours?

Nadia hesitated and then said, Prissy McGillis.

Bing said, So how many names is that now?

Nadia sat up and managed, after a slight struggle, to drink down the cup of hot sugary water. A lot, she said, and smiled. Do you collect for old man Gallegos?

Yes. Midnight Cowboy Theater man. Bing laughed. Right. I do your clothes. Bing shook out Nadia's tote. Eww, she said. They give you a homeless dress. Give me what you have on.

The homeless dress was almost like a prison uniform but she didn't care, there weren't going to be any Forensics officers coming in here, she didn't think. Nadia was happy to lie unstrung on the couch and watch the clothing shoot through the huge wire-screen tubes overhead, blown out of the dryers and onto the sorting tables. She was watching for telltale signs that hers were coming out of the dryers. The first sign would be her red canvas shoes with the black polka dots galloping along down the tube, one after another. It was noisy and clean and warm. The giant washing machines whirled and shuddered in a storm of clothing. Outside the great heavy rains had begun, and soon all would be changed, changed utterly.

Bing ate sunflower seeds and said. The showers are back there. If you are indigent they have to let you take a shower for free. Rules are rules.

Oh, thanks, said Nadia.

You need my daughter walk you back there? Hey, girl, Lia, come here!

No, said Nadia. I'm okay.

Nadia stood for a long time in the shower, gripping the soap basket to stay upright. The cubicle was made of warped beaverboard and the slats were slimy with soap but she didn't care; the water was almost clear, and it was hot, and she scrubbed her thick, short hair until it was a mass of lather, rinsed it, toweled it nearly dry with the thin gray towel.

And so, said Bing, regarding Nadia with her long black eyes. She handed Nadia some sunflower seeds. Bing's hands were very small but wide, heavy with muscle. She had tapered fingers and perfect nails. Do you know where you are now? She asked this in a low voice.

Nadia said, also in a near whisper, Yes, I'm here. She cracked the seeds between her teeth.

You are going on somewhere, said Bing.

Yes. Nadia watched the tubes overhead. A red canvas shoe came clumping down along with flying pieces of clothing. Her shirt, her brassiere and underpants. She said, There's my clothes.

It's raining out there, said Bing. A little snow like salt coming down too. You need warm clothes. I talk to the candy girl.

And so after Nadia retrieved her clothes from the sorting table they allowed her to look in the storage room behind the washers, where there were clothes people had left behind when they had been taken away, arrested, forgot them because they were drunk. Bing shouted at the attendant, If they are not for people like this homeless crazy woman, for who then? Eh?

In the storage room, which was where the candy stripers also drank their tea and ate their lunches, Nadia was delighted to find a heavy charcoal-colored wool coat, striped leggings, and lavender wool gloves inside the pockets of the coat. In a cupboard she came across three vials of Kero-Light and a folded square of some kind of plasticized material. She shoved the small things in her tote bag and pulled on the heavy coat and leggings. A good haul.

Thank you, said Nadia. She took Bing's hand. Thank you.

Bing said, Now, you, think about this, I scrap dishes. Find me some good dishes, no nicks, I pay you dimes. Bing affected that sort of pidgin English in which independent women traders always spoke. You could use some dimes. You buy good fry bread from Noria, just down by the dishes.

Yes, yes, I will.

Where are you going, Priss?

To find the love of my life, said Nadia. Who lives behind the North Wind.

The program switched to *Empress of the Golden Plains*. The adults sat down on couches with children on their laps to watch as the empress discovered a traitor in her midst, her favorite general: Banu Shan, a courageous, even noble general who had never wavered in his loyalty to his beautiful empress. Banu Shan stood before the empress alight with love for her, crushed by shame. Nadia fell back on the couch. Oh man, she said. He's innocent. That's so unfair.

Do you think he's gone over?

Over? said Nadia. To the enemy?

Yeah, the ones with the nose rings.

I don't know, really, Nadia said. Hard to keep up.

At last the program closed with the empress lifting a goblet full of an unknown liquid to her lips. Slow fade. An insect crept slowly down the face of the lighted screen, testing its luminous surface with long and thready antennae as if desperately trying to reach General Banu Shan. The insect's antennae sent out a questing signal backward through time and sideways in space, all the way to the steppes of Central Asia, to a time before the seas of grass were covered in cities and slums; before, when the Aral Sea existed and held out its miraculous reflecting surface from dawn to dusk and its shores were crowded with wildfowl and lone riders bearing sincere messages gazed out over the restless water while the wind whispered at their backs. *Banu Shan, your enemies in court have told the empress that you have gone over to the Rla's! Banu Shan! The liar is named Asdan, go, kill him, save your honor!*

The insect crawled on down the screen leg by leg and at last one of the children squashed it in a smear of fluids and a clutter of disconnected legs and so the message was forever lost. Somewhere in the realm of the imagination Banu Shan is shackled to his horse's breast-collar and is led away by the Household Guard.

Nadia walked down to the riverbed again, confident in the pouring rain, with the plasticized material over her head. The magpies rode the tossing bare limbs of brush and looked at her as if they had been expecting her.

Nadia, Nadia, do not lose heart, it will not be much farther.

She came to the dish heaps. The column of rain had swept on past and now the sleet returned. Nadia felt pinhead grains falling on her face. A large truck backed up and disgorged a roaring slide of more dishes and pottery. Far ahead was a building from which came a deafening, smashing noise. In it they were grinding up dishes for some use she could not imagine. She joined the hundreds of scrappers clinking among the breakage, slowly, turning over dishes and drained of strength.

She pulled at the corner of a cardboard box sticking out of the broken ceramics. It took her a long time to work it loose. Her lavender gloves were now full of nicks and tiny slashes. She pulled out the packing carefully. As the shredded paper scattered at her feet, an eye rolled out.

The box was full of glass eyes. Blue ones, gray ones, dark brown, black, hazel, and mild brown. They stared, naked and astonished, out at the valley of scrap and Nadia quickly slipped them into her coat pocket. The world was full of people in long draped blankets and cloaks among the broken dishes and in the distant sky a thin thread of oily smoke and a hang glider. The valley of Crow Creek was filling with water. It ran down between apartment buildings and splashed into the old drainage bed, the bed itself now a roaring torrent of live water, and the only bridge over it was a two days' walk behind her.

At sunset Bing came walking down the road with a handcart. It rolled along smoothly on high wire-spoked wheels that left wandering tracks in the mud. Two women walked with her, the young women who had laughed at Nadia at the Laundromat. They had rinds of light snow on their headscarves and stared at her as Bing counted out seven old dimes into Nadia's hand for five plates and three bowls, all good.

Bing regarded Nadia with her bright and ageless eyes. And now where you are go?

To the electronics waste.

Lucky you are on right side of river. Now, people have to think about, do I have to cross the river? New. She laughed.

How far is it?

One day walk. You give the guard five dimes.

Okay. Nadia knew it was time to walk on but she was reluctant to leave the company of Bing and her daughters. So she said, How did you start collecting, Bing?

One way and another. I was a color expert for C&E. For television sets, clothes. I did color suits and ties for people who say "studies show." Somebody wanted my job. But! I saw it coming. These my daughters, we got away. Long story. My cousin, she made it to the Northwest. She was a water tester. Bing paused. And you too are running. I know.

How did she get there? Nadia clasped her hands nervously. How?

I get one letter. She was on a train with chemicals, then snuck off, started walking. She says people up there speak by holding an egg and they have to ive in concrete prisons by the sea. But then, no more letters. Bing shrugged. And so you looking for somebody you love. Behind the North Wind.

Nadia turned up her wool coat collar. Yes, yes, I am. Do you do fortunes?

Yes. But I don't do fortunes and these hard looks into the other world for free.

Well, I'll give you back some dimes. How many dimes do you want?

I have lots of dimes.

So then Nadia reached into her pocket and brought out two clattering eyes. She held them out.

Take whichever one you want.

Aha! Oh, wonderful! Excellent!

Bing peered into Nadia's cupped hand and chose the mild brown one. She took out a handkerchief and wrapped it and put it away in one of her jacket pockets. She sat down on a small barrel that had fallen from some truck at the side of the road and put her hands over her face.

Nadia watched her. She said, Are you . . .

Ssshhhh! Both girls shushed her at the same time.

After several minutes Bing looked up and said, You met him in a hotel. It was made of glass. He could walk then. It was in the other world. Now you are coming together in this world. She wiped her hands together There. That's a good message. I made good contact. It was the eye

Nadia caught her sleeve and said, And so now I need words of wisdom.

Bing laughed. You want too much.

I don't care said Nadia, and then she said, What's too much?

All right. Bing reached out and patted Nadia on the shoulder and the light snow fell from her coat shoulder in flakes. I will tell you this,

Prissy, what I have learned, poor girl, poor homeless girl. What I have learned is that if you live long enough, all the old clichés become true wisdom. Those old sayings we laugh at when we are young. We become fifty years old, surprise, we see that they were all true. They grow up so fast, many hands make light work, there is no place like home, one man's trash is another man's treasure, love is blind.

Nadia passed an old woman who stood at the roadside, throwing leftover grains and biscuit crumbs from a bowl in broad gestures of great generosity, beautiful sweeping gestures. The birds slanted through the early-morning air and slid their dark legs in front of them as they landed, bearing to earth all they had learned of the upper skies and the birth of snow.

CHAPTER 33

E-waste trucks grumbled past. They spewed pink mud. It looked like paint thinner. The rubbish they carried was all square; monitors stared out at the nebulous day with lifeless but deep glass eyes. Tendrils of curling wire spilled out between the racks and she saw dangling mouses like little fists. On one she saw a digital clock. It was in a steel chassis with curling brass inlays, ornate and battered. It was wedged between a broken printer and a stack of flat screens. It said, *5 P.M. October 31 2198 Clouds and occasional drizzle.*

Maybe the clock was out of order, maybe it announced times and years that did not exist. But then again maybe it *was* accurate; maybe it was some sort of atomic clock steadily enumerating the advance of time and the burdensome accumulation of years. Nadia decided to believe it. To believe that she was in the valley of electronic scrap, on a real earth turning on its axis, in the current of time, at home in the galaxy. A local habitation and an hour. "I am time, grown old to destroy the world." She wanted the clock. She would say to James, Here I am, on November first, sometime in the twenty-second century. The Day of the Dead.

He would say, Give me your hand. I will be well. All will be well.

There is an island in the North Pacific waiting for us. We will be devoted to each other and to the forests and the orcas, the drifting fogs and the blue, dashing jays, to the great restless North Pacific that eats men and ships and airplanes, but not us. Not us.

At the guarded entrance to the e-waste heaps Nadia lined up with about fifteen or so people. The line moved forward alongside the trucks. People spoke together in alarmed voices about the sleety snow. A group of people had crowded into the guard shack against regulations and pressed close to a TV screen. Suddenly someone shouted, No! No!

What's going on? A woman beside her called to those in the guard shack. Is it another execution? The woman clutched her hands together in alarm as if the television had become dangerous to look at, dangerous to see.

The Facilitator's been arrested!

They made the confused noises of an alarmed crowd, spontaneous cries, turning to one another, the erratic light of the screen jumping across their wet faces.

Nadia waited in line, standing on tiptoe to see the guard with his handheld card reader. And so the beautiful egghead was arrested, all the more reason to get out of here as fast as possible. He stood under a porch cobbled together of wood and canvas. He was very young and nodded without cease.

Yeah, yeah, go on, okay, go ahead. The guard waved people on. Then it was her turn. He took the stripped blister card from Nadia and turned it over to one side and then the other.

What's this? he said.

Nadia dropped the plasticized material from her head. Individual issue, she said. Her lips felt stiff for some reason. Just slide it. Nadia placed the five dimes in a neat stack on the windowsill and then tucked her hand in a coat pocket.

The guard did not look at the money but put her blister card into the card reader and waited. The black screen said something to him in bright green text, and he read it and shrugged. He kept turning back to glance into the guard shack at the TV where people cried out, I can't believe it!

Wendy Hu, he said. I am to issue you a permit, one time only.

I want that clock, she said. May I have that clock?

The truck driver looked up with flat screens in either hand and the drizzle running from his canvas hat.

I can trade you this for it. She held out two eyes: a blue and a hazel. That would leave her with only one, a black one.

Hey! The truck driver reached out for the eyes. It's a deal. Hey, never seen these before. A Continuity Man will pay a mint for them. He handed the clock to her. We're supposed to account for everything but with this news the Facilitator is being arrested nobody's going to have their heads on straight. He smiled. This is a time for theft and flight and so on, got to play the cards as they lay, right?

Mountains of wrecked printers, computer towers and monitors, old television screens. Many of them had wooden chassis that were now splintered and broken. In the distance smoke rose from a mound of burning plastic refuse. Sellers and buyers, most of them probably black market, fingered through the piles of components in the stalls. I need capacitors, a buyer said. One hundred Ohm speaker parts. Resistors.

This is all I got.

Nadia hurried past dim figures picking at cell phones with needle-nosed pliers and others cooking circuit boards over charcoal fires to drain out the dregs of gold hidden within them. People in blackened rags smashed toner cylinders, broke them open with wooden mallets and dumped the remaining powder into steel barrels and then with a sort of lighthearted jollity flung the broken cylinders into great bins.

They did this under a shelter made of plastic pipe and canvas. It had originally been for shade but now the people worked under it for protection from the fine drizzle of rain and snow.

In the puddles forming at the edge of the canvas where the water dripped, beautiful marbled designs swirled in black and taupe as if the ink and toner were runoff from all the books that should have been written but never were, all pouring out in a discouraged and continual weeping.

Excuse me, excuse me, Nadia said.

Two human figures paused and looked at her. They were a midnight people, wildly busy, dark as anthracite.

I am looking for the truck bays.

A boy ran out and took her hand. He imprinted his hand on hers. He pointed with an inky forefinger. Straight ahead, lady, he said. You go that way.

The drivers of the square van with license plate number GAN-22VP1–928LES were listening to Big Radio. Nadia told them her name and they pointed to the back. She climbed into the back of the van and sat among restored and renovated electronics, all of them bundled in shrink wrap. Water ran into the cab through a window that seemed to be permanently stuck open. Written on the side in ornate gold lettering: *Fremont Exclusive Delivery.*

Don't drink it, said the driver.

Okay, I won't drink it, the relief driver in the passenger seat said. I never saw it rain in fifteen years. Then it just drizzled a little.

You're not allowed to drink it. It's called incidental water and the TV goddamn expert health people say it's full of rat hair and bird shit.

I said I wouldn't, didn't I?

They drove on through pastry-colored scrubland. The highway was excellent: two-lane asphalt with a yellow stripe down the middle, jumping with raindrops. Only a few other vehicles traveled the road and on either side the borrow ditches overflowed into the fields. There was a strong iced wind outside and its song was a signature motif of some larger, worldwide change in the weather, change in the sea.

The windshield wipers, never used before, jammed and rusty, seemed to be willing to wipe once but when they were up they wouldn't come down again. They stopped midwindshield. The driver stopped and got out. He found a length of cord somewhere and tied it to the passenger-side wiper, opened the passenger window, and handed the cord to the relief driver.

Now yank that back down, he said. It goes up on its own and you yank it back down.

With the window open? And me getting rained on?

You want me to go off the road?

Well, shit.

They drove on past great checkerboards of fields that had turned into shallow lakes. There were dead cornstalks and river and creek drainages plated with concrete and spilling all they garnered into the cornrows. Agricultural workers labored in the cold and the sleet; they rode puffing steam tractors and sat on ATVs pulling a machine with revolving blades that struck the standing cornstalks into shining fragments and sprays of rainwater. They stood on flatbeds stacking sacks of beans that those on the ground heaved up to them. They were emaciated, they were criminals and political arrestees, water thieves, color saboteurs with a crust of snow on their shoulders and hats and backs.

Some had been important agency people with cats and water features and they were now serfs. They had got caught at some minor infraction and somebody wanted their job. Nadia had been raised to think the prisoners deserved whatever they got but that notion had now, after her month in prison, disappeared entirely from her head.

Mountain peaks loomed to the left like white lamps in the moving, queasy clouds. They passed an enormous industrial plant of some kind. Great steel vessels many stories high veined with complex piping and from chimneys steam poured into the misty air in confused plumes.

The whole area was cordoned off by chain-link fencing that appeared hairy with the sagebrush and tumbleweed caught in it. Trucks loaded with workers drove through a gate as harassed guards tried to verify the numbers of prisoners exiting; sign here, worklists checked.

That's corn products, said the driver. Starches and syrups and oil and sheep food. They steal a lot of sheep food and syrup out of there. He watched the truck full of prisoners pull out behind them and speeded up to outdistance it. They'll get good rations there.

Right, said Nadia, from among the shrink-wrapped e-stuff. She wondered what the prisoners did with stolen sheep food. They ate it, of course. Nadia looked out at the landscape hoping to see sheep or any kind of animal. The world unrolled out of her imagination or from some deep source. She pressed her nose against the glass. Mountains, rain.

It snows up in the mountains, said the driver. To the west. There's a glacier up there. He pointed to the left-hand horizon and Nadia held out the compass to check out what he said and he was right, it was the western horizon. And then in the summertime it melts and runs down and it makes a lake behind the Fremont Glacier dam.

What if it overflowed? said Nadia. It's actually raining now. It could overflow. She drank down her second and last bottle of water.

Well, then we'd all drown, said the relief driver.

Now they were cruising through what appeared to be a small city of barracks, row after row, two stories high, mud splattered up to the windowsills. Thousands of people were getting into the backs of trucks, long lines of trucks. They unloaded sacks, transported machine parts, hung out stained clothing on clotheslines, or just walked along in a slow mechanical step, all in the wet, driven snow. Nadia looked into their faces. Could she possibly know any of these prisoners?

Then she imagined her own photograph, taken from a security camera screen capture, tacked up in the entryway of every guard shack and office. MISSING AND WANTED, ESCAPEE NADIA STEPAN AT LARGE. Then the trial, then the stack of sandbags.

Crowds of prisoners stood at the sides of the road to let them pass and the landscape was now a flat sheet of running water. The ditches were overflowing, running across the road.

The driver stood on the brakes. A guard was in the middle of the asphalt ahead, waving an orange flag. They stopped and sat and listened to the sleety rain drumming on the van roof as a long marching column of men and women crossed the road in the hundreds. They were all old-looking, including people who were clearly young. Water deprivation, dehydration. Some were scooping up ditch water with their water bottles, and the guards yelled, pushed, knocked the bottles out of their hands but some prisoners were fighting back.

I don't like this, said the relief driver. They're going to find those radio parts.

They wouldn't even know what they were, said the driver.

It was chaotic. The column wavered, fell apart, was pulled together again. Prisoners licked snow from their arms as they marched on. Then Nadia could hear loud shouts and the column broke and became a mob and a crowd surging around without direction and then she heard a sharp crack.

That was a firearm, said the driver. He shifted around in his seat, swallowing. It was a rifle.

Go on get out of here, said the relief driver.

I can't just drive through them.

A flying wedge of guards burst through the chaos with two prisoners in their grasp and flung them down on the bare dirt beside the road and as the two men tried to scramble to their feet the guards shot them in the head. One of the men on the ground sprang galvanically to his feet with blood bursting out of the exit wound in his cheekbone as if he had found himself on a red-hot stove and the guard lifted his revolver and shot again.

Don't look, said the driver. He stepped slowly on the gas. Don't look at them. Look straight ahead.

Nadia kept her eyes on the two-lane asphalt with her hat tipped over her eyes. She said some kind of prayer or verbal supplication to the unearthly powers that were transparent and, hopefully, attentive, and shrank back into the farthest recesses of the van. Her heel struck a shrink-wrapped packet that began to emit sounds and flashes. A solemn voice that said *The Trials of Fardan! You are in City III.* Nadia threw her tote bag over it and after a few moments it shut up. As they drove on they passed bodies by the roadside in prisoner gray, being rained on.

CHAPTER 34

At nightfall they came to a tiny shack by the roadside, where a green-and-yellow flag cracked stiffly in the wind. It was some kind of roadside eating place for truckers and van drivers. Other vans were parked in front. It was bitterly cold. Nadia saw three red-cheeked children dressing up a donkey in a ragged ball cap and a shawl for some kind of play or drama in which the donkey was a royal personage. They wiped the fly specks out of his eyes and he yawned. And as he yawned a lamp was suddenly lit inside the café as if the light had flown out of his mouth

A woman shouted, Come in here! It's cold out there! And the children snatched the cap and the shawl from the donkey and ran inside and the donkey stood bereft and naked in his fur.

All through the dim plains and up the sides of the foothills were house lights and rows of dim barracks lights.

Nadia went to stand beside the donkey and took in its wet, grassy odor. She was in need of reassurance, consolation. Her heart was still pounding from the terrible scene in the work camp. The woman came out of the little diner. The snow had changed back to rain and in the distance was a deep rolling thunder.

Nadia said, Can I touch him? Her?

Yeah, sure. You better come and eat. Him. It's a him.

Okay. I just wanted to touch him. Nadia put out her sodden lavender glove. What's his name? For a moment she thought the woman might say his name was Homer.

Sparrow. He's got all his papers and stuff in case you're a spy for the animal agency. You can check his tattoo number.

No, no, said Nadia. Not at all.

Nadia patted the donkey on his lower neck as the dark settled in on this high-altitude agro-world. *Cuando, en el crepúsculo del pueblo, Platero y yo entramos, ateridos por la oscuridad . . .*

Were you, at one time, Homer? Nadia said. Have you changed names, become somebody else? She reached across the great chasm of creation to stroke his neck. "In the very dawn of the city we enter, Platero and I, frightened, in the dark."

In the diner Nadia spooned up a clear, rich soup with slivers of crisps in it.

Those are tortillas, the woman said. We're different here. This ain't the global culture. She wadded up her skirt hem in her hands and watched Nadia with a distrustful expression.

They drove on and she woke up when the world was gray with dawn and the windows were running with drops. She felt better. An entire twenty-four hours of rest, and the food at the roadside inn. The rain came down in sheets. She found the little flashlight in her tote bag and shone it around; all in order, including the familiar dread in the face of authority. *Fear the masters, grovel, O churl,* said the electronic device. Nadia jammed it under a bulky keyboard and it fell silent again.

We got to go through the gate. It's where the higher-ups live. Where we're delivering this stuff including you.

Nadia said, Good.

It's restricted for the higher-ups. A million square acres. The driver put the van in gear and they moved slowly forward in the line on their spoked wheels. The guards were making people get out of each vehicle and stand in the rain, checking ID, going through bags and boxes.

Nadia said, Acres are already square. You must mean a million square miles.

Exactly, I knew that.

The guards wore crisp loden-green uniforms and brass buttons on heavy overcoats. They had billed caps with a lot of brass insignia that Nadia had never seen. It was as if they were officials of some other country or nation. Their breath poured out in clouds and a blue-and-white-checkered flag floated in artificial light, and in the shadows of its folds it glowed red from the light of the red zingers flashing down the fenceline. The flag bore a coat of arms in its center and despite the rain it flapped out with every gust of wind.

An officer came to them with a cold expressionless face and they got out. She stood holding the canvas piece over her head while he took the blister card back from her hand. He put it into a handheld reader and for a second she wondered if she were going to be stopped here and handcuffed, imprisoned, beaten, shot. Abandoned here in some alien neighborhood called Wyoming, striking off on foot through the endless villages of shacks.

You're good, said the guard. He handed the card back to her.

The houses stood far apart from one another, surrounded by areas of grass, tall thin trees, fresh air, silence. They blazed with electric lights and the lights illuminated the downpour so that the rain looked like flying wet tissue. There were no banners with Awareness Months, no billboards.

They drove on winding streets and pulled into a huge basement or carport. She had dozed off again.

The driver said, Here you are. They unloaded her and her tote bag and some packages of e-goods. The van doors slammed. She watched as a pair of great doors slid back with a repeated snicking noise and the van drove on out. She picked up her tote bag and walked over to a door and knocked. When there was no answer she opened it.

The house was empty of people. She walked down a long hallway on a thick carpet. One room smelled strongly of wood smoke and cold ashes and in it she found a stone recess with burnt ends of logs in it and realized it was a fireplace. She turned away and saw someone approaching her but it was only herself in a mirror with an ornate frame. She looked drawn and thin and the colors of her clothes outweighed her. A burglar in a bent straw hat and a look of desperation.

She came to a large kitchen and saw herself reflected long and strange in the steel refrigerator door. She opened the door to find packaged food in plastic containers with snap lids. There were bottles of Fremont Glacier Water and she took three and drank one of them down and put the other two in her tote. She ran her hand along granite countertops and touched the leaves of genuine green plants growing from inset slots and a polished wood breakfront on which was stacked a pile of damask napkins. There were porcelain sinks and shining faucets. Shelves of wineglasses. A tall water tower, a tube of clear plastic with the daily allocation but she thought, *They don't need it here. It's just because they like to have it. It's pretty.*

She came upon a room full of books and long windows with opaque glass. She went to the glass and pressed her ear against it but there was no sound or sight except the figure of a cat pressed against the outside and when it heard her it mewed. On a table she saw a framed photograph. It was Thin Sam Kenobi, in an aviator's uniform, young and handsome. He wore no eyeglasses.

She reached up and touched the photo and her eyes filled with water. The cat mewed again.

She came upon on an old lady in a bedroom. The old woman was sitting up in bed in the middle of a froth of lacy pillows and around her hung a canopy of net with butterflies woven into it that shone in the early-morning light. The light lay across the floor in a pale bar. The old woman turned her head toward Nadia. She had fine eyes. Large and gray as rainwater and still beautiful.

Yes? the old woman said.

How are you today? Nadia said it in a cheery nurselike voice.

You're not Heather.

No, I'm Wendy!

The old woman nodded. Yes, yes, Heather is dead.

I'm so sorry for your loss. I'm her replacement.

Nadia walked into the room and began to straighten things on a rich, glossy sideboard where there were photographs and a book of crossword puzzles. To one side a keyboard on a spindly-legged table.

I killed her, said the old woman. She stared into memories, confused and jumbled, that darted unrestrained in the air in front of her. No, no, Farrell killed her.

Well, Nadia said. I am sorry to hear it. What did James say about it?

Nadia took up a tissue from the woman's bedside and began to dust the keyboard. As she dusted she must have inadvertently hit some key or button, because the keyboard lit up and burst into "Oklahoma!" The volume was terrific.

Oh, "Oklahoma!" cried the old woman. My favorite thing! She sat up and then fell back again among the pillows. Nadia punched wildly at buttons and the keyboard broke into another song.

Oh, 'Beautiful Dreamer"! cried the old woman. She sat up and then fell back again. My favorite song!

The noise was overwhelming. Somebody was going to come and investigate. Nadia would be taken away in thumbless mittens to die in the dryers. Another hit on a button produced an oom-pa-pa rhythm, loud as a parade. Nadia felt as if she were falling into a lightless well of musical accidents, pursued downward by tubas and unseen chords and virtual xylophones. She got down on her knees and jerked the cord from its plug.

Oh, silence, said the old woman in a low voice. My favorite thing. She lay quietly in her pillows with her eyes closed.

Nadia tried to breathe evenly. Well, now, what are we doing today? she said. She picked up a day-by-day pill case from the bedside table with a shaking hand. Let's see. You've had your meds this morning. Nadia put it back down and wondered who had given the old woman her medications. Should I go and ask James?

You have to go help him in the pool. James is in the pool.

All right. Nadia patted the old woman on the arm. It was as frail and brittle as white candy. Where is the pool?

Why don't you know?

I'm new.

You're not Heather.

No, Nadia said. Heather is dead. Farrell killed her.

Farrell. Farrell. The old woman waved one hand. He missed his dental appointment. These avaricious tooth people.

Yes, but I have to go help James in the pool, said Nadia. But I have forgotten how to get to the pool. She smiled and fluffed a pillow. You have to tell me how to get to the pool.

I used to get in the pool. Now it's so much trouble. They lift you out and you're all wet.

Yes, it's inconvenient. Nadia felt panic rising. If I go out the door, do I turn left or right?

Left, said the old woman. To the kitchen. Where's Brat Kitty? He's so spoiled.

I'll go find him, said Nadia. She bent down and picked up her tote bag and walked out of the room and turned left.

In the kitchen she assembled some things on the tray; cheeses from the huge steel refrigerator and a package of crackers, glasses, a bottle of wine. If she ran into somebody who asked her who she was she would say, I'm the new maid.

She turned from one side of the kitchen to the other. No stairs. She went back out into the hallway, the opposite way from which she had come, and there was an entrance to the pool, the word written on the door, and stairs beyond.

CHAPTER 35

The stairway was of the rosy Crow Creek granite with recessed lighting. She ran down broad stone steps, a wheelchair ramp alongside. At the bottom she came to the pool.

James floated in the polished water with bright spikes of light all around him. The intense lighting flooded the walls with water radiance and his wet hands sparkled as they stroked the surface. The air was steamy with humidity and all was in rich and somber tones. Artificial plants held up skillfully designed leaves.

Nadia stood with her battered tote bag, her sagging hat, her striped leggings, and her shawl in the oceanic light. James drifted in the water, his legs white and unmanned, his gray eyes regarding her. Nadia felt like a mail-order bride with the wrong name who had been sent to the wrong address. The silk plants dripped slowly and his wheelchair was backed against the wall as if it had been accused of some crime.

James?

Nadia, he said. He gripped the bars of the ladder. Nadia.

She dropped her tote bag and hurried on the slippery tiles. She set the tray on a glass-topped table. The bottle toppled and broke in a spray of glass and wine.

James. I'm here.

He closed his eyes and pressed his forehead against the steel tubing of the ladder. I died several times over, he said. You're here.

Nadia flung off the coat and shawl, the striped leggings and the lavender gloves, her soggy hat, and then the disreputable tunic and skirt. She kicked off her red polka-dot shoes.

Before he could say anything she splashed into the water in her underwear. Her thin arms were like sticks. She touched bottom and stood upright in a burst of spray. She stretched out her hands and he took them and pulled her through the water with his powerful arms and gripped her body in a kind of seizure. He took her hair in one hand and kissed her mouth and her forehead and shoulders. Xenia, he said. The Lost Princess of Lighthouse Island.

Neither one of them said anything but only listened to the slight booming sounds of the water galloping along the sides of the pool. The water was warm and the air vents overhead made slow breathing noises. She was caught in his iron grip and his muscular chest and arms were like pistons and it seemed she could not take him in enough, his gray eyes and the plain face.

I was helpless to do anything but wait. He said this into her dripping hair. Wait, wait, wait. You made it. You're here.

I talked to the elderly lady upstairs. Who is she? How long do we have?

Not long. He put his hands on each side of her wet head and looked into her eyes.

She held on to his forearms. Can you walk now?

A few steps. My brother will fly us north. My baggage and the equipment are stored at the airstrip.

Won't Forensics know?

Not so far.

He kissed her again and she felt as if she would dissolve in the miraculous water that surrounded them and held them up in an effortless floating. The way water talked and spoke and the way shelled hearts opened in high tides. Finally she said, So much has happened.

He wiped her hair back from her eyes and stared at her face.

There will be time to talk later. We have to move. But still he touched her face and eyes as they drifted in the lighted water. The jumping waves threw planes of light across the recessed ceiling as they held each other, dangerously close to some irrevocable deadline.

She said, You knew my father. Thin Sam was my father.

No. Your father's brother. That's my mother upstairs. Is she saying I killed the maid?

Heather? Nadia still held to his arms.

Yes.

She says Farrell did it.

God. Who knows what happens to our souls when we fall into senility? He pressed his forehead against hers and closed his eyes. You can't know how I felt, waiting for you. Hoping to not be arrested before you arrived, hoping you would get through to here, unable to go and find you for fear of being taken myself. Unable even to run were the agency officers to come after me. I would rather die than live like this.

We're not going to die.

I know. It's all all right.

You're a friend. The only friend I have in the world.

Surely not.

I wouldn't lie to you.

He smiled. Let's go.

She climbed out of the water by the pool ladder and when she turned on her bare, white feet to help him, James impatiently waved her away. He pulled himself up with his thick forearms, and then stepped carefully and precisely on the grainy step and stood up holding the ladder rails. His legs were mere pipes of bone and he was pale as the water. Nadia clasped her hands to keep from reaching for him but his eyes were not on her but on his wheelchair with its prosthetic look and its grim spokes.

He clasped the handholds for a moment and then with a silent concentration took four steps to where his clothes lay over a chair. He leaned against the wall to dress himself and then sat in the wheelchair and pulled on thick socks and new heavy shoes. Then for a moment he dropped his head back.

Come. Put your bag on the back, there's a small shelf and an elastic tie. Get dressed. Hurry, you should never have jumped into the pool, hurry.

What about your mother?

My brother will take her south. The Facilitator has been forced out and storms are upon us. The confusion works in our favor.

His hands grasped the wheel rims and he turned and rolled up the wheelchair ramp with Nadia running behind him.

As they came to the kitchen with its amazing refrigerator they heard low voices and laughter. James stopped his right-hand wheel as they came through the door.

Two Forensics men were making sandwiches. They smiled at James and Nadia with a kind of mechanical delight. Tissue engineering made their eyes move in jerks and their faces were artificial with elaborate tattoos. They were big strong men and they smelled like snow and wool.

Hi! said one. Hi!

The other one said, We'll just make up these sandwiches here and then we'll get you arrested. We'll need your signature. He slapped mustard on a slice of brown bread. This is good roast beef. We'll need your signature.

Nadia grasped the door frame, her mouth stupidly open. Far down the hall she heard a newscast going on and on and briefly the face of a maid or attendant who was most likely Heather appeared in the hall beyond the kitchen door with her mouth in a round horrified O. Then she disappeared.

Very well, said James. But I will want a lawyer. He shifted in the wheelchair to get at his coat pocket. I have a right to a lawyer.

No problemo, said one. They began to wrap their sandwiches in waxed paper and they were all easy authority and threat. One of them said, This woman is Sendra Bentley. She'll have to sign the arrest form agreeing to official detention, and a copy goes back to Book Dump.

Nadia stood with one hand on the wheelchair push-handle. She thought for one second of fleeing alone out of the kitchen and down the hall and out into the luxurious world of Fremont Glacier Estates. Instead she looked around for something to throw, a kitchen knife, anything. She took up a framed photograph and threw it in a slicing motion straight at the man on the left, and at the same time James's hand appeared from his coat pocket with the dart gun. The photograph hit the shelf of wineglasses, they shattered, and he shot one of the agents in the eye and the other in the neck.

The dart gun made only a light pop. The darts were propelled by CO_2 cartridges and were loaded with four hundred milligrams of a conotoxin derivative that left both the Forensics men paralyzed on the kitchen floor surrounded by bread and mustard and broken plates and thrown pieces of roast beef, glass splinters. Their lips worked as the neurotoxin shut down their breathing. Light foams of blood and sputum bubbled out of their mouths. The taller lay on one side still as a mannequin making long snoring noises and the dart wobbled where it had lodged just to one side of the pupil.

James wheeled his chair next to the head of the taller one and reached down and grasped the snake-eye earbud and wrenched it out. As he did so a long string of tissue and blood came out with it, longer and longer, until he finally ripped it loose and flung it across the room like a loop of intestine. Blood spattered.

They'll be dead in an hour, said James. Time to go.

As they fled through the house, the electricity failed and the TV went silent.

CHAPTER 36

This is the end. We must come to the end. It can't go on forever, not like the endless soap opera of our dreams, that go on and on every night of our lives until we die. Then good-bye to the messy dreams of overpopulated rooms and brief, pointless conversations and darkened hallways. We are surprised and terrified by forks, by kitchen chairs, by falls down undefined spaces without bottoms, accused of actions that deserve the death penalty such as wearing white shoes after Labor Day, such as forgetting to fill the birdfeeder. Who stands in our defense? It is not about the birdfeeder.

—FACILITATOR BRIAN WEI

A DC-3 is a conveyance that leaves you wondering how human beings invented flight not to speak of the complexities of the flight deck: the hydraulics, the gear-flap activator, the throttle-prop mixture and fuel tank selector valves, as well as the overhead panel with its starting switches and radio gear and between the pilot and copilot seats a console with knobbed handles. And the man who has his hand on the controls, his eyes on the various instruments, the man who knows how to fly it, who invented him? What cunning hand or eye.

Nadia is unimportant among all these people, a girl whose only accomplishment is having memorized whole libraries of old poetry, whose only occupation has been evading the authorities, whose only distinction is that James loves her. He trusts her. She is a nobody. She has an eye in her coat pocket.

She stood at the edge of the long runway with her hands on the back of James's wheelchair. Small round clouds tumbled one over another at a low altitude, revolving, rushing away from something even more furious coming up behind them. She had never imagined she would be allowed on an airplane. She put one hand on her head to hold down her hat. The airplane's nose was in the air and its two motors socketed on the wings like giant biceps. It seemed blocky and trustworthy. Even if she died she wouldn't care. She would have been in flight over the earth itself, however briefly. In flight from killing and threats of being killed, airborne toward the unknown.

Farrell came running toward them, bent over, his earphones around his neck. He was dressed in a short flight jacket and khaki pants. He looked like James but stockier, his hair not so thick. A storm was stalking them in long, spectral columns.

Farrell said, We dragged them out and left them in a recycle pitch. My crew wanted to take the bodies and throw them out over Mount Fremont but I said we'd never get the door closed again. The dam is spewing overflow water at both ends. He turned to Nadia. You, Farrell said. He hooked his thumbs in his belt and stood in front of her. You talked him into this.

Farrell, said James. Stop. This is what I want. We're going to the island. James thrust himself about here and there in his seat. I never knew if I could do it if it came to it but I did.

For her, said Farrell. I've seen you fall all over yourself for a trollop before now. She's using you.

Nadia opened her mouth to say something. Then she realized it was a fight between brothers. She closed her mouth and tried to appear honest, competent, and resolute.

James said, You gave me a promise and I'm holding you to it. Do you hear me? He bent forward with his forearms on his thighs and his hands clasped so that his knuckles were white and the bitter, rainy wind beat at them. It brought the smell of aviation fuel and wet concrete and mud and distant snows. I said, do you hear me?

Yes, yes, I did, said Farrell. But it was a long time ago. If you want to die, it should be in a hospital.

There's a chance I'll live, said James. I've fallen in love. Both things can happen.

Farrell turned again to Nadia. You've seduced a sick man. A sick man in a wheelchair. When you get to Lighthouse Island you'll abandon him. You'll have got what you wanted.

Nadia bit her lip and tears started in her eyes.

James said, Farrell, I don't know what I can say to shut you up about this.

The medication will probably kill you.

I'm adjusting to it. What do I have to lose?

Your life.

Stay out of this, Farrell.

That is so untrue, said Nadia. Words were not enough but she said them anyway. What you said was totally untrue.

Farrell turned away.

The engines were roaring, the props spun. The mechanics carried rifles. They laid down their weapons on a wooden pallet and threw down a flat ramp from the door in the fuselage. They unbolted one of the rear seats so they could place James in his wheelchair in the slot.

James said, What about Mother?

They are putting her aboard a Tekkna 22. Elliot and Bob Morely and Findlay, they came in on foot. I called them on the last call on the dedicated phone. Elliot got Findlay out of the interrogation center in the bucket of a front-end loader. They took the wall down. His wife committed suicide. Forensics may be organized enough to track our flight and then again maybe not.

James said, I release you from your promise if you want to find another pilot.

No. Farrell turned to Nadia and stared at her with his hands on his hips. She is not who she says she is.

You are wrong. James ran his fingers over the keypad. About people you are often stupidly, furiously wrong. Stick to your engines.

Farrell studied Nadia's face. She's a con artist.

Nadia turned up her coat collar and watched the fluctuating sky. She could do nothing else.

James said, Then don't take us.

Don't be stupid. I ask you once more to reconsider.

No.

Farrell crossed his arms and stared at the concrete. When he looked up his eyes were wet.

The airstrip was thirty-eight hundred feet, surfaced, and at the end where they waited to board stood hangars several stories high with engine shops and arc-welding bays, all made of steel and bowed like the old Quonset huts; inside were the echoes of shouting men. Here and there smaller planes strained against their chocks and their un-locked propellers spun in the wind. The runway arrowed down be-tween houses. There was no margin for error. Nadia heard motors and shouting and once, gunfire. The tanker truck sat with its hose in the fuel tanks of the DC-3 and the air shook with the coming storm. Birds canted and swept sideways in the wind.

James turned his head up to Nadia. It didn't use to be like this, he said. Airports were cities unto themselves. You can see them in old films. Executive channel. The Facilitator's jet is about a mile away; it's in a guarded area. His head fell back and he closed his eyes.

Nadia looked up to see a small single-engine plane take off, dip, recover, flounder upward, and then turn and disappear to the south.

The great, surfing storm had stolen up on the northwest horizon and on its forward edge a low fog poured over the mountain peaks. Behind this was a wall of solid oceanic cloud of a deep, threatening marine color. The rain had ceased but more was coming.

Nadia, listen, said James. No matter what happens save my brief-case. Maps, binoculars, my watch. Do you hear me?

Yes, she said. I have a compass.

Good girl.

Hurry, said Farrell. He had a small radio in his hand. It's the Hous-ing Association. They are claiming this plane. The dam is giving way. Hurry.

Armored cars came down the road from the elegant houses, car-rying armed men, men clinging to the sides as well as inside and the ones outside were holding on with one arm and gripping rifles with the other. They drove straight toward the airstrip throwing wings of water on all sides.

One of the mechanics walked forward in the rain with his rifle and aimed carefully and shot at their tires. His rifle jumped and a thick cloud of smoke poured out, he fired again. One of the armored cars spun and drove its front bumper into the cascading ditch water. The mechanic shot again and a rear tire on the other car collapsed with a thin puff of expelled high-pressure air

The men jumped out of the armored cars and ran toward them.

One of them yelled. Stop, stop!

Farrell ran up the ramp and into the pilot's compartment with a sheaf of aviation charts and the mechanics wheeled James up the ramp, half turned in his chair with a grip on Nadia's wrist that nearly broke it. She ran to keep up and they made room for her. The men from the armored cars had broken into a series of running figures like spilled beads. Farrell pushed a throttle forward and the propellers began to roar at the highest RPM possible while Farrell and the copilot stood on the brakes and when the engines were at their highest pitch they suddenly popped the brakes and the DC-3 jumped forward as if it had been shot from a catapult. The asphalt runway had accumulated decades of oil and grime from exhausts and now the rain pounding down made it slick as glass. The DC-3 slid from side to side, burning rubber, and at the last moment Farrell and the copilot gave the engines all the power at their disposal, the fuel mixture on "rich." They skimmed rooftops, and the lifting wheels ripped the top from a Douglas fir. Then they were laboring up the altimeter, yard by yard.

CHAPTER 37

They told her to sit toward the front. They would not let her go back beside James's strapped-in wheelchair because she would be in the way. Nadia looked out the window and just before they rose into obscuring cloud layers she saw the world's authentic topography where Fremont Lake lay in a scrubby basin and the dam with two great spouts of water breaking through at either end. Then the dam broke; sections of the structural concrete turned over and over in a rush of what looked like glittering filth, dancing trees briefly upright, carried down by their roots. How heavy it looked. The massive rush of floodwater threw up ruffles of debris at its front edge and the rest came on heavy as molten pewter.

Rain continued to batter the square plexiglass window at Nadia's left hand and those in the cockpit. Farrell and his copilot were flying with all eight hands and feet. The altimeter said twelve thousand feet and then, suddenly, eleven thousand feet. They dropped like a stone, then began to climb again through vertical disturbances, one after another. She clicked her seat belt loose and got up and staggered to the rear from seatback to seatback.

A man clinging to handholds in the cargo area stopped her. He held up his hand. She saw a heavy-weave curtain flopping with weighted hem in front of the very back of the tail section and in another moment two of the crew came out with James between them. They managed to half fling him into the wheelchair. James gripped the arms with his powerful hands and arranged himself. The crew members returned to holding on. Then one went back to use the lavatory himself.

Nadia managed to crouch beside James and the look on his face was one of fury. You see, Nadia, why I am taking my chances with the medication. I'd rather die than endure this. He dropped his head back and got his breath. This humiliation.

She nodded and said nothing.

Go back up and strap in.

She found her seat, clutching seatbacks all the way up the aisle. She stared out the little window. She had walked so far, and now the earth rolled beneath them like the scroll of Revelation.

Fires had broken out in the city below them. The DC-3 fought from layer to layer of storm and they flew over the Rockies in impenetrable cloud. Thunder detonated on both sides and at fifteen thousand feet the engines screamed at full power. The port engine backfired and blew ice out of the carburetor airscoop like a glittering quoit. Nadia's eardrums felt pierced. When they broke free on the other side, occasional openings in the cloud layer showed mountains scarred with mining and clear-cutting.

After some hours she saw a polyhedral knot of towers in a city-mass along a snaking inlet, a mountain like a perfect white cone. As she watched, a multistory building in the knot of towers began to erupt in flashes. Bright sparks flared from the air-conditioning window units all along its sides and then jumped out of giant antennas and transmitting masts on its roof. At its base floodwaters galloped past carrying debris. Smoke began to pour out of the building and drift away.

Roofs peeked out of the dark floodwater along with uncounted numbers of upturned Buddy cars that lay washed up on the shore of a lake with their little wheels in the air. Streams of water poured down the mountains and their running tendrils resembled the human venous system.

She went back again to sit by James.

Over the noise of the engine she said, Is there nobody there? Why can we go there?

He folded his map carefully. There are people onshore. I have no idea what kind of people they are.

Savage hippies, said Nadia. A man named Chan with a china egg, a crazy person with a wallpaper book. I heard about it. I have secret knowledge, clandestine intelligence.

You, he said. The wanderer.

What's on the island?

No people as far as I know. James pulled himself upright in his wheelchair with both thickly muscled hands on the armrests. His face was a hot color, a fever color, and cracked with fatigue lines.

But there used to be?

Yes, yes, listen. I bought the position of lighthouse keeper. One buys management positions at present. He closed his portfolio of maps. My brother and I bought the rights. Interviewed people. A family I knew seemed capable, the Shalamovs, two children. So I hired them and sent them there. My brother, Farrell, shared the expense and had them flown up. He needed trustworthy weather reports. But ten years ago they decided they wanted off. Too isolated, they had kids, no TV. So they stored everything and left. Farrell asked them to store a year's supply of . . . he paused and ran his hand across his forehead. Store a year's worth of supplies.

He was having trouble breathing and fever burned in his face. Nadia was seated on a pile of duffel bags behind the last row of seats. I want you to hold on, he said. He bent forward out of the confines of his wheelchair and took her hand and placed it firmly on the seatback. You make me nervous.

From whom? said Nadia. Bought it from whom?

From your parents' estate.

She was stunned into silence. Then she said, My parents owned the island?

Were you not listening? He ran his hand through his hair, gripped it, and let go. They owned the lighthouse keeper's *position*. After they died it was part of their estate. There was a lot of legal juggling. I managed to buy the position. My father knew them vaguely. Knew Thin Sam.

What were their names? Why did they abandon me? Are they dead?

Mary and Leonard Dronin. They were not lighthouse keepers. They never went there. You were Raisa Dronin. Your parents were packed and ready to go, with you as a child, when they were arrested. They *attempted* to go there. They didn't make it. They were planning on escaping the big purges.

And so did they?

No.

And?

Another time, Nadia.

When?

We'll see. Stop. Be quiet. He wiped his sweating face on his coat sleeve. Get me some water.

They landed on a watery airstrip in several distinct crashes that nearly tore Nadia out of her seat belt. Farrell and the copilot were landing on visual alone. Mud erupted in dark wings on either side. It battered the fuselage with a sound as if people were hurling gravel at them. A fan of mud whipped over the window and Nadia jerked back as the glass was painted over with brown slush and the twin-engine wavered to a halt.

They had landed at a fire suppression station at what was at one time the American-Canadian border. They were among the tree farms. Inside the shack that served as a sort of airstrip waiting room she sat and leaned against the wooden wall. Still at last. On unmoving earth at last.

A television glowed with a broad yellow band with black letters. The crawl flashed on and off, on and off, under a still photograph of the new Facilitator. He was both old and handsome. Stay where you are, the crawl said. Emergency workers will reach you. Then an old episode of *Things You Cannot Say* came on.

Farrell leaned against a wall, exhausted, with a bottle of energy drink in his hand

Okay, brother? said James.

Farrell tipped up the bottle for the last drops. It was like flying a grand piano, he said. But yes, I'm all right. You'll have to go the rest of the way by helicopter. I'll copilot as best I can.

All right, said James.

I want you to get married, said Farrell. He had two days' growth of beard and his clothes were spotted with coffee and wrinkled. I won't be charged as an accessory under Square One. Plus, she will be legally obligated for your maintenance.

Nadia understood that Farrell refused to say her name. She was a "she."

James nodded. His head lay back on the wheelchair rest. I planned to, Farrell. Don't sound so arrogant. You know what her name is.

When? said Farrell. I haven't heard anything out of you so far.

We used to get along, said James. And then I met Nadia. Elementary sort of conflict. He closed his eyes.

Farrell laughed. How many times have you been in love? Every year or so. He paced back and forth across the dirty plywood floor. It was littered with crushed poplar leaves and twigs and cigarette butts and wadded papers. Outside the window, which was obscured with dust, a skidder engine roared and a helicopter lifted into the air under a halo of thunderous rotors. They'll charge me with something. Anything. They can't say it's because of the weather report. So it will be something else. Maybe I'll make it to the new execution program. Death's cabaret.

If there's anybody left to charge people with anything, said James. He had fallen slackly against the backrest and his face was flushed, his eyes closed.

Think not? Farrell threw his energy drink bottle out the door. So I'm your best man.

I suppose at some point, said Nadia, I will be consulted.

Be quiet, said Farrell. There is a Personal Concerns counselor under the Workplace Well-Being Office of Primary Resources who shows up with the skidder operators once in a while. She's probably drunk by now, if she's here, but I've sent somebody to look for her. Farrell pulled his ear protectors from around his neck and wiped them. Everything's damp, he said. I never remember this kind of damp.

What's the real problem, Farrell, said James.

She's using you to get to Lighthouse Island. When you're there, she'll let you die.

I'm at a loss for words, said Nadia.

You'd better not be, said Farrell. He turned his square, muscular body toward her and thrust his hands into his flight jacket pockets. You'd better be able to say "I do."

The Workplace Well-Being counselor wobbled into the camp on a bicycle dressed in many wet layers of green, turquoise, and mint, carrying a brandy bottle and the required papers. She read from the statutes including one very long one that established the counselor's authority to issue binding agreements between two people as to maintenance and care for each other and legal obligations of both parties. Then the legal consequences of not caring for each other. The legal consequences of neglect were severe. If that happened Nadia would be arraigned before a Personal Relations council and sent to a Severe Sanctions work camp to cook down fish guts under the charge of reckless marital endanger-ment and James ditto.

Nadia and James repeated various statements that began with "I affirm." The last ones required that they say "I do." Farrell bent his head and looked at his worn-out boot toes. The strange pattering sound of a thin rain surrounded the shack and a long crawl of leaking water sidled across the floor, pushing dust ahead of it.

CHAPTER 38

They spent their wedding night in a cubicle in the timber workers' living quarters where each man had his own small room. Their cubicle had a blanket hung over the doorway and a single cot and a chair. James's wheelchair was backed to the wall. Nadia sat in a bewildered amazement at this rapid transit from one part of the continent to another, from the desert city to this stormy logging camp.

James lay in his clothes under the blankets and they listened to the rain. He said, Hell of a wedding night. Dear child, dear Nadia.

Nadia closed her hand around his forearm and he laid his own over hers. She was married to him, to this body, this mind, this past and this future.

We're alive. She smiled.

Yes, we're alive. No small feat for a paraplegic in a general disaster. Someday you will have wedding bread. I promise you. He lay with his eyes closed. Down the hallway a television was on at full volume. It was the trial of the Facilitator and the prosecutor's voice droned on and on, going over legal technicalities. The timber workers groaned or shouted insults. Nadia, reach into my briefcase and find the medication.

She handed the blister pack to him and he broke one out. There were only two left.

What will happen when it's gone? she said.

Then just one leg will work.

James, she said.

He put the tablet in his mouth and drank from a water bottle.

Where are your people? Nadia said. You said they had gone south.

Yes, they went to the far south. I think they will be beyond the flooding. Cousins live in that gerrymander. Another pilot flew my mother and Farrell's wife and children there. He will join them. James struggled to sit upright against the lumpy pillows. So for your wedding night, to make it memorable, I will tell you about your parents. Hand me my briefcase.

Nadia took the photograph from his hand. It was herself at age two on her father's knee and her mother standing behind them. When her name was Raisa. At her father's shoulder stood a young Thin Sam Kenobi in an aviator's uniform. No glasses. Her uncle, Samuel Dronin. But Nadia could not take her eyes away from her mother and father in their blaring overdeveloped colors and wide smiles because they were faces spectrally familiar and known as deeply as one knows one's own face in the mirror. They were smiling out of the frame of the tattered photograph the way people smile at children, with unguarded expressions and kindliness. Smiling at her from between her two hands. Mary and Leonard Dronin.

Behind her mother, a distant white wall. Her father was in a good suit and tie with a bank of medals or awards on the right side of his suit coat. Her parents and uncle were in light coming through some tall window that fell not only on them but on containers of leafy, flowering plants. The background faded away into sequential shrinking mysteries. Little Raisa rested her head against her father's coat and she was reaching up with one hand toward her mother. She looked like her father. Auburn hair and straight eyebrows and a pointed chin. In the background, unseen Forensics agents step quietly out of a collection bus and walk upstairs on noiseless runners.

Leonard and Mary Dronin sit at their dining table making a list of what they need to take to Lighthouse Island. They are not sure how to get there. The dining room is their own, eight feet by fourteen. They do not have to share it with another family. Raisa sits on the floor and tries to entice the cat who regards Raisa as deeply suspect. The cat turns its head quickly because it has heard someone running up the stairs.

Children do not live long in the camps and it is said to be terrible for their parents to watch them lose their hair and waste away. To bury them in a dusty potter's field. Only two hours off to dig the hole, lower the tiny wrapped body. A neighbor shoves Leonard and Mary's door open and says, They are coming. They're downstairs.

Leonard and Mary take up their daughter and run down the stairs and into the streets, handing her a coin purse and a paper.

Look for the North Star and we will always be there. You will be lonely at first but things will get better.

Her parents were separated. In the grain fields Nadia's mother withered under the heat and the work and finally fell from the truck and was caught on the ball hitch. She was dragged turning over and over through soybean rows. The other workers yelled Stop! Stop! and banged on the truck cab roof but Mary Dronin had been dragged for half a mile and died the next day.

Her father survived a while longer. For all his faults he loved her mother more than was advisable in that kind of atmosphere. He was an impetuous man. He fought with the criminals in the barracks and after a while somebody killed him. Without her mother he had become somewhat lunatic, weeping and drinking the alcohol they distilled in the barracks.

Thin Sam was her father's younger brother, an aviator: Samuel Dronin. Out of the bedlam of an overpopulated world, despite everything, lines of continuity crackled here and there as lightning bolts out of the storm and strikes the same place once, twice, three times. Thin

Sam talked with Farrell about flight, the complexity and oddity of aviation. The families lived near one another and against all the rules they established lateral connections. In the computer world James had come upon Sam's photograph in some forgotten declivity and had printed it out and placed it there in the house at Fremont Estates for her, for when she arrived, if she ever did.

He was so good, said Nadia. I want to know about him. She wiped tears from her face.

Sam was arrested at the same time. James laid his hand on a sheaf of papers smeared with bad printer ink; he opened and closed his fingers on it so his fingertips were tacky and smeared. He didn't seem to notice it. He said, Sam began to lose his sight in the camp because of malnutrition. He escaped. He managed to break into Health and Child Care's computers and traced you through your name change. He decided to live near you and look after you. James's fingers closed on her wrist and left prints. You were loved, James said. Nadia?

I know.

He was interrogated that night they arrested him for water theft and I suppose he felt that he might as well tell them the whole story. I found his interrogation transcripts.

Nadia sat with a wet face, listening to the endless rain. I loved him, she said. Where is he buried? I think somebody once tried to get a message to me about where.

It didn't say. It didn't even say how he was executed.

Nadia placed the tips of her fingers together, delicately. James, could he be alive?

A million to one, said James. Don't think of it now. We have a lot facing us. He watched her face from his bed. He said, I wish I had known him better. Sam was older; he was sure of things in a way that most people were not. And here. This is a map of Sissons Bend, where you were born.

Born? she said. Me? She reached out for the paper.

James lifted one knee and made a tent of the covers and then dropped his leg down again. Darling, you didn't get to this world in a pod, after all. His voice was low and hoarse.

It was a page printed out of a much larger map. Some old suburb of Kansas City, where the Missouri River, long extinct, flowed through a bend and on either side it seemed there had been houses that sat apart from one another as if they might have had gardens. She looked up at him. He had fallen into a restless, fevered sleep.

Nadia wept into a thin, coarse towel and splashed water onto her face and after an hour she heard a radio in the next cubicle. It was Big Radio speaking. The last of the day's readings, Female Voice One.

Light plays like a radio in the iron tree;
Green farms fear the night behind me
Where lightnings race across the western world.

She stood and walked to the blanket curtain, pacing, unable to sleep. It was by Thomas Merton.

Earth turns up with a dark flash, where my spade
Digs the lovely strangers' grave;
And poppies show like blood.
The woman I saw fleeing through the bended wheat:
I know I'll find her dead.

A cargo helicopter dropped in a storm of debris onto a helipad. A vermilion-and-yellow sign said DUCK LOW WE MEAN IT. There was an alarming graphic of someone's head flying off their shoulders, ear protectors and all, surrounded by large, blooming sprays of blood. They wheeled James out, slack and semiconscious in his wheelchair. Nadia and the others ran for the open door, bent low beneath the rotors as if bowing to the God of Flight.

Bare velvet mountains of the coast came toward them like an enormous sculpture, earth giants made outside of time, running with water. *I see,* thought Nadia. *I see why.* She pressed the headset down over her hat. Why men labored for centuries to produce flying machines, constructed parachutes, leaped off cliffs with umbrellas and chased the sun in a chariot. The world swam beneath the skids. The odor of dry stone struck by downpours rose to them like the smell of a forge. They were in a hurricane of wind in a frail flying machine, Nadia and a crippled man and his despairing brother, going to some deserted island in the North Pacific. She was elated to the point of lunacy. The world tilted beneath their skids, columns of downpour paced the world.

Look! she shouted. The rain flowed in nets over the helicopter's plexiglass bubble windows. The ocean! I see the ocean!

Farrell jerked one of his headphones away from his ear. Shut up, he said.

If only they could get down now on that minute island in the grainy sea, which now appeared out of the storm clouds, and come to earth in one piece; if only James were not so ill. An island of twenty-two acres with a light tower and a tiny companion island, circled in lashing surf, just off the coast, sturdy and apparently unsinkable if only they could reach it. They were flying to a geography of the edge and she was not exactly sure where they were except that it was on the brink of the Pacific. They were in a borderland, an outer limit, one of the moons of Titan or a lost Atlantis sort of coast that had risen in ages past out of the sea bottom, cascading salt water and maybe it was rising yet. Floodwaters stained the river mouths with rotating, oily blossoms.

The instruments shone up on the faces of the pilot and Farrell, acting as copilot as best he could. Their heads were apostrophized by headsets. They were trying to keep the gale from driving the nose up, for then the full force of the wind would strike the underside and impel the helicopter up and backward and then permanently down and then everything would become permanent. Dump the nose down thirty degrees, full throttle to inch toward the island and the light tower.

Passing nine hundred, said Farrell.

Okay.

Passing seven hundred.

If only he would live and thrive in this place, the island of her dreams, the place she had seen when she could first see again in that dusty hospital and on all the television screens of her life, screen after screen after screen, inviting her to dream and hope in hot offices and toward which she walked all those perilous miles through the city. She held on to James's sleeve with an iron grip. *I am to see to it that I do not lose you.* Whitman, "To a Stranger."

They settled down like a drifting, rocking leaf on an overgrown helicopter pad with the rotors tipping first one way and then another. The landing lights illuminated the rain into a blazing aquarium. Nadia threw out their bags and jumped. The tree branches and wiry nets of vegetation all streamed one way in whipped, cowering motions.

The Pacific beat against the island like a heavy drum sequence played over and over. The mountainous waves spoke to the land in irresistible and sinister voices. At the foot of the lighthouse the Outer Rocks were a maelstrom of white water. The lighthouse stood resolute, unmoved, like something arrested, without light. It disregarded the assaulting waves at its feet, the waves that roared, We love you.

CHAPTER 39

They had to carry him in through the storm on a stretcher. Another man ran behind with the wheelchair and made hollow footstep noises in the empty house. Farrell bent over James on the narrow bed asking, Do you know me? James, can you hear me? But he did not, and Farrell at last took James's hand and gazed into his blank unoccupied face and said, Good-bye, brother. Until we meet again.

Farrell tore himself away and on his way out of the bedroom brushed past Nadia who stood at the door with round, alarmed eyes. He turned to her.

He took hold of her lapel in a wet heavy hand with something angry to say impounded in his head. He gathered up her coat in his fist almost enough to pull her off her feet so that she had to take hold of the door frame. Then finally Farrell really looked at her for a long moment with his hazel eyes. The other men impatiently blundered around the kitchen shaking off rain. He didn't say what was in his thoughts after all. He only said, Take care of him. And then he dropped his hand and walked away and they left, to catch the tailwind that would speed them back south, saving fuel, riding on the nose of the locomotive storm winds.

If only. She sat up beside him all night, watching water running from the join of the French windows. The house sang like an oboe in every crack and seam. Her breath fogged out in front of her face and condensed on her tangled strands of hair. By the light of a candle she watched his lean face for hours, the shadows of his eyelashes. She lay one hand on the coarse blanket over his heart. She counted beats. The dusty curtains lifted and fell, lifted and fell, as slices of wind slipped through the window joints.

It was a long night in which the wind and rain fell upon the steep-roofed house, having come from enormous distances. She listened to the peculiar sounds of water running uncontained everywhere. She felt the rise and fall of his breathing and took in the sweet smell of rain and wet wood and all this made her deeply happy, despite everything. Small traveling elements of joy passed through her like x-rays and lit up all her bones.

That next day she searched the house looking for food, medicine, matches, fuel. The house was empty, unused. She screamed when rats fled with stinking feet into holes chewed in corners. A long central hall that went up to the steep inverted V of the roof made her steps echo. On one side was James's room, next to it another she took as her own, for now. The first room she had ever had. She set out the photo of her parents, her garnet earrings. Next to that was a bathroom. On the other side, some kind of storage room and the kitchen. Rotted curtains at the windows and grease marks on the door frames. At the end of the central hall one of the windowpanes was blown out and water streamed over the wood floor.

She piled all the blankets she could find over James but he threw them off and lay with legs like those of a starved person, sticks with no muscle, wasted thighs in his loose shorts; his heavily muscled torso and arms. He was hot and scarlet and his hair stood up in sweated tufts.

She tried the faucets but they gasped and nothing came out so she set out buckets under the eaves of the porch and from there, through the pelting rain, saw a shed behind the house and ran to it. Fuel pellets in steel bins with a layer of dust and fir needles on top. She ran in through slashing rain with a bucket load, and filled the stove. It was called a Storm King, written in brass letters on its side. She found a jerrican of kerosene under the sink. She poured three cups of kerosene onto the pellets from a brown mug and set them on fire, then filled the kerosene heater in James's room.

Before long she had two rooms warm and hot water on the stove, a collection of tins of oysters and meat paste of some kind and pilot biscuits; more scavenging in the cabinets produced aspirin, cough medicine, earwax remover, and corn plasters. Flatware in a drawer, rusted, with *Celebrity Cruises* etched on the handles.

And now if only he would stay alive to greet her one of these days and call her by her name and turn his head with that mild intelligent look to ask her how they came to be here in this howling Russian folk chalet. If only they were together it would be all right and all their confused and unlucky lives would be redeemed and everything would come true. It could happen, it could happen, she said with a cup of hot weak tea in her hands.

James, could you drink this?

He couldn't because he didn't see her; he was not looking at this world of storms and broken windowpanes, noisy as something hit a window with enough force to bash in yet another pane. If only we two are together, she said to him, to try to reach him in his fever and unconsciousness, and we will walk along together, because you will walk, and be happy in each other's company, two friends together. It's so simple. It's so simple. That we could be happy together and delighting in each other's company. As long as you are here by me all is well and the world will look radiantly good to us as we walk along. Or is this otherworldly? Can this come to us on this earth? And if not, why do I know of it then, like some lost nation drowned beneath the flood. The phrases came to her as if she had not thought of them herself but had come upon them in some way. They were premade. That we could be happy together, two friends together, and delighting in each other's company.

She sat beside the stove waiting for the hot water and listened to the crinkling fall of fuel pellets burned in their own shape and collapsing and the stars far beyond earth's Venusian cloud cover moved intergalactically on their courses, exploding or imploding or just shining eternally, saying O earth, O earth, return.

In the middle watches of the night, nodding beside a candle, Nadia took the towel and wiped James's face and eyelids. Suddenly he said in a clear voice, Let's go for a walk.

Sure, said Nadia. In a little while. She drew the cloth over his forehead.

It's cold. James shivered and with his eyes closed tried to pull up the blankets.

Nadia tucked them around his shoulders and then tiptoed to her own room and took a blanket from her bed to put over him.

What do you want in life? He opened his eyes and seemed to be addressing someone at the foot of the bed.

Let me think about it.

Okay, he said. We need radios. Now his eyes drifted to the left and he seemed to faint into a half sleep.

I'll look. Nadia lifted his hand to her cheek.

Nadia, if I die, you must throw my body into the sea.

And then his eyes closed slowly and a droplet of sweat ran down from his hairline.

Nadia's mouth opened but she could not think of anything to say. She felt the blood drain from her face and a sudden paralyzing dread that he would die in front of her and his hands would open limp and unliving and for a moment tears scalded her eyes. She fell asleep in the chair beside his bed with one hand clutching his striped blanket.

About the Outer Rocks kelp streamed. It slithered in broad taffeta ribbons and bobbing balloon heads and medical-looking tubes that sank and rose in the breaking sea. Northward the headlands went on plane after plane, standing out like Bakelite, and the capes were foggy with the beating surf. Forty-foot waves struck the Outer Rocks in avalanches of foam and a noise like houses falling. Spray was ripped off horizontally over the elevated walkways that ran along the seaward side. Five cleared acres near the house were pooling in a big pond over what had once been a garden and in this floated empty containers and bits of boards.

The great light tower stood on the seaward bluff. It stood against all this visual noise and chaos unmoving, the tower narrow and the wide, glassed-in cupola. It looked very like a chalice, once filled with light, lifted to the storms. It looked out upon illegal fishing and scrapper ships flying past with patched, russet sails. Its rotating light had shone out at ten-second intervals upon the just and the unjust. The light came from the first-order Fresnel lens, a marvel of engineering never to be poured again. A helmet of razored visors three feet tall and inside it the light of a kerosene lamp or even a candle would be magnified thousands of times. When the heavy clockwork mechanism was wound up it would rotate three beams into storms or calm all night at ten-second intervals so that if you or any tourist on credits stood at its base at night you would see three beams like a crown turning on the axis of the tower and sweeping through the night, against the stars. *I am thinking about you,* the light had said. *I will not abandon you.*

But now it was the other way around.

She stood in front of the Storm King naked with both hands held out to the warmth and watched with surprise as her clothes steamed where they lay over a chair. All edges were clean and sharp and this was also amazing since she was used to dust everywhere, clouding panes and blurring surfaces and now all surfaces and verges were brilliant. So clean, she said. Everything seems so clean.

She looked up. James stood in the kitchen doorway in his shorts and a pair of socks drooping around his ankles, holding to the frame on each side. Nadia snatched up her soaked coat and held it in front of herself.

His head nodded forward and then he lifted it again and smiled. He had a four-day growth of beard and his tongue was hot in his mouth.

It's all right, he said. We're married. At least nominally. Stay with me, he said. Sleep in my room.

All she had to read was the old *Girl Scout Handbook,* 1957 edition. She lay on a camp cot and listened to James's regular breathing and lifted the book and opened it at random. *It is fun to send messages to your friends in all sorts of ways. This book is full of fun,* thought Nadia. *Do you know the types of signaling used by other people in their work, such as railroad men, sailors, aviators?* And following was a chart of Morse code. She whispered to herself and carefully worked out her name: _. ._ _.. .. ._ N-A-D-I-A. James would get well and walk and they could become Argonauts or astronauts flashing Morse to each other. Using the flashlight and some other flashlight that they would find somewhere.

Rain struck the window as if it had been blown from a firehose and James suddenly threw aside the covers. He turned to her.

You are reading, he said. You are pondering. By candlelight.

Yes. She sat up in her sloppy boy's shirt and smiled. In the wavering candlelight his lean face was alert, his voice was stronger. She wadded the blankets around herself and said, I was wondering what "naut" was. As in argo and astro.

Sailor, probably. Boat, vessel. James swung his legs out from beneath the covers and put his feet on the floor and grasped the bedpost. As in "nautical."

Don't, she said. She sat up and swung out one leg, one bony knee. What are you doing?

I am in my right mind, he said. Leave me alone. Don't help me. He stood up and then with disjointed movements he made his way to the bathroom next door. She lay back with her hands clasped listening. After a while he came back in, holding first to the door frame and then the wall and then fell into the bed. He put his hands each to one side, taking deep breaths.

I can't look, she said. She lay back with both hands over her eyes.

Good. Don't. It will just unnerve you. It is unnerving me. He slid under the covers again and shivered. Then he said, Actually, I feel great. Is it the middle of the night?

She turned and they lay regarding each other in the dim candlelight, where the kerosene heater stank of unburned hydrocarbons making the flames dull orange. Their breath clouded in the cold.

She said, Close.

You know, you don't have to bring in buckets of rainwater. In regard to the bathroom. There is piping, faucets. His eyes began to shut, opened, shut again.

They don't work.

Then the cocks have to be turned on the collection tanks outside. They are probably rusted. He subsided. He was sinking into dreams or sleep. Get me some vise grips.

Now?

No. In the morning. Go down and check on the stores.

First thing, she said.

Reach into the briefcase and get my medication.

And so she did. It was what was destroying his immune system. But it was allowing him to walk, or at least begin to walk, and there was only one left. So she got up to make him yet another cup of sweet tea from the kettle simmering on the kitchen woodstove and he threw the last tablet into his mouth and drank down the tea and fell asleep again.

It was a strange feeling to be wet all over. Her plastic cape drained and her red canvas shoes squelched gouts of water at every step. Her hat drooped and streamed. She explored what she could of their island in the needling rain; near the light tower the wind turbine spun off a daisy wheel of water, and close by she found concrete steps going down to the sea and on the north end a beach made of a billion broken shells that rolled in a coarse orchestration around a small boat shed. Inside the shed an elegant small skiff rocked on its painter as wave after wave boiled up under the trackway, impatient, as are all craft, to be at sea.

A rocky, overgrown path led through the forest to the south end, where the tiny companion island lay across a narrow chute. Through this chute the sea roared like a millrace and she realized it was natural. Human beings had not cut this slot; the power of the sea had done it by itself.

She hung over the rail of the elevated walkway to see the dotty little black oystercatchers dance up and down on the rocks with their long red beaks pecking away like sewing machines. Pink and blue starfish wallowed in stone saucers of salt water and the seaweed was thrown far up on the rocks, along with debris; shoes, a floating tea canister.

She stood beneath the great light tower. Everything smelled good; it smelled of wet and damp and pure water, of salt spray and cedar needles. Mussels grew like chain mail on the rocks. They were living in a noble ruin in an unmanaged world. Something that had survived inside her as a dry kernel now took on moisture and lived and throve. She was competent and smart and efficient. She could do stuff. She had more space to live in than she had ever thought possible, an island for just the two of them, and she had a photograph of her own parents on a packing crate in her own room. She was married and an adult. She was Nadia of All the Islands. And because she loved him James would live. She was sure of it.

CHAPTER 40

Nadia played the flashlight over the basement, standing in a pool of foul water, and naked rat tails fled into the dark. Twenty-gallon tins lay empty in the seepage, all the seed jars shattered and the seeds eaten, spices spilled in fans, cans tumbled off the shelves, jars of fruit smashed into shining pieces. Her flashlight beam flashed from the surfaces of pools of seep water and broken glass. It seemed like some Siberian tomb where there had been a final orgy for the dead. A few things were left. Meat floated in solution in glass jars, twelve to a box, several tins of flour and quinoa that had been wired shut. Vacuum tins of butter and a bottle of what appeared to be wine. The rats had destroyed and eaten everything else and Nadia stared at it with a subzero feeling around her heart. Curiously numb.

She found an empty wooden crate to sit on and put her head in her hands. This needed thinking out. This was entirely new. There was no food. None that they knew how to garner, net, search out in the tide or the ocean or among the firs that stood guardian on the island. At some time people had fed themselves with animal products and gardens but neither she nor James had any idea how to go about this. All her life and

in the lives of everyone she knew food had been issued. Now there was
no agency to issue it. It was not so much frightening as it was puzzling.
Behind her confusion was a growing panic. Don't tell James. Not now,
not just now.

She carefully searched out and stacked whatever was salvageable,
counting it all up and brushing away broken glass. She found herself
weeping. She wiped her face, lifted her head, and saw a stack of books.

Gardening North of 50°. Good. Nadia supposed they were somewhere around 50° north. Next was *Western Birds* and something called
A Bouquet of Best-Loved Love Poems, which did not sound promising.
Then in a blue cover was the crudely printed journal of an early lighthouse keeper.

This one she opened. She wiped her eyes on her sleeve and then
flipped the damp and wrinkled pages with the skill of an expert reader,
holding the flashlight in her teeth. The prose spoke in terms of unwavering and uncompromising confidence in all those virtues that were
right and good and made life worth living. A language more than a
century old. The journal was written with a kind of undiluted convic-
tion, the confidence of somebody who did not have real or imagined
censors looking over his shoulder and who was not facing starvation.
Other people's standards, including those of grammar and spelling,
were irrelevant.

*Your lite tower lins is your most important companyon and you must
gard it from brakeage for the lives of others and the fulfilmint of your duty
depends on it's remaining unbrockin.*

A white-bellied mouse sat holding up its pink paws as if to an-
nounce something. Perhaps, *I am not a rat.*

Nadia turned the flashlight on it. And when she did shadows like
persons appeared behind the empty tins on the shelves and behind the
stairway. And in these shadows she seemed to see the former selves
of lighthouse keepers from time immemorial, keepers who had lived
on lonely islands and unpeopled coasts, who had endured storms and
raised children and goats and stubbornly cherished their solitude,

whose job it had been to light the beacon to say, *Don't come here*, who had been keepers of the fire for those in peril on the sea. All these in the darting shadows that fled from her flashlight beam. The mouse ate a seed between its two paws.

Nadia, Nadia, read the book.

One: He stared at his kerosene-soaked hands and wiped them on his trouser legs. The kerosene heater was between his knees where he sat in the wheelchair and he had used the vise grips to remove the line from the tank to the pot. He put the copper pipe to his mouth and blew it out. Thick substances spattered on the floor and then the line was clear. He wiped his mouth on his coat cuff. Two: Where's my briefcase? He screwed the line back into place and placed the heater next to his bed and lit it. Bright, hot blue flames sprang up and he said, Good.

I set up the desk for you, said Nadia. She wiped at the kerosene on the floor with one of the towels. She said, That desk made out of a door in the central hall. I laid out your maps and notes. I put your briefcase there. As a handy-dandy wife-type person.

He reached for her hands and held them between his to warm them. Good. Three: Did you check the stores in the basement?

Yes, they're pretty good, pretty good, said Nadia. I'm a terrible cook. I should have told you that before we got married.

Food is food. Four: Take the binoculars and go up in the tower. Can you make it?

Yes. I can. And I am to look for enemies. Forensics agents, savage hippies, pirates, kraken, Oversupervisor Blanche Warren.

He regarded her in the damp boy's clothes and the wet red canvas shoes, a blanket over her shoulders and that slight, glad smile came to his face as it often did when he looked at her. He said, Also the Flying Dutchman. Jack Sparrow, Director Crumm in goggles. If they come here I will kill them. And then go out and cut me a sapling to make a cane with. He watched her widen her eyes and pause at the edge of saying something. He said, You don't know what a sapling is. A young tree; cut it at the bottom and just above the first branch. Then he released her hands. Then he said, Nadia, how are you?

How am I?

Are you troubled about anything, are you tired, are you frightened?

I can't lie?

Not at present.

Okay, well, the sea is rising. I mean the entire *level* of it. She gestured with nervous little movements of her hands.

They're called tides, darling. It's all right. It will go back down. He held to the arms of the wheelchair as if he would stand but then sank back down again.

This is a new life, Nadia thought. She sat beside the stove, exhausted, and massaged her knees. A life of the ocean and endless rain and someday a garden when lilacs first in the dooryard will bloom. She remembered thinking, in the hot streets, that when she came to Lighthouse Island she would be herself. And so she was, a person grateful to be alive and slowly unfolding one new mind compartment after another, which happens when people begin to believe they might be their own masters and are forced to find their own food and shelter. *I'll worry about that later.* She had a photograph of her own parents, a map of Sissons Bend, where she was born, unique in all the billions, and a window looking out into a world of leaves, trees, and curious unshaped stone. And therefore, choose life, however appalling that might become.

A cat had come to the island on a pile of floating debris. He came ashore the day before the helicopter arrived. The debris was mainly a roof of pinewood with rustic cedar shingles from some higher-up's house in the Columbia River Valley. A gated estate home with dormer windows. It came meandering up the Pacific currents, far out on the gray and heaving sea. Around the stub of its chimney a fishing net had clung in a thousand tangles of purse seine. In this were caught empty containers and a child's plastic lobster toy with very white ominous cartoon eyes and more busted lumber, door frames, parts of trees, and Buddy car tires.

The orange-and-white cat lived under a dresser drawer held in place by the edge of the seine net and all day and all night the salt water lifted the roof and all its hangers-on high into the air and then down again. The cat had been soaked wet for five days and had nothing to eat but the remains of fish caught in the net.

A man had swum up and clutched his neck and then let go and sank and then a woman and a child had tried to entice him onto a rubber raft. Eventually the cat crawled out to drink the rainwater washing around in the Buddy car tire. Worst of all were the arms and hair floating inside the dormer windows, rising and falling and gesturing. He clung to his insignificant life under the drawer as if it were as valuable as that of a prophet or a king.

And then the debris broke apart in the surf on the mainland side of Lighthouse Island and somehow he swam ashore. There he ran headlong into the head rat of the engine house burrows, ten inches long with a ten-inch tail. The orange cat was nearly without strength but he managed to run up a tall fir to the first branch and hold on.

From there he saw the house and its lighted windows. Inside were royal personages, a king and queen of heat and food and life, who were probably also homicidal, guarded all around by terrible enormous rats, and he called out from his fir tree, Help, Help. Help.

James began to pace, hesitantly and slowly, up and down the long central hallway. He walked to the storage room and went through its tattered piles of discarded things. He had trouble placing each foot in front of the other. A slight fever lingered in his body. The Shalamovs must have had some kind of arms, if only a shotgun with rat shells. Broken chairs, a roll of canvas, rusted kitchen tools, scraps of sheet metal. He dragged out the roll of canvas and fell at the door.

Okay, okay, he thought. *Okay, I fell. No problem. Get up.*

He pulled himself up by one of the long support beams that rose to the ceiling in the central hall. His eyes were spasmodically winking with pain. He left the canvas where it was. His central nervous system fired a billion neurons and misfired and fired again in an interior series of little detonations. It was an assault on the unused muscles of his thighs and lower legs, the wasted quadriceps.

He waited for the pain to slide away, bit by bit. He checked the atomic clock against his watch; if he could find Greenwich mean time and set the atomic clock to it, and if it would hold steady, he would be on his way to finding their longitude and placing themselves on the invisible grid of the planet, he and Nadia. The book of their lives had opened to a new and difficult font. You are on your own, said the opening line. On an unknown coast, and on that coast a strange people.

CHAPTER 41

Nadia lifted the binoculars to look out through the glass of the cupola. She was sixty feet above the island and below her the firs appeared to be conical, flashing with ravens. She traveled her lenses across the coastal mountains and its bursting surf. She focused on flood trash thrown above the tide line, the prow of a wrecked ship in an inlet. Nadia could not make out its name or why it had come to grief. Farther north tall black things stood near the shore. She spun the focus wheel. Chimneys. Blackened stone standing out of a mass of dark jumbled timber. A village that had been burned and destroyed.

She lowered the binoculars.

That meant trouble. Bad trouble. She wouldn't tell James about that just yet.

She focused on something glittering that rose and sank with the waves: a collection of debris loosely held together—boards, barrels, billowing cloth or tarps, tires. This whole world seemed to be in a state of anarchy as parts of the megacity floated past and the rain fell unregulated. On their island everything just grew anywhere it wanted. The sea did whatever it liked. This coastal world made inhuman noises on its own. Beyond the partly open door to the catwalk she heard the wind tearing through fir needles like the reeds of a musical instrument and from somewhere a singing howl: a beast, an unowned and unlicensed animal.

And on the Outer Rocks, playing in the crashing surf, seals appeared. They were blond and glossy; the waves broke over them and they reemerged without drowning. They were like unsinkable bathtub toys playing in the dangerous ocean. Nadia watched them for a long time until they disappeared into the absorbing and alien sea.

She studied the radio console with its microphone the size of a potato, decorated in brass. She clicked all the buttons and slid the sliders. A dial jumped once and fell back. She threw off bird's nests and tried to wipe it clean.

I made it! Nadia spoke into the microphone. She threw out both arms and cried, Ta dum! We're on the fabled Lighthouse Island, everything is going to be all right. We are going to make it.

She eased down the steep and ringing metal steps and passed by the big green metal consoles at the base of the stairs. Their lights still glowed, powered by the wind turbine. She had no idea what they were for. She was thinking about how to find books about the sea, instructions on fishing, edible plants.

The yellow cat ran through the rain for the engine house. There he came upon the head rat of the engine-house burrows, the margrave, bruxing and guarding his rat hole, a foot long from nose to tail. On the concrete surround and in the whipping rain, both stood on their hind feet and threatened each other. The yellow cat burst out into the demented screaming of a desperate feline at such a volume that the head rat flattened its ears, wavered, and finally gave way. It scrambled over the side of the surround and dropped into the brush. The soaked and starving cat shot into the rat hole and gained the shelter of the engine house.

They took apart the old television camera that lurked in the long central hall. James unscrewed the lens barrel and the lenses dropped into his hand, Nadia held a tea mug for the screws. They spoke of their journey through the city, evasions, narrow escapes. James told her of life in Fremont Estates and its luxuries and its dangers. Ponds for skating in the winter and a sailboat in the summer, pet goats and ducks, arrests and abductions in the middle of the night. They spoke of Nadia's gray days in jail, James's fall from the balcony, and the day that Nadia threw her diary into a mixer of hot tar. The short day slid into darkness and unrestrained vegetation lashed at the windows. James slid the lens over his maps, down the Missouri River to Sissons Bend, where she had been born. There had been gardens there in centuries past with gleaming leaves of sweet corn and bean vine tendrils. Smoky little houses teetered on the bluffs looking down on the river and animals stared over the fence into the fresh edible leaves and fruit.

We will have to get domestic animals, he said. There's no use trying for a garden in this rain.

And soon, she thought. *Before we starve.*

The Buddha said, One can't always go through life saying, "Not this, not this." At some point you must say, "This, this." At least I think that's what he said. Don't quote me.

That night Nadia dreamed of mythical animals returning two by two with all their trouble and all their messiness and dubious loyalty, bearing unknown to themselves the gift of food, half of one world and half of the other. They had waited up in the constellations for a long time and they stepped back down in a long procession to be with human beings again: Capricorn, Taurus, Sirius the Dog Star, Draco, Pisces, Pegasus, Leo, and children. The twins. One named Man, the other named Twin. And the Milky Way to feed them and the pastures of the hurricanes in which to play and die.

The sun sank below the sea horizon as if it were wet and had been drowned.

CHAPTER 42

The deep interior glow of the Zircon radio dial band shone on their faces. Nadia had found it in the engine house, along with a bale of used clothing: rain gear and sweaters. She had found wet paw prints in the engine house as well as rat sign and stinking nests. When she came upon a rat head she grabbed up all she could carry and fought through the rain along the elevated walkways. Some gruesome thing lived in there. She would tell James about it later. Not now.

The kerosene heater flickered ornate patterns on the ceiling; the chalet smelled of fumes and the chemical tang of fuel pellets. Beyond the windows they could hear the roaring surf and the light pattering of a thin rain striking the collection tanks in their cradles.

James ran the needle down the band, searched for the TV audio and news of the megacity, the world and all the people they had left behind, either drowning or starving. She pulled a kitchen chair up beside him and he listened and absentmindedly stroked the hair from her face.

It was heavy, said James. Carrying all that back in the gale.

I could do it, she said. I mean, I did it. It was so you will love me and be forever grateful.

He looked at her a moment and smiled; her lashes seemed to have grown thick in the wet and cold, her gray-green eyes half hidden in the parka hood fur, a cautious animal.

Now here is the chill map. An announcer's professional voice. *We can see the isobars coming down from the northwest so some areas are being hit with successive waves of isobars.*

Oh my God, said James. He doesn't know what an isobar is. He threw himself against the backrest of the chair. Nobody has told him.

There are some floods that are exhibiting extreme flood behavior in certain areas.

That's it, said Nadia. The TV audio for sure. She was nearly engulfed by the big yellow parka but she didn't care, it was warm. Life was warm, just sitting here beside him.

An investigative panel has been tasked with looking into several instances of dam malfunction but the panel is finding it difficult to meet and the chairman has objected to the lack of a clear mission statement. In the meantime WETEMERG is considering requests for Type II Incident Management Teams and on-scene incident command structures . . .

Stupid sons of bitches. Louts. Hominids. Illiterate cretins. James shifted restlessly in his chair and turned the dial carefully. Odd how people who love abstract language also want to kill you and cut your legs off.

Listen, said Nadia.

They heard a simple folk tune, eight bars played over and over, ceaselessly.

What's that?

James bent his head and listened. I think it's a numbers station. Has to do with intelligence stuff. Spy stuff. He turned the fine-tune dial slowly.

Then a man's voice speaking in a foreign language, a patient, explaining voice.

That's not Spanish or French, said Nadia.

No. I think it's Japanese.

Do you speak Japanese? Nadia looked up at him.

No. They listened, as intent on the dial as if it had been a human face. And so, said James. He sounds close, so close.

But the Japanese speaker faded away into a distant Pacific of radio noise. Then they picked the TV audio again at 720.

Next! The trial of Director James Orotov and Sendra Bentley, the sexual brigand who seduced a paraplegic director of demolition.

Far overhead rats cried out in ultrasonic chitters. James and Nadia stared at each other.

Sendra Bentley has been repeatedly charged in the past with adulterous affairs, Tom, really sordid stuff here, and we obtained an interview with a subdirector in Cactea Opuntia Supply named Earl Jay Warren who was one of her, well, conquests and he . . .

Is he charged . . .

There's no charge on him as far as I can see here, and he said they went up on the roof, I mean really, right? Vet Supply in the same . . .

Supplying what, Ethel . . .

Looks like supplying gophers and pigeons to some kind of street zoo . . .

Nadia clutched her thick auburn hair in both hands and it sprouted up in tufts between her knuckles. A street zoo! she cried. It's all confused.

Hush, said James. I am dying to hear about me. Shoved back into my wheelchair. I suppose I will beg for my life. His face was set with fury. He took up a pen and flipped it from one hand to the other.

. . . and then apparently moved on to other conquests. Now it appears that Warren's wife, Nadia, maiden name Stepan, is missing from their residence and may have been murdered.

I'm not dead! Nadia cried at the TV audio coming out of the old Zircon. I wasn't his wife!

Oh, come on, James said to the radio. What about Director Orotov, you slovenly bastards?

This trial has the highest ratings since . . .

It's sex, Ethel, sex and death, new audacious programming, we're taking chances here but life is chancy, you take risks and sometimes they pay off . . . here's the courtroom audio . . . And then from the Zircon loudspeaker came the putative voice of director James Orotov: *You can't imagine the things she knows how to do! I was her slave!*

James fell back laughing and threw the pen across the desk. Well, shit, I am sorry to miss it.

Nadia closed her hands into fists. Sexual brigand!

He bent forward to relieve the pain in his spine but instead it flared into something resembling an intense electrical shock so he sat up straight again. You will introduce me to all these vile practices?

Oh please.

And who was Earl Jay Warren?

Nadia flushed bright red. A dreadful affair at the office. A total mistake. I should never have done it. First clue: he had eyes like ball bearings. She put one hand over her eyes. I'm an orphan. I'll take up with anybody.

Then she was instantly sorry she said it.

But I'm not anybody, said James. I'm apparently Sendra Bentley's sex slave. Or somebody's sex slave. They're not quite sure. Lots of indefinite pronouns here. You would be a kind of celebrity except they don't have your name. Be grateful. You've only been murdered but I, worse luck, am being groped by Sendra Bentley.

Nadia placed her hands flat over her eyes and created a private darkness full of regret and rage. Tears leaked from the heels of her hands.

Bentley and Orotov were attempting to escape on a private jet when they were apprehended by a local housing authority . . .

Nadia pulled the big parka hood over her face and said, Get away from it, James, it's poison. It's evil.

I am, I am, *shhh.* He put one hand on her arm and spun the dial again, searching for Big Radio. And there it was at 88.3, clear and reassuring.

There it is, there it is! A glad voice from inside the hood.

James reached out and pulled it down around her shoulders. How can you hear anything inside that parachute?

November, said Female Voice One, *is the time for sea tales and shanties and ballads of the sailor's life, for winter winds and the sound of the ocean at the eaves of the house. Now let us listen to excerpts from the heroic true story* Endurance.

Yes, yes, let's listen, said Nadia. Heroism and no sneering. She wiped tears of sheer fury from her cheeks. Just mindless heroism.

The radio said, smoothly, in the voice of reason and storytelling, *At the time the boats were launched from Patience Camp, Clarence Island lay just thirty-nine miles due north. By sailing northwest, they had reduced that distance to about twenty-five miles NNE, Worsley estimated. However, it had been two days since the last observation, and during that time the strong wind out of the northeast had probably blown the party a considerable distance to the west.*

James got up and limped to the tattered old couch with his long legs stretched out before him and held out his hand to her. Take off that parka, would you?

She shed it and threw herself beside him.

It's all right, he said. He put the blanket and his arm over her and so she pressed against him and put her hand on his belt buckle, close to his human warmth and out of reach of the accusing powerful invisible eye that even now lurked in the radio dial. She heard his heart, thumping away in steady and heroic thumps.

The trial may have been prerecorded months ago, he said. They may be all drowned. I like to think of them drowned. He kissed the top of her head and then fell back in a relaxed slump against the couch and his eyes drifted shut and opened again.

It was worse for you, she said. It was your real name. They had you back in a wheelchair.

But here I am. Here we are. James was drifting into sleep. Arms, legs, everything. Including rats.

Canvas from the tents was stretched over each boat and with great difficulty the small primus stoves were lighted so that some milk could be heated. They drank it scalding hot, huddled together under the flapping canvas of the tent cloths. They were enjoying the luxury of a moment's warmth, when a new menace appeared . . .

She lay with her head on the heavy old sweater she had found for him. They were alive and here and the news was not alive and somewhere else and they were holding out, the two of them, against the gales and the sea much like the light tower itself. She said, You know, it always seemed to me that there was a man and a woman up there, reading. I mean a live man and woman.

No, it's sent up there from here on the earth somewhere. Called an uplink. From NASA. It was geeks fooling around at NASA. Place called Houston. His eyes drooped. He said, Your hair is growing out. You have such beautiful hair, Nadia. Such beautiful hair.

They fell asleep on the couch listening as Shackleton and his men made their way toward Elephant Island through enormous icy Antarctic seas in a twenty-two-foot boat. The kerosene stove broadcast its patterns over them and sparkling streams of rain ran down the panes. They fell into dreams that took place in old-time places, strangely altered. James and his brother, Farrell, were looking for their dog, Bandit, and James slogged through deep snow in boots far too large for him and then suddenly the dog was behind them, silent, stalking them with teeth like a ripsaw. Nadia was on trial in the old high school auditorium; she stood destroyed because the prosecutor knew her intimately and it was all true and he despised her; he held out his hand to point at Earl Jay Warren and his wife Oversupervisor Blanche Warren and two weeping children. She was guilty and done for. But then her father came through the crowd dressed in his old work clothes and greasy apron, a person whom she had never seen before but still was her father, and said, *Get out, all of you, get out now. This is over. She is my daughter.* Her sense of relief was overwhelming. Near dawn she woke up and remembered that her father had been killed a long time ago.

James leaned aching and weary on the kitchen counter and poured hot water from the kettle into a basin. The greasy soap foamed up and he scrubbed a pot with a rag, which from time to time he dipped into a saucer of sand. Wet trousers and shirts hung from the drying rack. Wild onions, which survived the sleet, had been chopped into fragrant green dice. They lay in a heap on the counter ready to go into a soup made with the last of the bottled beef.

He dried off the counter and his hands with one of the thin towels and then took up his cane and steadied himself.

And so why did you not tell me about the mess in the basement?

She stared at him, at his expressionless gray eyes and the flat planes of his face. She inhaled deeply in order to come up with some explanation and then stuck.

He sat down on a kitchen chair, one hand on top of the other on the handle of the cane. I went down to the basement to see if I could negotiate the stairs. Never mind. I know. And you have been eating very little. You are diminishing by the day.

They sat and listened to the gusts of wind tugging at the house as if it would collapse at last and be thrown into the sea. Finally she said, The rats. Rats got it.

I saw that. How much do we have?

Ten pounds of flour, about ten of quinoa, five pounds of rice, a gallon of cooking oil, a tin of sugar. Some glass jars of wiry chicken thighs and bluish beef. One brick of tea, some citrus powder, a good supply of soap and biscuit powder, two boxes of candles and kerosene and batteries.

This is catastrophic, he said.

She shut her hands together into a bony knot. What are we going to do?

Leave.

Oh no. Nadia's hands dropped limp as rags in her lap. We just *got* here. This is our island.

We have to.

A slick and weighty rat stared at them boldly from a hole in the kitchen ceiling and made a little chipping sound as it ground its teeth.

CHAPTER 43

He had to be able to walk and run and sail before they ran out of food and starved, before they became too weak to handle the skiff and too malnourished to think straight. And whatever sort of people they would have to deal with at Saturday Inlet, he would prefer they didn't stand around the dock watching a lurching gangling six-foot-two cripple wallow out of the skiff and sprawl at their feet.

He walked with iron resolution down the elevated walkway as shots of pain ran up his spine, his long feet squelching in the good shoes. Then down again into the paths through the island, an unpredictable world. Things streamed past Lighthouse Island in the storm winds: flights of petrels, gulls, a bright-colored piece of awning from somewhere, a trailing glitter of plastic weather balloon, a faded handbill advertising a Squid Fest. He fought the wind and his own pain to load the wheelchair with pellets and bring them into the house. Nadia hid and refused to watch.

Once he caught the smell of wood smoke being blown from the coast, another time a long dark ship with russet-colored sails coming up from the south. He stopped to watch it, leaning on the wheelchair handles, and wondered if it had been blown off course, maybe from Japan or Kamchatka, wondered if it was a friend or an enemy.

He tripped on salal roots and plunged into holes, fell, lay there looking up at the soaring firs, the fog and rain that misted their crowns. A banana slug crawled past him, laying behind it a highway of slime. Then the orange cat appeared, staring down at him and when he put out his hand to it, it disappeared.

Come back! he said, but the dollar-shaped salal leaves closed around it. He rolled over to his hands and knees and then got up slowly. He must not break a bone or knock himself out because this would put Nadia in danger; he would become a fatal liability.

On every side the North Pacific pounded and polished the small island into secret beaches and tide-polished volcanic stone. In a tidal pocket was a stone that had been rolled round as a cannonball over the centuries. In other pools were green shapes like dollars and hairy, lifting things with pink fur. They had few names for anything here except desire, rain, love, the sea. *I heard the sea roar past in white procession filled with wreck:* Masefield.

It was a miracle that he should be walking at all, swinging one leg after another. In all the cold and rain he often felt the unstained joy of people who have been granted miracles. It was neither digital nor chemical but you had to know the dwarf's secret name; *miracle* or *dwarf.*

He stood below the blazing fan of the wind turbine and knew it had to be sending power to the big green battery chassis at the foot of the ladder inside the light tower, and then to the radio console up in the cupola but when he attempted the steep stairway he fell ten feet onto the concrete floor with one foot twisted under him. He lay there in the reek of his steaming clothes and gazed out the open door at the gray sky and the gray sea beyond. He got to his feet and put weight on the foot. He had not broken it.

From time to time would come moments when he was actually striding along the flat places, along the walkways, at the shelly beach, spinning his cane with long reaching strides. He was suspended with joy and fear of falling. He was a biped again among all the normal bipeds on earth, listening to the jingle of the seas loose change as the salt waves thundered into this protected little pocket and ran all the billion broken shells clattering through their fingers. He listened, listened, as the surf exploded in foam and the distant currents ran deep and unseen and he heard the sea call his name.

Nadia handed him a blanket warmed on the rack over the stove and a bowl of broth. The lighthouse keepers' book lay on the counter. She had been reading about the wrecks on a dangerous coast called the Graveyard, which was apparently nearby.

Good broth, he said. Warm blanket.

She tucked it closely around his neck. Rain drained from his hand as he tipped up the bowl.

You're hurting, she said. She lay her hand on his neck.

Let's not talk about my falling down and wallowing in the rain, he said. Water dripped from his nose and his brown hair was all awry like splinters. Let's just consider wallowing an occupational hazard at present.

Okay. Nadia turned back to her cooking. She dropped a spoonful of baking powder into the flour. Not a word. Now, James, listen, do you have to train chickens to lay eggs?

He fell back laughing helplessly. For a moment he couldn't stop.

I resent that, she said.

He managed to stop laughing and cleared his throat. No, Nadia, you don't. They just sort of lay them naturally.

And what about mussels?

He shut his hands around the blanket. Listen, Nadia. Listen to me. Don't go down on those rocks, Nadia, I mean it. You don't understand the sea. I have no way to help you if you fall or get hit by a rogue wave. You hear me?

Yes.

I mean it.

Okay. Nada's hands were gloved with sticky dough. I promise.

James sat watching her work. How thin she was, how thin they both were. They were not getting enough nourishment; they were losing weight, losing ground.

Now, as for the mysterious noises, it's a cat.

Oh! Nadia's mouth dropped open. Oh, a cat! They kill rats, right? She did a quick dance with her skillet. Yes, yes! Murder and mayhem!

Yes. James smiled. He's completely wild so don't get your hopes up. He's terrified.

James handed her the empty bowl and stood up and shucked off his coat and then his shirt and boots. He stood beside the stove with both arms out to take in the heat and he was steady on his feet and his skin flushed red from the warmth and his desire for her. *This, this,* he thought.

Nadia stuffed the bathroom rocket-stove water heater with wood splinters and struck a match to it. The match lit her face and the tips of her auburn hair, the hirsute wool of her giant sweater. The wood took fire and roared and within minutes hot water gushed out of the faucet and into the tub and the harsh soap powder foamed. Even though they were both yet hungry after a meager dinner, they still had hot water.

She said, And so what do we know about this place on the coast? Saturday Inlet?

Not much. Looks like ten houses or so.

And Banefield? There's black squares for houses there. South of here, right?

Yes. They are supposed to grow their own everything. It is some kind of an experimental ag station. Mislaid biologists. But I suspect it is long gone.

He unbuttoned his shirt and pushed his shoes off with his cane and then shed his trousers and underwear. He was weary and his sentences were collapsing. Used to be called Bamfield, I think. Are you embarrassed?

We're married, she said and held her hand out for the trousers. At least nominally.

Soon I will drag you kicking and screaming into my bed. He stepped into the tub. I will turn into a savage, you will be my sex slave.

Okay. She shook out the trousers, flicked off wet leaves, and went over the seams for tears.

He sank into the hot water and said, Ah. After a moment he said, Maybe it's a fantasy village.

Which one?

Banefield. He felt around for the hard bar of yellow soap and lifted it in foamy hands.

Like, fantasy how?

As in people so many times have this romantic idea that there is someplace where people reward each other for good work. I'm not being sarcastic. Independent yeomen who hold town meetings and build cider mills. The old noble savage cliché. James's eyes closed. He said, We dream of fresh milk and eggs, honest folk. Unicorns. There will be meat, bread, bells, amiable big men who can lift timbers to their shoulders and build a barn and sing some kind of hearty work songs, grapevines, homemade wine, people who play instruments.

And so why not?

He was silent for a moment, a wry smile, and finally he said, Good point.

Nadia turned over his wool shirt looking for rents. James felt the pain in his back and thighs diminish, fade. He ran the sliver of soap over his face and its two-day beard and searched her face as if wondering how a blind orphan child had become this ardent young woman with her face now smoothed out by wet and damp. To him she was erotic and steadfast and endearing and if she were not this to other people, then he alone held the key to her being. Sometimes love is blind and sometimes it is sighted, perhaps with a third eye.

That night on Big Radio was the old ballad "The Wreck of the Edmund Fitzgerald." They warmed their hands at the Storm King and heard again the story of the sinking freighter, the loss of the twenty-nine men, and how all the church bells of Lake Superior had rung out twenty-nine times. She bent over a torn-off coat sleeve in the soft steam of the teakettle and tried to wipe tears away without James seeing her. Her emotions were dangerously close to the surface of her mind and her eyes.

James and Nadia ran the little skiff down the trackway into the waves but a rogue wave lifted up the bow high into the air and turned it over on its side. James fought with it, managed to drag it back onto the crushed shells of the little beach and then he and Nadia righted it.

Then he nosed it back in, up to his waist in freezing surf. The little beach was being swallowed by the tidal surge, wave upon wave.

Nadia struggled in the crashing, leaping salt water, spray in her face, her hands clutched to the stern and then a larger wave struck her full in the face and she went under. She tore her arm on something below the surface, something steel, and salt water rushed into her mouth. James shut his muscular hand around her parka hood and dragged her out. She stood gasping and shaking on the shells while James struggled the little skiff back onto the track and back into the boathouse. He was surprised at the buoyancy of it and at the sucking power of the sea. He came to Nadia and put his arm around her and helped her into the house.

Ow. Ow.

Be quiet. James wound gauze over the iodine. It was a puncture wound. Then he put his chin on top of her head and held her close against him.

He was so much taller than he had seemed in his wheelchair and she felt all the length of his body against hers and his collarbone against her temple. They both smelled of salt water and wood smoke. He unbuttoned her wet and disreputable khaki workshirt to reveal the female within, her thin, pale skin. Then her trousers. I knew you were in there, he said. Beneath all this. I suspected it all along. He wrapped them in a blanket. She was naked and salty with her feet to the fire. He ran the tip of his forefinger along her shoulder and up to her mouth, watching her.

They abandoned the blankets. Then they were in the bedroom with the covers thrown back. Nadia burrowed under them, shivering. Bright pinheads of wet snow flicked at the windows. She heard James unbuckle his belt and strip off his soaked trousers and then he was beside her in the bed with its curtains and pillows. His long pale body tight against hers and after a while they were warm. The room was warm. The kerosene heater threw its floral patterns of light on the ceiling. He sat up, relaxed and loose on the sheets. He leaned on one elbow and ran his hand down her face and torso and thighs.

Darling, you are very thin, he said. And beautiful.

She smiled up at him and lightly touched the tip of his nose.

They lay face-to-face and put their arms around each other. In the other room the stove cackled loudly over its load of fuel pellets like an enormous fiery hen. The voice of Big Radio was deeply engaged with a biography of Doc Watson and played illustrative clips of his music: *Was blind but now I see.* They did not hear it, nor did they hear the Pacific seething over the Outer Rocks. She forgot about the gauze and the iodine on her arm. He bent over her and lifted her against him with his powerful arms for he was starved for her and had been starved for her for all these months and distances.

They woke early in the morning, swamped with rucked sheets and quilts, to turn to each other yet again.

It was midmorning before she got out of the bed. I'm so hungry, she said. I'm famished.

He watched her dress. No kidding.

Yes. There has to be something left in one of those jars. If not, not. She bent and kissed him.

Tant que je vive, he said. However long that is.

They lay together in bed every night and she ran her small, strong hands over his back, his thighs and ribs. He was building muscle, slowly. Too slowly. She brought iodine and ran a bath and they sat together with bright hot skins; steam pearled the bathroom window, and afterward they slid into the bed where hot water bottles had heated the sheets. They were hungry. Still hungry for each other and for nourishment.

CHAPTER 44

He climbed down the sea-facing rocks that were laddered with mussels gasping in the climbing waves, seawater draining from their jaws. He pried them loose with a screwdriver. The wind was not so bad. He filled a bucket with them and with difficulty clawed his way back up to the elevated walkway, the surf slamming into his knees. He sat with Nadia opening the mussels until the kitchen was cracking underfoot with splintered shells and rank with the smell of shellfish.

Now, he said, like this. He threw away mussels that were open and cut the beards from the closed ones with the knives that said *Celebrity Cruises* on the handle. He put the saucepan on the stove and in it simmered the last four tablespoons of butter with wild onion swimming in bits. Nadia watched.

Where did you learn mussel cooking? said Nadia.

We had a cook, said James. I watched her do this.

. . . *the four Pickwickians assembled on the morning of the twenty-second day of December. . . . Christmas was close at hand. . . . And numerous indeed are the hearts to which Christmas brings a brief season of happiness and enjoyment. How many families, whose members have been dispersed and scattered far and wide, . . . meet once again . . .*

They listened to Male Voice One and his reasonable tones. After fifteen minutes the mussels opened and they used steak knives to take out the meat, and they dipped the morsels into the sauce and ate them all. They broke the beaten biscuits into the liquid with its swimming bits of wild onion and were happy together and smeared with butter.

Merry Christmas, James said.

She lifted a mussel on a fork. Happy New Year.

Nadia packed the traveling bag. She had made up ship's biscuit with the last of the flour. She wrapped it in the shrink wrap in which the radio had been packaged and put in the last can of meat paste, a can opener, and a plastic jug for water. She added two kitchen knives, dropped in the compass, and then wrapped his change of clothes in the plastic shower curtain.

He sat at the FM radio. At 98.2 he found he could pick up a distant and static-distorted broadcast of some maritime transmission. Maybe it was a trick of the storm.

Chan the Uncanny at Saturday Inlet. What did he . . . local criminal activity unregistered . . . Sigint relays pirate radio Nootka. . .

What's sigint? said Nadia.

Signals intelligence. James bent to the radio listening intently. It means they are monitoring radio transmissions.

A voice broke in very loud, very clear. *Mayday mayday mayday this is M.V.* Primary Enforcer *at 49 degrees, 10 minutes and 30 seconds north and 125 degrees 53 minutes and 25 seconds west, ship white and orange, one hundred ninety feet, fifty-two people on board repeat.*

Primary Enforcer *this is* Nutrition Valor *we have you at 49–10–30 and 125–53–25 we read you unable to assist.*

What's Mayday? said Nadia.

A ship in trouble. Somebody's going down.

He tied on the sagging life vest. It leaked stuffing like dandruff. Only one of them would go. If he should overturn at least she would still be alive. If he could not get back this night he would signal from the coast with his small flashlight, the black tube he had given Nadia long ago on the rooftop. In Morse: T for tomorrow. Then OK.

What if you're not okay?

James said, I will be okay. He turned to her and bent down and kissed her, his long hand on the back of her head, tangled in her thick, flying hair. Don't run off with anybody while I'm gone.

Right. Some guy with a bigger boat. And then with difficulty, she smiled.

He kissed her again and they ran the skiff down the tracks.

A sharp and level wind came from over the sea to fill his sail and send him flying headlong into the long rollers. They were crowned with froth and drift. He found a kind of wild suicidal joy in the salt water pouring over the bow and the lift, the rise, then skidding down the far side of a long roller, and all the sea before him.

As he pushed on he saw that he was heading to land too far north of the wreck. He had to come about and get out to sea and come back at another approach. Now he could see each separate rock half buried in surf and the distinct limbs of the drooping firs. There were tiny pocket beaches of pewter-colored sand. The firs that had survived clear-cutting in the ravines stood like drenched persons with their arms hanging down and draining rain. As he watched, a great fir waved its drooping limbs and teetered in the wind and then fell. It came down the cliff end over end, snapping branches, its roots flinging dirt and stones and it shattered on the rocks at the bottom. The surf swarmed up to take it to pieces.

He came about: he ducked and slipped to the other side and then the sail went slack on top of a wave crest and spun, caught the wind again, and then he was burning along the surface on a beam reach and headed out to the great sea. The melonseed was so far over to port that the rail was under. James went on, far to the southwest so that the wicked and beautiful coast receded and became indistinct. Lighthouse Island was only a line of trees and the great tower and within it Nadia, her hand on the Fresnel lens.

A cross wave struck him on the port side and buried him in foam and salt; James took the can in one hand and began to bail.

After a long reach he brought her about on the northeast tack and this one took him straight into the inlet and the wrecked ship and at last a feeling that he was truly sailing, in flight on the surface of the ocean and despite his weakness a sense of uplift and joy, of speed.

He ran the skiff into the small inlet where the ship's prow and bridge thrust up out of the waves. The rollers lost their momentum here. A small sandy beach shone like satin in the gray daylight. A small doglike animal trotted across it pressing in shining paw prints that were neatly washed away by the thin, shelving waves. There was a safe half buried in the sand, a great deal of storm drift, some enormous logs and ranks of smaller wood, torn fabrics that seemed to lift and simmer in the waves, bottles of all kinds, net floats, seashells, and a sodden, discolored novelty chicken hat thrown overboard from some cruise ship.

He stood up in the dancing boat and felt in his legs a colorless sensation. He had tired more quickly than he knew. The prow and part of the ship's bridge and crew quarters were abovewater like a slanted and half-drowned block of apartments, rising far over his head. Far below the surface the railings plunged down into the depths and disappeared. Indefinable things waved in the current. Her name was painted in bright letters on her side: M.V. *Nutrition Packer.*

This was yet another Primary Resources ship gone aground, a fish processor.

He dropped the sail on the skiff and then tied on to the angled rail at the point where it came out of the waves. The ship seemed about two hundred feet long but he couldn't tell with two-thirds of her underwater. He swung up on the rail. On the white wall of the bridge rising above him someone had painted, *Bargaze Maru salvage rights. Mitts off.*

Damn. Salvage people had already been here. Damn, damn. He stood looking at it, trying to gauge the freshness of the paint. Disappointment left him with a feeling of outrage, as if he had been robbed.

He walked carefully up the sloping deck to the bridge where the glass panes were smashed in and rain poured onto the consoles and the monitors. His rubber-soled shoes gripped the grainy deck. He climbed in. Most of the navigation devices had been pulled out and the wires stripped. He pulled out the map sliders but the charts had all been taken or perhaps destroyed before it was abandoned. Secretive bastards.

James climbed out again. They would have had warning before they struck and so did not leave much behind and whatever they did leave had been salvaged.

Where would the galley have been?

He eased through a tilted and destroyed cafeteria; the furniture and dishes were underwater at the far end where the steep slope made a pool. The water was clear and not silted and when he shone the flashlight into it he could see dishes and glass jars and cutlery heaped up against the downward bulkhead. The place was awash in squid and rubber gloves. It was growing dark.

One or two jars seemed unbroken and it took him a long time to take hold of them. His feet were protected by his shoes but he had no gloves. In the dimming light he dropped into the freezing water up to his waist and shone the flashlight down into the water and kicked aside the broken glass until two jars were lying clear of the glass fragments. He placed the flashlight on a shelf, held his breath and went under and felt slowly and carefully. After a while he had the two jars and a bowl. He took them back up through the galley where forty-gallon pots had tumbled against one another and giant jars of mustard and pepper and mayonnaise had all fallen into the water, the contents washing away.

He found two large Mylar packets. They were not broken and he read the labels: *Rotini Pasta* and *Scrambled Egg Powder,* twenty pounds each. He had no idea why the salvage rats had missed them but they were a gift, treasures. He would return with something to show and this made him happy in the increasing dark.

He groped up the sloping deck and then out.

He could see the island from the prow. There stood the lighthouse tower with a pinpoint of light in it and the entire island surrounded with a haze of spray. He turned the flashlight toward the tower and made one long dash. After an interval he made another dash. T: tomorrow. Then OK.

He knew she would pass her hand or a sheet of cardboard over the light if she saw his signal. There it was; three dashes, then a dash, dot, and dash. OK. The light of a soul and human speech in a stony world.

That night he sheltered in the bridge and instrument room, wrapped in everything he had, including the life jacket, listening to the rain. He lay on the wet, sloping floor. It took forever to get the top off one of the jars. He carefully turned the contents up into the bowl. Then he took up some of the objects on his knife. It was okra. He ate it, and also the next jar; some kind of fish fillets.

And so, he said to the empty ship. I have learned to sail on the open sea and I'm coming back with rotini and scrambled egg powder. So there you go.

CHAPTER 45

Nadia remained in her cold tower for a few minutes after she had sent her Morse signal with the kerosene lantern. She nervously flipped the microphone switch and slid the sliders. Then in the blue evening snow she saw the cat trying to paw the door of the house open.

Wait! she shouted. Wait! She ran down the steps of the light tower at top speed. When she held the house door open he darted inside and hid.

She poured in fuel pellets to make a large, hot fire in the stove that would last all night and went to bed without supper. Let the cat make up its own mind, come when it would. She named him Edward because they have to have names, as far as she knew.

She put out some of the bottled beef for the cat but nothing for herself. She wasn't doing much hard work. She didn't need to eat. But she felt a draining in herself, a sort of systems crash. She listened to the wind that sang like an oboe at the windows. Something beat regularly against the side of the house as if to draw her attention while another thing forced the front door. Nadia imagined Terminal Verna landing on the shelly beach in the nocturnal surf in some podlike Jules Verne nautical thing, with her teeth like burglar bars, stalking creepily up to the house with her truncheon. She imagined James trapped inside the wrecked ship. Then the skiff going down under a great wave and its sail overwhelmed. She jumped out of bed in flight from her thoughts and went to the junk room and found a broken chair. She took up a chair leg. If Terminal Verna or anybody else showed up they would have a fight on their hands.

She carried the FM radio into the bedroom. She used up fuel pellets as if there were no tomorrow. She got back into bed. "At night the old world comes into its own," said Dr. Maturin and he was right. She laid the chair leg alongside her body like an extra arm.

The pellets were disappearing from under the woodshed roof. Soon it would all be gone. Then they would have to go drag in driftwood, hoping the sea would bring them more. Then they would have to cut down trees and run away as they fell, and then cut them up limb by limb and saw through the great solid trunks and then split them. But they were not strong enough.

Then she sat up, dressed in many layers of underclothes and one of James's flannel shirts, listening to a thin, high sound.

The cat. He was at the door to the bedroom, crying in a small voice. Now that James was gone, now that there was just one person, he had decided to take a chance on not being strangled and drowned.

She sat up and made enticing sounds. The cat danced around with his front feet a few steps and then looked up at her and began to purr. He was dressed in a marmalade tuxedo with a white muzzle and an orange mustache that made him look as if he had been eating tomato sauce.

He stood beside the bed and glanced up at her for a few seconds at a time, and away again. Then he jumped up and stalked across the blankets purring with his green eyes fixed on Nadia and clearly thinking about the 98.6 degrees of warmth he would sleep next to, not to speak of the hot-water bottle.

Edward, *catto de tutti catti,* you are a he. I knew it. She reached out to him.

He became brazen and adoring. His purr was thunderous and he gripped and ungripped his paws on the blankets, saturated with happiness. Then he lay on his back with his front paws doubled on his chest and fell asleep. He quivered in dreams. His tail jerked and lashed and he woke himself up and stared at her and then fell asleep again. Nadia watched him for a long time in a fascinated amazement and wondered if she ought to pet him. When she did he seemed very happy. An advance into the world of animal communication.

She turned on Big Radio to find where in the reading cycle they were now but suddenly it had taken on a hollow, booming background noise as if the satellite had broken out of its orbit and landed on another planet that suffered from an electronically troubled atmosphere, broadcasting from the bottom of a Venusian ocean. It was now arriving at the time of year for the end of *Pickwick* and the beginning of the easterners but it was hard to listen to. This was very worrisome.

She sat up and shook the receiver. Edward woke up and also stared at the receiver. In the background there was a sound like gulls, some kind of birds, who twittered behind the strains of Handel's *Water Music*. How could that be? The predator birds of space. The reception had to be connected to the console up in the tower and she had ruined something.

Well, damn, she said. The quality of the sound was not only grating but hollow in a scary kind of kids' horror story way but she listened anyway. The nighttime music was selections from Boccherini. It seemed that it was now being broadcast from wherever the satellite had fallen, its orbit degraded, into the depths of some Magellanic cloud.

In the morning she carried the radio back to the desk, made herself some hot water and citrus powder and picked up Edward and told him he was a good cat, to keep watch in the night as he had.

She climbed the tower and pressed her face against the glass. She could see the little melonseed, tied up on the rail of the wreck, lifting and falling, riding the high and icy waves, snatched about by its painter. It appeared to be the size of a hazelnut shell.

Now I see you, she said. I see your boat. Not yet in peril on the sea. At the sound of her voice the dials jumped once and then fell flat again, like her barred handheld counter that counted nothing, which she had used to pretend to be checking cable in that distant escape time, the flight through the endless city, which was not endless and which was actually only two months ago.

As she came in the house she heard a crashing sound in the central hallway. Edward had trapped a large rat behind the radio and with screaming noises he flung himself into the narrow space where the rat had slithered. He knocked off a cup that spun and broke on the floor. Behind the radio the rat stood on its hind legs with that peculiar rodent wavering motion of its low-necked head trying to see where Edward was.

At the last moment the rat shot out from behind the radio and scrambled up one of the supporting beams. Edward went up after him in a flash of orange and white and got him by the hindquarters. The rat turned, shrieked, and began to snap and they both fell nearly one story and landed hard. The rat got away. He raced across the floor and into the kitchen with surprising speed.

Edward and the rat both flew into the woodbox fighting in a frenzy of screams and flying fuel pellets. A last shriek and Edward stood with the bloody rat hanging from his mouth. He wanted neither praise nor petting. He was Conan the Barbarian, he was Banu Shan the Warrior of the Golden Plains, deadly and merciless. He trotted away to the bathroom, where he ate it. He killed rat after rat all day with Nadia cheering him on. And she found herself stepping on small round things that proved to be rat eyeballs, popped out of their heads when Edward crushed their skulls.

There he was, her first animal, slaughtering other animals.

James worked in the boat shed with what tools he could find to construct a kind of cabin on the eighteen-foot skiff. He took off the splash guard and fitted in planks cut from the door of the junk room, planed on the edges and cut in graduated sizes to slide in the narrowing gunnels of the cuddy. He was going to have to try to sail to Saturday Inlet twenty miles to the north.

Outside the shed, snow fell lightly in a kind of incredible purity he had never before seen. The snow slid off the roof of their house in long slanting sheaves. Nadia came to the boathouse, carrying something hot wrapped in a blanket. The orange cat marched behind her for a few steps and then became alarmed by the snow and turned and ran back to the house.

They sat together and drank hot steaming citrus-powder drink from a jug, passing it back and forth. The snow made the firs with their drooping limbs appear to have been quilled in white. It fell in layers along the launching trackway into the sea and the weak sun cast sparkling colors along the drifts.

It won't be long, he said. I should have this finished before long.

I don't want to leave, James, she said. She began to cry. It burst out of her in painful sobs and she was helpless to stop. She put her hands over her face and cried and could not stop herself. I don't ever want to leave this island, not ever, not ever. Please.

Baby stop, he said. He slid his hand into her collar and caressed her neck. Darling. We have to.

She took a handful of snow and pressed it against her eyes.

He stirred the lanky dark-red hair from her face. She turned and looked at all the great fir standing in wings of white. Their island a snowy outpost of the continent surrounded by flooding surf the color of pearls charging up the rocks and a hissing sea where the snow spattered lightly and died in drifting columns.

CHAPTER 46

Far away to the east a great landmass called Siberia was throwing weather at Lighthouse Island and the northwest coast at velocities that were beyond description. Creeping acres of debris rose up on the waves and glistened with bodies, propane tanks, truck tires, barrels. Cliffs collapsed into the surf. The waves piled up to thirty and forty feet, streaming with foam, and struck the stone-bound coast in a haze of spray, and the atmosphere was dense and gray. Lethal surprises awaited them every mile.

The *Bargage Maru* flew north six points off the wind with a sail like metal, hard, full of hurricane. Captain Gandy and a redheaded man whose face looked as if it had been boiled were seized on the wheel. Their feet skidded on the wheelhouse decking. Gandy was glad of the storms. He and his crew could live through them and Primary Cruisers could not. Primary's charts were outdated but Gandy knew his way from shoal to cape and far beyond, and far beyond. They climbed up the striped waves living out the fearsome grammar of the sea with sliding, creaking cargo.

Something came over the side riding a wave and struck the cookhouse and washed off the port side.

What? Gandy shouted.

Barrel!

The sixty-foot schooner was a traveling junk yard, a floating thrift shop that sailed up and down the coast carrying anything Gandy could make a profit on, to all the little settlements both hidden and disclosed. Gandy had kinky blond hair and an earring made of woven gold wire. He was short. He had an underbite that made a fence of his lower teeth shining out of his beard. His hair sprang out of his head in corkscrews as if it had been wound up inside and then released. He would buy and sell almost anything and so on the deck of the *Bargage Maru* crates of stolen hair dye, twists of hard tobacco from the far south, expired pharmaceuticals and engine parts surged against their straps in the storms. A pile of scrap metal shrieked rust on rust and steel on steel. In the hold crates of stale rations and rope, bales of used clothing, illegal fish, and a contraband crate of rifle and shotgun parts slid and smashed at their bindings.

The schooner tore north at ten knots, sank with the dropping motion of a boat in a following sea, and then she began to rise again. Wet men appeared out of the rolling white water, along with the engine parts, the stolen hair dye, the expired pharmaceuticals, and so on.

The smell of fuel-pellet smoke; Gandy signaled another crewman to take his place and lifted his binoculars. They slid past the lighthouse on the small island. Gandy saw a man struggling along the elevated walkway in a blowing coat and his head down. He was pushing what looked like a wheelchair with a load of something. The man lifted his head; his face in the binoculars' wallowing lenses was lean and the eyes deep shaded. Gandy thought he saw a figure moving about in the glassed-in cupola of the light tower. And then the *Bargage Maru* slid past and Lighthouse Island and its two sinister occupants disappeared in the tearing rain.

How long have they been there? the mate shouted.

Saw them last time, Gandy cried. There's a directional antenna on top of the light tower.

I know it, the mate yelled. Been there forever.

They're going to starve if they aren't being resupplied.

Inspectors for Primary. Spies.

Maybe.

They left the lighthouse behind and after an hour they passed the ruins of Left Hand Bay. Only the black chimneys were left standing on the gentle slope of a delta, running cascades of ashy water into the sea. A Primary gunship had shelled the place for noncompliance and assaults on inspectors two years past; ten dead, many injured. The men stared at it and one of them lifted his streaming watch cap and held it briefly to his heart and then put it back on.

Another scrapper ship was coming past to windward on the opposite tack, a triangle of jib and a shortened mainsail. She trembled and sprayed and slid along on her side. Light flashed from her bow. It was the *Closed Third,* under Captain Britt Contreras. She signaled:

Primary processor xx'd up on Goat Shoals R there people on Lighthouse Island?

Confirm primary processor claim salvage Yes people on L.I. Cruise ship grounded Barkley Sound, per overland news, take it.

Will not chance the graveyard. Light up at Sat Inlet. B.v.

B.v.

Bon voyage.

Gandy went below and sat with Sparks at the VHF marine radio. Hot tea rolled out of their cups and scalded their knuckles. They drank it down like molten amber. Gandy dried his hands on a bunk blanket and rolled a cigarette. The air in the cabin was thick as a fabric with smoke and cooker fumes and wet hair.

Did you pick up Primary?

I think their dispatch station is washed out.

Okay, then turn that off, said Gandy and Sparks reached for the

FM dial where Big Radio was playing. Female Voice One was announcing the end of December's Christmas Week with Charles Dickens. *And so we move through the year to the short days of January,* she said, and behind her voice was the sound of gulls and a murmuring. Another voice.

What? Gandy grabbed Sparks's hand. Listen.

Sparks stared at the FM. What is that?

It's changed. Is there another voice in the background?

They listened but the ship was noisy with wind and water. Gandy put his scarred hands into his armpits to warm them. The voice said, *Now I see you. I see your boat. Not yet in peril on the sea.*

It sounded like Female Voice One but it was speaking *behind* Female Voice One.

The bastards have grabbed Big Radio, Gandy said. They are breaking it up. Some other station is breaking in.

Where's the uplink? said Sparks. I thought it was down in the south of the world.

You wonder, eh? You wonder.

CHAPTER 47

Saturday Inlet was a dwindling settlement of ten cinder-block houses. At the shoreline trash seethed and lifted in the wash of the sea. The houses, lined up at the water's edge, held on to their roofs as if by the hat brims. They were the color of smoke and jittering light poured out of the small windows from television screens. Wind chargers spun in the hurricane winds, driftwood knocked with timid sounds at the ruined dock.

Up on the steep sides of Saturday Inlet waterfalls spouted and roared and the streams ran around the cinder-block houses sweeping away oily liquid refuse. Nearly all the people had been moved here ten years ago from somewhere in the endless city to work on the dock but Primary Resources had misplaced the paperwork; the repair supplies never came and the foreman never arrived, so no one worked at repairing the dock. The people lived like lost domestic animals, slow and indifferent. They sat all day and watched scenes of hygienic people in designer interiors pour down refreshing drinks, somewhere far away in the great city and now the unbelievable new program where they executed criminals on live TV. It made them understand something deep and primitive about the agencies. Their paralysis grew.

They survived on supplies delivered once every two weeks by truck. They regarded the landscape as alien, incomprehensible, treacherous. The mountains rose straight up all around them in a still and silent wrath, hackled with dead fern.

It was said that once a woman walked up the mountainside and had met her double and was led away, and her body was not found for two years. A man had set an illegal net without applying for net privileges but when he pulled it from the water something charged out of it and took his leg off at the knee. So they heard from the truck driver. They stayed in their houses, close to shore. From time to time children shouted over the water at the far cliffs to hear the echoes, they climbed out on the collapsing dock, they set fire to the schoolhouse as if to make themselves a childhood out of charred boards, floating trash, broken metal; stories to tell in years to come, wild escapades. In the end the children went back inside and shut the door. The abandoned echoes called and called.

Sometimes at night the people heard the voices of the great horned owls that sounded like a soft, otherworldly jeering. Steller's jays shot like blue rockets down the inlet screaming and a river fell into the far end of the inlet in a series of furious, white cascades. Seals like silkies rose and stared at the lights onshore and sank again and when they were underwater they became magical beings. Fish both big and little and squid with wormy arms went creeping about the sea. A blacktail deer up in the mountains strolled among rusted and abandoned skidders with all the vanished rain forest shining in her eyes.

Now great storms had arrived. They melted the soil, and rocks came tumbling down through thick stands of ferns, gorse, the whins and stubby alders, like rolling heads. The wind ripped off parts of the roofs and water drained into their beds. The truck had not come in for a month and hunger stared in their windows.

And so the Five Companions met together to decide what was to be done.

Colin the Radio Guy ran into the storehouse. Inside three others shifted from foot to foot to press water from their rubber shoes. The storage bins were empty and the tools gone except for a carpenter's level and a come-along.

What's that you got, Colin? Hey, hey, Colin?

Colin wiped rain from his glasses. It's, um, a bannock.

Where'd you get the flour?

From that barrel in the battery shed.

The inspector classified that as spoiled last trip.

Well, we've got to eat something, you know. The road is out.

I don't believe you.

Colin stepped to the doorsill to run out into the cold rain, out of this dank storehouse with hungry people running spoons along the floor of the bins to scrape up grains of quinoa and grits. Septic tanks had overflowed in their sodden graves and blue sewage with fibrous wavering tissues slid in sheets among the houses.

Nobody believes me, said Colin.

Why do you meet up there? a woman said. You're going to get us in trouble. She splashed from foot to foot. Why don't you fix the door so the rain don't come in? You Five Companions. What a stupid name. Do something besides give yourselves stupid names.

Fix it yourself, said Colin.

With what, said the man. All the tools traded off to Gandy. He's a hard man. I wouldn't have taken a place's only tools.

But you traded them, didn't you.

Well, I wish we hadn't. And you up there messing with a radio. This place is going to get a reputation. We're going to end up in reports, here. Then the man shifted his padded coat collar closer around his neck. His damp white breath poured out. God, God, God, what are we going to do?

You could get fish, then, said Colin. Set nets.

That was tried, said the woman. A man tried it once. She stared down into her steel bowl and its handful of semolina. So I don't know.

Colin bolted through the rain and wind clasping the bannock under his coat. It was warm against his heart. He scrambled uphill on a path like a running stream and far above him the bottle house winked with light through alder leaves. It was a clean light shining and chased with ferns. Sweet wood smoke rolled out of the chimney and downhill under the whip of the wind. Up there were friends, there was light and talk and a hot drink. Colin, Colin, where have you been?

CHAPTER 48

The Five Companions had begun to meet together three years ago after the failure of the midnight Squid Fest. Each of them had been sent to Saturday Inlet from some other place except Chan. It was understood that Chan had escaped from a labor camp somewhere far inland because his hands were blocky and stiff from years of heavy work and a puckered scar ran down one forearm, and his upper lip on the right side had been deeply cut. He had appeared one morning sitting on the dock, without a ration card or an ID or work assignment papers.

People came out of their houses in the early morning and stared at him.

Fell off a processor, he said. Swam ashore. You never saw me.

Right, they said, and sat on their doorsteps for a smoke and tea and looked the other way.

When Chan first arrived in Saturday Inlet he lived under a rock up on the mountain for a while. He was a broad, strong man with curling black hair frosted with gray from hard times and hunger. He hiked up the mountain and from there he saw a long white beach and beyond that an island with a lighthouse. He came back down to Saturday Inlet with a backpack load of bottles that had washed up on the white-sand beach and then went back for more. Before long he had enough to start the walls of a bottle house. The cinder-block people watched him stride off into the unknown mountains and come back alive.

Chan sang aloud and wrapped his broad head and curly black-and-gray hair in a pirate's bandanna. He traced out pig paths in the thick undergrowth. He walked up the south arm of the inlet, a jutting cape, and stood on the gleaming black of a coal seam and watched clouds in lengthy rafts skimming the sea and its foils and its shining. On the distant horizon he saw a Primary Resources heavy cruiser plowing through the rollers, throwing spray. He saw the supply truck lurching down the switchbacks at the head of the inlet with its load of supplies. Chan held out his palms to the sun.

Lord, he said. Great and powerful Lord, help me kill my enemies.

He fished without a permit and gathered driftwood. He came down through the bracken, the parchment-colored fern, through the spiny gorse, carrying a backpack of coal and cloudberries in season, traded some to Captain Gandy for an FM radio. He made pig traps and butchered what he caught; their blue guts rang with chiming flies. He roasted the piglets slowly, lovingly. He wove nets and lifted them streaming from the sea rocks. He searched the long white beach where the waves came all the way from the Sea of Okhotsk and were choked into the Aleutian Trench and then rolled into the gyre that circled the North Pacific so that net floats set sail from Japan and came to the scattered inhabitants of the northwest coast like happy rubber unbirthday presents. Many things washed up in Saturday Inlet and Chan knew how to make something useful from all of them except the Feet. For some unknown reason they were always left feet.

The people who lived at the shoreline were nervous about him and did not like him but didn't know what to do about it. And so he was called the Uncanny.

Four people finally hiked up the hill to help build the bottle house. Colin the Radio Guy; Oli the schoolteacher in her wide flowered skirts; the Toastmaster in his top hat; Everett bald and ink-stained and anxious. Boredom and idleness had worn them down to a chronic disquiet, a pointless unresting anxiety. Each one of them felt privately that he suffered from some kind of mental disease that had to be hidden from everyone else.

So they came up the hill and helped to lay in rank after rank of sparkling vodka bottles and whiskey bottles. They became entranced by the project. It was the pointless, happy play of children. It was like playing house. Nobody was making them do it nor were they being paid in credits or coupons. They cemented a bond among themselves just as they cemented bottles layer on layer until the walls rose over their heads. They found themselves laughing together with sticky hands among the crushed ferns.

Chan taught them how to weave nets, how to dig a pig trap. So from time to time they feasted and took in the sweet smell of a driftwood fire and said this was good, the hot shower device was good, and the roof planked with mill sidings and the fireplace and the stone floor. It was all good. As they worked they listened to Chan's FM radio and the voices of Male and Female One, the immortal stories, the yearly round; *Blood and Sand,* Carton mounting to the scaffold, Akhmatova's *Requiem.*

We don't have a permit for this, said Everett.

So? Chan looked around at the bright new leaves of the alder brush and springing fern surrounding the bottle house, piles of chips, sludging cement waste, pig remains. He took up his ax to bring down saplings for the walls of a compost bin. It's done already. Who is going to tear it down?

Maybe. Well, no one.

We got to get something going here, said Chan. People down there living on food deliveries, waiting for some year Primary realizes,

Oh shit! Here's the paperwork! Dock not fixed! Slap foreheads, look around, move those citizens! How many years? Let's have a bonfire, roast something. Chan's pronunciation of *f* and *r* was slightly off because of the deep scar through his upper lip. Oli, the former schoolteacher, noticed it. She found it appealing somehow.

Chan's ax flashed and he made three expert slashes, three alder saplings down.

A Squid Fest! cried Oli. She gave a half turn that made her pieced bright skirts fly around her ankles. We will boil squid and sing. I know a song . . . "Adrian's coming, over the sea . . ."

But nobody came to their Squid Fest. A clean spring night, a thin moon. But the people in the cinder-block houses were not used to the taste of shellfish and the squid looked like entrails and tasted like seawater. There was no reason to sit outside in the cold air when inside there was light and music and beautiful people and the soul-gripping new execution program. The camera shots that made them want to scream or flee but they did not.

The Five Companions with their hopeful fantasy name sat alone at the shore; Chan and Oli the schoolteacher, and Everett who longed to produce books, Colin with his homemade FM receiver and his father the Toastmaster who wore a top hat. Oli lifted her bright soprano voice in three lines of a remembered lament and then fell silent. The bonfire burned down and they were left with stars and waves in a lonely celebration by the sea.

They met again at Eastertime, when the fawn lilies bloom, and the blackberry and cloudberry are covered with minute, shattering blossoms, when the broom up on the naked mountains over the inlet is swept with yellow flowers, when *Alice in Wonderland* and segments of *Lord of the Rings* come on Big Radio, the time of fantasies and quests. From those departed voices stories flowed and ran in caverns measureless to man, beyond the sunless sea.

And so what if, there now? said Chan. A blackened kettle sat on the fire. Flame light winked from all the bottle ends as he jammed a length of rebar in the coals, shifted a stick. What if? Look here. He held up a shining china egg in his hand. Here. Found on the long beach. Take it and speak and as long as it is in your hand, nobody will interrupt you or else. Say I. This is so your head can run loose, hey, a getaway car.

What if what? Everett wiped his balding head. You mean what if people came to a festlike gathering, a better one, something more kind of happy fun?

Affirmative. Nobody owns your head, said Chan. Nobody's eaten your brains. Who will take it? The china egg shone in his hand and the kettle grumbled and spouted.

Yes, they have eaten our brains, my dear sir, said the Toastmaster. He lay down his net shuttle. Too late, too late. Long ago human beings could make up stories. He gestured at the radio with a bony old hand like a signpost pointing to a dead past. No more. They were different, sir, and possessed different brain lobes.

No, no, said Oli. She lifted one foot and stamped it on the floor. Imagine it, it's free. Imagine a midsummer night festival and people who can sing; it would make echoes, and the bonfire light would shine on the waves. There. I just imagined it. She picked up her knitting needle and stared at her work through a slippery fall of hair come loose from its braid.

Colin the Radio Guy said, Make them up, why not? It's just voices. I hear voices all the time.

Tell us stories about China, said Oli. Chan? China, across the sea. She did not look up from her knitting. She had unraveled old torn sweaters from the clothing bales. I have looked it up in my only volume of *The World Book,* which is C.

I'm Kazakhstani, said Chan. He handed Oli the egg. Go.

She took it from his big, scarred hand slowly so that she could feel his hand on her own if only for a moment. Oli's hair was a rich, sliding brown and she was not much over thirty and her rubber shoes, squamous as they were, were laced with bright ribbons.

What if we called ourselves the Five Companions? she said. And sang every night? Well, once a week. Oh, if only we had a tuning fork! She handed the egg to Colin.

What if I asked Gandy to bring me a dog? said Colin.

My son, said the Toastmaster. You would have to hide it. It would bark. They bark.

No interrupting, said Chan. No disagreeing, because then everything turns into an argument. He got up and rolled a teacup between his battered hands and then lifted the kettle. You got to get a grip on how this works, fellow companions. We did it in labor camp. Common in labor camp, relief, hope which springs eternal in April, usually. Chan turned to see the caution in their faces. Yeah, labor camp. He reached down and took the crackled china egg. Listen, I imagine a system of justice that is just. Hearty men who rise at night to the sound of a bell to take up arms. I imagine a snowy night and a bottle of wine. Cloudberry wine. You don't think we can do it?

We can do it.

They met night after night and passed the egg from one to another and it clattered on Oli's copper rings, it made a dry sound in the hands of the Toastmaster, Colin tossed it in the air and caught it again as he spoke of a new antenna and voices from other continents. Everett brooded over it before speaking, like a hen. They invented a village of people who made their own houses. They gestured from hard uncushioned chairs and said, What if there were chickens and we could get a shipment of chickens? What if we built a fish smoker? What if houses could not be entered by Primary inspectors without permission? Imagine that people came together and cleaned up the trash. What if we had a map of the interior showing where the roads go? They spoke their new thoughts and shells broke loose from their wits like the casts of nameless sediments. They imagined daring journeys and distant kingdoms, lights on the water sent out in quavering lines from midnight ships, voyages to splendid coasts, courage and bravery, people who sang.

Oli imagined people building their own houses up the mountain on seven levels and that every level had a name. That spotted dogs sat upon roofs and barked up and down at one another. That the lights that shone out of rainy windows were the golden lights of lamps. Through the umber and rust colors of alder brush and broom, in the steep up-and-down world of leafy odors and glinting rainy roofs and ochre nap of bracken, glimpses of the shining sea, people would file down the seven levels, carrying lanterns, singing, to come to a festival at the new-made dock. She imagined a schoolhouse with a mossy roof whose teacher had old books with maps that showed the polar snows and the drainage area of the Columbia River and the palms of California.

Everett dreamed of printing books. The only one he possessed was stitched together from wallpaper. He would record the stories of old people. He invented the old people. Everyone has a story they must tell, everyone has lived through events they have not chosen but they must make of these events the plots of their lives and Everett would record them all. He imagined his book in people's hands, all the people of the coast sinking down into their beds at night with candles lit and moths circling like planets and they would read and read and read.

The elderly Toastmaster had found his top hat and tuxedo among the used clothing carried in on the supply truck and had always thought of himself as a celebration arranger. Now he spoke his dreams aloud and planned spectacular Squid Fests where he would be master of ceremonies and tell jokes, convincing everyone to donate to those in need.

His son, Colin, reached for the china egg to invent technological tales of radio waves but then Colin saw them squint and brace themselves for imaginings they could not understand. Well, he said. I imagine a message board on air. Where people can radio in and say, Apples for sale. The salmon are running. A Primary gunship is on its way to Nootka. Now hear this, Nootka: Get together at the dock and chop their lines when they tie up. Tear up their applications. Set their ship on fire.

The other four Companions stared at him in shocked silence.

Where will this lead? cried Everett.

We're getting wild here, said Chan He rolled a cigarette and lit it, took two puffs and threw it in the fire.

CHAPTER 49

Then the hurricanes arrived, typhoons of wind that did not stop. Winds drove white-topped waves up the inlet in violent ranks and they could no longer set nets or make a way through the whipping bracken on a pig hunt. Like everyone else, they were hungry. Like everyone else, they were unnerved by the news that the Facilitator had been executed. It was not broadcast because of his rank but the people in the cinder-block houses had now seen at least five executions and so they knew. They could imagine. In fact they could not unimagine it.

The new Facilitator, Standford West, was supposed to be reassuring but he was suspect, probably a computer-generated image.

Chan the Uncanny stared out his window at the tempest and when electrical storms struck, the bottle house was filled with an illumination like the methylated spirits of lightning decanted throughout the rooms.

Then in the middle of the night a shock of stunning thunder roared down the inlet with a force that shook the windows. The next morning Chan went up the road on foot to see what had happened, slogging foot by foot through the mud, head down against the wind. At the end of the inlet, as Old Number Four Road began its climb upward, he came

upon the site where an avalanche had come down along with half the
mountain. The rains had loosened the scree on the treeless mountainside and the road ended in a great rockfall, spattered with the wiglike
bracken torn up by the roots. They were out of food and cut off from
any deliveries and Chan knew that no more would come. He stood at
the foot of millions of tons of fallen rock with his ax in his hand.

As Chan looked at the barricade, a man in a uniform came climbing
down the tipped and smoking stone. He was soaked dark and his lips
were white. He was netted all over with thin streams of blood as if he had
been hit with rat shot. The wind shrieked among thin edges of slabs and
boulders freshly broken and pale as doves. The man's khaki pants were
torn at the knees and elbows. He paused on a slab, looking down.

You, he said. Rain cascaded all around him, stone to stone.

They stared at each other.

What? said Chan.

I know you I know your face. It's on the flyers. Escapee.

Yes, said Chan.

You low-life shit. You scum. Important big man higher-up. Convicted of abusing children. I read it.

They made it up, said Chan. His face was expressionless and he
leaned on the ax handle, casual in the tearing rain.

Yeah, yeah. Get up here and help me with Inspector Grandin. He's
injured. The truck is smashed. It's on the other side of the rockfall. We
barely escaped it.

No, said Chan.

Yes, you will asshole. You're under arrest. That ax is classified as a
weapon. Put it down.

Come and take it, said Chan.

There were no more fuel pellets, no soap or citrus-drink powder, tobacco, or baking powder or the heavy flour from unknown grains. The children were hungry and a father sat behind his leaking cinder-block house and wept into his hands. What could you do, what could you do?

Others in the leaking houses could hear him and their hearts ached for him but that night was the trial of James Orotov and his accomplice, Sendra Bentley, the sexual brigand. They sat riveted; it was something to take your mind off images of the Facilitator in handcuffs, the flooding. Sendra Bentley had escaped from a maximum-security prison by shoving a guard into a giant clothes dryer and turning it to "permanent press." She and Orotov had been arrested while trying to board an expensive and luxurious private jet in a tony higher-up estate. The crime was so serious there was extreme pressure from the watching public for their televised execution. James Orotov bent forward in his wheelchair and put his hands in his face and cried out, *You can't imagine the things she knows how to do. I was her slave!*

And Sendra Bentley in a beret and tight sweater and red lipstick struck him and said, *Shut up, you fool.*

After that, the television failed. It winked several times and the picture shrank to a point of blue light and went dead.

Colin stood in the doorway and handed the bannock to Oli and then hung his dripping coat on a nail. Best I could do, he said.

Everett the printer wrote on the first page of his wallpaper book: *The Five Companions met on the 25th day of continual storm.* I suppose this is a kind of chronicle now, he said. It seems a little overambitious. I mean, are we that important?

Yes, said Oli. We're alive and we have souls. She laid the bannock to one side of the fire to warm it and then turned back with a whirl of her skirts, stitched together from the brightest scraps she could find in the used-clothing bales. You matter to yourself anyway, don't you? The stone floor gleamed with water and mud.

"The Chronicle of the Five Companions." Everett hesitated. This was supposed to be for my interviews with old people.

We don't have any old people, said Oli. So just go ahead and keep a chronicle of . . . She paused. Well, of us.

I'm old, said the Toastmaster. He slipped the shuttle into the net weave, his tatty coat shining with stiff nap. But, sir, I would be willing to not be courted as old. Verily, I forgo the honor.

We just made ourselves up, said Everett. He was still hesitant and a deep layer of doubt writhed about in his mind over the audacity of making yourself up. It was kind of a little clandestine amusement.

But we *are* the Five Companions, said Oli. She draped her wet shawl on a chair back and turned it toward the flames. Because we say so. We get to say. She laid her hand on Everett's steaming sleeve. Have courage.

It could be found, said Everett. My handwriting could be identified. They sat in silence.

We could assign somebody to throw it in the sea, said Colin.

I will, said the Toastmaster. If it came to that. And me with it.

It was another night of hammering wind and the surf whipped into volcanoes of snowy water hurling boards and barrels and roofs at the shoal rocks at the mouth of the inlet. Chan held the egg in his hand as if it were one of those Celtic eggs that had inside it a falcon and inside the falcon's beak a ring and engraved on the inside of the ring some magic word. He revolved the egg between two palms and said that the time was upon them to both pray and do.

We have to leave, he said. The five of us. Or starve.

To where? said Everett. Where *is* there?

Banefield, said the Toastmaster. The agricultural station at Bane-field.

How? said Oli.

Chan said, We hire Gandy. We hire his ship.

He isn't a taxi, sir, said the Toastmaster. And he's a hard man.

What have we got to pay him with? Chan sat with his thick forearms across his knees. We must have something he needs. Listen up.

There is great peril facing us. Chan slapped the egg from one palm into the other. They could hear the booming of the surf beyond the windows as it tore the old dock to pieces. Great peril and starvation. We have to imagine striking out, onto the land, or the sea.

There may be limits to thinking things up, said Everett. I don't know what they would be but they're probably *there.*

Chan said, So let them come and confiscate my imagination, go for it, bring it on.

The Toastmaster gripped the arms of his chair. They'll do worse than that, my dear sir, he said. Take care what you say.

Bring it on, said Chan. His Oriental eyes were fixed on the leaping flames, the deep scar through his lip was outlined and his expression was hard. Here I am, I'll tell them my name, that's my front door. We can sit here and do this huddling thing. But if we think and plan and move, I tell you we will dance before the gates of our enemies.

Silence; they thought about it. None of them knew how to garden and it was too wet and too late in the year and there were no tools, there were no seeds. Where to get seeds? No goats or sheep or donkeys or cows or chickens and anyway they did not know how to feed animals or take care of them. They had no way to leave except on foot. They would have to fill out applications for travel permits to go anywhere. None of them knew what lay in the interior. And where was Primary now? Where were the inspectors? Who would accept their applications?

We don't even know how to make soap, said Oli. How do you make soap?

With ashes, said Chan. He shoved the rebar poker into the coals again. Every time has its time and this time's time is now. His hair drifted in frosted spirals in the heat of the fire. I imagine a dragon will come out of the sea and it will attack us but we will defeat it. We will set the dragon's body on fire and out of the fire something mean and small screams and flies away. Nothing left but ashes.

Everett said to himself, *Then the Companions set the dragon on fire.*

Chan turned and stared at the other Four Companions and a gust of wind roared down the chimney and blew evaporating sparks out of the fireplace. He said, We are going to have to find out if Banefield is real because hey, news to you, otherwise we are going to starve.

Everett thought for a moment. His expression grew dreamy. He said, A journey by sea, to strange countries. He ran his hand over the flocking and garlands of the wallpaper pages, generic birds that flew from edge to edge and far beyond.

They handed around triangles of smoking bannock and ate them carefully. They considered Banefield, the mythical village of Barkley Sound. Oli had heard that it was called Barkley Sound either because of barking seals sliding from the rocks there, or because of a black-and-white dog that sat on a headland among the gorse flowers and barked at boats going past. It was some unknown distance to the south, on the edge of a dangerous coast called the Graveyard. It was there that scientists or perhaps magicians had saved all the old heirloom seeds and knew how to raise animals, the secret chemistry of yeast breads; they knew how to build cider mills and presses, which is to say, how to make a wheel roll on an axle.

Gandy says there are people on the island with the lighthouse, said Oli. We need more people than just us, don't we?

Yes, said Colin, and I triangulated . . .

Exactly, said the Toastmaster. Sir, I know who they are. That Orotov man, the crippled one, is a cartographer, sir. He would know the way. The Toastmaster tied off the last warp string of the net and laid down the shuttle. The Shalamovs, talkative people that they were, told me all about the Orotov brothers when they shipped out of here. Said the Orotovs might come someday. Indeed, it must be them.

We can't take a crippled man, said Chan.

Gandy said he saw the guy walking around, said Everett.

Let me speak, said Colin. He made a nervous gesture at his elderly father.

Chan jumped up and put the china egg in Colin's hand and took the top hat from the Toastmaster's silvery head, jammed it onto Colin's, and said, Everybody shut up.

Colin said, The uplink to Big Radio is in the lighthouse tower. He returned the top hat to his father and sat down again with a determined look and crossed arms.

What? said Chan.

I triangulated it, said Colin. Yes, for sure.

Big *Radio*? In that lighthouse?

It is, it is, and there's a transmitter that feeds through the satellite uplink. The woman there, probably the crippled man's wife, must be messing with the radio transmitter. I think probably by mistake. She's turned the mike on by mistake.

I thought it was down in Houston! Chan stared at him. Or what used to be called Houston.

Trust me, said Colin, and took off his taped-together glasses and wiped them. It would be so nice if somebody would.

Oli took the egg and said, The sea has many voices, many gods and many voices.

The Dry Salvages, said Everett.

Then, we go to the lighthouse and get them to come with us, said the Toastmaster.

Everett jumped up, clutching his book in his fingers stained with experimental ink. Why not? The television is dead, why not?

Why not! cried Oli. The inspectors will never get past the rockfall!

The inspectors are *dead,* said the Toastmaster. Squashed under the landslide!

Chan hesitated a moment and then said, Yes, the inspectors are dead.

They all began to yell and dance up and down. Oli cried out, in a fit of daring, We'll just leave! I don't care if I die, it would be worth it!

Colin stood by the FM radio, his hand on the bar dial.

Think of sea-journeys to unknown coasts and risk and discovery and all those in peril on the sea. Think of curious and vigorous people and the ridicule they have endured, now standing on the prow of a ship shaped like a raven skimming into the fog of Barking or Barkley Sound with a black-and-white dog running along a shoreline after them because the first shall be last and the last shall be first. Think of the brave crews and a person who has a chart and explosive thoughts and azimuth compasses and sextants, master of longitudes.

We have to go, said Oli. And I will not be left behind.

Then let's start figuring this out, said Chan. Supplies, stuff to offer Gandy.

Something was gathering in the room, ghosts, or things of another world, bodiless visitors out of the storm or the people who had belonged to the Feet who had walked all the way over the ocean bottom to say, *Now, now.*

Chan said, To the lighthouse. And then to Barking Sound. The time has come. He stood up and spun an unlit cigarette between his fingers. They know it and we know it; the time has come for the kingdom of dreams to go on the offensive.

To Barking Sound, then, said Everett, with his blank book in his hands.

Colin the Radio Guy said, To Barking Sound.

CHAPTER 50

Colin lived for words and signals floating out of the stormy air and into his headphones, up on the mountain in his radio shack. He traded for point contact diodes, capacitors, and breadboards from the black market scrapper ships. Late at night he listened to the pirate station in Nootka and the TV audio and numbers stations with his thin shoulders hunched and his taped glasses askew. Once upon a midnight he had heard the legendary "Lincolnshire Poacher," eight bars of a folk tune played over and over, coming from some distant place. He could not figure it out and so left it. He stalked Primary transmissions and handed on the information to the Five Companions. They had all cheered when he brought the news that the *Primary Enforcer* had gone down, and they gloated over her Mayday.

Colin was an adept at lines of sight, a Druid of invisible talk. In his suffocating shack he put on his handmade headphones and smoked cheap tobacco. He ran his antenna up a hundred-foot Douglas fir that the loggers had missed, and then strung it sideways to another. It was powered by a jerry-built wind charger. His antenna swayed and sprayed rainwater as the Douglas fir was battered by winds.

Colin could receive but not reply to anyone, nor could he call for help or ask where the supply truck was or determine what was happening elsewhere or ask for local weather or find out who had charts. All FM and VHF radio traffic was coastal, broadcasting no more than thirty miles up and down the coast and nothing could reach the interior. This was because all FM traveled line-of-sight and so struck the sides of mountains and rebounded or was absorbed by wet bracken or eaten in flight by lightning. But Big Radio, from its satellite relay twenty thousand feet above, could reach all the coasts and the interior and all the ships at sea.

Chan sat patiently with his thick forearms on his thighs and his coat collar turned up. Outside the radio shack the winter bracken was starched with frost and the mountaintops sprinkled with their first winter snow. Colin's wind charger purred like a cat. Chan listened and smoked. Colin turned his FM dial to 88.3 and Big Radio told them of the Christmas celebrations at Dingley Dell, but around and behind Male Voice One was another voice, barely audible. It sounded like Female Voice One, as if they were together.

Is that her?

Colin nudged the bar dial. That's her. She's breaking in, Chan. There's a transmitter in that rig and she's turned it on by mistake. The people living there. Her. She doesn't even know it.

You're amazing, said Chan.

Oh, thanks, said Colin.

You did this triangulation thing.

Yes, said Colin. And see, see, if we could *get* it, we could *transmit*. Oh, oh, transmit. Colin grabbed his own cheeks. I could die. Transmit.

Yes, and if a Primary gunship picks us up? Forty-millimeter mortars, right through the lighthouse tower.

And before they hit us I would say, "You are evil, we are going to kill you all, come to us, we are waiting for you." Colin smirked a nerdlike murderous smirk.

You are bloodthirsty, said Chan.

I dream bloodthirsty things, said Colin. I want that uplink. In an avid, personal sort of way. If Forensics or Primary gets a fix on the tower, yes, then they'll hit the base and the sea will roar past in white procession filled with wreck. He crushed out his cigarette in an oyster shell. Chan, where did you get that egg?

Chan smiled and punched Colin lightly in the shoulder. Son, I laid it.

The next night Chan jumped out of the rowboat into the surf that surged around the little island at the mouth of the inlet. Colin and Everett jammed the oars in sand as he fought his way through the freezing, sucking undertow and hung the light on one little juniper. It was a signal for Captain Gandy or Captain Britt Contreras. They hoped it would not be drowned out or blown out, and that one of the captains would see it.

Afterward Chan sloshed up the path through the dark and the lashing fern, the spiny gorse. He hoped his fire was not out. He slept alone and would always sleep alone because when some woman discovered the false charges that had sent him to the labor camps she would gasp and turn away. Door slam, so long, how could you? Beast. A tiny rose of light gleamed out of the streaming bottle house, the last of the fire.

The Five Companions sat at the table in the main cabin of the *Bargage Maru*. The schooner rocked on its lines at the collapsing dock in the noise of the beating sea. Chan and Colin had managed to net one sockeye as a gift for the lighthouse people and it thumped steadily in a tub.

Gandy regarded the pile of coins, the sack of coal, a new gillnet woven of some kind of stolen and valuable nylon line, a carpenter's level, and a come-along.

Any of you get seasick?

None of them did or none of them would admit to it.

Gandy leaned forward and said, Miss Oli, are you the only woman?

I can sleep anywhere! she cried. She weltered anxiously in her bright layers. I don't need a cabin!

Chan said, And Colin can fix your radios and there's more coal if you want it to trade.

Gandy said, I can use the coal. My radios are fine. He shifted in his chair and his waxed yellow slicker made cracking noises. His lower teeth gleamed in the blond beard of his undershot jaw. They say there was an old experimental station in Barking Sound but I always thought it was defunct a long time ago. Called Bamfield. Changed to Banefield. Maybe because it turned dangerous, like "bane." Barking Sound is south of here, past Lighthouse Island. It's just before that coast they call the Graveyard. I have no charts, just my rutter.

Just a rutter, said Chan. Oh man. Handmade, sea-level observation.

Yes. And if we pass the entrance to the sound by mistake in the night or in a fog, we end up in the Graveyard. The storms are pretty steady from the northwest now and they'll drive us onto the coast. It's all cliffs, straight up and down as a wall. It will smash us like a sawmill. So we cannot miss that entrance, eh? Beyond that, I have no word. I think this Banefield place is supposed to lie inside the sound to the northeast. You make your own deals at Lighthouse Island with this uplink, but I would give some vital part of my anatomy for charts.

The Toastmaster cried out, Well, sir, well now, the Shalamovs said the man on Lighthouse Island is supposed to be a cartographer as well as a demolition expert.

Ah, said Gandy. You don't say.

Yes, the guy in the wheelchair.

He's not, said Gandy. Or one of them isn't.

So, we should find out, said Chan.

The Five Companions tried not to look at Gandy but at their hands or somewhere else for fear of a refusal. The Toastmaster turned his worn silk top hat around and around in his hands. He had carefully waxed the seams in all their shoes against the salt water and Oli had stitched travel bags for each of them out of pants legs with her avid, winking needle. The bags lay in a pile beside all the food they could collect, wrapped in a rubber sheet and tied. They had fashioned for themselves clumsy sea hats. Into each of the travel bags they had portioned out their treasures: matches, a metal mirror, a knife, a spoon, squares of chenille for towels, slivers of coarse brown soap. When they had pulled the drawstrings shut they felt like Argonauts.

Well then. Chan regarded the glow of his cigarette.

Finally Gandy said, I have a shotgun and a rifle. Are you prepared to shoot?

Chan said, Damn straight.

The others looked at one another nervously.

Captain Gandy spread his hand on the table. And what about the people here?

I showed them how to set nets, said Chan. And traps and where the pig trails are. He lifted his shoulders. They'll do it if they got kids.

Gandy shook his head. Maybe, he said. He turned to Colin. You better take care of those glasses, he said. Because there's a big breakdown in the city. Bad, bad flooding. There may never be any more eyeglasses.

Colin took off his glasses and wiped the lenses and stared at them thoughtfully.

Chan said, Then you'll take us? Yes or no.

Yes.

The Toastmaster said, Gentlemen, and lady, we must all swear on something in immortal and gripping phrases.

And so they sailed away from Saturday Inlet and the long black schooner's keel bit into salt water the color of jade and her patched sails filled with storm and tore her onward and south, her prow bursting into the cresting rollers.

CHAPTER 51

After a day and a night they came to Lighthouse Island. It was a clear, rainless day. The sun shone out between slats of clouds in ladders of radiance on which gulls and petrels sailed up and down, up and down. The lighthouse stood like a white shaft in the air, seen from the rise of a wave. They carried gaff-rigged sails on the two masts and the sails full as moons in the moderate wind. The *Bargage Maru* leaned to one side and a fountain of foam sprayed along her lee as she slid down the boiling scree of a long wave, sent by a storm surge from a distant tempest out in the Pacific, beyond sight except for a hard slaty bank of cloud far to the west.

When they came to the Outer Rocks, they saw at the top of some sea stairs a man and a woman watching. Sails hung out to dry on railings above them, belling in the wind, and the Savonius wind turbine blazed as it spun. The man lifted a pair of binoculars.

Well, he isn't crippled, said the Toastmaster. He held to the rail with one hand and gripped his top hat with the other.

So which one is he? Oli's bright headscarf flapped in the wind.

I think he *used* to be crippled.

The man and the woman seemed bleached as they stood there in their parkas and mufflers. They were people reduced by hunger and the salty wind to a pair of strange and faded angels. The man lowered the binoculars and then stood with a cane in one hand and the other jammed in his coat pocket.

Take care, said Gandy. He has a weapon.

Chan saw the man and the woman staring with the intensity of people who had lost all idea of their own appearance before others, the way animals are who have no sense of how they themselves look, whose minds live only in their eyes and what it is they see. In human beings it is an odd and dangerous look. So the sea beat and spangled on the gray volcanic shelves and threw sequins into the air and overhead the gulls sailed and watched.

The Five Companions climbed into a small skiff and were lowered into the water and came threading through the Outer Rocks with a crewman at the helm. Colin leaned over the side and was seasick, making horrible animal noises. Oli brought with her a canvas carrier with gift food and the salmon.

Permission to come ashore! yelled Chan.

The man handed the binoculars to the woman and put down his cane. Chan thought, *He wants to appear stronger than he is.* Then Chan shouted, Are you Orotov?

Yes! The man put his hands around his mouth and shouted, Who are you?

I am Chan the Uncanny! he called out. We are from Saturday Inlet!

Oli gestured with the salmon, which shone like metal. The Toastmaster lifted his disreputable top hat and bowed. Beside him Everett, bald and ink-stained, held up his large book of wallpaper. Chan shoved his bandanna more tightly around his thick, curling salt-and-pepper hair and his gold earring sparkled.

Orotov and his wife now appeared alarmed. Chan had to admit to himself that the Five Companions looked like lunatics. He shouted again, Permission to come ashore!

Orotov turned to the auburn-haired waif beside him. Their coats were marked with charcoal and salt scum and they were as thin inside these coats as clothes poles.

What do you want? shouted Orotov.

Your help! Charts! Demolition! We are going to Banefield!

There was a long pause as Chan the Uncanny hung on to the tossing gunwale and rose and fell with the chop.

How do you know of us? the man shouted.

Long story! Chan bellowed.

The Shalamovs! screamed the Toastmaster.

And finally Chan shouted, Well, there's more, then!

What?

Now the woman came down three steps to stand behind Orotov; she carried a chair leg.

The uplink! The uplink to Big Radio is in that light tower! Somebody has turned on a mike and you are transmitting!

Nadia stared at them. She was silent and blank for a moment and then said, I was *transmitting*? Transmitting what?

Come ashore, said James. He remained at the top of the steps. Get out of the boat and come ashore.

One of Gandy's crewmen jumped out onto the lower steps and tied onto the bollard and so they all got out one after the other as James watched with the dart gun held openly in one hand. They sloshed up the steps and at last they reached the top gasping for breath and all that they wore blew in the wind while behind them on the sea the dark schooner rode up and down with bare poles and on the horizon was the coming storm.

Chan lifted a flat palm. He said, Peace.

Likewise, said James. He lifted the dart gun and pointed the short barrel at Chan's face. And so tell us all about yourselves.

And so, said Chan. Right now we're travelers. From Saturday Inlet, like I was screaming at you out there in the boat, then. Which is a Primary work station up on the coast.

Okay, said James. I know it from my chart. Nadia stood behind him with the chair leg and now it embarrassed her but she didn't know what to do with it.

A chart! said Everett. He turned to Chan. You see, he has a maritime chart.

Chan crossed his thick arms. We need your charts. Saturday Inlet is all out of food and out of ideas. I hope you weren't counting on sailing up there for steak and eggs.

Actually, yes. We were just about to leave.

Nah, forget it, supplies delivery stopped a month ago, no more soy cheese and so, cheeseless, we five here decided to save ourselves and try for a place called Banefield. So put the gun away. We need you.

James lifted his head to the Pacific behind them. Is that your ship?

No, no, said Colin. That's Captain Gandy, he's a scrapper and a trader, like, illegal, sort of black market, we kind of hired him and it was me, okay? And you are transmitting. He waved both hands in the air like brushes as if to scrub the air of all doubts. It was me, I triangulated on the tower there; it's the uplink to Big Radio and it transmits. Colin then pointed both forefingers at the light tower.

Big *Radio*? Nadia was stunned into blankness. Her big yellow parka beat like a tent in the wind. From the *tower*?

James didn't look up at the tower. He kept his eyes on the group in front of him. I thought so, he said. I couldn't get up the steps.

I was transmitting, said Nadia. Oh my God. And you thought so. And you didn't tell me.

It doesn't matter! said Oli and gave a little leap. It doesn't! Where is Primary now? Lost, no orders. And television is dead.

So, said James.

Long story short, said Chan, we decided to form a company and hire that ship.

We are the Five Companions, said Oli, presenting the fish.

We imagine things, sir, said the Toastmaster, and lifted his top hat.

I build radios, said Colin. So we can hear radio talk and, so, be encouraged, then.

A better life, said Everett holding his wallpaper book. "And on either side of the river was there a tree of life, and the leaves of the tree were for the healing of the nations." *Fahrenheit 451*.

They built a fire of driftwood and looked at one another's faces in the endlessly altering radiance. Light speaks to us and holds us, flames or glowing TV screens, moving illuminated shapes seize human minds, a gift, a ball and chain. They spoke and explained themselves to one another, a tortuous process because they had all spent a lifetime in a suspect world of overlords and beautiful celebrities, and now bloody and terrifying scenes on the screen; a world of deaf, opaque social structures and contaminated language crushed by fear and boredom and awareness weeks. They were just people. They had no script.

Oli brought out her flour and baking powder and made bannocks and the salmon lay upon the coals. Gulls hung overhead as if suspended on wires, turning their yellow eyes from one person to another as they spoke and interrupted one another and explained and then the gulls cried out as the red salmon was torn apart and handed around. The air was full of gull cries, hungry, always hungry.

And so tell me about transmitting, said Nadia. She stared at them with her gray-green eyes fringed in wet black lashes, as if she were guilty of some grave social error, which she was, having muttered death wishes against Earl Jay Warren in the imagined privacy of the light tower, *muttered only,* she told herself, *a mere whispering muttering.*

Couldn't hear! cried Colin. I swear! All people heard sounded like murmuring and the birds!

No indeed, said everybody else.

Be easy, young woman, said Chan. And eat. Here, take another bannock.

Still, her murmuring had gone out all over the Western Cessions, but who now would care? She lifted her head to the light tower, now something other than it was, something *more* than it was, far more, radiating all the great stories to a drowning world.

The flames raveled like neon threads and streamed southeast and threw sparks and old nails glowed in the timbers as they talked and ate. And so these strangers on an island in the North Pacific sat down together on the magnetic lines of dire necessity, a collection of jesters gathered at the far border of the Western Cessions in top hats and over-sized parkas.

Now, said Nadia. She went to the house and brought out the bottle of wine. There was enough for one drink each. They clinked their enamel cups together and said, To Barking Sound.

On January fifth the Companions started for Barking Sound, Everett whispered to himself. He must go on and write the chronicle as if they were a kind of royalty, founders of kingdoms. Their faces were turned to the beckoning wind that came out of the drowning megacities and then over the bare mountains, out of the dissolving tundra. It blew from the remote country known as Japan or Kamchatka, come over the sea to sing to them. In all directions were danger and hunger but also things unexpected. Things that would astonish them. The world unrolling like a scroll or a map of the unexplained and within that another maplike thing equally inexplicable, like the beyonding compulsion that seizes people as they stand looking at an unknown shore with a ship out on the sea waiting for them, and the smell of salt water and rain.

As they tipped up their heads and drank they heard the report of a shotgun. James grasped his cane and stood up and saw a puff of smoke at the rail of the schooner.

That's the signal, said Chan. We've got to board in under an hour. The storm is coming.

CHAPTER 52

Colin, who had been seasick from the hour they left Saturday Inlet, would stay behind and work in the light tower to build a relay transceiver that would transmit on one frequency and receive on another. He had already found the hype-zipped CDs of all the readings, moving with infinite slowness inside the green battery units at the bottom of the tower and was carefully taking the console apart. They agreed that he would transmit whatever information he had at ten o'clock every night. For food he had a pallet of the expired foodstuffs from Gandy's hold, mussels, and the net contributed by Gandy and set in the slot. For company he had Edward the Cat.

Gandy and the crew threw down a boarding net as the skiff bumped against the strakes. A tall thin man shipped his oar and came up first, thin to emaciation but yet he reached down with strong arms and hoisted the young woman aboard with little trouble. James's cane fell from her hand, turning over into the rising sea and was lost.

Let it go, the man shouted. Let it go.

Sparks called up, Sir, sir, come down, sir.

Gandy and Sparks sat at the radio table. The marine radio was set at FM, 88.3. Male Voice One said, *This is the last excerpt from* The Pickwick Papers *before we go on, with the arrival of the New Year, to the tales and poems from the Mysterious East. So let us begin with our final selection. "It is the fate of all authors to create imaginary friends, and lose them in the course of art. Nor is this the full extent of their misfortunes; for they are required to furnish an account of them besides."*

And then Colin's voice, breaking in: *Captain Gandy do you read? This is Lighthouse Island. Try band 16. Do you read?*

Sparks glanced at the captain, not knowing what to do.

Gandy picked up the VHF mike and turned the knob to band 16, clicked to transmit, and said, Read you loud and clear, Lighthouse.

A nerdlike scream of triumph erupted from the speaker.

They set sail in a cold, hard wind and light snow racing across the deck in gusts. Nadia held to the rail and watched as the lighthouse tower disappeared, pouring out the great stories and poems of the world, and in their interstices, messages from the present disaster.

The *Bargage Maru* drove on southward with only occasional glimpses of the Velveteen Mountains of the coast. Here and there on the sea the rafts of debris streamed up the crests, stringing along torn roofs and clothing and bodies.

In the dark hold the passengers huddled around a vial of Kero-Light that Nadia had placed inside a jar, braced with shoes. They sat in an alley between strapped-down pallets of expired rations and bags of fuel pellets and rolls of screening, bales of rags and children's toys. James and Nadia broke open packets of anything readily edible even if it were expired or stale.

They considered what to do if Banefield were either there or not there. James said first they should *be* something. A club, a moot, a council. So if there were people at Banefield they would not think they, we here, were a sloppy gang of raiders. He looked over at Nadia. What do you think?

Nadia said, That would be better. It would mean we had sense enough to organize ourselves.

She had found a bag of roasted wheat berries long past their shelf life and was eating them by the handful and even though there were sour looks and dubious frowns and small negative gestures about being a moot or a council and so on (it seemed to invite creeping bureaucracy) Nadia suddenly liked them all, in a kind of surprise rush. Because they were doing something together, because they had set out on the wild sea on a chancy mission and thus they made themselves beloved to the great, dangerous forces that offered fire to humankind. They had a mission. It makes all the difference in the world. In this they would become dear to one another, she was sure of it.

In the end, tossed back and forth in the dark hold with the sea roaring past the bulkhead and hands reaching out to grab the glass jar with its small flame inside, they decided to give their group a name.

And they would make a flag, and have a written purpose, which was to learn to plant things and raise domestic animals, to make their own living, and make good maps of the coast and the interior and share them with whoever needed them and fight off whatever agencies tried to stop them. This founding charter would forever forbid them from any other purpose and would convince the Banefield people that they were not mere helpless refugees or pirates. After a long controversy they decided to call themselves the Lincolnshire Poachers after the strange and distant numbers station.

But my good people we must not forget about radio transmission from the lighthouse, said the Toastmaster. And Chan's coal seam?

" . . . make good maps of the coast and the interior and share them with whoever needed them and look for coal seams and maintain radio transmissions and this founding charter will forever forbid us, etc.," said Everett, writing in "coal seam" and "radio transmissions."

What about . . . said Oli.

Stop, stop, said Chan. He leaned back and laid his thick hands on his stomach. Stop. It will never end. We'll end up adding weaving, composting, plumbing, shingles, naval architecture, and geriatric hygiene.

We're going to do all that? said Everett.

Depends. He glanced over at James, who had burst out laughing. James stopped and cleared his throat. This is going to be harder and dirtier than any of you imagine, said Chan. Sometime I will tell you about the timber camps.

I would like to hear it, said Oli. She combed back her wet hair and smiled at him and she began to braid it.

Later, said Chan. He did not look at her.

After a while all but James and Chan fell asleep, exhausted by the talk and the unpredictable movements of the ship. They placed the shotgun and rifle nearby, slotted between two pallets of tattered ration boxes, and leaned back against the bulkhead that wept with damp. They talked long into the night, about James and Nadia's flight from arrest, about what news they had of the catastrophic flooding inland, about the rifle and the shotgun and the possibility of finding ammunition, about staying alive in a world in which some things were going to be new and other things would return, altered but recognizable, such as numbered years and maps and animal husbandry.

We need maps of the interior. Chan pulled out his last packet of tobacco and rolled a cigarette. He bent over the jar with its wavering flame and sucked air and smoke. You'll have to travel. And I need you to blow out my coal seam. And then new marine charts. Chan's agile mind leaped from one thing he wanted to another thing he wanted.

That's hydrography. I'm not a hydrographer.

You're not stupid, said Chan. You could learn it in two weeks. The agencies are gone, okay? They will show up again in a few hundred years. We will all be happily dead. So it is with the world. Bureaucracies have been around since Mesopotamia. Chan drew on his cigarette and turned it and looked at the glowing end as if it were a world on fire.

Eventually they always fall apart, segments, crash, ends up with somebody living in a cave, "Hey, I'm an assistant director for the general director for information systems!" Like, no shit.

James found a pallet of canned oysters, pulled one out, and rolled back the key. And so?

The times in between are the good times. I know. I listened to it on Big Radio. The good parts in *Lucifer's Hammer,* eh? And so, there's got to be other people like us on this island.

James held on to the pallet beside him as the ship rose up and then plunged down again with a roar. Then he went on eating the oysters. Sorry, let me get this straight. What island?

Chan lifted the hand with the cigarette in it and indicated the mainland, beyond the bulkhead. The island, he said.

James frowned. That's the mainland east of us, yes?

No, man no, that isn't the mainland; this is a gigantic island. Chan moved one hand in a circle. I escaped labor camp in a hang glider, came right over a big strait, you could see forever, I about froze my Kazakhstan ass off. Crash-landed and some old guy helped me. He said it was known to be an island. Huge, absolutely huge. He said it was called Vancouver's Island.

Be damned, said James. Worlds unknown.

Yah. Chan smoked. It's as good as space travel. The smoke wound around his ragged bandanna and his gold earring glinted. There's got to be a map of it somewhere.

There is. But I would have to get to a connection.

Okay. List of priorities needed here, one-two-three.

And that uplink is valuable. Incredibly valuable.

I figured that out, said Chan. Brain engages, gears grind.

The tower has to be guarded at all costs. Or we transport the radio equipment up a mountain.

Either way, a white-knuckle thrill ride.

A cross wave hit the schooner and they jerked sideways and James caught the jar with the Kero-Light just before it slid off the pallet. He shoved the empty oyster can into a trash bag and ran his hand through his spiking, lengthening brown hair. He looked down at Nadia's face with her lips slightly parted and the auburn blaze of her hair strewn across her face. She slept exhausted on a folded sheet of canvas in her vast yellow parka. He reached down to move her hair away from her nose. If they all managed to live and break the bread of celebration, he would be working with a scratch crew drilling blast holes in a coal vein and then months aboard scrapper ships, struggling with sextants and azimuth compasses. Nadia would have to keep the island alone for weeks at a time with their animals, and hopefully, someday, the inevitable children. She would need help. He would have to search out old hydrographic surveys, compute magnetic variation and tidal races, and this would be a lifetime of work were he granted a whole lifetime. He would stand upright and walk among people, one among many on two feet. This thought left him with a lifting feeling of gratitude as if a hot-air balloon were taking him into a stormy sky. And there would probably be shooting. Errol Flynn, in tights, leaping over the starboard rail.

Chan tipped up a water bottle and poured a few drops on the end of his cigarette to extinguish it. Not the old kind of life, is it? No promotions, no weekend seminars in elegant resorts. Maid service, hot tubs. A good apartment and water features. All gone.

James looked carefully at Chan's heavy face. He recognized it from a time when it was much slimmer and unscarred. He said, You know a great deal about the agencies.

Yes. I was very involved with them in my former life.

You were? How?

Chan rolled another cigarette. He turned it in his thick fingers and put it in the pocket of his parka.

Yeah, he said. I was Brian Wei.

CHAPTER 53

The schooner drove south through waves like glass where fish shapes poised in the rise and petrels struck the foam to carry them away. James and Gandy braced themselves at the gateleg table in the main cabin, the atomic clock secured to a shelf overhead.

How did they do this? Gandy said. There's Goat Shoals, like you were looking down on it from above.

James ran his finger down the coastline. He said, It's a copy from the old GPS readouts a hundred years ago. But much of this has changed. Is changing. With the floods and avalanches, and now silting you're going to get prograde deltas. Tell me to shut up if I go on. I do go on.

Well, go on, then, said Gandy.

Here's the old Amphitrite Lighthouse, twenty-five miles south of us, on the north shore of the entrance to the sound.

I've seen the ruins, I know where it is. Weird name. What does it mean?

It was the name of the daughter of Oceanus. Greek.

Now, this chart is off north. Gandy's thick finger pinpointed the compass rose on the chart.

Magnetic north, said James. It indicates magnetic north instead of true north and so you can see it's twenty and a half points east of true north when this chart was made. Magnetic north moves around and so there's no telling where it is now. James grabbed a shelf overhead and his chair slid beneath him.

No wonder the idiots go aground all the time. What does your compass say?

James compared Nadia's little compass with Gandy's. Its bulb of plexiglass shone queasily in the binnacle light. I'll know as soon as I can get a fix on the North Star.

God give us a clear night, said Gandy.

But a storm front moved in again and within the naked mountains repeated lightning strikes sent echoes that doubled back on one another and so made strange and frightening harmonics that did not sound like thunder but like roars coming from beasts as big as moons. They sailed past ruined docks breaking up in a long delta, the spilled slants of fallen buildings that had slid down an eroded slope, a fallen microwave or radio tower awash in the surf. Stony headlands revealed themselves one from behind the other. They sailed at the foot of these gigantic forms, their prow like a raven's beak cutting its black way into the sea.

James and Nadia sat together in the shelter of the cabin, watching the white line of breakers against the coast in the darkness.

What does Amphitrite mean? said Nadia. The ruined lighthouse.

Sea goddess, daughter of Oceanus, said James. They shared a package of crushed Savory Circles. He shook out a whole one for her.

Then, floating through the layered clouds, a glare of shifting light in the mountains: a transport helicopter with stalking searchlights that blazed like an electric wig. It ran its beams over the mountains, lit up a plated collection of angles, the walls of a collapsed building. The helicopter hit the walls with a hissing blast of cannon fire and red shards flew up into the foggy night in slow expiring arcs. Nadia dropped her

Savory Circle, her mouth open. They watched it thunder on to the north.

Primary, said Gandy, beside them at the rail. He put down his binoculars.

The dragon, said Everett. He held his book against his chest. Remind me to get this written down.

Looking for who? said James.

Forensics, said Chan. He lifted the rifle and followed the disappearing lights of the helicopter gunship. I tell you, we will dance before the gates of our enemies.

They shot at empty cartons thrown overboard to get the feel of the weapons and after the hard crash of the explosion lifted their heads to watch the splintered boxes lifted on the waves and floating past as high as the rail.

Another, said James, and tried again, then lowered the shotgun and watched the broken boards and gun smoke float past.

Let me show you something, said Gandy. They followed him down to the cabin where he laid the shotgun on the cabin table and took up a twenty-gauge shell. This shoots in a broad pattern, which doesn't have much force. You need a hard-hitter, do this.

He took a shell and cut small perforations all around it just above the wadding. His penknife pecked at it like a gunpowder bird.

This is called a cut shell. When you fire, the brass case at the bottom will be all that's left. The perforations let that sleeve bust loose with the shot and it stays intact; it flies out in a solid mass. It's like bar shot, like bar lead. You'll knock a hole in something as big as your fist.

They went out again and Gandy aimed the shotgun at an old telephone spool made of heavy timber and knocked a hole in it as big as his fist.

Little extra firepower, there.

Gandy and James and Chan and Nadia and Oli leaned toward the maritime radio receiver and the hour was ten at night according to the atomic clock. It was the first week of January, time for excerpts from Chinese and Japanese novels, poems, and plays.

From the Middle Kingdom and its delicate music, its enthralling land-scapes, the poetry of Tao Qian, said Male Voice One. *"Mistakenly I fell into the worldly net and thus remained for thirteen years . . ."*

Bargage Maru, do you read? Colin's tenor voice broke in.

Captain Gandy thumbed the transmit button and his breath smoked out cold and fogged. I read you, he said. Reply.

Bargage Maru, do you read?

Gandy shook his head. He can't hear me. We're out of range.

So now I want to head to the southern lands . . .

I can't pick you up, said Colin. In case you are reading me, there is a Primary gunship bearing north toward Nootka. I am sending out a general notice that the *Bargage Maru* is heading south to Banefield with an explosives expert, a cartographer, coal supplies, and seven willing hands.

Before the hall are gathered peaches and plums . . .

If that gunship hears Colin he's in deep shit, said Gandy. We're in deep shit.

I could do it, said Nadia. She looked around at them. I could broad-cast information when Female Voice One is reading, I can imitate her. They'd never know. I could, I really could. She pressed her hair back and was alarmed at herself, volunteering like this, emerging from con-cealment, having ideas as herself, Nadia, in front of a group of people. Yes? Listen, when she's speaking, I switch off Big Radio, relay messages in her voice as if it were part of what she was reading. I could make it sound sort of like whatever she was reading. Then when I've relayed the messages, switch back on. Back to her reading. It would be seamless. They don't listen to Big Radio anyway but if they did they'd think it was part of the reading. She paused. I'm repeating myself.

Damn, said James. Of course you could. He thought for a moment. You'd have to have earphones to monitor what she's saying so you'd know when to break in.

But first, Banefield, she said. First food.

Beyond the dark and distance lies a village . . .

James turned to Sparks, who was jammed back in a corner listening. The radioman sat with his earphones around his neck, smoking, and he looked up at James's sudden attention with some alarm.

Listen, said James. If you could home in on their dispatcher and imitate *his* voice you could transmit a fake set of coordinates to that gunship and send him straight into a mountainside. If we had a map. If we knew what mountain. They'd never think ordinary people could do that.

Gandy and Sparks stared at each other in a slow, private thoughtfulness.

It's called spoofing, said the radioman.

I like the way you think, said Chan. He slapped his hands together. I like the way you think.

The weather cleared the next night and those on deck could see the stars; the wind had blown all the storms away and set fire to the constellations and in their thin acidic illumination and that of the binnacle light James took a reading on the polestar. Magnetic north had shifted in the hundred years since his chart had been made and it was now fifteen degrees west of true north. He buttoned his wool coat tightly around his neck and went below.

Nadia and Oli stood together at the rail and grasped the shrouds. They drove on into the blackness and above them sails hard as metal forged by the wind, lit by starlight. Sirius white-hot in the east, Orion a blaze of jewels. Nadia ate fragments of musty Almond Delights and listened as Oli spoke enthusiastically of cloudberries and blackberries, of fruit leather and teas from wild mints and the nannies, the hens, the competent and friendly people of Banefield. They'll have dogs! Oli opened her hand in a gesture of magical production; canines, leaping from the imagination as if through circus hoops. Dogs to herd the goats and chase off foxes, just animals all over the place.

Nadia had a flash image in her mind of herself setting out a brown fragrant loaf of yeast bread on a table and hungry people tearing into it, of standing in a strawy barn with a goat baby in her arms. Heidi of the Alps.

Yes, she said. If it would come true. I think about it a lot. It's complicated, Oli. It's not simple.

But we can learn! We can do it. And when we learn how to live, and we get back, you will speak over Big Radio, said Oli. Her face was serious and sprayed with her unraveling hair and scarf fringes.

The lights from the cabin shone out onto nearby rising waves and lit them as they formed and sank and fell beneath the prow; they sailed on into a wall of night and a rising moon.

And so what's the story about Kazakhstan? said James. He handed Chan the gun oil and the stiff little wire brush on its rod. I'll just play straight man here. They braced themselves at the bottom of the companionway, in the hold, where the dove-gray light fell down in moving bars from the deck. They were taking apart and cleaning the weapons.

A ripping and fascinating tale, said Chan. My great-great-grandfather, tough guy, notorious liar. Eat your lunch. He escaped from the Baikonur Cosmodrome, they were about to shoot him into orbit as a test case, ka-boom, straight to the moon. Then, Urban Wars. So he scarpered to London, which he said was all of south England, stowed away on something, ended up in a titty bar in Seattle. Family warrior tradition, here. Possibly totally untrue. Everett wants all this for his Book of Amazing Personal Stories. My name is actually Abay Qunanbayuli. Don't try to spell it. Chan stood up and started up the companionway, the rifle across his chest. Man, I would love to get a shot at a Primary helicopter. Bango, right through the plexiglass.

James stood up as well. So how did you get to be Facilitator?

I looked good. They wanted somebody that looked Eastern and wise. I just read off a teleprompter. Remember the shit about the bird-feeder? I had great scriptwriters.

They scrambled up onto the deck and bent against the wind and spray.

Chan, said James.

What?

Don't draw fire. We have two old people and two women.

Ah, said Chan. He stood on deck and regarded Oli hanging out her underwear on the lanyard of the jack staff, and the first mate hurrying toward her, shouting that we do not hang our underwear from the jack staff, if you please, ma'am.

Right, said Chan.

Colin and Edward the Cat occupied the light tower like secret squatters among the radio waves. Colin ran through the kilohertz and the megahertz on a hunt for voices while storms splattered the glass and far below the old wooden Russian chalet unloaded waves of snowy rainwater from its eaves and the fir trees appeared conical when he looked down on them. He adjusted the antenna at the risk of his life, clambering up to the roof of the cupola while Edward meowed at him through the glass. He dropped down and began again to gather news of the flooding and the voices of survivors.

The Antarctic polar jet stream kept on spiraling out of its regularly assigned route to circle the South American latitudes at 550 miles an hour. It sent off cyclonic back-eddies that seemed they would rip all the snow from the Andes. In this alternative world of overpopulation and man-made greenhouses the northern polar jet stream whipped itself into meanders called Rossby waves that would have looked like the fluting on an Elizabethan collar had there been any scientific equipment available to track it, or meteorologists to read the instruments. All gone like *les nieges d'antan* and all the old familiar places as time went by. Weather was a kind of faerie, a land of mystery and peril that nobody could control or even understand.

The Rossby waves brought front after front tearing across North America, gathering moisture up from the Pacific in megatons and flinging rain onto the already-wet northwest coast, onto the parched Great Basin of Utah. The rains filled the dry bowl of Lake Mead. Water crawled up the cracked structures of Hoover Dam. When the rain hit, at first it stirred up a rolling front of dust clouds so that people watching from their packed apartments thought they were seeing another sandstorm.

The cyclonic storms filled the rivers of the central Great Plains, the Kaw and the Platte, and fed into the Missouri, which tore out of its banks and charged into the Eighth Gerrymander, formerly known as Kansas City, which now stretched all the way from Omaha to Des Moines to St. Louis. The floodwater brought down with it workers' barracks and any loose wood and at the bottom of the channels, unseen, Buddy cars and nameless scrap rolled over and over on themselves. Also the bodies of people and rats. The silos full of soybeans swelled and burst. Rotting grains surged downriver from the storages of the great Denver-Kansas field systems in floating putrid islands. At first people watched the progress of all the flooding on a few shaky-cam shots slipped into news reports and sat staring, fascinated, but since nobody knew where any of this was taking place they often heard the locomotive sound of oncoming water and stood up to find that the televised flooding neighborhood was their own and floodwater was coming through the windows.

Within a month Little Radio broadcasters appropriated parts, stole antennas, and cobbled together a network that radiated laterally like a sparkling network of unofficial news, some of it true, some not. They listened to Big Radio, they relayed all they could gather. *Nutrition En-*

forcement Teams and Black Ops from Furniture Supply are at war with each other, fighting going on now in Gerrymander Seven, Neighborhood Seventy-Two.

Among the listeners was Farrell Crotov, far in the south where he and his mother, his wife and two children lived in a mansion formerly inhabited by a Mariculture executive, on Les Isles Dernieres, which were once again becoming islands.

Farrell pressed the earphones to his head.

From the Middle Kingdom and its delicate music, its enthralling landscapes, the poetry of Tao Qian, said Male Voice One. *Let us begin. Mistakenly I fell into the worldly net and thus remained for thirteen years . . .*

Then without warning a different male voice broke in. Bargage Maru, *do you read?* A pause and then it said again, Bargage Maru, *do you read? This is Lighthouse.*

Farrell began to laugh aloud. Thank God, he said. Thank God.

So now I want to go to the southern lands . . . Again the new male voice broke in. *You are out of range. Primary gunship bearing north toward Nootka. I am sending out a general notice that the* Bargage Maru *is bearing south to Banefield with explosives expert, a cartographer, coal supplies, and seven willing hands.*

Then Male Voice One returned. *Before the hall are gathered peaches and plums. Beyond the dark and distance lies a village . . .*

Down in the ship's cabin the elderly Toastmaster, much worn by the voyage, sat with his knobby hands clasped one in the other and listened to the radio. Smoke from the galley streamed forward with the smell of a thick pudding and from farther up in the pointy nose the racketing sound of a hand-cranked sewing machine as a sailor ran a piece of white cloth under the needle. Oli and Nadia decided they would design the flag. A round blue circle partly covered by a yellow star. That seemed noncommittal and generally peaceful. Later they could add things like leaping salmon, the Big Dipper, lightning bolts. On top,

"The Lincolnshire" and at the bottom, "Poachers." Nadia and Oli sat in the captain's bunk, with quick and furious stitches, hemming the circle and the star by hand.

Female Voice One said, in delicate tones, *And now it is time, in the beginning months of the New Year, that we turn to fable, legend, and myth. We step into the land of mystery. We move on to the graceful and moving Nō plays of ancient Japan.*

The night grows late. Eastward the bells of the three pagodas toll. By the moonlight that gleams through the needles of the thick cedar trees I begin to put on my armor.

Do it, said Oli.

Nadia said, in a perfect Female Voice One voice, *The night grows late. In case you are reading me there is a Primary gunship bearing north toward Nootka. By the moonlight that gleams through the needles of the thick cedar trees I begin to put on my armor.*

In the slanting afternoon light the *Bargage Maru* passed the remains of the old Amphitrite light station; the ruins sat, a low square stub, stained with the sea fogs, draining rain, at the top of a mass of volcanic rock. It warned of shoals and the entrance to the sound. The Pacific swarmed white at her feet.

That night James and Nadia lay together in a space between secured pallets of hydrated lime packages on a bed made of sacking and what blankets they could find and felt themselves rising and falling with the *Bargage Maru* as she rode like a dark swan over the eastbound waves. Coats and bags hung from overhead beams; they swung forward and back, forward and back, a water bottle galloped down the hold until somebody grabbed it, whispered voices from the others came to them over the creak of strakes and the rush of the sea. A light gleamed. The others were still talking, Chan and Oli and Everett and the Toastmaster. Talk of hopes and plans and dreams and dangers but in all that happy imagining you still had to hang on to your courage and your traveling bags.

Nadia, said James. Listen to me.

Nadia lay with her arm thrown across his chest and her nose on his shoulder.

He said, If I were to die I think we will meet in another world. Some other life.

James! Her hand shut tight on his biceps. James, how could you? Die?

Shhh. People die. They will do it, sooner or later. I just wanted to tell you that. James's hand stroked her back under the blankets and the yellow parka. You are destroying my arm.

She loosened her grip on his biceps. Don't say that. Don't talk like that.

Shhh. The medication could allow for tumors, he said. Various blood cancers, there's that. We are in danger now of a great many things. I just want you to know what it means to me that you chose me when I was still in that wheelchair. I remember how you stood back so I didn't have to look up at you. And so many things. Seeing you running in from the rain in those red shoes. I can't tell you how much I love you. So I want you to know that if something happens to me we will meet in another life. This can't be all. I know it is not all.

The colors of the nighttime hold were all dark beams and the gold of the distant flame shining in bars through Chan's cigarette smoke and the errant sparkle of seawater as it dripped through the seams of the deck overhead. Up on deck the watch called out a line of song and was answered by a thin chorus, and the Pacific roared past on the other side of the hull, only six inches between themselves and the great ocean.

Yes, said Nadia. I know, I know.

And so both of them, having been so close to death, knew it was not themselves but something beyond the universe they had been left with and also the human voices among the cargo pallets, the Toastmaster telling a story, Oli laughing.

Chan turned and regarded her, and then laid his hand on her shoulder. Oli sat very still, feeling the weight of his broad hand.

CHAPTER 54

The *Bargage Maru* ran under a jib and a sprit sail as they moved up the channel into Barking Sound. The waves became shorter, then came on faster. It was close to dark now and it seemed to them that ahead, the bottoms of the racing clouds were faintly lit as if from some sort of lights or maybe fire. Nadia's hands shut around the heavy lines. It was spitting snow still. They were all worn and stained by the long days of hard sailing, their hair salty and bound down with wraps of spare cloth under the sea hats, but their flag streamed from the mainmast declaring a blue moon and a morning star.

To their right the volcanic mountains slid past and the broom and gorse and the endless bracken were all weighted with snow. Before them lay perhaps an end to hunger, maybe an end to constant fear, and all their future and their fate.

Nadia stood in the jib shrouds with one foot on the bowsprit and around her neck she wore Thin Sam's silver dangle as an appeal for good fortune. James stood beside her and grasped the back of her parka. Then she heard Oli shouting.

Look, look! A horse, it's a horse!

A white horse stood stiffly in the tall snowy growth, staring. It had enormous black eyes. It snorted and then turned and ran in the most amazing fluid movements and galloped away through the golden fern as if it were made to run and born to run and as its long white legs struck out in flight it scattered snow like powder. It ran headlong upon some familiar path it knew well as if it could not bear to let them out of its sight. The horse's mane streamed out like a rippling banner, rising and falling. It leaped over stones and logs and galloped on. Now it was ahead and it seemed to be leading them on into some country of mystery and peril. It was leading them toward the brightness ahead, now reflected on the wave tops.

And the horse stopped and turned and looked back at them with its ears up.

Nadia James, I have looked for you since the beginning of the world.

James took hold of Nadia's arm and said, Go to the cabin. He held the old Mossberg twenty-gauge shotgun loaded with cut shot in one hand and Chan stood beside him with the medium-caliber rifle. Gandy was in the crosstrees conning the strait. For some reason the horse gave James a thrill of fear. As if it were some illusion, something projected and made of pixels to lure them on. Some new kind of illusion that went far beyond mere television.

Wait, James, she said. Not yet, not yet.

They came around a headland. Before them was a grinding white surf of shoal water and a town or village spread along a low shore. The horse pelted into the town and disappeared among houses with mossy roofs, scattering dark-faced goats. A bonfire was burning on the shore. There were people in bright clothing staring at them, standing in front of the small houses and others walking out onto a wharf. The snow sifted from the low sky. Among the crowd was an old man with thick glasses and steel front teeth, waving his hat, on his arm glittering bracelets made of woven foils.

Sam! Nadia screamed. Sam! Sam!

A man with a halo of wild frizzy black hair paddled toward them in an orange kayak. The paddle blades flashed with fire reflections. His eyes were wide and anxious. He brought the kayak up to the side of the *Bargage Maru* and bobbed in the foaming sea.

He shouted up at them, We thought you would never come! We thought you were just our imagination! Then he smiled and the light sparkled around his edges and on every hair of his head.

Chan leaned over the side. The *Bargage Maru* went up on one wave while the kayak sank with another and their flag snapped out overhead. Do you know who we are?

Yes! Yes! You are the Lincolnshire Poachers and you know where the coal seams are! You have a cartographer! You have the uplink! We need your help! We heard about you on Big Radio! Welcome, welcome!

A bell began to ring. A big bell, with a deep tone. James and Nadia moved to the rail. She wiped rain from her eyes to see better and James pulled the load from the Mossberg, slid the bolt home.

Tie up, he shouted. We are having a Pig Fest in your honor!

The people onshore gestured; Come on, come on. The old man waved his hat and in the light of the bonfire his eyes shone behind the thick glasses. Come on!

Thanks to my editor, Jennifer Brehl, and my agent, Liz Darhansoff, for their encouragement and attentiveness to this new work, and the new direction I was taking, over three years. Many thanks to light-keepers Jeff George and Caroline Woodward on Lennard Island Light Station, three miles offshore Vancouver Island, dear friends for many years, for their hospitality and terrific cooking and granting me the privilege of experiencing life at a lighthouse. Jeff's photo of the Lennard Island Light graces the cover of this book. Caroline's books and Jeff's photography tell the stories of the North Pacific. I owe a great debt to Laurie Jameson, poet and novelist, for her attentive line-editing and suggestions, hard work done out of friendship and love of writing. And thanks to Shane and Blake Kurtz, two ingenious and hardwork-ing boys, for cutting cedar and their brilliant conversation. Writers are always in debt to their enablers and we know no other way to repay than to express gratitude in these acknowledgments, inadequate though they may be.